I0824323

QUESTIONS 27 & 28

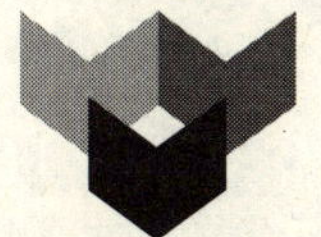

ALSO BY KAREN TEI YAMASHITA

Through the Arc of the Rain Forest

Brazil-Maru

Tropic of Orange

Circle K Cycles

I Hotel

Anime Wong

Letters to Memory

Sansei and Sensibility

Dark Soil

QUESTIONS 27 & 28

A Novel

KAREN TEI YAMASHITA

Graywolf Press

Untitled still life (April 20, 1943) by Chiura Obata. Courtesy of the estate of Chiura Obata.

Published by Graywolf Press
212 Third Avenue North, Suite 485
Minneapolis, Minnesota 55401

www.graywolfpress.org

Published in the United States of America
Printed in Canada

ISBN 978-1-64445-381-0 (cloth)
ISBN 978-1-64445-382-7 (ebook)

2 4 6 8 9 7 5 3

Library of Congress Cataloging-in-Publication Data

Names: Yamashita, Karen Tei, 1951– author
Title: Questions 27 & 28 : a novel / Karen Tei Yamashita.
Description: Minneapolis, Minnesota : Graywolf Press, 2026. | Includes bibliographical references.
Identifiers: LCCN 2025045181 (print) | LCCN 2025045182 (ebook) | ISBN 9781644453810 hardcover | ISBN 9781644453827 epub
Subjects: LCSH: Japanese—United States—History | Japanese Americans—Fiction | LCGFT: Novels
Classification: LCC PS3575.A44 Q47 2026 (print) | LCC PS3575.A44 (ebook) | DDC 813/.54—dc23/eng/20251121
LC record available at https://lccn.loc.gov/2025045181
LC ebook record available at https://lccn.loc.gov/2025045182

Jacket design: John Gall

Jacket art: Japanese American National Museum (Gift of the Mine Okubo Estate, 2007.62.241); Shutterstock

For John & Asako

CONTENTS

BOX 3: Residue

EPILOGUE

QUESTIONS 27 & 28

BOX 1

SALVAGE

1.1 Yone Noguchi
1892–1904 San Francisco Stoddard & Miller
Russo-Japanese War poetry, Bohemians

1.2 Kyutaro Abiko
1885–1925 San Francisco / Livingston Ishi & Kroeber
Christianity settlement, journalism, salvage anthropology

1.3 Etsu Inagaki Sugimoto
1903–1904; 1910–1932 Cincinnati / Nagaoka Mead & Benedict
Bluestocking, Seitō female friendships & daughters

1.4 Tsutomu Dyo
1906–1923   Chihuahua / El Paso   Pancho Villa & Pershing
Mexican Revolution   prospecting & espionage

1.5 Yamato Ichihashi
1921–1923   Stanford / Saratoga   Jordan, Stine, Yamamoto, Bywater
Washington, D.C., Conference   war games & eugenics

1.6 Haruko Obata
1912–1943   Berkeley, Topaz   Chiura Obata & D. Thomas
Great Nature   arts & crafts

YONE: American Pillow Book

While we look not at the things which are seen, but at the things which are not seen: for the things which are seen are temporal; but the things which are not seen are eternal.

—2 Corinthians 4:18

I become a transparent eyeball; I am nothing; I see all; the currents of the Universal Being circulate through me; I am part or parcel of God. The name of the nearest friend sounds then foreign and accidental: To be brothers, to be acquaintances, master or servant, is then a trifle and a disturbance. I am the lover of uncontained and immortal beauty.

—Ralph Waldo Emerson, "Nature"

Yone's new life is dawning as he leaves Tokio for America.

This is the 26th year of our Emperor Meiji.

Yone, born into this Restoration, time of Westernization, will be propelled beyond Nipponese shores to embrace a new language and a new land.

Yone is a tender seventeen.

He exchanges his kimono for Western attire. A silk tie and bowler hat. He struts forward, looking down at his shiny leather shoes. What an elegant young man!

He rereads Longfellow. And Emerson. He will be a New Man in a New World.

Boarding the *Belgic*, he waves a tearful farewell to the Bay of Yedo. Sayonara, dear city.

Passage across the ocean is a long difficult birthing. Seasick, he struggles to the deck to witness the infinite expanse of oily-looking waters and a lone star on the darkening horizon. He vomits into the Pacific.

Aboard the ship, he meets a stuffy old Japanese gent with a stovepipe hat on his way to be our Japanese minister to Mexico. Oji-san repeats his cups, tongue loosened, expounding on the Chinese question, then declares that the future of the Japanese people lies in Mexico. What does this man know of the Spanish language? Through the air drifts cursing voices, red-faced sailors at work or gambling.

But one evening, Yone awakes to see the ocean moon at its fullest, and it is then that he knows the moment of his loss. Distant in his homeland, he imagines the same moon. He weeps.

Back there, in Tsushima just outside Nagoya City, his father sells paper umbrellas, wooden slippers. He has left everything behind for his first love, an English spelling book.

On the next morning, the *Belgic* arrives at the port of San Francisco.

Yone, filled with anticipation, shaves, combs his hair, dresses to perfection. Primping in the mirror, looking this way and that. He will arrive in America a young prince.

Oh, by the way, as it happens, every now and then, a character rises from the page and writes the life of her author. This is nothing new, and, to be clear, I am simply sharing my intentions. I am Asagao, Miss Morning Glory, and this is my story about the poet Yone.

As you may know, Yone wrote my diary, *The American Diary of a Japanese Girl*, and now I, Asagao, will write his. I write this as a corrective to other false impressions of my hero and to substantiate his portrayal of me, who, for as he knew, was not a foolish character in the *Mikado* or a pathetic geisha doomed to take her life or a Chinese Canadian pretending to be a Japanese authoress.

Ah America! The dream is a complete failure. Upon the docks, smoky air and the putrid stink of sweaty humanity. Cars chasing cars in cavernous streets, shadowed between the highest of edifices.

And what of that street beggar? Yone has imagined even the poorest American dressed in swallowtail coat with a book of Emerson in hand. No such personage. Where is his Emerson?

The Cosmopolitan on Fifth Street, a shabby yet palace-like hotel. Yone rises miraculously by elevator to a room with high ceilings and electric globes. He enters at dusk and pushes a button. Light dazzles from above. But the bed is soft like water, once again rocking him, nauseated, at sea, sleepless.

In every corner on every floor, a spittoon, but wandering out to the street, a red-faced man claps him on the shoulders. *Hello, Jap!* And spits in his face.

Life in America begins with a letter of introduction from Shiga Shigetaka, Tokyo benefactor and editor of *Nihonjin*. Sugawara Den is the clerk for the Aikoku Dōmei located in a gloomy house on O'Ferrell. It's a patriotic league like Russian anarchists, something Yone's read about. Here is adventure for the boyish mind. Join our movement! Sell our paper, *Sōkō Shimbun*.

But what sort of job is this? Petty change for pancakes made from flour and water. Go without dinner except occasional free food at the Chinese restaurant on Dupont Street in exchange for ads in the paper. No bed but a tabletop spread with newspapers, encyclopedia for a pillow, in a house full of rats.

But who cares, if Yone can read. Food for the mind. In America, you can read books for free from a library. Shakespeare's *Hamlet*. Poe, Byron, Blake, Keats, and Shelley. He cannot make his spoken English understood, but his mind swirls with its most lyrical language.

Then one day, the Enseisha guys with their opposing paper, *The Golden Gate*, fight the Aikoku, and Yone's dear friend Hinata Terutake beats up an Enseisha man with an iron bar. Young Japanese only talk politics. Yone craves poetry. Time to move on.

Put an ad in the *Chronicle* soliciting work. Menial labor in private homes in exchange for food and board. Stoke their fire, cook their meals, wash their dishes, scrub their floors, and maybe there will be time to go to school. At Stanford's Manzanita Hall, Yone cleans the classrooms and serves the student-boarders in exchange for a lecture or two.

But Yone's shoes have become heelless, his socks shot with holes, his shirt threadbare, his jacket dirty. Exchange of This for That cannot buy him respectability.

Yone washes dishes at the Menlo Park Hotel. The poet's delicate fingers turn blue and swollen. Even in America, money does not come easy.

Then, all at once, life takes a turn. Hike to the Oakland Heights where Joaquin Miller lives. Miller, *the hermit who lives on dews, God's gardener,* raising roses and carnations. He's a rugged white-bearded mountain man in top boots, cloaked in bearskin, a cap of ribbons. A red crepe sash about his waist, he's named himself Joaquin after the Mexican revolutionary Murrieta.

Miller is, they say, *extremely fond of Japanese.* Yone is Japanese. Just go up and meet him. In the Heights, *nature never hurries.* It is here that East meets West. And it is here in the Willow Cottage where Yone will live, caring for the old poet and his mother and their guests, their meals, household, and gardens across acres and acres of field, forest, and canyon. Living in the mists overlooking the San Francisco Bay, Yone enters his dream of romance and poetry, apprentice to the Poet of the Sierras.

Yone resolves: I will become a poet. But was he not already a poet *reclining heart-to-heart on the breast of Mother Nature? True poetry is not in writing, but in the union with nature.*

Set a table in the dappled summer sunlight. Sprinkle rose petals over linen. Pop the cork on a bottle of claret and linger, talking of men and books.

The literati come and go, and Yone, by attachment, becomes a Bohemian. This does not mean he enters the Club. White men only, please. The only honorary other is Club librarian, to be California poet laureate, Ina Coolbrith, but this will happen later.

Miller declares that Yone is *one of my class, the best blood in the kingdom, an avowed admirer of Whitman.*

Ah, indeed!

The dawn of Yone's American life: poems published in the *Lark*. Critics write: *His composition is queer, baffling Japano-English . . . like Stephen Crane . . . like an Oriental Walt Whitman.* What do critics know, attaching their precious language to our exotic race?

Yone has laid bare his naked soul to the heart of nature. Who but Yone, a homeless snail, home upon his back, exiled from the island of Basho; who but he can know this infinite solitude cast over a grand and rugged, endlessly fertile and industrious continent? East connected to West by a transcontinental railroad, the Iron Moonhunter.

One of the Bohemian Club, Charles Warren Stoddard, has followed Mark Twain and Robert Louis Stevenson to the South Seas. Charles writes its idyll, his delight to have seen, to have touched and be touched by the savage islander, their *sleek dark forms glistening in the spray of the reef.*

Now from his D.C. Bungalow, Charles learns of the Japanese poet, broods, and ponders.

With Miller's assurance, Yone introduces himself to Charles, sending a poem with pressed flowers.

Charles replies: *Dear friend of the Orient. Long have I waited to hear from you.* And begging Yone for his photograph, *The muse has brought us heart to heart.*

Thus begins their loving epistolary. Long distance between Heights and Bungalow. Pals of the pen.

Yone gathers poppies and buttercups to offer to his still imaginary Charley, throws kisses to his Bungalow, hungers for the next letter. *We are like two shy stars, east and west. Let us love each other as heavenly twain.*

And Charley: *O Yone! My sad poet. Like the weary bird, torn from the Garden of Spices. Thy songs are tear-stained, singest the song of exile.*

Yone to dearest Charley: *My sweetheart, I dreamed a dream. You were a dragonfly, I a butterfly. Needless to say, we loved.*

We floated down the canyon, our path suddenly barred by dense bush. We couldn't attain to The Garden of Life without adventuring in. Then, you stole in from one place, I from another. Alas! We parted forever.

Charley invites Yone to the Bungalow, and Yone replies, *Tell me when we may be together with sweet love. Tell me when!*

But with what money will Yone travel and for what purpose other than to be with Charley?

Perhaps the continental trip can be made on foot.

Give it a try. Make the pilgrimage of a vagabond, a book of poems for a walking stick, into the Yosemite Valley.

Camp under the trees by a brook with its silver song. Sleep under starlight.

Sleep over fragrant hay in a barn between the legs of a horse.

Find lodging in a Japanese farm, exchanging translation for laundry and a hot bath.

Wash dishes. Chop wood.

Ride with gypsies under a bright moon.

Sit under balconies serenaded by banjos and the lilting voices of Spanish girls.

Following rail tracks into a dark tunnel, Yone falls into a ditch, but escapes. Sleeping near a coal fire, he passes out and is taken for dead. News travels. Kosen Takahashi, another admirer left behind, draws memories of Yone, *charming as spring blossoms, my love forever.* Kosen drowns in his tears, losing Yone to *naughty spring.*

Two weeks later, it's a miracle to see Yone returned to San Francisco alive.

A letter comes from Japan, a reminder of Yone's obligation to serve in our Imperial Army. This poet is not cut out to be a soldier. The decision is made for Yone. He will stay away in America.

But may not the poet serve the nation as poet?

Finally one day, Yone finds himself east in Charley's Bungalow.

To Yone, Charley is a white Chinoiserie, a sainted porcelain.

To Charley, Yone is far too Westernized. If only Yone had come to him barefoot in kimono.

Yone complains, *Am I to be another South Sea sea god, shaking spray from my forehead like a porpoise?*

No matter. They sit and doze in *one huge chair with a deep hollow, its long arms appearing but a pair of oars carrying them into the isle of dream.*

The Bungalow is its own idyll. Ivy creeping up brick into a broken window. Coconuts from Fiji. Fans and feathers from Hawaii. Weapons and dancing skirts from Tahiti. Persian pillows and cut-glass punch bowl. And most seducing of all, a great library of books, each autographed.

Yone is *dream child, clear as glass, pure as water, sweet as milk.*

Then enter journalist, historian, and Alabama belle Ethel Armes. Playing the piano in the Bungalow reception room, Ethel greets Yone for an interview in *The Washington Post.* As the story goes, Yone is smitten.

Charley mourns his lost Kenneth, too young, fickle, and unfaithful. He nurses a glass of Madeira, stroking tender fingers through Yone's thick black hair.

Languidly, Yone puffs cigarette after cigarette. Then taking his cues from Ethel, he too addresses Charley as Dad.

Yone wants to marry his sweetheart Ethel, and Charley must come and live with them forever. But Dad disapproves of Ethel and warns Yone: *I pray you do nothing rashly! You should both be free!*

Besides, Ethel also loves Alice and Annie and Daniel. Everyone plays breakup and makeup. Ethel and Yone engage and disengage.

Meanwhile, Léonie Gilmour answers Yone's ad in *The New York Herald* for an editorial assistant. She's studied at Bryn Mawr and the Sorbonne. Léonie edits Yone's book, a diary of a Japanese girl in America. All about me, Miss Morning Glory. *Charming, isn't it?* She brings me to life. She makes the writing perfect. Retains Yone's unique style. Campy and oh so modern. The invisible writer behind the writer.

Léonie moves into East Twenty-Sixth Street, marries Yone in his work.

Yone travels, and from London, he receives news of his book's success. The reviews are favorable, but who is this Miss Morning Glory? A Japanese coquette with snippy attacks on the American bourgeoisie, *with lightness and such frivolity . . . even frothy*. It's an exotic secret, but is she authentic? But of course I am authentic. What would Lafcadio say?

A highly fantastical diary of an imaginary Japanese. Fantastical, indeed!

Her piquancies would be possible in a Japanese man. Ah, American readers cannot discern a Japanese man from a Japanese woman?

But can a Japanese girl be a New Woman?

What about charming Ada, who fans herself in *Japanese chic*, then, hooking her arm around Morning Glory's neck, squanders kisses? *Two young ladies in wanton garments roll around happily on the floor.* And so we did.

As there is no plot and barely a suggestion of a love theme, the book is evidently genuine. Ah there you are!

This is a happy benign tale, while Yone's poetry is so mournfully sad. Sadness turns to satire. Satire is fiction. My fiction. Satire is American, but Yone can only be an American for so long.

Invisible, how can he be made visible to the world?

Yone and Charley, invisible to each other.

One poet moves west to find the East.

Another moves east to find the West.

Léonie is pregnant, but Yone loves Ethel, loves Charley.

After thirteen years away, Yone returns to Japan to great clamor, to celebrity. Now he is a full-grown man of thirty years. Yone is a famous poet. He writes for *Yomiuri Shimbun*, publishes his memoir, his poetry, his essays, teaches at his old school, Keio University.

In her mother's garden home in Los Angeles, Léonie gives birth to a son.

Ethel cancels her trip to Japan. She won't come. Neither will Charley. Didn't Ethel know? About Léonie, the other woman? Never mind Charley. Never mind any of the other boys. Yone must confess. He has betrayed her.

Our Meiji Japan is victorious in war, defeating Russia, extending our Empire.

Yone is changed forever by America's gaze. Now a man of many worlds, he can never fully return to embrace origins. Yet old privilege and power are comforting.

Yone marries his housekeeper, Matsuko Takeda.

Even so, Yone writes to Charley: *Oh, Dad, if you were here with me now! Write to me. I am lonesome!*

For the pleasure of his company.

Charley has moved to Monterey on the bay. His misses his Bungalow. He lies in bed. Rheumatism pains him. His heart breaks.

One day, Léonie arrives in Tokio with three-year-old Baby.

Baby has no name until Yone names him Isamu.

As I said, I am Asagao, and this is my story.

KYUTARO: Come, Japanese!

He is not dead. I open his mouth, pinch the nose, pull back the chin. My mother drips her medicine onto his tongue. Just a few drops slither to the back of his throat. He gags, then coughs, a good sign. And we wait.

My son, in this year of my kanreki, as I complete my sixtieth year, I bequeath this confession to you to use as you become the good man I wish you to become. Here, see me as I have been.

I was born in the first year of Keio, 1865 in the Christian calendar, on the 23rd of June, in Suibara, on the Japan seaside of Echigo-no-kuni. The village of my ancestors is surrounded by wetlands, flooded centuries ago to create a reservoir in which thousands of northern Karafuto swans seek refuge in autumn. My strongest memory of my homeland is of these swans, in elegant white clusters floating over the clear reflection of snowy Mount Gozu in the near distance. Sadly, I have no memory of my mother, who died seven days after my birth. My memory of my father is also dim, as, upon my mother's death, I was returned to the household of my maternal grandparents and there raised.

The era of Keio would be the last of the Edo bakufu, the restoration of the Emperor Meiji commencing in 1868. I was born into these tumultuous times, times that overturned the fortunes of my family, reduced to paper- and candlemaking. As a young boy I peddled our wares from village to village. Given this responsibility at a young age, I gained confidence and learned skills that serve me to this day: salesmanship, the art of negotiation, managing time and money. Rolling my cart from place to place, I met an English missionary who became a regular customer and, over time, also my teacher. It was his instruction that inspired me to seek a life beyond Japan.

Perhaps my plan might have been delayed, except that a local magistrate came to our house and addressed himself to my grandfather with an arrogance that shamed me. My grandfather, however humble, was a scholar, dignified and honest. One day in the middle of the village market, I hoisted myself onto my cart and gave a speech denouncing the magistrate. As the crowd gathered, I became animated until I saw my grandmother staring at me in shock. Until that moment, my rebellious spirit had been suppressed.

And so it was that, days later, to escape my shame, I grabbed a bundle of my belongings and the scarce funds I'd saved over time, and walked away from my cart and my home forever. From Niigata, I found my way to the docks of Yokohama with the intention of crossing the Pacific to America as a stowaway. I was seventeen, only a few years older than you today, full of energy, completely fearless, but also foolish. There were no ships, and in time I spent all my money.

來たれ日本人

近来北米合衆国に於て鐵道事業の大に進歩したるか爲めよ隨て勤勞者の新需要を威するに至りたる次第は大に日本政府及其人民の注意を惹くに足るものあり現にモントリー、サンライス、オピスポー、サンタ、バルバラ、ウヰンツゥラ、ロースアンゲルス、等の地方に於てはソレデートよりの新線路の落成したるか爲めに數百萬エークルの美田を得るに至り又之れと同時にサスタ、レスキオン地方もカリホルニア及オレゴン線路ノ竣功に由て其地に產する木材を他方に運送するの便を得たり然るにかくの如く土地物產の開くるに隨ひて玆に一の困難と云ふは勞役者の不足なる一事なり之れか不足を供給するは支那人の勤勞こう適當のものなるに何故か兎角米國人は支那人を忌み嫌ひて之を逐斥するに至れり今日本人か之れに代りて其需用を充たす可きや否は日本人の宜しく熟慮す可き所なり今日の所にては米國人は毫も日本人を忌嫌するのは偏頗心なしと雖とも逐々其數加わりて一ヶ月に千人も二千人も渡航するやうにならは恐らくは亦支那人の如く忌み嫌はるゝに至らん然れとも日本人は支那人の如く執拗ならすして能く俗と興に推遷る性質を有し米國の衣服を着け米國の食物を食し日常生活の事亦皆米國風に従ひて吝かならされは固より支那人と日を同うして語る可からす且日本人は勉强、正直、節儉、怜悧の好評あり果して然らんにはこの新開の土地に取ての珍客と謂う可し近年日本人の布哇に移住する事實と先頃メール新聞の報したる日本國內の不景氣の狀況とによりて觀察を下すに數十萬の日本人を米國內に移住せしめなは外に移る者の幸福は勿論內に留る者も亦爲めに利益を得て實に一擧兩得の策と謂う可きなり

Come, Japanese!

In the United States of America, the railroad business has drastically expanded and created new demands for labor. Hence, it is worth bringing to the attention of the Japanese government and the people of Japan. Indeed, places like Monterey, San Luis Obispo, Santa Barbara, Ventura, and Los Angeles have attained millions of acres of fertile land as a result of the completion of new rail lines near Soledad. Because of the California–Oregon line, the Shasta Siskiyou region has acquired the transportation to carry its lumber to outside areas. With further development of land and products, the lack of labor will become a severe difficulty. Although Chinese could fill this demand, Americans hate and repel them. Today, Japanese should seriously consider meeting this labor demand as a replacement for Chinese. Americans have not yet unfairly shown their contempt for the Japanese. However, someday, if as many as one or two thousand Japanese arrive in America every month, Americans might loathe the Japanese like the Chinese. Nevertheless, the Japanese are not obstinate like the Chinese and tend to adapt to new customs. If the Japanese wear American clothes, eat American food, and follow American ways of living without complaint, Americans will not treat them like Chinamen. The Japanese have received a favorable reputation because of their diligence, honesty, frugality, and intelligence. Thus, they are rare and welcome guests in this newly developed land. In recent years, I have observed Japanese migration to Hawaii and Japan's economic recession. If we encourage hundreds of thousands of Japanese to migrate to the United States of America, those migrants will gain happiness, and those who stay in Japan will also obtain benefits. It is truly like killing two birds with one stone.

She sends me to the stiller waters of the creek that slide in swirls around stones where I can spear a toad. We wrap the toad to the snake bite, poison to poison. And we wait. He is not dead.

In Tokyo, I supported myself with odd jobs, peddling noodles and the like. Eventually I found my way to a Christian church under the sheltering wings of a Japanese pastor who impressed me when he confessed his previous skepticism for all religion and said he had found his way to the faith through translating the Bible. I wanted to know the words that had moved such a change in this venerable man.

I studied with great eagerness English, French, and classical Chinese. My grandfather, your great-grandfather, was a scholar of Chinese, and I came to understand that his Confucian thinking supported the old way of bushi, the samurai. The Restoration had brought an end to filial piety and to class distinctions of lord, samurai, farmer, and merchant. Those of us who lived under the old way were lost. I could not follow my grandfather. I understood that if we Japanese were to enter the modern world to take control of our destinies, we would require new principles, spiritual and moral guidance to light our way. In the next year, I accepted the Lord Jesus Christ as my Savior and was baptized. In the year following, I became a student of the Fukuinkai or Gospel Society, and, three years after leaving home, under their auspices, boarded a British ship, the *Gerrick*, bound for San Francisco.

渡航の心得

商用や修業や其他の諸事用向にて日本より外國に渡航せんとする者は總て海外旅行券下附を地方廳へ出願して其下附を待ち之を所持して乗船せさる可からす若し乗船の際火急にして旅行券の下附を出願するの暇なきものは無届にて渡航し着後當地の日本領事館に出願して新に旅券の下附を請ふものあれとも日本にて其下附を願ふ時は五十錢にして着後當地の領事館より下附せらるゝ時は二弗なり

Instructions for Voyage

All people who plan to go abroad from Japan for business, study, or any other reason must apply for a visa at the local office, wait for approval, and hold it when embarking on the voyage. In case of an emergency that does not allow this proceeding, you can travel without a visa and apply for one at the local Japanese consulate upon arrival. However, the application fee costs fifty cents in Japan and two dollars at the local Japanese consulate.

He is not saltu, not white. My mother looks from him to me. We are the same but different. Nose. Cheeks. Hair. Briefly, his eyes open. What does he see? He nods and returns to his dreaming world. Between here and there, his confusion turns to relief. He is safe. We are not saltu.

I arrived in San Francisco on January 23, 1885. In those days, the Fukuinkai was located on Washington Street in the basement of the Chinese Mission. There I found boarding and like-minded friends. In the next years, I gave my greatest energies to our fellowship. I served as prayer leader, speaker, presiding chair, night school instructor, then superintendent, treasurer, and eventually president of the Fukuinkai.

I studied at the Boys High School on Sutter, and upon graduation dreamed of heading east to college to study sociology at Chicago or Columbia. However, my friends came to ask me to postpone my plans, to enroll in the meantime in the University of California and remain in San Francisco in order to help establish a firmer footing for our fellowship, to which, it is true, I was faithfully devoted. In those days, the study of sociology was very new in America, the first department in the country being established in Chicago in 1892. I was eager to be at the forefront of this research. At Cal, I chose my courses with an eye to moving on, but it was not to be.

After five years of study, interrupted by my many activities, I felt the weight of my dreams. My many promises heavy upon my shoulders. I was already thirty years of age, without a secure position or true career, unmarried and beholden to a struggling lot of Japanese schoolboys who looked to me for mentorship. And there were my impoverished grandparents in Suibara, to whom I could send only a pittance of my small earnings. If I could not continue my studies, had I lost my purpose? What was my purpose? I confess to you my loss of direction, though my feelings may only become meaningful to you much later in life. I spoke to no one, but gathered the necessary implements—tent, rope, axe, tin pot and cup, dry provisions, matches, knife, fishing pole, bedding, Bible, equipping myself for a short journey away. I slipped away in the early dawn and took a train north toward the Sacramento delta with a spur into Oroville and set off on foot into the forest beneath the sleeping volcano, Mount Lassen.

There, camping and fishing near a river, I sought solitude and meaning. I remember my retreat into the mountain forest to have been but a few days, nothing extraordinary except for a chance encounter with a rattlesnake. But my friends claimed that I was gone many months, that they had sent inquiries to every possible destination, even a search team to cover the city, posted my absence in the newspapers and with the police. When I appeared again at the fellowship, they looked at me as if seeing a ghost, having supposed the worst.

However long I had been away, I returned renewed. I understood now that I no longer needed to leave for further studies, that my place and true study would be here within our brotherhood, tested over time by our accomplishments and contributions to our future in America. God had given me this sign.

製服の事

日本人の如きは白人に比しては身体骨格の不規律なる頸筋の短小なる大腿骨の彎曲なる其威儀容姿の美ならさるに服飾其節ふ適せさるときは其風姿甚た不恰好にして觀るに足らす況んや流行外れの粗服を着して之を米人の目下に披露するに於てをや吾々日本人の品位風采を損するや知るへきなり

On Clothes

Compared to white people, the Japanese have little visual appeal because of their unbalanced physique, short neck, and bent legs. As a result of their unattractiveness, it is unbearable to see the Japanese wearing ill-fitting clothes. If they wear clothes that do not fit their postures, their figures look awkward and embarrassing. You should know that presenting yourself to the eyes of Americans with shabby and outdated clothes harms our Japanese dignity.

貨幣携帯の事

日本より貨幣を當合衆國へ持携するには最初墨西哥弗を持越す者甚た多かりしか後來の渡米者よ「メキシコドルラル」をは決して携帶すへからす當時桑港にての通用貨幣はUnited States of American One dollarにして墨西哥弗にあらす其兩替屋ハ横濱海岸通りにある支那人の「エキスチェンジ」に於て兩替す可し

On Money

In case you carry money from Japan to the United States, never bring "Mexican dollars" like your many predecessors. As of now, the currency used in San Francisco is the "United States of American One dollar," not Mexican dollars. You can exchange money at the Chinese shop on Yokohama Kaigan Street.

We find his camp. His tent. Rope. Axe, Tin pot, Cup. His fire. The things of his world. We take it all away, hide everything, to make him vanish. If they come to search for him, they will not find him. We keep him safe.

My friends pressed me for an explanation; I had none and I lost no time to outline my plans. With the exception of odd jobs, I had little previous real experience, but gathering the various skills of others, I opened a laundry, then a restaurant. I began to understand my role as an organizer who might bring others together.

From time to time, I had the opportunity to write my ideas and put them into print in a small fledgling Japanese newspaper, *Sōkō Shimbun*. My friends in the Aikoku Dōmei, excited by our generation's emergence in a new Japan, founded this paper. I realized that here was an opportunity to express, debate, and spread ideas. Japanese wanted to keep abreast of world news, to find ways to meet each other, to advertise their small businesses. Men in search of work often came to me, and so I became a labor contractor. I had a continual need to post and announce work opportunities. But these men were also in need of spiritual and moral guidance. Moreover, our increasing numbers roused jealousy and fear among white laborers, and we required a way to establish good communications and friendly relationships. Finally, I negotiated to buy this newspaper and, joining it with another, established the *Nichibei Shimbun*.

I formed an industrial corporation for the purposes of arranging Japanese contract labor. I traveled to Ogden, Utah, to establish a branch office, and we began to hire men to work in mining, on the railroads, and in sugar beet farming. We sent three thousand men to work in Idaho, Nevada, Wyoming, and Utah. In this business, I saw that what little money these men earned was mostly sent to support their families in Japan. But among the sojourning, money was also spent recklessly in gambling and other pleasures. There was no thought of tomorrow. Our Japanese bodies had become laboring machines, divided by and exploited on both sides of the ocean. I knew from my own experience that as long as we set our sights elsewhere, whether in Japan or some other future location, we would never find peace or a home. Our dream of return was a chimera. The decision to settle, to become a part of the land and place, would bring the prosperity we sought.

Still, this was not an easy proposition. We faced many obstacles. On several occasions, I approached American banks with financial proposals, but I was turned away, unless I could procure the indemnity of a prominent white citizen and the certification of my legitimate intentions, business acumen, and reliability. Japanese required a way to collect our earnings to make it possible to finance larger projects, to invest and install our businesses and organizations, to buy houses and land for farming. We were yet a small community. We knew each other and whom we could trust. And so we founded our own savings and loan bank.

船中便所の事

西洋の便所ハ一段高き所に圓き穴ありて此の穴に腰を掛ける趣向なり此便所の模様は家の内にある者と毫も異なることなし唯諸君の注意すへき要點は他なし各其用を達するの際大小便を日本流に一時にヤラカシテ便所を汚すものなきにあらす

Bathrooms on Board

Unlike Japanese toilets, the holes of Western toilets are located on a platform, and you need to sit on them. Bathrooms in homes are no different than bathrooms on board. Needless to say, the point you must note is that you should not dirty toilets, doing your business in a Japanese way.

食事の心得

食巾は專ら食事の際に口に拭ふに用ふるものとす是を以てハンカチーフの代用を兼ね額、鼻等を拭ふへからす

Table Manners

Napkins are to wipe your mouth during meals. You must not use napkins like handkerchiefs to wipe your forehead and nose.

テーブルに對しては指を口中に入れて食物の齒牙に挾りたるを直ちに取るへからす食巾を以て口を掩ひて之を取り去るへし決して衆客列坐の中にて指頭を以て唇歯に觸れるしむへからす

At the table, do not put a finger in your mouth to remove food stuck between your teeth. Cover your mouth with a napkin and remove it. Never touch your lips and teeth with the tips of your fingers in front of others.

Clear soup. His chest heaves. Tears dribble in happy meeting. Tears to soup. After this, the salmon is good.

It was during a trip to Lake Tahoe, stopping around Placerville, that I rediscovered Gold Hill, the site of Wakamatsu Colony. You know this place where you, with your mother, also visited. In 1869 it was a brief experiment of twenty-two samurai to settle the land, planting tea and mulberry for silkworms. None of the tea plants or mulberry trees had survived. The land was now owned by a family, the Veerkamps, who kindly showed me the gravesite of Okei, the only girl of the group, who, left behind, died at age nineteen. This first colony failed, and yet I felt a stirring. Perhaps Okei, buried in this distant land, spoke to me as I prayed for her spirit. From that moment, I carried within me the seed of a promise. In the next years, I searched the delta and valley for a settlement of my own.

In April of 1906, the Great Earthquake shook, and San Francisco crumbled and burned around us. As we worked to recover our losses, we were physically assaulted and boycotted, as if we Japanese had caused the quake. Of small notice was the rebuilding of the primary school in Chinatown, renamed the Oriental School, with the edict that all Japanese students were to be segregated there with the Chinese. Japanese parents filed suit, protested to the Japanese consul and ambassador, inflaming an international conflict. You must understand that this was a year after Japan's defeat of Russia at Port Arthur. It was an insult to segregate Japanese with Chinese. The political jargon had become alarmist; such humiliation might ignite war.

The Gentlemen's Agreement between America and Japan settled possible hostilities for the time being, but with the result that, in exchange for nonsegregated schools, Japanese laborers were now barred entry into America. I was reconciled to this outcome, believing that we should not become like coolie labor, but rather immigrant settlers, with a purpose to contribute our labor to build the nation. Thus, in this same year, I made an offer for three thousand acres of undeveloped land in Livingston, California, surveyed and divided into forty-acre lots. We began with a handful of investors and two settling families. We sold the lots at $35 an acre, financed through our Japanese bank. Thus began our dream of the Yamato Colony in America.

桑港上陸手續の事

船太平洋の航海を終り右に「シーサー」を望み「ゴルデンゲート」を過き左にオーグランドを見又右に桑港を望みて船の進行漸く緩く汽笛一聲の合圖と共にカスト

ム、ハウス（關稅局）より小汽船にて醫師稅關吏巡査等十數人來船して乘込を調へ稅吏は乘客船員より其他殘る限なく嚴重に調ふることあり此際若し密輸入品を認定するものあるときは誰れの所有品たるに論なく沒收或は課稅す可し船進んて棧橋に至り此に船を停めて上陸す此時も稅吏來りて乘客の手荷物を一々默撿するを常例とす

Landing at San Francisco Port

Toward the end of the voyage in the Pacific, you will see the seaside at the right and pass under the Golden Gate Bridge. The ship will slow down when you see Oakland to the left and the San Francisco Port to the right. Following a siren, a dozen medical doctors, customs officers, and police officers will come on board for inspections. Custom officers will thoroughly inspect passengers and the crew. If illegally imported items are found, regardless of ownership, they will be confiscated or taxed. After the ship arrives at the pier, it is routine for customs officers to check your luggage.

粧飾の事

元來香油香水等の如き艶髮石鹸の如きは粧飾品にして婦人の外は日常重要の品にあらさるものゝ如くなれとも文明國の人程清潔艶麗を好み且人自ら健康を保たんか爲に衛生上尤も缺くへからさるものとして之を使用する者男女共に多き事なれは後來渡米の諸君も此邊に注意して頭髮亂散のことなく每朝美麗に梳るへし（白人に雇はるゝ者は殊ふ然り）然らされは支那人の如き輕蔑を受くることを免れさるへし

On Hygiene

It used to be that perfumes and shampoos were not considered daily essentials for anyone other than ladies. However, civilized people prefer cleanliness, and both their men and women use them in order to maintain hygiene. Those who plan to come to America must keep this in mind and comb their hair every morning (especially those who will be employed by white people). Thus you will avoid being despised like the Chinese.

We sweat together. The stink of old life leaves the body.

I had the occasion to meet your mother in San Francisco as she began her foreign travels with her older sister in 1907. Your aunt, as you are aware, founded the first women's college in Japan, where your mother was also a teacher. Our meeting was brief but I felt it fateful that I should meet such women of stature. Your aunt had been educated in America, and both sisters spoke English fluently. They continued east, crossing the country to Washington, D.C., then across the Atlantic to Europe, circling the world. Occasionally I received a postcard from somewhere, and I treasured these small insights into their travels.

Upon your mother's return to Japan, we began to exchange letters in earnest. I wrote about my aspirations for my fellow Japanese in America, my dream of distinguishing ourselves in the modern world. Your mother agreed with me, but added that we should not abandon our Japanese culture. Experiencing many marvels across Europe and Asia, she felt even more strongly her appreciation for Japanese traditions, its art and music. When I suggested that she may have been homesick, she countered that she was not discussing homesickness but those Japanese abroad who mimicked Westerners, attempting to hide being Japanese. She found them rude and ridiculous. And furthermore, it was impossible to hide within Western clothing; others always saw a Japanese. Japanese must learn to stand proudly. I read her words with both pleasure and anxiety: pleasure to know our philosophical connections and anxiety to wonder if she would be willing to leave Japan to make a home in America.

My purpose in traveling to Japan in 1909 was to find investors for the Yamato farming colony, but I also hoped to meet your mother again. Through my newspaper, we promoted settlement, encouraged Japanese men to exchange photographs to arrange for brides. In our Japanese system, conjugal arrangements were usually decided between families with the help of marriage makers; often couples were united between villages, over many miles, never having met. In this case, they would marry across a great ocean. Without such arrangements, family life, the basis for settled living, could not begin. We Japanese would remain sojourning men, prey to loose morals, to gambling and prostitution, fostering odium and disrespect toward us. I myself had put off this responsibility for too long. It was time to find a wife.

英語研修の事

西洋人に接して對話中不意に質問を受けて直に答辯するは困難の事なれとも交際上に用ふる言語は通例限りあるものにて之を記臆するは容易のことなり米國に渡來すれは何事を爲すにも皆英語を以て用便を達せさるへからされは日常交際上に應用する英語を記臆すへし其語の種類三千餘も記臆せは普通の談話位には差支なきものとす

Studying English
Needless to say, answering random questions when approached by Westerners is challenging. However, it is easy to memorize English speech because the vocabulary is limited. You will have to use English to do everything once you migrate to America. Therefore, you should memorize words for daily conversation. You will be able to converse regularly if you learn approximately three thousand English words.

He watches carefully to make his body move as my body, to see and hear and smell as I see and hear and smell. My little brother. But there are other stories remembered in his body. He is confused. These stories must take him away, back to what was.

In the summer of 1909 I returned to San Francisco with your mother, and you were born in the following year. I also brought your uncles, my stepbrothers, to America, and they began to run our newspaper. On the one hand, the newspaper, top in circulation among Japanese papers, thrived, but for the farming colony, these were the most difficult years. I traveled back and forth between San Francisco and our valley farming community. Twenty pioneering families had settled permanently, building homes and barns. Initially they planted peach trees and grapes, but these trees would take several years to give fruit, and in the interim, they were stretched for cash. Fortunately, one enterprising woman began to plant eggplants, which were exceptional in quality and taste. Everyone began to plant eggplants, then sweet potatoes, asparagus, tomatoes, and melons, and thus the colony struggled but survived.

While the colony created a cooperative and its own form of management, my one recommendation was that there should be no businesses created to compete with existing white businesses; we would use their stores—grocery, dry goods, hardware, clothing, restaurants, petrol—and promote civil society between and among us. Despite our utopian example, in 1913, the Alien Land Law ended our hopes. It proposed to prohibit aliens ineligible for citizenship from owning agricultural land. Japanese, Chinese, Korean, and East Indian—all of us were such ineligible aliens. In print and publicly, I protested vigorously, arguing that the right of naturalization should be granted to the parents of American-born Japanese, and in so doing, nullify this land law, to the benefit of all Californians.

禮式心得の事

東西其風俗人情を異にするかゆゑに我日本に禮法に合へる事も米國にては却て無禮とすることあり日本にては總て男子を尊み婦女を卑しみて交際社會に加へさる事なれとも當合衆國にては却て婦女を尊敬するを以て常例とするか故に若し街上往來の際誤てなくとも婦人に衝突をする事あれは忽ち巡査にせられ違警罪を以て處分せらるゝなり

On Manners

Because the East and the West have different manners and customs, things that make sense in Japan are sometimes impolite in America. Unlike the patriarchal society in Japan, ladies are commonly respected in the United States of America. Because of this, if you accidentally bump into a lady on the street, you will immediately be arrested by a police officer and charged with a minor offense.

During the last days of hot summer air, one night, I uncover his tent, rope, axe, tin pot, cup, the things of his world. I place everything back as I had found it, but in a wooded place near the beginning of his trail. It is the end of the way to where the saltu came, but it is the beginning of his. I arrange the cold fire just as it was.

Your mother quickly became involved in the church and worked to establish a boardinghouse with classes in English, cooking, and sewing for Japanese women, most of them recently arrived picture brides. In her work, she was my most impassioned counterpart. This organization eventually became the first Japanese chapter of the YWCA. Your mother moved with ease in all social settings, so it was not surprising that we received invitations from Mrs. Phoebe Apperson Hearst to special events at the anthropology museum. It was Mrs. Hearst who introduced your mother to the architect Julia Morgan, who has been contracted to build a new Japanese YWCA. Your mother was also acquainted with Mrs. Henrietta Kroeber, the wife of Professor Alfred Kroeber, director of the museum.

You probably have no memory of your museum visit. You were perhaps only three years of age, but you were fascinated with the Indian Ishi, who crafted for you a small arrowhead. Ishi was said to be the last living person of his tribe and emerged from the forest to cross into civilization. Now he had come to live in the museum, surrounded by the tools and artifacts of his lost life. He had become himself an artifact. I read his tragic story with an aching heart. I thought I understood his confrontation with this rupture in time. Had I not also experienced such a rupture? But I now know his pain, unlike my own, was unspeakable. He placed the arrowhead into the small palm of your hand, looking up to see me. Face-to-face, both of us in the trappings of our Western world. His exile, my embrace. In that moment, a dream passed between us.

They have enacted an immigration law that finalizes our isolation in America. I have advocated for peace between our two countries. Two great empires have risen on either side of the Pacific. You were born here, an American. Now you must be the bridge. This year, 1925, we will inaugurate in our newspaper an English section, and we will sponsor nisei study tours to Japan. To you, I bequeath an unknown future. My son, may God bless and keep you.

桑方西斯哥府繁昌記

桑港市中の往來には便所の設けあらす故に日本人の内には随分困却を感することあり若し他出して中途にて兩便の催すをある時は己を得す歸館す迷惑至極のことあるへし

Notes on San Francisco

Some Japanese are greatly perplexed that no public bathrooms are installed on the streets in San Francisco. When you have an urge to go to the bathroom, returning home to do business is a huge nuisance.

倶樂部通則

當クラブは専ら在カリフォルニア州の日本人より組織し内は相互の利益を計りて其交誼を親密ならしめ外は異邦人に對して我日本人の位價を高むるを目的とし救濟法を設けて不幸者を援け貯金法を立てて會員の資産を富まし体操場を置て會員の体育を進ましめ臥房を裝して其止宿に便し及讀書室、交談室、遊戲室、を設くるの外漸次會員の志望に依り兵事課、商法課、音樂課、學事課等の分科を置て益其規模を高大にすへし

Mission Statement of the Japanese Association

Our San Francisco Independent Nippon Club, entirely organized by the Japanese in California, seeks to foster mutually beneficial friendships, and aims also to elevate the status of the Japanese among the non-Japanese. We have established a relief plan for those in need, a savings plan to increase members' revenue, a fitness studio to encourage exercise, and sleeping quarters to be utilized as lodging, along with a reading room, meeting room, and recreation room. Hereafter, we will further expand our scope to military, business, musical, and scholarly affairs, depending on members' requests.

He follows me to the river to spear fish. He follows me to the meadow to hunt rabbit. He follows me to the beginning of his journey where he finds his old campsite. He searches for and picks up his old things in disbelief, but when he looks for me, I am gone.

English translations from the guidebook *Kitare nihonjin* (*Come, Japanese!*), 1887, by Yuki Obayashi.

ETSU: Woman Samurai

February 2, 1903
Nagaoka, Japan

My dearest Etsu,

Upon your departure, the snow began to fall lightly but continuously, and I remember your small figure with little Hanano cuddled on your back under your quilted coat, tufts of her black hair at your neck. You paused to turn and wave, then hurried to follow Matsuo, who walked ahead. Even now I see you slip away into that quiet whiteness. I believe its hush is a prayer for your safe journey. After many days, a deep feathery layer of snow blankets everything. Ishi tells me it is a late winter storm, just to remind us of winter's power.

So it is that Ishi, your mother, and I find ourselves confined, huddled together under the kotatsu and blanket. I am reading, practicing my hiragana and katakana, and writing you this letter. Your mother is busy pulling the threads from an old kimono. She and Ishi are repurposing the silk for a smaller version for Hanano. And Ishi, despite her age, is never at rest, keeping us fed, tending me with tea and stories. I am so grateful for Ishi whose happy memories of you bubble up so spontaneously. Your mother, a more reticent person, is thus happy to chime in with details. They are both very patient with my questions and my poor Nihongo, and in this way I am learning about your childhood here in Nagaoka.

The other day, I learned that Ishi came to work for your mother as a girl of thirteen. She also grew up in your family. I asked Ishi about her name for you, Etsu-bo. Why does she add "bo" to your name? She chuckled. I had some difficulty understanding, but I believe she said it was because you were raised like a boy. Is this true? I myself was considered what we call a tomboy, but for you, it seems more purposeful. Now, I will pay more attention to children, how boys and girls are differently raised, and think of you.

My writing was momentarily interrupted. Ishi came to take me to the threshold of the house, putting a handful of warm roasted peanuts in my hand. A racket of revelers in demon masks chased by drummers ran by, and we threw the peanuts at them out into the snowy road. I hurried back with Ishi out of the icy cold. She slammed the door and looked at me significantly as if to say, now we are quite safe. Daily I have such surprises.

Etsu, how can I convey my gratitude to you for inviting me to accompany you to Japan? And now, to continue, even in your absence, to live in your family home? It is for me a small miracle that I am here, partaking of the everyday. I now live the very cadence and attention to routine imagined from our conversations and sweetly remembered in your person. Every day I awake in anticipation—for what, I am unsure, but I know I feel my senses heightened, and I have been given new eyes and ears. I am happier than I've felt in many years. Happier only if you and Hanano were yet here.

You, of all friends, know my discomfort with life and society in Cincinnati. Now that I think back, I feel embarrassed to have pressed myself upon you in those early days when you first arrived there for marriage. I was more needy of you than you of me. My attentions to you were selfish, and you would have been just fine without my intrusions and constant excuses to show and tell. Now that I am in the lap of your family, I begin to understand your hidden strength. This harsh cold winter, for example—your people move within it with determined grace. I hope you will excuse my trespasses. You have been patient with me, my foolish enthusiasm and my desperation. I will get my Japanese education, I will. Please continue to be patient. I promise to be a better friend to you.

This letter follows you to your destination in Cincinnati, so you may read it at your arrival. I hope your American home welcomes you back. Please give my loving regards to Mama and my aunt and uncle and allay any fears they may have about my remaining behind in Japan. You will laugh since how often have I heard you complain of the restrictions of Japanese life, but here I find the very freedom I have dreamed of. While you have gone West to find your freedom, I have come East to find mine. Well, perhaps it is a different freedom. I might call it peace. I will return in due time, and—who knows?—as a truly new woman.

With love and affection,
Your Flo

March 3, 1903
Cincinnati, Ohio

Dearest Florence,

Ohio! Your mother, now ours as well, anticipated our return. She lighted the fireplace and greeted us with her hearty beef stew. Mama was especially surprised to see Hanano, who left a baby and returned a little girl, and we realized that an entire year had indeed passed. In tears, she embraced us, and I saw how much we were missed. Hanano has been fussy throughout our travels, but now I can put her to bed quietly without complaint. I am again settling into our house, and Matsuo is busy with business. Yes, I think we have come home.

But then, to read your lovely letter and to know you are also there at home. I felt anxious to leave you behind, but it is really you who hold hidden strength. And it is I who must thank you for accompanying Hanano and me to Japan. As you know, Mama did not think it wise to travel so far with a new baby, but you helped to convince her that we would be fine.

I'm not surprised to hear of the heavy snowfall upon our departure. Nagaoka winters are famously snowbound, continuing even into March. But here in Cincinnati, there are but patches of snow across the lawns, and small green signs of spring are appearing.

As you know, my mother carefully packed with me my doll collection. We unwrapped each doll and placed them on their pedestals with cookies and small treats. Hanano is walking! You should have seen her delight and clapping hands to greet her lovely imperial court. And so we greet the coming spring and pray for Hanano's happy future. Now we've celebrated Hinamatsuri, and in February it was Setsubun for you with Ishi driving away bad spirits. How time passes.

I smiled to read your question to Ishi about her name for me. Yes, I was Etsu-bo. Let me explain further. I was the third child born. The first, my brother, was to inherit the family name. Then there was my sister before me. My great-grandmother desired that I become a priest, and so my training began at an early age, and my education was more formal than usual for a girl. "Bo" means priest and also boy. As you realize, I did not become a priest. This is a longer story with some twists and turns. A marriage had been arranged for my brother, but when the bride arrived, traveling from a distant village, my brother refused this arrangement and left the family. This was a great embarrassment, and my father never spoke of my brother again. My studies, already begun, continued, but with the different purpose of making me heir, which meant that I would be married to an adopted son chosen to carry our family name. My brother left for America and tried and failed to make his way there. About the time he returned to Japan, our father died, and he was called back to Nagaoka by our grandmother, and so regained his position and became the head of our family. Thus I did not become a priest nor was I married to an adopted son.

On our ship returning to America, I was, as in previous voyages, quite nauseated, but this soon passed, and while Hanano napped, I began to read with great interest the book you lent me by Mary Wollstonecraft. I can understand your excitement for her words from long ago: "What were we created for? To procreate and rot?"

You need not ever apologize for your friendship to me. I will always treasure your sweet attentions. As you said, you have set yourself to study Japanese culture and have much to learn. I will be interested to know your discoveries, how you perceive our strange world. You are ever in my thoughts. I miss you very much.

With loving affection,
Etsu-bo

~❀~

May 5, 1903
Nagaoka

My dearest Etsu-bo,

Today it is the most beautiful spring day. And your sister arrived with her young sons for the holiday. They have grown much taller since I last saw them. Your mother placed your family samurai helmets in the tokonoma, and Ishi hoisted two beautiful paper carp to fly above the gate. Ishi kindly allowed me to help make the mochi cakes with sweet an. I am not that tall in comparison to other Americans, but I feel oversized in Ishi's kitchen. I suppose she is, in her old age, shrinking. I hope she is not too annoyed with me. At first, I followed her around the entire day, but she very handily introduced me to neighbors. I have become friends with a farming family where I am learning about farming silk. Then there is the family with a mercantile shop. They have asked me to teach their children English in exchange for stories about their lives. I've become daily busy, going here and there.

Your sister is a younger version of your mother, with the same gestures and elegant polish, making me imagine that perhaps you were more like your father. Not that you do not have polish, but you are a different strain of this family. For example, I cannot imagine your sister or your mother in anything but kimono. They are of another time and place, whatever this Restoration would like to decree. Your sister, when she is not occupied with her boys, enjoys remembering your childhood together. She speaks fondly of you as her little sister and remembers you as she left your family home to marry—your worried face. She has never forgotten the look on your face, and says that she turned in the palanquin to hide her tears. She says you were given a very different education. She does not say this with any particular approbation. I think of the good fortune of your education and your immigration to America, but your sister and mother are quite content to be here at home with the familiar. Knowing this, I try to be quiet and observant, although I cannot ever be invisible. I feel, I will be honest, a pulling attraction to these elegant women, but I fear my ideas are cluttered with exotic imaginings, about which you have admonished me.

I read with great interest your explanation of Ishi's name for you. But now I am curious about your brother's wedding that never was. I tried to broach the question with your sister. I did not follow all her meaning, although I understood that to break the promise between families of the wedding engagement was a deep shame. I thought of my own broken engagement, a very different matter. I know I caused Mama consternation and some sadness, but in the end she understood the impossibility of the match. And after that, Uncle Obed invited me to join him on his travels. That was my first encounter with many places but most memorably Japan. To be finally living here is a dream. But, I digress. From what I understand, your brother was disowned. Responsibility to tradition and to right conduct is much more consequential for you Japanese than for us.

Please send me word of you and especially of Hanano, my namesake, our little flower. While I am savoring my every day, I most regret not being there to watch Hanano grow. I can see from the changes in your nephews that time passes quickly. We must not squander our opportunities to live as fully as possible.

With loving embraces, I am
your affectionate Flo

~ ✿ ~

June 6, 1903
Cincinnati

Dearest Florence,

We seem to be past the rains but headed for a very humid summer. Matsuo has been traveling constantly for business. We see him so rarely these days. Meanwhile, I am spending many pleasant days with Hanano in our garden. Some days, I close my eyes and see all of us here together. You, and my sister, Hanano, playing with her boys.

I do remember my sister leaving our house, that tearful goodbye. Unlike me with my curly hair and plain features, my sister, as you know now, is very pretty, and I saw her transformed into a beautiful bride with a white powdered face. On that day I believed her lost to me. I was little and wanted her for myself. Well, she and Ishi will describe to you all the particulars. This was truly a traditional Japanese wedding unlike those Nanki-Poo–Yum-Yum spectacles that Cincinnati brides plan for themselves, with torchbearers, tea servers, and sake drinking. Can you imagine tossing rice? Such a sacrilege and bad omen. I suppose Matsuo and I were the first real Japanese to wed in Cincinnati, and in a very traditional Christian ceremony at that.

Sometimes I wonder what sort of priestess I would have made. I suppose they would have shaved away my unruly curly hair! Can you imagine your bald Etsu-bouzu?

You have set me to thinking about the unexpected turns that brought me to Cincinnati, and it might have begun with my brother's broken duty, which forced him to make his way on his own to America. You see, it was my brother who arranged my marriage to Matsuo. In San Francisco, my brother was beaten on the street, a cruel incident of senseless hatred from which I believe he never fully recovered. It was Matsuo who aided my brother. How fortunate that a passerby but fellow Japanese came to my brother's rescue, taking him to the hospital and following his care. I was engaged to Matsuo when I was twelve years old and began my education to become his wife. Do you know I learned to cook his favorite foods? When I arrived in Cincinnati, there was no way to ever make such dishes! And yet I had been made to live in his absent presence, a strange fantasy, for ten years until I came to America. I, Etsu, was my brother's and our familial promise and gift to repay a great debt of kindness.

Now I look up at Hanano chasing her dreams around the yard, and

I think I could never put her in such a place of obligation. But I myself followed my brother's wishes without question. I do not fault him. He sent me to Tokyo where I learned to speak and read English with American teachers and where I made the reasoned decision to become a Christian. From the example of my women teachers, I was given the confidence to think for myself. It was not simply my mind. For the first time, I realized freedom from even the carefully trained movements of my body.

I have had to reconcile the Buddhism, with which I grew up, with Christianity, but I have not entirely given up my sense of Buddhist resignation to my circumstances. Matsuo and I together attend Sunday church services, and I feel on those days the renewal of hope and freedom. The traditions of the past have pushed me forward, and yet the intricate patterns of Japanese duty as a mother and wife continue to mark my way. This is the strict training that you observe in my sister and mother. I suspect I will always be admonished while guided by their examples.

Forgive my rambling on. I do miss our long walks and talks. I think of you every day.

Until we are together again,
Etsu

August 8, 1903
Nagaoka

Etsu dearest,

Your mother and Ishi have sewn me a special yukata for Bon festivities. I have abandoned wearing Western dresses in this heat. The cool cotton lies softly on my skin. As you know I am prone to rashes, and this is a great relief. Ishi supposes I will learn the Bon dances. She has been singing and clapping and urging me on. You would laugh to see me. I go left and she goes right. But Ishi is insistent, and I must mimic her movements exactly over and over again until they become habit. You speak of your mind and body's movements trained from childhood, the release from which you have felt freedom. And yet I am learning a freedom in ritual.

I have been thinking about your picture-bride marriage to Matsuo.

I believe you have turned your obligation into good fortune. It might have been very different. The man who rescued your brother could not be a bad person. At least that much your brother recognized. I, for one, am thankful for these happenstances that brought you to Cincinnati. I don't mean to be impertinent, but I am curious to know what you felt when you finally met Matsuo in America. And today? I see Matsuo as busy and industrious and, having left Japan, certainly adventurous. I suppose he also took a chance. Do you think that he, too, was preparing all those years to finally meet you? This is only to say, I pray that you are happy.

But now I wonder about the young lady who was engaged to marry your brother. What happened to her? And why did your brother refuse? After all, he assumed he could make the arrangement for your marriage when he himself refused the one made for him. Is there no place in the world where women are truly free? You and I have had to leave our homes and the people we love to know something of the freedom men take for granted.

I understand that the coming festival welcomes home the spirits of the dead. Your mother anticipates the return of your father's spirit. I have been copying names and dates from the gravestones in your family cemetery and have made a genealogical map. I point to names in my map, prodding your mother, hoping for stories. Who, for example, was your father's mother? She is not buried here. And there is one stone that is nameless. Today I asked about this stone, and I felt a small shudder in the room. Your mother looked away in discomfort. I felt as if I had broached some unspeakable memory.

I returned with Ishi to the gravesite to wash the stones and pull weeds. I took some care around the unmarked stone. I know it is presumptuous to think that is my stone, yet I feel attached to its mystery. Ishi left and returned with incense and flowers.

Ghost stories fill these hot August nights, with the low drone of cicadas, my mind chasing fireflies flitting in the dark. I think of us sitting silently in the warm darkness after dinner rocking on the swinging bench on the veranda, looking into the pine and cypress across the lawn, the shock of the full moon.

With affection always,
フローレンス

~❀~

September 9, 1903
Cincinnati

Dearest フローレンス,

I believe under Ishi and my mother's tutelage, you are becoming Japanese. But still I hear my old friend raising the banner for the rights of women. You cannot change my mother or sister. Of course you would never presume to do so, but I think you are learning that they are, in their way, strong women, even if their strength is their stubbornness to change.

You have brought to the surface several stories I had forgotten about the women in my family.

If I remember correctly, it was on the very day of his wedding that my brother left our household, just as the bride arrived with her belongings in a palanquin. I supposed it would be like the groom fleeing the church just as the bride makes her parade down the aisle to the altar. Such a scandal! The bride had been conveyed to our household. That is, she was no longer a part of her old family but now belonged to ours. My mother kindly brought her in, and she lived with us for a long while after until another marriage was arranged.

There was another young woman who lived in our household. She had been sent by her family to be educated in proper etiquette, and she left the house abruptly. I imagine it was she with whom my brother had had a relationship.

I am sure there is an official map of our family genealogy as this lineage is a mark of our old prominence as a samurai family of the Nagaoka domain. I believe we must have come from elsewhere, cast to the snowy seaside perhaps in exile, because of political rivalries. This history is important to the story of my father's mother, whom I never knew and who lived in Edo serving as governess to a princess of a high-ranking clan. She, too, left our family because of another disgrace, and, again, not of her own making. Her own father and my grandfather, to whom she was married, were on opposing political sides, one supporting the continuing rule of the shogunate and the other for the restoration of the emperor. When my father was only seven, his father was likely poisoned in this political intrigue. Considered complicit in her husband's death, though she had nothing to do with it, she left our household in disgrace, leaving behind her son, never to see him again. As a child, I received many elegant gifts from this grandmother whom I never met and whose story I never understood until many years later. Her absence was never spoken of.

It occurs to me as I write that today in Japan is Chrysanthemum Day, a day to celebrate the imperial flower. And here, in our garden, the mums are beginning to flower. This is due to Mama's green thumb. I can see through my window clusters of orange and purple and yellow against the back fence. I have to smile because of their happy disarray, falling this way and that. In Japan, you will see enormous blooms standing in single pots held straight and high by little posts, each perfect flower carefully cultivated. However, in our garden in Nagaoka, where you now reside, you will see no mums, I am quite sure. They were long ago banned by a great-grandfather of generations past. This brings me to the story of the unmarked stone. The name that should be there inscribed is Kikuno, named for the chrysanthemum. One day, Kikuno was caught alone in the garden with a young man. This was absolutely forbidden. She was the beloved of this great-grandfather, who mourned her consequent death. Thereafter no kiku flowers were ever again planted.

My grandmothers are all long gone. That era is passing into the very air you breathe. Like it or not, we become modern.

Lastly, you've asked about my feelings meeting Matsuo for the first time. He met me as I arrived at the train station in Cincinnati. His first words to me were to ask why I was dressed in kimono. Even though I had dressed very carefully, I felt the shame of this. The next day, I dressed as a Western woman, and I have never looked back. That is my short answer.

My mother has written of you in her letters to me. She worries that the food is strange to your taste. I have assured her that you enjoy Japanese food more than I.

With hugs from Hanano and me,
Etsu

~ ❀ ~

December 12, 1903
Nagaoka

My dearest Etsu,

Winter has returned. How quickly the year has passed. It seems as if only yesterday I saw you depart in the flurry of snow.

You are so right that the world of your childhood is rapidly changing.

In my journal, I try to document everything before it may vanish. For example, the daughter of the farmer I visit regularly suddenly left amidst much gossip. She had intimated to me her intentions to live in the city, but this was a secret, and I must pretend to know nothing. I feel for her mother who cried when she told me.

But you are also right to point out the hidden strength of your mother and sister. I do not believe their strength is stubbornness to change but, rather, resourcefulness despite. I have understood from your sister and other wives, farmer and merchant alike, that they all hold the purse strings in the household. I was very surprised. No doubt this responsibility for household finances affords Japanese women a certain power. Yet it is still true that Japanese women, like Western women, are made dependent for their lives on the earnings of their husbands. We must all be married off, become casualties in the larger events of men. I am so grateful for my small inheritance. How many letters have I received from friends who want to know why on earth I am in Japan? And these are women who wouldn't never ask such a question if I happened to be housed in France or Italy.

I have got Ishi to fill out the story of Kikuno. I suppose your mother did not think it appropriate as it is rather bloody, one of those mukashi-no ghost stories. Kikuno was a young second wife of the lord, your great ancestor. She fell in love with a youth serving her husband, who was after all an old man. The two were found out, but rather than being exiled they were given the honor of seppuku death. As she drew her short sword, the lord interrupted, indicating that she should have the honor of dying by his personal sword, which he pushed toward her across the tatami. In the act, her blood cascaded from her throat and she flung her hand against the wall, leaving a mark that could never be removed. It was said that her ghost restlessly roamed the household.

I have been these many days contemplating the nature of love, how we have created our societies to control our desires. And then we are encouraged to believe in romantic sentiments that I've seen so often fade with the reality of married life. Knowing now this life of yours and your journey, I am envious of the equanimity in your manner. You write of resignation yet hope in your marriage. It seems a contradiction, but I find contradictions are built very usefully into Japanese life.

After I read your letter, I asked permission to gather mums from a neighboring garden, because just as you said, there are still no mums in your mother's house. I placed them before the unmarked stone with a small prayer.

Affectionately always,
Flo

P.S. I have taken to writing a bit of poetry.

Every season gifts a flower:
Springtime Daffodil, summer Susan, autumn Mum.
Wisteria, climbing Rose, and sweet Clematis
—my constant bower.

Yet beneath white winter hidden,
Snowdrop, intrepid and inquisitive,
Seeks the sun, a tiny bursting extravagance,
My epic-center yet unwritten.

January 1, 1904
Cincinnati

My dearest Florence,

I write to you today on the New Year with auspicious greetings. The house has been full of food and friends, children running about, with Hanano at the center of everyone's attentions. Now I am sitting in the glow of the fireplace, catching the twilight as our guests have left. I want to savor a few moments as if you were here, snug in the sofa with some book.

Matsuo had sweet rice delivered, and he fashioned a large mallet, then carved a smooth hollow out of the stump of a fallen tree in the yard. I joined him outside, turning the hot steaming rice in a good rhythm to his punching. Hanano watched from the window with Mama. Our mochi was quite good.

I am impressed that you left mums for Kikuno. Her spirit must have stirred. By the time I was born, the old house and the mark on the wall had burned to the ground. The rebuilt room, however, was still thought to be haunted. My mother had to close this room, which no one wanted to enter. I have been reading Japanese ghost stories told by Lafcadio Hearn, but there are many more stories to tell. I have been thinking of you and your journal. Yes, I believe you must write what you've learned.

This brings me to a story about that reticent woman, my mother. This happened before my birth, but my sister will certainly remember it. During the overthrow of the shogunate, my father was summoned and imprisoned. With his death imminent, my mother gave directions to prepare the house, then gathered her children, my brother and sister, and escaped into hiding. She returned at night to the house and set it on fire. In my imagination, it is all very dramatic. The blazing fire, and my wild mother in her white death kimono beneath her peasant disguise, prepared to die. In the meantime, my brother was discovered, and he was sent to die with my father. But my father and brother were saved by history, by the restoration of the Emperor. My father returned to the charred remains of a burned house.

My mother does not think of freedom. When she sent me off to marry, her counsel was to be loyal to my husband, brave in defense of his honor, and to find meaning in my life in my duty to him. She advised that only thus would I find peace, but it was a declaration of her own experience. Appearances deceive. She is not in any way docile or as one might describe some American women, a shrinking violet.

I do not mean to worry you, but Mama has not been feeling very well these days. She tires readily and does not seem to be her old self. She misses you very much.

I have a secret to tell you. I believe I am again pregnant.

Sending wishes for a prosperous New Year,
Your loving Etsu

March 3, 1904
Yokohama

My dearest Etsu,

I have been alarmed with your concern about Mama's health. And now that they've started a war with Russia, I sense a certain zeal in the air. What this means I am unsure. A warrior past stirs here. I do not want to believe that this war is in any way necessary. In the end, it will be women who must make the peace, for the bloody end will come, and more important to know is how we will live together each day.

Several days ago, I bid goodbye to your mother and Ishi and am posting this letter from Yokohama. I do not feel there is danger to us in Nagaoka, but I take the war to be a sign. I am sad to leave Japan, but then I can hardly wait to see you again.

I just looked up to see my reflection in the glass and realized I am back to wearing my old dress, the blue one you must remember so well. It had been put away all these many months. How strange I look to myself. I had become, I thought, just another villager cloaked in warm kimono layers. Suddenly it comes to me, what I will most miss. It is the bath. Ishi and I crouched together naked in the big steaming tub. Our cheeks are flushed and ruddy. Sweat dribbles down our foreheads. We are silent, listening to the water. I feel safe and something sublime. The bath speaks to everything I have learned these many months, my life and foolish expectations turned completely around, what I have come to know, to be.

Now, I shall be returning, and nothing for me will ever be the same.

I am yours forever,
Flo

~❀~

August 8, 1910
Chicago

My dearest Etsu,

As I write you today, my heart fills with sadness.

You will have already received in Tokyo the curt telegram about Matsuo's sudden passing—such an abrupt and unkind communication. While my letter will not make Matsuo's loss easier to bear for you, I hope a slower telling may ease your heart.

When Matsuo did not return from his trip to Chicago, we began to worry and made inquiries by telephone to hotels and vendors there, and, after a week, to the police. Finally, we received a return call from the county coroner, a Mr. Peter Hoffman. It was Friday evening and the ringing interrupted dinner. My aunt looked from the receiver, clearly upset.

Unsteadily she motioned to me, and my heart skipped. The man announced that the body of a Jap man was in the morgue at the county hospital, and wondered if this was the person I was looking for. His words were drawn and lax, and I was in great shock. I blurted out: "Sir, Mr. Matsunosuke Sugimoto is my brother. If you would please speak with the dignity his death deserves." I could sense the man stand at attention. He read his dry report: cause of death: acute appendicitis. Then added that, soon after being admitted to the hospital, Matsuo lost consciousness. He must have been in pain many days before. His appendix had burst, the poison spreading throughout his body. If he had attended to his pain earlier . . . but such conjecture is now useless. He explained the difficulty of distinguishing a stomach upset from appendicitis. I thought, Oh Matsuo, so occupied by his many business concerns that he ignored the seriousness of his condition until it was too late.

I arranged for a train ticket to Chicago the next morning and arrived in the evening. The morning after, I went to the hospital to meet Mr. Hoffman, who bade me identify Matsuo. I had hoped we might transport the body back to Cincinnati but decided it best to put Matsuo's poor body to rest until we are able to bring him properly home. I made arrangements for cremation and temporary interment in the Oakwood Cemetery in Chicago.

Etsu dear, this is not the letter I hoped to write to you these days. Your summer wedding seems to have been just the other day. Hanono is twelve, so that was many years ago. Please hug Hanano and Chiyono for me. I will do everything I can to help. You are all so dear to me.

With loving sympathy,
Flo

September 9, 1910
Tokyo

Dearest Florence,

I write from Matsuo's family house in Tokyo. As you know I have been living here for many months waiting for Matsuo to join us. I am at a loss.

Returning to Cincinnati is no longer possible. And Matsuo's tentative plan to migrate to Brazil is also out of the question. I realize what a restless soul he was. Now our back-and-forth has come to a sudden stop.

The girls miss you and their home. They ask about you constantly. Little Chiyo wanders from room to room asking where her bed or table is or her chairs, this or that. She cannot understand our empty tatami rooms. And Hanano is quietly mourning her papa.

With the news of Matsuo's death, my mother has decided to come with Ishi to Tokyo to live with us. I feel nervous about making her comfortable here. My mind has been diverted to making preparations for her arrival.

Then there is the question of school. The girls are quite behind in Japanese, and these questions must be decided, in Matsuo's absence, by his uncle, the head of his family. I will have to tread very carefully. Yes, I know my proper station, my duty to Matsuo's family and to my mother, but after so many years away . . . I must balance my words carefully and act obediently, and yet I must find a way to protect my daughters. My mother will have proper advice. I so wish you were here to counsel me as well.

I am so grateful to you for your attentions to Matsuo. I miss you very much. Please send my regards to our friends and family.

With love always,
Etsu

~ ❀ ~

April 4, 1911
Cincinnati

My dearest Etsu,

We finally arranged for a small service for Matsuo at our church on College Hill. I include here the program. It was made simply but always with you in mind. I also include a list of the guests. You have made many friends here, and so many came to honor Matsuo's memory. Many wreaths and flowers were offered.

It has taken until this past month to clear all the documents related to Matsuo's business. My uncle as executor and I were surprised to know of his many dealings. I believe he was slowly liquidating his assets and paying off his debts, and with this purpose in mind, we tried to complete this work. I went daily to the stores on Race Street and Seventh Street and gave notice to his two last employees, keeping them on until we could sell the remaining merchandise. Buyers came from everywhere—an antique dealer, a museum curator, and a decorator among them. Mr. Oyama, who owns the curio store in the Emory arcade, came to help, and in the end, I asked him to take the remaining items as payment for his kindness and friendship. He is also experiencing financial difficulties, and I wonder how long he can continue. Finally, we wrote to and spoke by phone with the remaining creditors, pleading the circumstances of Matsuo's unfortunate and sudden death. We obtained signed letters accepting the final terms of our negotiations and hope that is the end of it.

I have also been, as you have instructed, giving away your belongings and selling your furniture. All of this has been helpful to settling outstanding debts. I will keep some more valuable items and pack them for you.

There is much correspondence in Japanese, I assume relating to business concerns, but possibly family matters. I will bundle these for your eyes and discretion. However, there are also stacks of Japanese newspapers and newsletters, mostly posted from San Francisco. Mr. Oyama identified the papers as *Nichibei Shimbun* and *Jiji Shimpō*. He did not want them, so I will burn them along with some old ledgers and other unnecessary papers. As for your many books, I have approached the library to donate them. Those in Japanese may become useful to newcomers to our city.

On my end, I have put my house up for sale and have purchased passage to Japan in a few weeks. I've instructed Uncle Obed to place the funds from the sale in trust. Yesterday, I visited Mama's grave and explained everything to her. I'm sure she would understand.

Here at home, I have placed Matsuo's urn on a table with his photograph. In clearing out the office on Race Street, I found the girls' drawings and their small crafted gifts to their papa. He kept them all, these many childish items filling an entire drawer. I've placed a few around the urn to keep him company until our departure. I will bring Matsuo home to you. I am bereft in my responsibility.

With affection,
Florence

November 19, 1932
Aoyama, Tokyo

My dearest dearest Florence,

In this world, you will never read this letter, but, with faith, I put it in your hands to take with you to the next.

You were my maid of honor at my wedding in Cincinnati. Little did I know that day that Reverend Schenk married me to both you and to Matsuo. It was June 8, 1898. This might be to speak a sacrilege, but we have lived together so many years longer than I with Matsuo. I count twenty-two past my married years to Matsuo. You have never wavered in your friendship and support. You have been there for me at every juncture, the birth of our daughters, the death of my husband and my mother, the education and graduation of our daughters, and their marriages. I do not know how I have deserved your care and company through all these years, sharing our trials and making with me the trek back and forth from Japan to America and back to Japan.

To be frank, when I first met you, I was of two minds: that I needed your help but that you were too eager to help, and I should not impose my need on your eagerness. You and I had both just arrived from Japan, you from traveling with Uncle Obed and I for the first time. I was twenty-four when I married Matsuo who was in his late forties, and you were forty-two, both more mature. I had been thrust out on my own to Tokyo and felt emboldened by my education and my conversion to Christianity, but really I was very young. At first I thought of you as like one of my teachers in Tokyo, but the difference in our ages became inconsequential to our growing and deeply felt care for each other.

In 1910, when I left Cincinnati with our two daughters, I thought I would not see you again, that I would have to settle somewhere in Brazil as Matsuo was planning. Though exactly what he planned I do not know; as you were the executor of his business concerns, we both realized he was likely in financial straits. It was most difficult for me to say goodbye to you, but Matsuo's death changed our lives. When you arrived with his ashes in Tokyo, I wept with mixed feelings of sadness and joy. You stepped through the threshold into our house, the girls wrapped in your arms, and we became a family, our own small island. Together we combined our efforts and plotted an escape that would assure the girls of their education and future independence. It would be three years in Tokyo where you and I both taught. Eventually we found a way to move to New York City, where we lived for twelve years, raising our daughters, teaching and writing. With Hanano married, Chiyono in college, and our book published, we returned to Japan, as you had always desired. Your last years here were a gift to both of us.

I am surrounded by your books. This one about Cochiti Indians of New Mexico by Ruth Benedict. We knew Professor Benedict at Columbia. On top of her book is perhaps the last you were reading, about Samoa by Margaret Mead. Was she not a student in those years when you attended classes in anthropology while I taught Japanese? The bookmark peeks out from the page where you left off. I think of you as a lay anthropologist, that you came to know the Japanese as no other American I have ever known. You said you were happy to lead a vicarious life, but your living moments were so much more. You could intuit and interpret the feelings and actions of others. While others gravitated to the strange and exotic, you interpreted value and meaning in the everyday. I have been constantly surprised and grateful for your comprehension of all the subtleties of our impossible social interactions and strictures. It was you who was most discerning and strategic as we carefully navigated a way to return to America to complete the education of the girls. Together we found a way. You have loved Japan, your final home, but you have also always believed in freedom, in the rights of women, especially for our girls.

Our next book, *Daughter of the Narikin,* has just been published. We fought over your stubborn desire not to be recognized as the author. I know we have written these words together. And our memoir could never had been possible without you, your curiosity, and your persistent and prodding interest.

Now my mother has passed, as has Ishi, and many of the people whom you met in Nagaoka. What if you hadn't captured their stories all those years ago? What if you had not asked your prying questions? Perhaps I have lent authenticity to our books, but you have crafted the stories, interpreted the complicated patterns of our lives. Even though you joked that you were only always trying to understand Etsu-bo, like you a living contradiction, you really believed in the vindication of Japanese women, and I will do my best now to continue on alone. It will not be the same.

I have read through your journals, marveling at your perceptions. It is as if you had a special set of glasses through which you saw more clearly. You have made me see ingrained habits taken for granted, ways of thinking learned, all the simple patterns of our lives that give pleasure but prejudice our opinions, stymie freedom. Moreover, you have shown me that it is where and when we deviate from our rules, test their limits, that we experience change. Indeed, we have woven your many thoughts into our books. Perhaps, in the future, some reader will decipher knowledge there. I have tied our letters and these journals within a silk furoshiki to accompany you. It will be as you requested.

There are small things I will miss. Your craving ochazuke at the end of any trip. Your policing of my grammar. Your love of opera. And you dozing over a book or manuscript with a pencil slipping through your fingers.

We have grown old together, you and I. I did not believe I would lose you so soon, and yet I see now that you have been ready for some time for this last journey. I will keep you forever in my heart until we meet again.

Your loving Etsu

TSUTOMU: Code Name Storm

Storm was a little man with a big heart.

Storm was a diminutive man bigger than life.

No no no. Storm was huge but invisible.

Storm was the toughest, most agile ninja warrior kick-ass borderlands fighter before Bruce Lee.

What?

Storm challenged Pancho Villa to a fight, mano a mano.

It was a shoot-out.

On horseback. Samurai centaur versus Mexican centaur.

Kung fu fistfight.

Chess match.

Storm almost killed Pancho Villa.

No no. Storm saved Pancho Villa's life.

But when did Storm meet Pancho Villa?

Some folks think Storm was a great revolutionary.

Others think Storm was a great bandido. A thief and outlaw.

Some say he was an oriental Robin Hood.

Debonair, a Zen Zorro.

But not an aristocrat; he was working class.

A working-class samurai. You know, lost his old warrior job. Like the rōnin.

Maybe more like a drug lord or mobster boss.

No no, nothing like that. No merry men. No famiglia.

Storm worked alone. A lone wolf.

Secret agent.

A silent Storm.

You got to be kidding.

This is a true story with true exaggerations.

STORM 1

Let's start with the Revolution.

You mean the Restoration.

Okay, start there. Meiji Restoration. Commodore Perry sails into Tokyo Bay on his black ships and the Edo is over.

Good-bye samurai. The Emperor rules again.

By the time Storm is born, the Meiji is into its second decade. Modernize. Militarize. Build ships and railways. Build the nation.

By the time Storm comes of age, Japan's got China in check, and it's time to go to war with Russia.

Storm's the son of Kumakuro, the black bear, and his second mistress. Second mistress, Kura, is young and pretty and gets her way. This means Storm gets a commission with the First Army under General Kuroki. Storm spreads out the maps and serves Kuroki tea while forty thousand Japanese cross the Yalu and defeat seven thousand Russians. Storm gets a taste of war.

More like a whiff.

You've got it all wrong. Storm actually fought with General Nogi's Third Army at Mukden, in Manchuria. An American captain named John Pershing just in from fighting the Moros in the Philippines was a military attaché sent to observe Nogi's army. That's when Storm met Pershing.

Serving tea?

No, artillery. In the trenches.

Then the fall of Port Arthur, the Battle of Tsushima, and the Treaty of Portsmouth, and Storm is back home, victorious.

But soon Storm packs his bags. Kura, his okaasan, tucks the Rising Sun, the flag of the nation, between his shirts, and Storm takes the train from Sendai to Yokohama and catches the first ship out headed for America.

You mean Mexico. Acapulco.

Actually Salina Cruz. He's supposed to head to the Japanese colony in Chiapas, Escuintla, but on the boat someone asks, *So you want to be a farmer? That's what they do in Chiapas.*

True, Storm's no farmer. Didn't he study mining?

Another says, *You're young, what's the hurry? Hurry up and farm? Where's your sense of adventure?*

They point to a map: La Sierra Madre. Barranca del Cobre. Copper, gold, silver. *You find it, it's yours.*

He makes a reckless decision.

At the docks at Salina Cruz, some guy under a sombrero greets Storm. He pulls off the hat and bows yoroshiku. He's a Japanese named Juan Sato.

They wander through the dusty clamor, a sea of sombreros. Peons hawking corn and bananas. Women with baskets and water jars on their heads. They walk through an old adobe laced with strings of hanging chilis, and Sato sits Storm down at a table in a bar. Pours Storm an aguardiente.

Welcome to Mexico! He announces two choices. *I point you in the direction of the Escuintla farms and off you go, but you got to promise, you never saw me. I never came to meet you.*

Second choice?

You come with me. We go north to Ciudad Juarez. Cross the border to El Paso before the Americans close it to the Japanese.

Hey, are you crazy?

It's 1906. Sato has his ear to the ground. Next year, they'll call it the Gentlemen's Agreement. Sato spits. He's no gentleman.

By the way, where is La Sierra Madre?

North in the desert of Chihuahua. *We pass her on the way to the border.*

Storm looks at Sato's calloused hands, grime under the nails, hiding a sunbaked face under a sombrero, pretending to be Mexican. Storm's no farmer.

They head for the railway. Women stoop over braziers, roasting tortillas. A fews centavos gets them a hot stack, and they hop on the next train headed north.

Cross the Rio Grande and knock on Uncle Sam's door. Come on in. You made it just under the wire, but now what?

Storm says, *We are young and strong. Here to make our fortune.*

Sato shakes his head at the dumb greenhorn. *Please sir, we are good workers in need of work.*

See that big chimney stack yonder? Follow that road paved in gold to Smeltertown. Talk to Mr. Towne or Mr. Guggenheim, partners in American Smelting and Refining.

Storm and Sato get to work, making lead bullets contracted to the US military. Back and forth between Fort Bliss and Smeltertown, delivering ammo.

Storm announces, *This is our ticket to riches!*

Hmmph. Juan Sato pulls out his empty pockets and gestures with empty palms. He doesn't see what Storm sees.

Storm points south. There is La Sierra Madre, where the mines are. The Americans get the minerals there. *See the railroad? The tracks run from there and stop here. Here they smelt the minerals into metal, then sell it to the military who make guns.*

Sato pours the whiskey. Storm swigs it back. And by now Storm's got a habit: Lights his cigar. *Don't you see? That's why we fight the war with Russia.*

To get the minerals in Manchuria, smelt them in Korea, build the railroad, send guns and ships to Japan.

Sato says, *I'm not going back to Japan.*

Storm says, *No need. This is America. Everybody gets rich.* We know where the minerals end up. Now we need to get to La Sierra Madre, the source. We need to learn how to prospect.

Sato's got ears like antennae. *I heard they're sending out a prospecting team.*

Storm sucks his cigar, then puffs. *You speak Spanish. You know the way around. And besides, you know, in Tokyo I studied some mining engineering.*

They talk their way onto the team.

Storm is a quick study. When he doesn't know, he inserts Japanese, like he'll get back to you with the translation. His eyes twinkle. He's a trickster.

You got to love that Storm.

Sato's his backup, feeding the fiction, asking the questions.

They learn geography. They learn geology. Earth has history. Rocks tell a story. When Storm and Sato can read the story, they peel away from the Smelting and Refining guys. Get some burros and Tarahumara guides. Climb into La Sierra Madre on their own. La Barranca del Cobre.

Miraculously, they strike pay dirt. Stake a claim. Set to mining. Hire more Tarahumara.

Eventually they buy a hacienda just outside Chihuahua, a stone's throw from the railway. They call it La Tormenta, grow corn and beans, raise burros, pigs, chickens, and cows. Feed the miners who collect the pay dirt for delivery to the smelters.

Back and forth, a trail of burros loaded with provisions up to the mines and then back down again, loaded with—who knows?—gold, silver, copper.

Hey, but it's not that easy. For example, there are bandits.

That's when Storm meets Pancho Villa.

One day Pancho Villa steals two burros from La Tormenta.

Storm tracks the burros deep into the mountains. Discovers Villa's hideout. He's about to reclaim what's his, but then he has to go into defense mode. Kick ass kung fu style with six barefoot bandidos. Bandidos got no clue. Villa sees it all. Storm's a tormenta. Grabs one guy and holds a knife to his throat. *This one,* he yells at Villa, *for my two burros.*

You should slit his throat, says Villa. *That one's not worth two burros.*

Okay, I kill him and then you.

Tell me, how does a little guy like you fight like that?

So that's how it starts, the little hat dance of Storm and Pancho Villa, circling each other.

Burros and horses for protection. Yakuza style. Pay dirt gets safe transport, mine to railway.

Now and then, depending on which dastardly rich guy, Storm joins the bandido raids on haciendas, just to prove he's in with the crew. He gives Villa his cut of the precious loot, but distributes everything else to the miners.

That's the Robin Hood myth.

Keeps his miners from stealing and striking. It's a win-win situation.

What's Juan Sato doing in the meantime?

Actually, Sato's a good medic. A bonesetter and handy with a scalpel. Even treats Villa for a gunshot wound. But on the side, he's distilling sake from corn. Mining moonshine.

Japanese hospitality. Villa must get blasted.

No, no. Villa never touches the stuff. Sato serves Villa tea and lemonade.

Arnold Palmer?

Didn't you know? Sato invented it.

By now Storm's got a Mexican mustachio. So does Sato. Even though Storm is the guy with guff and bravado and Sato's the stiff and silent one, no one can tell them apart. This way Storm is always in two places, the mine or the hacienda, at work or on a raid, keeping control.

Then one day, *pow pow!* Storm gets shot in a raid. Sato drags him away, cradles his head. Cuts and lights him a cigar for a final drag and puff.

Storm says, *American Smelting wants to buy us out, buy out all the small guys. It's a lousy deal. I tell you, they got 2.7 million dollars to spend!* They can afford to acquire everything in Mexico and hold on until the price is right.

You want to talk about this now?

This is important. Listen. Don't sell out to the gringos. Bury my ashes in the mine. Sato-san, you are my brother. I promise I will keep our treasure safe. Storm's eyes glisten. *Do you see it?* Storm sees a vision, flying up above the great copper canyon, rocky outcrops, majestic falls. Green, charcoal, orange, gold, pink, blue, purple, mist. *There,* Storm whispers and reaches.

Word gets around. Storm is dead.

But people see Sato. They panic and run away. He's Storm's ghost!

If everyone treats him like Storm, he must be Storm. Storm is alive. It's Juan Sato who's dead. So that's how Sato becomes Storm. The myth fits him like a glove.

STORM 2

It's 1910, and Porfirio Díaz is eighty. The Mexican dictator announces on American radio that maybe it's time for new blood.

More like: more blood.

Francisco Madero makes a run for president. Díaz says he changed his mind and chases Madero across the border. Madero declares his Plan de San Luis Potosí. *Oust the dictator Díaz!*

Now you're talking. Finally, the Revolution!

Villa shows up with his men at Storm's mine, makes a patriotic speech. All the miners get charged up and leave to join the fight. They are Los Mineros de la Revolución.

Actually, Villa promises to pay five centavos more.

Villa says to Storm, *I need your money for my army.*

Storm says, *You just emptied my mine. Who's going to do the work? We've got to close it down now. Come back later for treasure.*

Okay for now, says Villa. *Don't forget. That treasure belongs to México.*

What would Storm do? The hacienda is already taken over with pacíficos pretending to be revolutionaries. Storm saddles his horse, tips his hat to the secret treasure and the grave of his old compañero. *Vaya con Dios.*

Storm crosses his chest with thick leather bandoliers—polished bullets nestled in baby cradles side by side. He secures his rifle and sword, tucks knives into his boots, folds the Rising Sun respectfully into a satchel, mounts his horse. A cargo of moonshine and dynamite follows him in the wagon behind. *¡Viva la Revolución!*

Storm marches with Villa, who has teamed up with Orozco, to take Ciudad Juárez, peeking momentarily over the Rio Grande into El Paso. So close to America again; so far from Dios.

Díaz flees into exile, ending his Porfiriato. Francisco Madero's the new man in the seat of government.

Storm lights a cigar and pours a toast to the ghost of Storm. *Kampai!* Now we go back and uncover our treasure.

But not so fast; nothing lasts forever.

Here's the long story short: Orozco, who's got thin skin, feels insulted and stages a rebellion against Madero, who gets the old general Victoriano Huerta to go after Orozco, who limps away to Los Angeles. But then Huerta gets greedy and stages his own coup, assassinates Madero, and installs himself as president. But since Huerta is the usurper, the U.S. condescends to back Venustiano Carranza, who commands Álvaro Obregón to march against Huerta and, by the way, against Villa and now Zapata too.

Against Villa and Zapata? But what's a revolution without bandits and peons?

You ever read John Reed? About this time, Storm meets him.

Juan Reed, prying around with his notebook for four months. He's the original embedded war correspondent of revolutions. Starts with the Mexican, then graduates to the Bolsheviks.

Reed writes about Longino Güereca, Villa's first captain. Consummate vaquero and number one sharpshooter.

See now, that's really our hero Storm.

More tall tales.

No really, 'Gino aka Storm takes Reed to the lost mines of the Spaniards, but of course they never get there.

Right. Storm number 1's ghost is guarding the territory, keeps the gringo away by enticing him with the natural habitat and Mexican cheese, doing R&R before the next bloody battle.

Wait, Reed says here that 'Gino shot six Colorados before they got him.

Yeah, Storm did that. Taught Reed to dance and gamble, drink and sing, roll macuche into fat cigars too.

About this time, D. W. Griffith sends a crew across the border to make the silent *Life of General Villa.*

Could be a prelude to *The Birth of a Nation*. Mutual Films makes a contract with Villa: exclusive rights to shoot the Revolution.

That's how Storm runs into Suzuki and Fuzita. These Japanese got picked up as crew to lug cameras, set up camp, cook the refried beans.

Suzuki is Enzo, but they call him Enrique. Fuzita is Takao, but they call him Taco.

Storm's got the moonshine and the macuche. He's got the stories.

Enrique Suzuki's impressed. He says, *Storm, we're gonna catch you in the moving pictures. One of these days, I'm going to make movies.*

Taco Fuzita looks up from his book. Taco's what you call a bookworm. But he's paying attention, says, *Movies are the future,* and goes back to reading.

Suzuki continues, *But for now, we take photographs.* He pulls out his vest pocket Kodak. *Make you famous.*

Taco looks up again, points to Storm. *Wasn't that you on your horse leaping from the train?*

Suzuki shakes his head. *Too bad. The director yells, cut cut cut!* The sun is coming from the wrong direction. *We have to film it from the north. They'll get you next time.*

No one ever sees the cut scene, left on the cutting room floor.

It could be a lie. But for sure that was Storm, running across the top of the runaway train, jumping into the locomotive to bring the smoking black beast to a halt. Did they really get that on film?

Are we making a movie or making a revolution?

Storm rolls a fat cigar and says, *There'll be a raid tonight. What's your plan?*

Suzuki waves him off, pours another shot. It's in the contract. *No war at night.*

Storm guffaws. *You know the old story of Oda Nobunaga? At Okehazama? The warlord's odds were one to Imagawa Yoshimoto's ten.*

Suzuki whistles, draws his hand across his throat. *That night, Yoshimoto lost his head.*

Storm raises a wise eyebrow. *And Nobunaga's advantage?*

Suzuki nods. *Night attack. This your idea?*

Taco takes a husk and rolls himself a nice joint, lights up, and says, *But it's true. Villa can only go to war between 9:00 a.m. and 5:00 p.m., with some flexibility for sunsets.*

Naa-ni? Storm gets up. Where's he going? Off to a night raid, surprise guerrilla attack on Torreón with Los Mineros.

You're breaking the contract! Suzuki yells after him.

The Constitutionalists take Torreón, then Zacatecas. It's over for Huerta.

Villa captures it all: heavy artillery, half a million rounds of ammo, eleven cannons including the most famous, El Niño. Plus, he takes hundreds of railcars—armored, passenger, freight, cattle, and caboose, *toot-toot!*—and forty locomotives, turns the railways into a moving hospital and traveling fuerza armada.

Cattle cars fill with horses, supplied with alfalfa hay, grain, and water. Soldiers, soldaderas, their families, all travel along or atop the iron monster, El Niño, perched on its angry head, a black ribbon of smoke sifting into Mexican skies.

It's magnificent!

From the North, Pancho Villa and the División del Norte, thousands of centaurs under sombreros. From the South, Emiliano Zapata marches with

Ejército Libertador del Sur, peasants in white handspun cotton. Fifty thousand strong. Villa and Zapata converge at Xochimilco, then parade into Mexico City. Can you see it? It's the most glorious romantic revolutionary moment of the Revolution.

Villa and Zapata sit side by side in the presidential chair of the Palacio Nacional. It's December 6, 1914, commemorated in a famous photograph. If you look carefully, Storm is there at the very edge of the photo, a slice of his head, maybe his nose, his big thick black mustachio.

A Japanese nose in the picture? What nonsense.

Well, for certain, Rodolfo Fierro was in the picture, standing big to the right. El Carnicero.

Is it true? El Carnicero who sent Colorados running to a wall, and if they climbed the wall before he shot them, they got away?

How many got away?

Better question: How many shot? Maybe hundreds. ¡Qué pistolero!

They say he lined up prisoners, three in a row, chest to back, shot three hearts at a time to save bullets.

They say he smashed in the head of British haciendero William Benton and created an international incident.

No, it was Villa who pulled the trigger.

But for sure, wasn't it Fierro who assassinated his own compadre, Villa's other best man, Tomás Urbina?

Storm was there. He might know for sure.

Up there on his way to Sonora, in Casas Grandes crossing a river, Fierro fell from his horse.

The hated most feared El Carnicero drowned.

Maybe even his men allowed mother nature to take her victim.

It was quicksand. He drowned sinking into sand, a slow death, reaching for unreachable ropes.

Didn't you hear the story sung in corridos?

But our corrido is this: Villa sent Storm to retrieve the body. Suzuki and Taco follow. The Japanese are resourceful. They cut down mesquite, spread out their ponchos, make a bridge, dig into the slipping sand, tie an arm to a rope to a horse, and drag the body out. Storm brings Fierro home.

Enrique Suzuki takes the photograph.

Three months later, a train, chugging away through Chihuahua south to Santa Isabel, is stopped. The Americans on board are not worried. They got the railway running in return for a pile of coal. Villa is in their pocket. Even so, Pablo López, in the name of Pancho Villa, raids the train, kills a lot of folks, including eighteen gringos.

Storm has joined the raid but recognizes his old friends Watson and Newman from El Paso American Smelting and Refining, geo-engineers who taught him how to read the rocks. These guys are on their way to start up the mines again. Mining can fund the revolution. *Stop!* he yells, but it's too late.

Storm is on the wrong side now. *Pow pow!*

Suzuki and Taco drag their friend away. They bring a canteen of his moonshine to his parched lips.

Storm says, *The map is wrapped in the Rising Sun. You know my story. Now it's yours.*

Somewhere outside Santa Isabel, they bury Storm. Pour libations. Make their solemn promises.

STORM 3

Suzuki and Taco make it to the border at El Paso. But there's a problem. They're aliens without papers. It's customs control with its stinking badges. Enrique Suzuki pulls out Storm's identity and walks across, but Taco Fuzita stays behind in Ciudad Juarez.

Suzuki heads over to Fort Bliss and boldly asks for an appointment to see its commander, General Pershing. A captain intervenes because, who is this Japanese anyway?

Suzuki claims he met General Pershing in Manchuria during the Russo-Japanese war, and he has important intelligence to relay.

That's right. Now, Enrique Suzuki has become Storm.

What's the important intelligence?

That Francisco Villa will attack Columbus, New Mexico.

Impossible.

The captain who receives Storm speaks Japanese. Observed the war at Port Arthur, then Mukden, enjoyed the Ginza in Tokyo. Left some madama butterflies behind to be sure.

Storm and the captain enjoy a tête-á-tête, as if Storm could be the last samurai. Storm is into his role. The stories roll off his tongue as if they are his own. Every Storm is different but the same. But still, no one believes the nonsense about Mexicans crossing the U.S. border to attack a sleepy no-account town of mud, shacks, and rattlesnakes.

But just as Storm warned, on March 9, 1916, at 4:45 in the morning, four hundred men charge into the town of Columbus. *¡Viva Villa! ¡Viva México!*

One detachment shoots into the barracks of Camp Furlong. The other charges main street—the local bank and Sam Ravel's Commercial Hotel. They kill seventeen Americans, mostly civilians. They kill more horses than soldiers. Then retreat back across the border. For Villa, the results are shabby: a hundred of his men dead; no supplies from stores; no money from the bank; no arms from the garrison.

What was the point of that?

Possibilities:

Americans invaded Veracruz.

Revenge.

Americans leave Veracruz, then choose Carranza for president.

But America used to support Villa.

Fickle America. Plus, Villa hates Carranza. And maybe Carranza says to America, be my guest. Come on in. Go after that upstart bandido Villa.

Revenge again.

America stopped selling Villa guns.

More revenge.

Villa's gone psycho.

Villa's manipulated by the Germans, who want to distract the Americans from World War I.

Villa's paper money is worthless.

American mines aren't paying their taxes.

Villa can't pay his army.

Broke.

So maybe Villa pays with dreams: Sting the Americans into chasing Villa back into Mexico to rally the people to the true revolution. *Mexico for Mexicans!*

Who knows? But by now, the people are tired of war. Tired of being conscripted with only two choices: fight or die, which is the same thing.

Find that Japanese. Find out what he knows.

The American captain who speaks Nihongo has to go looking for Storm.

Problem is how to find Storm. All Japanese look like Mexicans.

And all Mexicans look alike.

Maybe it's the other way around.

Never mind.

What's El Paso in the day? A sleazy Mexican boomtown at the wingtip of Texas, filled with hacenderos, priests and pacíficos, miners and AWOLs, all fleeing the Revolution, and everyone else trying to make a buck from the confusion: mercenaries, smugglers, arms dealers, gamblers, pimps and prostitutes, and informants of every persuasion.

You could buy or sell information from or to any of the following: Carrancista, Constitutionalist, Huertista, Orosquista, Maderista, Magonista, Reyista, Villista, Zapatista, plus Germans, Plan de San Diego, Smelting and Refining, Texas Rangers, and the U.S. of A.

Find your mole. Name your price. Business is good.

Find Storm.

It's like in the movies. Storm's nursing a beer at the bar.

No. Storm is propped back in his seat, biting a stinky cigar like it's a lighted fuse, eyeing his cards.

No again. Storm's in bed with a beautiful muchacha.

Better. Or Storm's just thrown a guy twice his size. He's walking away from a fight.

True lie. You don't find Storm. Storm finds you.

The American captain lays out his cards. He's been around. He can't trust Mexicans. Can't trust Indians. Can't trust Chinese. Trusts his black Buffalos, but there's the problem of visibility. Ah, but the Japanese. The captain knows the Japanese. *You,* he points to Storm like he's uncovered the rare spirit of bushido, *come from true warriors with a code of loyalty.*

Storm puts on his grave face, his inscrutable eyebrows, rubs his mustachio, playing a role.

The American captain bends into conspiracy. *Are you aware of the stories of the ninjas of Iga?*

How did you know, Storm replies, *that I am from Iga?*

It's settled. Storm will infiltrate Villa's camp. Send back intelligence.

And one more thing. *When this is over, would you consider doing a little surveillance in Little Tokyo?*

Storm rises to leave, indignant.

The captain demurs. *No no, just testing you. For your loyalty, you know?* The *one more thing* is really this: *How close can you get to Villa himself?*

Pretty close.

The captain pushes over a bottle with twenty little pills.

Medicine?

They say two pills will take down a goat. Six for a cow. For a man, who's to say?

You do the math. If Storm fails, plenty of pills left over for himself.

Meanwhile, Villa's provocative raid on Columbus sets a war machine in motion. President Wilson sends General Black Jack Pershing with a punitive force of five thousand to go get the terrorist Villa.

That's right. It's personal. Go find and kill one man disguised in the camouflage of millions of Mexican peons, concealed in the secret heart of mountain crevices, not to mention the corazón of the people, further disguised by desert cactus, shrub, and slipping sand.

It don't matter. The USA is mighty. Give it everything they've got. Start with two columns: cavalry and infantry decked out with Springfield rifles and semiautomatic pistols, artillery and convoys of trucks loaded with machine guns, medical and signal corps. The general and his officers head the caravan in a team tag of Dodge touring cars. And flying overhead: a squadron of eight Curtiss JN-3 Jennies. There're five regiments of cavalry; that's men on horses, including the Buffalo Soldiers. Then five regiments of infantry, two regiments of field artillery, one aero squadron, Apache scouts, the National Guard, five hundred Chinese laborers to cook, carry, and repair the railroad, and a handful of Japanese spies. It's a technological and segregated prelude to World War I.

In war, it's the first time they fly planes and the last time they ride horses.

This is no surprise attack. Villa can hear the roar of their approach from miles away.

You want Villa? Maybe your better bet is sending an invisible Storm.

Storm crosses the Rio Grande into Ciudad Juarez to find his old pal Taco Fuzita, cooking chop suey in the back of a café and still reading between jobs.

Where'd you learn to cook Chinese?

I bring a wok and fire it up. They call me El Chino.

Storm says, *Taco, let me see your books. Hey,* he notices, *you have two copies of this one.*

American Diary of a Japanese Girl by Miss Morning Glory. Good for practicing your English.

Get ready, Storm says. *Grow a mustache, and bring both copies.*

We going back for treasure?

That's right, but first we got to take care of some business.

At command central in the city of Dublán, Storm and Taco find the captain. *We have a gift for you.* Storm hands him the diary. *As you have knowledge of our authentic Japanese culture, we believe you will find this book of interest.*

He introduces assistant Taco Fuzita. Taco can read. He points to the book. Taco cooks too. He points to the wok. Taco says, *At your service, sir.*

Storm bows and leaves.

Storm packs his burros with a flock of caged pigeons and heads south like a disinterested pacífico. He spots the Jennies flying over, back and forth with their cameras, searching from the sky. The Jennies can't spot a Japanese and two burros; how are they going to find Pancho Villa?

Somewhere around Guerrero, Villa scores a victory against the Carrancistas, but he gets shot in the knee. The leg's a shattered mess. Storm tails the wounded general to his hideout at cueva de Coscomate. Storm still has his special prescription, shakes the bottle like a maraca. Maybe Villa will die anyway of gangrene.

Storm gets comfortable waiting out on a high plateau under Douglas fir, opens the *American Diary* to read the life of Miss Morning Glory. The words are all there. *Evil fox. America. Chinaman. Jap. Mexico. Revolution.* Storm dips his pen in lemonade and pens his invisible intelligence onto thin rice paper: page, line, word number. Gojugo, ichi, roku. Hyaku niju nana, juyon, ni. Etc., etc.

Evil fox wounded, hiding but not dead. Dorados killed. Weapons cache hidden in Namiquipa. Folds the missive, tucks it tiny and attached to a stout pigeon, and off it flutters to the other copy of the *American Diary.*

Two months pass, but Villa doesn't die.

Storm pens: *Evil Fox in hole at Hacienda Torreon de Canas.* Or, *Evil Fox on move to storm chicken pen at Hacienda Coralles.* Or, *Evil Fox Independence Day plan for Chihuahua.*

Back in Dublán, Taco-san heats up the rice paper, deciphers the kanji, and makes his reports.

Villa is very much vivo. Taco writes back: *Enough lying low. Activate the plan.*

Storm steps into the heart of the Revolution: Villa's red caboose at the end of his revolutionary train, with chintz curtains, walls decorated with photos of lovely ladies snuggling virile portraits of God-rest-his-soul-Madero and the valiant Villa himself. In the day, a command center with generals, a kitchen to one side. At night a bunkroom of snoring, dreaming men.

It's Luz Corral who sends Storm to her husband with her recommendations. Villa has many wives and many kids, but Storm knows she's la númera una. She says, *We are partial to Japanese, a great warrior people with nice manners. It was a Japanese who introduced my Pancho to tea and lemonade. Can you prepare it as he likes it?*

And Storm serves up tea just the way Villa likes it.

Villa smiles at Storm. *You remind me of a Japanese I once knew.* Only Villa knows we don't all look alike.

Storm bows and takes his leave. Hoofs the burros back up into the mountains to check out the old mine. Camps out and decides to finish reading Miss Morning Glory's American adventures. One of Pershing's Jennies flies overhead, breaks his concentration, then suddenly chokes and smokes. Storm watches Jenny careen downward.

Storm pulls the pilot from the wreck, throws him over a burro, and conveys him back to Dublán. Before that, he releases the last pigeon with a last message. *Evil Fox medicated by Dr. Nodko.*

Days later, someone dies of a tummy ache. Funny thing, it's not Villa.

Fast forward.

An encrypted telegram from the German foreign minister Zimmermann is intercepted by Americans. It proposes an alliance with Mexico. The Americans flip out. Mexico is for Americans! Time to teach the Germans a lesson.

Enough chasing villains into borderlands. Get out of Mexico and over to invade Europe to fight the Germans. April 4, 1917, America declares war. Black Jack Pershing, having penetrated four hundred miles deep into Mexico, is forced to withdraw, losing Pancho Villa, who escapes into the crevices and caves of Copper Canyon's mother lode.

Storm and Taco Fuzita cross the border back into El Paso.

This time, Taco Fuzita enters as Eduardo Fung. Having served the American army, he's one of Pershing's Chinese.

Storm marries Taco's sister Masayo who arrives as a picture bride. They open a dry goods store, Las Mas Baratas, in El Paso. And Taco, now Eddie Taco Fung, marries his Mexican sweetheart and opens the China-Mex Café for Chinameshi.

Las Mas Baratas and the China-Mex are convenient covers as Storm and Taco cross the border back and forth, prospecting to reactivate La

Tormenta del Rey Mining Company, lost treasure of La Sierra Madre hidden in the Rising Sun.

In the meantime, history happens:

World War I ends. Zapata is killed. Carranza is assassinated. Obregón becomes president.

One summer day in 1923, Taco rushes into Las Mas Baratas, his greasy apron flapping, face flushed, to tell Storm the news: *Pancho Villa murió.*

That medicine took its time: six years.

Storm brings out a bottle of his best moonshine sake. Pours it like liquid silver.

To Francisco Villa! ¡Viva la Revolución!

Storm, Taco asks, *Whose side were we on?*

Storm lights a cigar, puffs a sweet doughnut into tepid air, and peers through the bullseye. *See that border? That's the Revolution.* He lifts his glass, eyes focused beyond, like it's the magnificent movie he will never make. *Wide and endless. One day, may we get to the other side.*

YAMATO: Rising Sun

The warlike nation of to-day is the decadent nation of to-morrow. It has ever been so, and in the nature of things it must ever be. . . . the great marvel of Japan's military prowess after more than two hundred years of peace . . . In times of peace there is no slaughter of the strong, no sacrifice of the courageous . . . The virile and the brave survive. The idle, weak, and dissipated go to the wall . . . The nation which has known least of war is the one most likely to develop "strong battalions" with whom victory must rest.

—David Starr Jordan, *The Human Harvest,* 1907

The present strategical conditions in the Western Pacific are favourable to Japan; but where the militarists go wrong is in assuming that the United States would accept an initial reverse as final. If, as is all but certain, the struggle were to be protracted, no facile successes achieved in the beginning could avert the most ruinous consequences to the Island Empire. The United States could afford to wait; Japan could not.

—Hector C. Bywater, *Sea-Power in the Pacific,* 1921

Woody, a child of three, could not be expected to remember anything about that day. It must have been in the spring of 1923, in April when the cherry blossoms were most abundantly in bloom. The previous weekend, Isabel Stine had staged in this garden a private performance of *Madama Butterfly*, and his parents, Yamato and Kei, had attended, as had other notable Japanese and their wives, among them the Japanese consul, the publisher of the *Nichibei* newspaper, and the artist Chiura Obata. However, by the following week, most evidence of the commotion of the operatic production had been cleared from the grounds, and the children returned to the garden: to set their canoes in the pond; hide and seek in and about the maple, cherry, and bamboo; brandish sticks in samurai sword play. Their playground was a replica of a Japanese garden designed by Naoharu Aihara, who had transformed fifteen acres of land, logged of oak and redwood, into this California replica of late seventeenth-century Japan.

Little Woodrow crouched in stocking feet on tatami, watched paper folded into origami boats by the two Stine boys, Johnny and Tommy, who lived in the Japanese garden. They followed the stern instructions of a Japanese man they'd nicknamed Fifty-six. Isoroku, he'd told them, is written like the number fifty-six. He pointed to the journalist visiting from London. *And he is Mr. Bywater. His name*—the captain paused to find the right word—*means Seaworthy.*

Tommy, the younger boy, age seven, ran in with a box of fat Crayolas. *Captain Fifty-six, sir!* He stopped short and saluted. *Are these what you asked for?*

Captain Fifty-six took the box. *Yes,* he nodded. *Excellent.* He selected a black crayon and two large sheets of paper. *Here,* he instructed the boys. *You will build the hulls.* He demonstrated, rubbing the black wax across the back of the paper. *Careful, now, not to tear the paper.*

Yes, Captain, sir, said Tommy, taking the crayon.

Come, Woody-chan, Fifty-six said to the little boy, handing him a red crayon. *Our hulls must be impermeable to withstand the long voyage and possible attack from torpedoes. Shikkari shite.*

The journalist sat cross-legged on the deck just outside the open sliding doors overlooking the garden, puffing his pipe. He scrutinized the pond below. *Are we building submarines, too?* he asked, an English lilt to his words.

Tommy responded, *Mr. Seaworthy, paper submarines will not be possible, but we have the koi fish.*

The journalist smiled and gestured with his pipe to the pond. *I wonder whose side the koi will take?*

Definitely Japan! Tommy spoke enthusiastically. *They are Japanese! Isn't that true, Captain Fifty-six?*

Older brother Johnny, just turned thirteen, sneered. *Tommy, so you're fighting with the Japanese?* He wiggled his paper warship in the air. *Mr. Seaworthy, I will join you and the Americans. What is our strategy?*

Seaworthy spoke conspiratorially. *Lieutenant John, when it comes to strategy, we must confer in secrecy.*

The Japanese captain paused in his folding duties. *May I remind you this is a hypothetical battle? Our countries are at peace.* He looked over the paper fleet stretched across the tatami, then said to Tommy, *How about this? Spotted koi against solid color koi. For a fair fight.*

Yes! Tommy exclaimed. *Japan will take the spotted koi!*

Have you counted them? Seaworthy interjected. *I would surmise that there are more solid then spotted.*

Tommy rose to the task and ran out. When he returned, he complained. *It's hard to count them. They keep moving.*

An estimate?

Ten solid and five spotted, Tommy decided.

Seaworthy announced, *In that case, I suppose Japan can build more ships.*

The Japanese captain raised his eyebrows. *Ah, then we will build two more cruisers, a carrier, and a second battleship.*

Seaworthy asked, *What sort of battleship are you building here?*

Fifty-six pointed proudly to his paper extravaganza. *This ship has a replacement of seventy-two thousand tons with nine forty-six centimeter main guns.*

Johnny and Tommy, kneeling on either side of the battleship, nodded seriously. Fifty-six continued with more details. *This ship is two hundred and sixty meters in length and travels at twenty-seven knots maximum speed for a distance of seventy-two nautical miles.*

Seaworthy cut in, *That's outrageous, completely outside of your limitations!*

The treaty limitations only encourage our will to technological innovation, Fifty-six pronounced. *Beyond the main guns, here four turrets of fifteen-point-five dual purpose guns, plus six twin twelve-point-seven and eight triple two-point-five anti-aircraft guns. Not to mention the machine guns over here.*

Seaworthy snorted. *Preposterous. A single battleship is quite enough.*

Another cruiser and carrier, at least. The captain stood his ground. *With a fleet of ten bombers. To represent one hundred,* he said parenthetically.

Five. You can't get more than five on those carriers you are constructing.

Seven, said Fifty-six. *And throw in two more destroyers.*

You drive a hard bargain.

In any case, destroyers and submarines are outside the treaty.

Is that so? Seaworthy raised his eyebrows and snapped, *Get to work, Johnny.*

Yes, sir. More destroyers!

What about bombers? Tommy pointed to Woody, having abandoned crayon hull work, was diligently making plane after plane. *Now we got too many planes.*

Johnny said, *Let him be. He only knows how to make planes.*

Fifty-six glanced at Seaworthy and announced, *Airplanes can be outside the treaty.*

Tommy queried, *What's a treaty?*

What, indeed. Seaworthy knelt to organize the growing naval accumulation. The room was great and spacious. On the far end, the ladies sat on cushions in a small huddle, sipping tea, Woody wandering back and forth to show his mother his latest creation. And between them, the paper fleets faced off over a vast tatami ocean.

Fifty-six stood to admire their handiwork, and Seaworthy suggested, *Shall we have a practice go at it, right here on dry land?*

Tommy pouted. *I don't think that's fair. We don't want to reveal our strategy, do we?* He looked at Fifty-six, worried.

Johnny addressed the two men. *Earlier, you were telling the story of Admiral Togo at the Battle of Tsushima. And you,* he pointed to the Japanese captain, *were really there.*

Tommy jumped up. *Crossing the T!* he exclaimed.

Yes, said Johnny, *Show us how it happened.*

Fifty-six and Seaworthy, men now transformed into boys, excitedly rearranged cushions and low tables into land and sea. *To the west, Korea, to the east, Japan, and through here, the strait of Tsushima opening to the Sea of Japan. Now, follow the coast of Korea north to Vladivostok.*

But see here. Seaworthy pulled forth a large piece of paper and drew upon it the geographic hemisphere. *This is Europe. The Russian fleet must leave the Baltic Sea, at Saint Petersburg. How do you suppose these ships will reach Japan?*

Johnny said confidently, *They should come through the Mediterranean here and cross the Suez Canal.*

Ah, said Seaworthy, *you know your geography. But, the English control the canal, and they've a treaty with Japan, so the Russians may not come through the canal.*

Treaty? asked Tommy.

Agreement.

Johnny said, *Then, they will have to travel around Africa?*

Yes, around the Cape and through the Indian Ocean. Eighteen thousand nautical miles.

That's a long way. Tommy pondered. *How many days?*

Seven months. The captain returned to their cushion archipelago on the tatami and pointed to the narrow strait between Korea and Japan. *On May 27, 1905, Japanese fishermen and merchant marine sight the Russian fleet, send telegraphs to alert the Imperial Navy. Admiral Tōgō calculated that, after such a long voyage, Admiral Roshestvensky would come through the Strait of Tsushima by way of the Japan Sea, a shorter route to Vladivostok than to travel around Japan into the Pacific and,* he pointed, *over here, through the Aleutians.*

Seaworthy began to place battleships in a row through the strait. *Let's see. Eleven battleships. Nine cruisers. Nine destroyers. There.* He observed. *The Russians.*

And the Japanese sail from Korea, here. The captain situated the Japanese paper fleet. *Five battleships. Twenty-nine cruisers. Twenty-one destroyers.*

Captain Fifty-six, Johnny asked, *on which ship did you serve?*

On this cruiser, the Nisshin. As proof, he lifted his left hand.

Tommy noted the captain's missing two fingers and said gravely, *Eleven Russian battleships to five Japanese.*

Seaworthy nodded. *But remember, the Russian ships are older and slower. And the sailors on board are sea weary.*

And, Tommy announced, assisting the captain in maneuvering the Japanese fleet, an impressive parade across the strait, *Admiral Tōgō in the Mikasa-maru crosses the T!*

The boys and men-turned-boys played out the battle. *Load the torpedoes! Sssptt! Sssptt! Fire! Fire! Boom! Boom! Boom!* The Japanese fleet cut off the Russians as they moved single file through the strait. Eleven Russian battleships sank.

Woody ran around throwing his paper airplanes, and Tommy yelled after him. *No no, Woody, there weren't any planes in this battle.*

Seaworthy affirmed. *No planes yet. In those days, the battleship ruled the seas.*

The captain asserted. *The battleship still rules the seas.*

They all looked across the Japan Sea riddled with sunken battleships, respectfully silent. Then Seaworthy asked, *Are we ready to test these ships in real waters?*

Ay ay, sir! Tommy said. They divided the battleships, cruisers, carriers, and destroyers—Japan versus America—and trooped down to the pond.

Tommy, said the captain, *Japan will take her position at this end of the pond.* They commandeered a small canoe, filling it with paper ships and war matériel. War matériel meant bamboo sticks and a bucket of small pebbles.

Seaworthy and Johnny, with Woody following, marched to the far end beyond the bridge and readied themselves in a second canoe. They set off paddling, skirting the edges of the pond, hiding under hanging wisteria.

Purple wisteria climbed a sturdy trellis over a small pier, built as a covered outlook with a bench. Woody's father, Yamato, sat there in that shade beside an elderly man with a bushy white mustache under his large nose.

Yamato addressed the old man. *May I offer my congratulations for the publication of your autobiography?*

Ah. When you are my age, you write your memories.

Two volumes of memories. Quite impressive.

It's been a long journey. Had to write them before I forget. The old man chuckled and changed the subject. *How are things at my old haunt Stanford? You realize it will be a decade this year since I stepped away from the presidency?*

Yamato mused, *Has it been that long?*

I see your chair is now endowed. Japanese history and government. A smart move by the Japanese Consul.

I find myself in a difficult—Yamato paused. *A delicate position. Not quite independent. Hired by Stanford. Endowed by the Japanese.*

I know you well enough, Yamato. Not one to dodge the challenge. You've always wanted a position in economics, your field, but as a Japanese scholar who has made his home in America, you are in a special position between two worlds. He pointed toward the Japanese house beyond the pond before them. *Mrs. Stine has joined our Japan Society of America. We've got to counter the anti-Japanese forces.*

It is because of you that I am at the university.

The old man waved away Yamato's gratitude and said, *I heard they called you to Washington, D.C.*

The conference on naval disarmament. I interpreted for Baron Katō, who headed the Japanese commission. I plan to write about it.

Very admirable work.

We negotiated a five-power treaty. Limited tonnage.

I believe you've prevented war. You know my thinking. A people engaged in constant war kill off their best and finest men, leave behind the unfit and disabled, destroy the gene pool, reverse the natural selection of their kind. You Japanese had the right idea, closing off the country during the Tokugawa. You yourself are the result of over two hundred years of isolation, an example of the excellence bred of racial purity.

Yamato shifted and crossed his legs in the other direction. *During those two hundred years, the strife of war between rival prefectures was continuous, and entire houses were decimated until finally the Tokugawa, by then ingrown, finally fell.*

Exactly! The old man slapped his knee. *This is why I advocate staging civil wars to get war out of our system, to gain the benefits of war: military rigor, heroism, duty.*

Yamato peered over at the canoe hidden nearby, his little son wedged between the older Stine boy and the English journalist the boys were calling Mr. Seaworthy. He'd read this journalist's book, a very knowledgeable account of sea power in the Pacific, and he had followed the journalist's reports of the Washington, D.C., conference, reports that seemed to anticipate negotiations and outcomes. Yamato wondered about the journalist's contacts, and now there he was with that young Japanese captain, a naval attaché he'd met briefly at the conference, playing naval games. The Japanese captain had fought in the Russo-Japanese war, then came to study at Harvard. He was traveling in California after visiting his alma mater. Yamato supposed the captain was curious about Stanford's reputation, which the old man was always proud to show off.

The boys had fashioned crayon-colored flags, and his son's canoe waved the red, white, and blue. Yamato sighed and returned to his conversation. *Some would say we lost two hundred years—*

The old man interjected, *To modernize in a mere fifty! Do you not see how your people were ready for the task?* He stood up, stepped to the railing of their deck. Yamato rose and compliantly joined him. They were quiet, looking at the close horizon as if from a ship, then observing the koi below, glint of colors surfacing in sunlight, slipping into darkness. *Species: Cyprinus rubrofuscus koi,* the old ichthyologist announced. He closed his eyes and intoned: *Genus, Cyprinus, common carp. Family: Cyprinidae. Order: Cypriniformes. Class: Teleostei. Phylum: Chordata. Kingdom: Animalia.* He turned to Yamato and smiled. *The order of the world. Where would we be without it?*

Yamato could now see beyond the red arched bridge, catching sight of the young Japanese captain, hiding behind the reeds among the water lilies with the younger Stine boy, their opposing flag hoisted—the red sun centered on white. Yamato smiled wryly. The Japanese captain and the English journalist probably missed their own children back home. They were younger men than Yamato, who felt too old to play such games. He saw his son Woody squirming, the journalist lifting the boy precariously from the canoe back to land, back to his mother.

The old man mused, *Interesting. Domesticated carp cultivated for their color.*

Yamato replied with restrained deference, *I would venture to say that the koi is more than a domesticated carp. Japanese revere the koi, not only for its beauty and serenity, as here in this peaceful garden, but for its strength and perseverance. Koi are said to travel upstream against any current, undeterred, never distracted. And resilient, living many years, possibly a hundred. Today, we sit under wisteria and cherry.* He pointed to petals scattering, skiffing across the pond's placid surface. *Blossoms—ephemeral. Koi—resilient. Perseverance despite a fleeting life.*

The old man repeated. *A fleeting life.* His shoulders hunched forward, but he continued. *Do you know a fish has been given my name?*

Is that so? What an honor.

A mistake. A German naturalist discovered it before me, but we published first, so the name's stuck. Algonomalus jordani. I've discovered thousands of species, but my name's attached to this one. Found that spiky devil in the Sea of Japan. He gestured to the pond. *Nothing like your revered koi.*

Woody ran back up to the house and called from the deck into the open room. *My airplanes! Mama, I need my planes!* Kei hurried forth to prevent Woody from entering in his shoes, then gathered all the scattered paper planes and put them into a large basket. She paused on the deck with Woody, taking in their bird's-eye view of the pond, the two national canoes stealthily creeping from their hiding places.

Kei returned to tea. Isabel Stine was explaining the story of her Japanese house and garden estate. A third woman, the soprano who had performed as Madame Butterfly the previous weekend, also took her tea. *I was inspired by the Japanese pavilion at the Panama-Pacific International Exposition. You remember, in 1915 to commemorate the opening of the canal,* Isabel said. *Oliver and I bought this acreage on the spot. It was our dream. I am bereft that he could not be here to see how it has all come about.*

Kei said, *I am sure he would be very proud of your achievement.*

Isabel smiled sadly. *Johnny and I traveled to Japan, but Oliver could not. I so love Japan, its culture and arts. Have you seen the art of Mr. Chiura Obata?*

Kei nodded respectfully, and Isabel turned meaningfully to the soprano. *Next year, I want to help stage* Madama Butterfly *at the Civic Center. Mr. Obata must create the scenery.*

Satisfied with his basket stash of bombers, Woody ran back to the American canoe, but it was already pulling off for battle.

Woody, said Seaworthy, seeing the boy's disappointment, *your charge is to meet us there.* He pointed toward the red arched bridge. *Be quick and careful about it!*

Woody crept back and climbed the bridge, watching the two canoes approaching from either direction. The Americans stalled in a bed of lily pads and launched their ships, pushing them forward with bamboo sticks. The Japanese paddled forward and under the bridge. One by one, the battleships, the cruisers, the carriers, the destroyers, all emerged. The moment of contact. The battle was on, Tommy and Johnny flicking pebbles from their positions, the Japanese captain and the English journalist prodding the paper ships, this way and that, seeing them sink or float, crayon-stalwart. *Fire! Fire! Shoot! Shoot! One destroyer down, sir! A hit! A hit! Come around starboard! Watch your flank!*

Seaworthy looked up at Woody on the bridge, observing the commotion with wide eyes. *Woody, Woody,* he yelled. *What about our bombers? Bombs away!* he yelled.

Woody took a plane from his basket and tossed it into the pond. It hit the water and floated away.

Johnny looked up. *Woody, keep it coming for America!*

Encouraged, Woody tossed his planes into the fray. They whooshed around this way and that, plowed under the bridge, stuck to the big battleships and cruisers.

The battle waged furiously, but like all wars, while the preparations were long and calculated, the battle itself was over in a matter of minutes. Eventually the paper menagerie all sank.

It was at this moment that Woody found the koi pellets at the bottom of the basket and began to toss them into the pond. From every corner of the pond rushed every koi, their golden, red, black, white bodies glimmering and spinning—great behemoths roiling beneath the bridge, folding and churning the water. And, it was also at this moment that the soprano at tea with the women, persuaded to reprieve her role as Madame Butterfly, emerged with parasol under cherry blossoms, stepped down onto the bridge and belted the most florid and anguished notes of Puccini.

From his post across the pond, under wisteria, Yamato saw little Woody, basket in hand, a miniature conductor on the red arched bridge, presiding over ravenous koi, tortured Puccini, and the death throes of the greatest paper battle of the Pacific.

HARUKO: Mother Earth

My ikebana sensei was an old man, maybe older than Papa when Papa died. It was summertime, warm air sticky and slow. It's hard to believe I could be only ten and sit so quietly. He put three leaves of baran okame in my hands. Baran grow simply from moist soil in leafy bunches. Ornamental leaves, not flowers, not so special you would think. But these narrow elliptical leaves had white stripes moving through dark green, each the same and yet different. I felt the glossy smoothness and the soft veins flowing from stem to tip, frontside and underside, the delicate strength and peculiar curve of each leaf—this one longer, this shorter, thicker here, paper-thin here. Stand the tallest leaf upward to heaven, the midsize leaf to one side as man, and the shortest to the other side, nearest earth. A triangle of life. But take care. Turn this leaf to face forward, but to which direction the others? And their white stripes, how do their patterns flow? How would you come upon these leaves in a shaded grove, dappled in sunlight? Wet with rain? This was my first lesson.

HEAVEN

Do you see that beautiful woman there in the painting? That is me.

I came with my father to San Francisco in 1910 to live at the Nagasaki-ya. This was a boardinghouse for Japanese on Geary Street run by my aunt. My aunt wanted me to work at the house, but I refused. I told her I had come to America to learn to sew. I might have said that I came to America to be free, free of tight kimonos, but what did I really know? I was eighteen years old. In those days, I might have been the only single Japanese woman in all of San Francisco. News travels. Men came to the boardinghouse to check me out, followed me on the street. What a nuisance. Every month there was another marriage proposal.

Oh well, finally I married Papa. He made a proposal to my father, said his plan was to study in Europe, then return to Japan. I wanted to go to Europe, so I said yes. To this day, I have never been to Europe. We got married at Ogawa-tei, a restaurant on California and Grant. This was just after the New Year in 1912. We had a difficult time finding a place to live. First, we rented an apartment on Bush Street, outside of Nihonmachi. I cleaned it sparkling and made a vegetable and flower garden in the yard, but just when my seeds were sprouting, we were evicted. Papa and I packed everything in a big truck with nowhere to go. Papa said, *Let's have lunch,* to cheer me up. My stomach wasn't feeling so good, but anyway we went to eat. Sakai-san was there at the restaurant too and asked us about the truck in front.

That's how we moved into a room in the back of the Uoki fish store on Post. It was a room where the employees went for breaks and naps, very cramped, smelled of fish. During the day, I took care of Shizu, Sakai-san's baby daughter. This was temporary. Next, we moved to an apartment down the same street. Same thing. I cleaned it up, and we were evicted again. So much discrimination. Finally, Papa found a house on Sutter for thirty-five a month. Too expensive, I thought, but Papa rented the extra rooms to others: a koto teacher, a painter, and a shop worker. Their rent paid for everything. Papa chose a big room for his studio with a smaller room next to it for our bedroom.

That first year of our marriage in March, I thought maybe I was pregnant, but by April I was sure, so I told Papa. He said, *Well this is going to be a problem. Get undressed right now. Women lose their shape after they get pregnant. I need to paint you before you lose your shape.* Lose my shape? Look at me now. Four children. First Kimio, then Fujiko, then Gyo, then Yuri. Have I lost my shape? Well, of course I have, but what sort of response is that? That is what it was to marry an artist. But Papa was resourceful and smart enough to use his talent to support our family, drawing for books and magazines, making the backdrop for the windows at Gump's department store, even the grand scenes of opera. *Madama Butterfly.* Well, in my opinion a silly story, but never before did they have such an authentic set. And at every chance, he took us all away to places where the children could play and he could paint and draw. For many summers we stayed in a farm in Santa Cruz in the redwood forest with trips to the beach. You know the landscapes Papa painted, all famous now, like Hiroshige in California.

You see the ancient redwoods, their branches bending to earth, the twilight softening and making that misty glow, wispy fog in the warm air around the pure blackness of my hair. One night, the farmer at the house in Santa Cruz began to cough blood, and Papa ran through the dark woods to find help. He thought, *My friend is dying; his spirit guides me by moonlight.* See where he paints wet on wet, his hand guiding three different brushes to make that glow. Precisely, deftly, with each breath. He cannot make any mistakes. My son Kimio inside of me then must have known our arguments. What was Papa going to do with his naked paintings of me? He said, *All wives of artists pose nude.* Nude! As if this was my duty. Scandalous. How embarrassing. I would not become a spectacle. Over many days we argued and argued. I refused. He pleaded. *I will make a painting to preserve your beauty.* Such nonsense.

Four children later we got the letter saying Rokuichi had died. He was both Papa's brother and father. This is the complication of yoshi practice in Japan. A family's name must continue in order to hold on to its property and legacy. So Rokuichi married into a family in Sendai and took their name, then took his younger brother to be his adopted son. The story is that Rokuichi practically had to capture his little brother, and Papa went screaming and crying from his birth mother and home in Okayama. Who is to say where and from whom we come? Papa is known by this name, and it will always be so. When Rokuichi died, Papa decided we must all go to Japan. Kimio, Fujiko, Gyo, Yuri, me. Papa painted, showed his work, oversaw a series of woodcuts of his California scenes. He wanted to show California as he saw it. Kimio missed his friends and left early to return to high school in San Francisco. Papa, who as a teenager had run away from home himself, thought this was best. The rest of us learned to live in Japan, but it was not forever. After two years and before we left Japan, I took Fujiko to my mother's home in Fukuoka. Maybe Fujiko, so sweet and innocent, even at thirteen with a child's mind, understood, or perhaps not. I placed three baran okame in her hands, embraced her for one last time and turned away. I could not show my tears and heartbreak. When I was a good distance from the house, I could finally look back without showing my distress. I saw Fujiko sitting facing the garden, her legs dangling over the wooden deck extending from our old house, twirling those leaves.

Papa said, *No one will see this painting. But I must paint it.* He made a big easel for his sketches. He unwrapped a special piece of silk, woven from the first spring threads of the finest silkworms. He stretched this precious silk over a giant frame that almost filled our room. He dissolved a special glue made from deer hide, carefully simmering it in water, then straining it through fine gauze to remove all impurities. Into this nikuwasui, he added finely ground hydrated alum. This solution, this dosa, he then spread tenderly with a flat brush over the silk surface. He prepared the paints. Got oyster shells from Uoki, smashed and ground them into a fine white paint. *This,* he said, *to paint your soft skin.* He separated his best sumi and sent for special colors from Japan. Paint made from stones like lapis lazuli or crystal agate, also coral and flowers. Finally, he prepared his special brushes made from the hair of deer, rabbit, badger, bear, fox, and cat. He placed the silk frame with its empty white surface on the floor and readied three brushes in his hand like many chopsticks. Nothing more to argue. Every night, we closed the windows, the curtains. Closed the doors. Many nights.

MAN

Papa painted this scene after he left the hospital in Salt Lake City. It was while we stayed at Larry and Guyo's house for a few weeks before moving to Saint Louis. In the hospital, Papa had no paints or brushes, and the doctors strictly advised him not to work. But it was impossible to prohibit him from drawing. As soon as he had a pencil or pen and paper, he was sketching. We thought we could stay in Salt Lake, but there were no jobs for Papa there. Larry and Guyo were nisei reporters putting out the *Pacific Citizen*, so they wanted to know what happened. Perhaps it's not fair to say so, but if you did not live in camp, you cannot really know how it felt. Larry and Guyo might not understand. If they wrote anything, it could be interpreted in different ways. Papa listened to our conversation and painted. Meanwhile I rubbed the sumi stick on stone and into ink. This was often my job. Prepare the ink just so. Pass Papa the correct brush. Wash the brush. Pass the next brush. How many public demonstrations? For the show, I was Papa's assistant, in proper kimono. Like an operating room nurse. If you think about it, half of those paintings are also my work. No ink, no painting.

Papa could see something and never forget it, never forget a face or flower, its shape and color. He came close to losing his sight and losing his painting arm and hand. This would have been like death to him. What he saw the night he was attacked he would never draw or record. The truth of what one sees and what one draws might not be the same. Do you not notice that he rarely painted portraits? He drew what we all experienced in camp together because we had no other way to record what happened. But after we left camp, Papa was even more dedicated to the faces of nature. He thought that art in nature could save us. He was an idealist. When we arrived at Tanforan in that cold, smelly horse stall, I cried and cried. What did we do to deserve this dirty prison? We'd had a pretty house with a well-supplied kitchen, our garden with vegetables and fruit trees, so lovely, Papa's work at the university, our art supply shop, now with a bullet hole through the window. My flower-arranging classes, all Papa's paintings, everything left behind. One suitcase. But Papa drew our hopeless and sad surroundings and still found hope. That was his purpose.

Papa blamed the questionnaire. It forced people to take sides. What side were you on? Were you the enemy? Could you be trusted? What did this mean? Good people were loyal on both sides. Good people were spoiled by evil events. Even today, no one wants to talk about what happened. They feel ashamed. But what do we have to be ashamed of? We did not do anything wrong. We were wronged. At Larry and Guyo's, Papa looked at my strained fingers rubbing the sumi stick as if to draw blood and said, *That's enough.*

The man who followed Papa from the bathhouse in the dark had even put on a kind of uniform, a military cap. He had already taken sides, and he believed Papa was a traitor. Poor Papa, an idealistic artist, accepting painting supplies from hakujin friends outside of camp. Organizing the artists to make an art school in camp. What did this man think? He must have thought it absurd. At a time like this, accepting our cruel circumstances with painting lessons? We were at war. Which side was Papa on? This man's suspicions and anger must have overwhelmed all his senses. His weapon was a metal pipe. *Kono yaro!* he yelled and plunged the pipe into Papa's head. Papa held his left arm up to protect his right. He could not lose his painting arm. The man hit him again and again. Papa threw off his geta to get away, running around Block 5. I could hear shouting in the distance. Papa, blinded, grabbed a fistful of sand and threw it at the man, who screamed and retreated. Reaching our barrack, he was soaked in blood. I wrapped his head in a towel. *Lock the door!* he commanded. *Stay here!* Our block was in the first row across from the hospital, but it was still a good distance over dirt roads. I peeked through the window to see Papa limping toward the hospital and realized that he was barefoot. His forehead and brows had to be stitched back together. His corona damaged. How, the doctor asked, was his left arm not broken, his head not crushed?

Every day people came to see Papa at the camp hospital. All the artists who taught at our school. All the students. Papa's friends. The newlyweds from the wedding party where Papa had come from that night before his bath. Papa worried about the art school. Matsusaburo and Hisako told him they would carry on. Did Papa know we already had six hundred students? So many from the few children who came to our door that first cold rainy day. People repeated rumors. We were tossed back and forth between the banality of everyday surviving and anxious fear. If this happened to Papa, it could happen to others. Who could we trust? Then seven days later, a man walking his dog at the far end of camp was shot by an MP from the tower lookout. The MP said he shouted four warnings, that the man had crossed the barbed wire. Perhaps the dog had run under the wire, but the man could not have crossed. And they said the man was hard of hearing. He fell to his death inside the barbed wire. The guns were pointed at us. Horror and anger intensified. Two thousand people went to the funeral in protest. Three days later, the camp director came to tell us that he could not guarantee Papa's safety, and in any case, he should be seen by doctors in Salt Lake City. In the dark of night, Papa was removed from camp and driven away.

Larry said that Papa should speak out. Others had been attacked in other camps, and it was time these guys were punished and separated. True, the FBI had come to visit Papa, but he remained silent. It was midnight. Who could see in the dark? Papa shook his head and painted the dying man at the barbed wire falling next to his dog. Papa said, *I am alive. You cannot make me a martyr for your cause.* I watched Papa's careful strokes on paper. *Mama,* he asked, *what was the date?* I knew the day Papa was attacked and counted seven more days. *April 11,* I said. Papa nodded and wrote down that date. This was the last record of events at camp that Papa drew. Of course, we did not personally know the man who was killed, except we heard his name, Hatsuki. But Papa could not draw just any face. His hand could reveal the smallest but special details that marked recognition. And so, in this painting, he drew his own face.

EARTH

Probably the tower is much too tall, but Papa could envision it at the center, the barbed wire fence at the bottom, the barracks and distant mountains beyond, clouds and moon above, yes, always the moon no matter where we might be, in Yosemite or Topaz, everything wrapping around the book. Dorothy sent from Berkeley, with her letter, a postcard photo to show Papa, but he only glanced at it. He made a pencil sketch. He picked up a book of haiku that Asano-san had left next to his hospital bed in the morning and folded this sketch around it to demonstrate. He squinted through one eye. *The title can go here. Here, the author name. Here, on the spine, title and name.* And then, Papa took a large piece of paper and began to draw. If Dorothy were there, she would have watched in surprise. It was only a suggestion in her letter that Papa could draw the cover for her book. She had written with concern about his injuries. The book was a proposal or perhaps a promise; she, her students, and many collaborators were researching the camps as it was happening. Now I understand that we were her research. Did Dorothy know that just by writing to Papa, he and the Japanese who helped her research became targets of suspicion? All those questions, like the questionnaire, all this prying and spying. What would the government do with our answers? How could we trust the questioners to make sense of our answers? How many of us pretended or simply lied, said things to make them feel better, entertained their ideas to make them go away? Probably Dorothy did not expect him to draw this book cover for her, but Papa needed to work to feel useful. He did not care about being under suspicion. His drawings could not record everything that happened in camp, and he believed that Dorothy might be able to tell our story so that we would not be forgotten.

Around the same time, Mr. Nickel came to the hospital to see Papa and me. He brought two branches of flowering apricot and a bouquet of yellow daisies. Only Nick, the town undertaker in Delta, had any flowers. In this place you had to die to see flowers. They must have come from his wife's garden. When we arrived, we looked around, and it seemed that nothing could grow in that silty soil except greasewood and weeds. They say we were at the bottom of an ancient lake, all dried up. Yet beauty could come from this desert. In a woodpile, I found a beautiful piece of dead juniper wood. I asked Papa to cut a piece. I made a hammer with a stick and nail and every night chipped a hole out in the center, little by little. Someone sent us a box of walnuts. I crushed the shells to expel the oil and wrapped them in an old cloth to polish this vase. Then I looked for flowers. My ikebana students in Berkeley sent us books and special materials like matagi and tomegi and kenzan and, the best surprise, camelia branches. When I opened the boxes, I felt my heart swell, then sadden to see branches without flowers, but Yuri pulled away a piece of colored tissue paper cushioning the package. Yes, of course. We began to work with the paper to make flowers. Petal by petal and with a little glue, the branches were in bloom. Nick was impressed by our paper camelias. From afar, you could believe they were real. I taught him something about ikebana, and he understood. He helped Papa go into the hills to find plants and soil to bring back to camp. Papa and others found an old twisted pine tree, dug it up, and planted it in front of our barrack. They went back with a dump truck and got a load of rocks and stones. We had to create gravel walk paths to keep from sinking into the clay silt that turned into slimy mud in the rain. You can imagine us like catfish swimming in sludge. Papa made a fine garden at our place, Block 5, Barrack 9D. I planted flowers and so did Mrs. Hibino who lived next door, but they did not survive. We planted geraniums in pots and, later, bulbs. Some don't like geraniums, say they stink, but Nick said his wife had lots and they would grow with bright color. Tulips and daffodils arrived in April just as we were leaving.

Papa sat in the visitor's chair at a small table, drawing Dorothy's book cover. Papa's head was bandaged, and he worked with one eye only, hand steady, each line straight, precise. He would prove that he had not lost his skill. First, he penned the tall tower and the armed soldiers at the barbed wire. And beyond, our barracks appeared as if floating among mountains and clouds, a sleeping village in the distance. Perhaps he remembered the last night he walked there. These images were impressed in his mind and in our dreams, never forgotten. All around was the quiet commotion of the hospital, several beds of convalescing men, sleeping, reading, staring into space, attended by nurses and aides. I arranged a vase of flowers on the nightstand next to Papa's bed. Every few days I changed the arrangement. I placed the apricot branches in heaven, the geraniums for man, the daisies on earth.

Papa's work will last forever. My work must disappear.

BOX 2
SPOILAGE

2.1 Isamu Noguchi
1942 Poston Mori, Fuller, Ray, et al.
Modernism Utopia & mental health

2.2 Violet Kazue Yamane Matsuda de Cristoforo
1942–1988 Tule Lake Hankey
Feminism hysteria / trauma

2.3 Joe Kurihara
1942–45 Tule Benedict
Militarism patriotism, masculinity

2.4 Miné Okubo
1942–1943 Topaz Frank A. Beckwith
Citizenship sketching / ethnography

2.5 Charles Kikuchi
1942 Gila River Adamic, D. & W. I. Thomas
Resettlement diaries & oral history

2.6 Richard Nishimoto
1943–1956 Poston Tsuchiyama & D. Thomas
Loyalty Questionnaire social engineering

2.7 James M. Sakoda
1945 Minidoka Joseph Kitagawa
Game Theory computational social science

ISAMU: Becoming Nisei

APRIL

Isamu checked into the desert asylum. Out there, the war was ongoing. They said it would be safer inside. Looking as he did like the enemy, he'd avoid hostility, be protected, be together with his own kind. And since he was volunteering to enter, it was an act of loyalty, in support of the cause. He wasn't as crazy as the others; there are degrees of crazy. He was on the lower end of that spectrum, functionally superior by contrast, and certainly famous enough, or, let's say, marketable. He brought his work with him. Those were his conditions: bring in his tools, machinery, supplies, set up a workshop studio. Of course, he wasn't asking for special treatment; he'd live just like everyone else. Fair enough. Eventually he'd build what he required, get the others involved, inspire and train, create a working community. It was like starting anew. The desert terrain was a blank slate. Anything was imaginable, but you had to have imagination.

All this was John's idea. He'd met John in San Francisco where John's friend Alfred gave them a personal tour of the anthropology museum.

Isamu peered into a glass case of Indian artifacts—bow and arrow with arrowhead.

Alfred said, *Those were made here in the museum by Ishi—last living man of the Yahi people.*

What's that? Isamu pointed to what looked like a hollow wax candle.

Wax cylinder for recording. That one recorded Ishi's voice, his stories. Alfred's voice faltered, and he suddenly strode away, lamenting the paucity of space for the current collection, too large for appropriate display, but it was their luck that he might take them into the storage behind the scenes, peruse the extensive acquisitions of Egyptian and Peruvian artifacts. He pulled forth a ceramic double jar excavated from a tomb in the Moche Valley. *This is a Chimu pot dating*—he looked for documentation and confirmed—*around 1400. The design is clever. Two pots are connected here at the hip like Siamese twins, and this connection serves as a handle.*

Isamu examined the animal head on one side and the spout on the other. He could feel the artist's hands there, tools carefully manipulating the once-soft clay. He looked at John, whose face was radiant even in the shadows.

You can feel it, can't you? John spoke with reverence and as if he knew Isamu's thoughts.

Then John urged Alfred to show them the California and Southwest collections, after all Alfred's specialty, gravitating to tribal life along the

Colorado River. As they entered deeper into the museum's bowels, Isamu felt an itch at the neck near his left ear, exacerbated by John's excited voice, its suddenly higher pitch.

Alfred pried open the cover of a long box and, pulling away protective excelsior and paper, exposed a skeleton. *We date this maybe at five thousand years, matching the artifacts in the same archaeological dig.*

Isamu saw John's face strain; his eyes seemed to pierce through to an unknown place. At first, he appeared agitated, then serene. *The river is the source of life,* John intoned. He wandered away, speaking as if in conversation with someone.

Isamu caught pieces of the dialogue. *Yes, yes, how true. Tell me more . . . by the way, I'm here with a friend, a man with great skills. I'm trying to convince him. If he goes there, you'll take care of him. I'm counting on you . . .*

Isamu turned to Alfred for some explanation, but Alfred only blinked and paused the tour, unfazed. He said, *You didn't know? He hears voices. Whoever they are, they speak in ancient tongues. I know how it sounds, but John believes the voices speak great wisdom. Who's to say?*

John returned still in animated conversation but in a language Isamu, who spoke also Japanese and French, could not discern. At this point, Alfred translated: *Look for mesquite. Beans to eat. Hard wood. Medicine bark.*

Alfred looked with interest at Isamu. *Are you really going out there to the desert reservation? You know John's the Indian commissioner. They tolerate him since he sincerely believes in the work, and he's in touch with the elders. At least he thinks so.*

At that point, Isamu hadn't decided, and the man trying to convince him was crazy, conversed with voices that seemed to arise from bones.

When John surfaced from his parallel world, he said, *Well, it's settled. They're waiting for you.*

MAY

Good thing Toshio arrived before him. Good to be greeted by a familiar face. Not that he knew Toshio that well. They'd met just last year. Isamu realized that before Toshio, he'd never known any nisei. He himself had grown up in Japan, then moved to the Midwest, then to New York, then to Paris. No nisei in those places. What about Lafcadio Hearn's children, whom his mother tutored in Japan—were they nisei? He didn't think so. Toshio's folks immigrated at the turn of the century, ran a bathhouse until they could get a piece of land to grow flowers. Toshio seemed to be a dreamer, head stuck in books, and a self-taught writer. They could talk about literature. O. Henry, Sherwood Anderson, Chekhov, Gogol. Isamu could have been a writer; his parents were poets. He mentioned this to Toshio, but he didn't say his father knew Yeats and corresponded with Ezra Pound. Or maybe he said his father lived with Joaquin Miller in the Oakland hills, and Toshio didn't really believe him. It was better to keep things simple for the time being.

Every evening Toshio sauntered over to Block 5 and sat on Isamu's stoop. Sometimes he arrived earlier and accompanied him to the mess hall for dinner. The food was pretty awful, and it was better to have company to forget about it or to complain. *Don't eat that,* Toshio warned, and good thing he obeyed. Everyone else had the runs the next day. No room at the latrines.

Back on the stoop, he poured tea and they talked. He asked Toshio about their group of nisei artists and writers. *Have you heard from the others?*

I get Larry's newsletter over from Salt Lake. He's fighting the good fight. I'm writing something for him. After that Toshio came with drafts of his essay about democracy and the Nisei. They discussed the topic endlessly. This was an opportunity for the Nisei to create an authentic democracy. *Maybe we were imprisoned for a reason. Or we can take control of our own reasons.* They both got excited. *It's our anti-fascist contribution to the war.* Generate ingenuity and creativity. *To serve the art of peace.* Their plans rose in a great dream cloud above their heads. Toshio would start a literary magazine. Isamu would start an art school.

Then, one day Toshio slumped onto the stoop. *I got this letter.* Toshio handed it to him. *They say they've got to delay publication of my book.* Maybe they'd publish after this war was over, but who knew when that would be? Toshio tossed the letter and walked away. Isamu didn't see him for a few days. When he decided to go looking, he found him digging around in the dirt, planting a garden. Toshio looked up with a weak smile.

After a while, Toshio started up his daily stoop visits again, but it was like that, up and down. Time and again, Isamu would see the shadow pass across Toshio's face, an uncontrollable sadness cloud his eyes, and he knew Toshio's necessary retreat.

It was during one of Toshio's retreats that the kid Jack showed up. Jack lived next door, crowded into a barrack with a family of seven. He was maybe fifteen. Isamu knew he skipped school. *Don't you have any friends?* he asked.

Nah. I'm no good with friends.

Jack started hanging around, watching Isamu carve stone or wood or build furniture. It was intrusive to have an audience. He required a concentrated solitude. Isamu sat the kid down with pencil and paper and told him to draw.

Draw what? he asked dumbly.

Anything. Just draw.

Turned out he could. Drew Isamu working. This was even more intrusive, but what could he do? This was part of the plan, to create artists. Kid wasn't going to school. This would be his schooling.

Toshio came around earlier than usual with a worried, excited look. *A little boy's gone missing,* he announced. *He just walked away. No fences out there, so who knows where he's gone? They're out there searching. I thought since you have that kayak.*

They rushed to launch the kayak. Maybe the boy wandered into the irrigation system and on to the river. It was a possibility. Even so, Isamu hoped they wouldn't find him floating. They pushed out into the water, Isamu rowing, Toshio's eyes scanning.

They spent the day out there. At some point, they stopped searching, lost themselves in the soft ripple of water, horizon of rock-carved hills against the stark blue cloudless sky. They could have kept rowing and escaped. They talked as always about democracy and freedom, about art and literature, about finding meaning in a time like theirs.

When they returned, Jack was waiting. He was sitting on a stone under a mesquite, digging around on the shore and playing with the wet clay, making random statuary. Isamu looked over Jack's figures drying in the sun. He felt the clay and nodded. *I bet we can use this. Ever throw a pot?* He got excited. *Maybe we could produce our own dishes. Chinaware.*

But Jack asked, *Did you find the boy?*

JUNE

Why hadn't anyone else thought of this before? He'd had a long conversation with Bucky about his Dymaxion designs: affordable housing, an aerodynamic aluminum structure that popped up like an umbrella, 1,600 square feet of living space weighing only three tons. Low-cost, factory-built, modern, earthquake- and stormproof, heated and cooled by natural means, perfect for the desert climate. Bucky explained that the downdraft ventilation system drew dust into baseboards and through filters. No need to dust.

Like flying saucers, you could drop modular homes anywhere into barren landscapes, build planned communities. They could be the first to initiate this experiment.

Bucky was out there living in the third district. Toshio commandeered a truck. The truck was full of harvested daikon to be delivered to District 3. *No problem. That's where we're headed.* And they drove off, but looking in the rearview, they saw Jack had jumped into the back with the daikon. Isamu couldn't shake the kid ever.

Toshio said, *You got a protégé. Where'd he get that sketchbook?* These days Jack carried a knapsack with spiral sketchbook and pencils. Any chance he got, he'd stop to draw what he saw.

Isamu shrugged.

Just as well. He can't be with others. Say he goes nuts.

Everyone is nuts. Just he shows it.

Bucky was running around in a sweat, giving instructions. Toshio looked at Bucky's tin saucer and asked, *Do you remember Orson Welles's radio drama?*

Isamu nodded. *Space aliens. That's us.*

It was at least a hundred degrees, and the shiny aluminum panels blinded them with hot light. Bucky ran up and said, *It's a prototype. I'm going to live in it and make adjustments.*

Isamu and Toshio walked around the structure, afraid to get too near it, and Jack sat on a rock and sketched.

How many of these do we need? Isamu asked.

Well, they've rounded up about seventeen thousand of us. You do the math. Toshio smirked.

If this works, it's going to change the way Americans live! And we'll be at the very forefront! Bucky was ecstatic. He kept wiping his brow, sweat streaming endlessly. *Isamu!* he exclaimed. *Where are those plans?*

They unrolled Isamu's renderings on butcher paper in the sandy dirt, and Jack came over to look at the gardens swirling around the saucer houses, the recreation center with a children's playground, swimming pool, miniature golf course, baseball field, basketball court, and gymnasium.

Bucky pointed to areas Isamu had designated for the school, hospital, bank, chapel, restaurants, and market. *This is a flexible plan,* he explained. *Beyond this area and along the river, we'll irrigate and plant. In this section, craftsman workshops. The urban and rural will be seamless and connected. Main thing is to create a new life in a contained world that's self-sufficient and sustainable.* Bucky beamed with exhilaration.

Isamu grinned but noticed Toshio's reticence. He thought to himself that Toshio was a nisei that way, or maybe it was his depressive side that never hoped too much. That's where they were different. Isamu and Bucky thought big. Wasn't this why he'd turned himself in? To be part of a social experiment larger than himself?

When they got back in the truck, they remembered the daikon. They drove away, and through the dust cloud revved up in the truck's wake, Isamu saw Bucky in the mirror waving them off, then disappearing into his saucer house.

It's down this road, said Toshio, making the turn. *Hey, what's that?* In the distance, they saw a small figure. *Maybe it's the boy,* he exclaimed. *Over there!* Toshio hit the gas, and they sped down the road, then stopped to search.

They ran into the desert toward the hills. Nothing. *Maybe we imagined him.* Toshio shook his head.

Jack said, *I thought I saw something too.*

Maybe it was a coyote, suggested Isamu.

Maybe.

The truth was that he and Bucky could make extravagant plans, but they needed a school now, not tomorrow. Isamu corresponded with John and arranged to meet with the Indians. After all, it was Indian land; the Indians had been forced to receive and house this asylum, a population much larger than expected. No wonder they were angry and reluctant to talk. But maybe they heard John's voices too, because eventually they came around and shared their knowledge of the land and their skills. Showed them the right mix of clay earth and straw for adobe bricks. Isamu was gratified to see that everyone got to work, but this was because it was a school, something they could agree about. The children needed an education; what sort, they'd argue about later. By the time the requisitioned wood planks arrived, one school building was up, and everyone agreed that the adobe structures were cooler and insulated. By contrast, the wood and tarpaper barracks where they lived were ovens. Dust and scorpions seeped through the crevices. Now it was daily a relentless 120 degrees. They didn't know it yet, but the Indians knew that in the coming winter they'd freeze.

JULY

Ray came around to watch him working in wood. *When are we going to get our art school going? Over there in Utah, Obata's group is in full swing.*

Isamu shook his head. *I got one student.* He nodded in Jack's direction and continued carving.

What's that? A bust? Ray circled him.

Commissioned by a movie star. Got to make some money.

What do you need money for in a place like this?

Supplies. As it is, we got to go scavenging.

So what? See that ironwood you got there? Look at that grain. Ray purred. *Now that's beauty.*

You're right, but paints, canvas. You're the painter. Don't you need paint?

I'm working on some plant dyes, then I steal oil and eggs from the kitchen. But I tell you what, if you can sneak in some film, I can make a pinhole camera. Hide it in a can. Heck, hide it in a piss pot. They'll never know.

Isamu stepped away from his work. *Ray, what the hell are we doing here?*

Hey, I didn't choose to be here.

Okay, okay. Isamu raised his hands. *It's just surreal. All this.*

Well, maybe you made a mistake.

I think they hate me.

Who? The nisei? They think you're a stool. Who can believe that nonsense about volunteering to be here? Then trying to organize them for creative democracy.

You're a nisei. Do you think that?

I'm just saying. You are kind of a prick.

So are you.

Ray smiled and patted Isamu on the shoulder. *We get along. Artists suffer the same insanity. What can I say? Nisei are so American they're pathetic. But really they're neither Japanese nor American. Here we are in this booby desert trap.* Ray spat. *Pathetic Americans.*

Isamu shook his head. *The issei I get. They know how to work with their hands.* Isamu held up his chisel and hammer. *Even now, they're busy making things, carving animals, polishing stumps of mesquite, making broaches and necklaces from shells. Soon as they got here, they got to work. The nisei can't handle anything but a spoon and fork. I don't get it.*

Ray walked over to see what Jack was drawing. *Not bad,* he said. He announced, *He's good, really good!*

Jack grinned, then looked past Ray to see Toshio in the threshold.

Ray turned and said, *Hey Toshio, you're just in time. I got an idea. We should show Jack's work. Give him a chance. Give everyone a chance. How about it? We put on an arts and crafts show.*

Toshio took off his straw hat. *Sure. Why not? Ray, you gonna show too?* He picked up the portfolio Ray had left at the door, slapped it on the table, then carefully untied the strings. Jack came over to see. Isamu peeked over his shoulder, and Toshio turned over the paintings, one by one. They were all paintings of the same outcrop of rock, the one everyone could see in the blue distance. In one series, only the tonality changed from orange to red to purple to blue. There were maybe fifty of them. Then there were other series of the same, some meticulously etched, some abstractly rendered. Hundreds of them obsessively repeated. If Jack was trying to capture everything he ever witnessed, Ray was hopelessly stuck on the outcrop.

The next day, hot winds started to blow. Isamu felt it start like a whiff, like the brush of bird wings that fluttered on with gradual intensity. Across the sky, lightning thundered and struck, and he waited for rain. But no rain, only pelting dust blasting across the landscape with the hot wind. It swirled around them, day and night, for days, sand seeping between the wood slats as if into an hourglass. He wondered if their flimsy barracks would hold and for how long,

On the second day, looking out the window, he thought he saw the boy in brown overalls. He ran out, battling to see through the storm, running this way and that against the wind. A mirage, he thought, and struggled back to his stoop in Block 5.

When it was over, he shoved the door open a crack, then had to push a broom through to sweep the pile of dust wedged against the stoop.

Toshio came by with the requisitioned truck, and they drove out to check on Bucky. There it was, the tin saucer sitting on a heap of sand. Dust had pelted the windows and worn the sheen on the aluminum, but it was still intact.

Bucky! they yelled. *Bucky!*

There was no answer. Isamu could see some movement within. Bucky appeared at the dim window, and he could hear a muffled *Go away!*

Let us in, he yelled back.

Go away!

Toshio climbed over the mounds of sand and tried to pry open the door. *Give me some help,* he called.

Jack and Isamu got on their knees and scooped away sand, then put their bodies into the job, slowly sliding open the door. They saw Bucky slumped into a round sofa in a living room filled with the desert. *Why'd you open it for? Never get it closed again,* he muttered.

You okay?

Leave me alone.

What happened?

Bucky closed his eyes, but Isamu could see. The downdraft ventilation system had been too effective; that is, it drew in the dust but couldn't expel it fast enough. Bucky had tried to close the thing, but with all the grit, he couldn't get it to slide closed. Bucky had been three days and nights caught in a spinning funnel of dust. Isamu wanted to laugh, and maybe at another time Bucky would have howled too. But now the lights had gone out of Bucky's eyes; his mania had been replaced by a sinking darkness.

Come on, he urged Bucky.

Yeah, said Toshio. *You got to leave this place.*

Bucky wouldn't budge.

Jack came from the kitchen with a bottle of Coca-Cola. *This place is amazing. He's even got an ice box in there.*

Isamu went to check. Under the dust, plenty of food in the pantry. He left a canteen of water on Bucky's lap. *We'll be back,* Isamu promised.

Bucky grumbled. *We plan a city and look for nails.*

AUGUST

Isamu woke with a numb arm, having slept on his side. Turning, he felt Yuriko pressed against him in the narrow cot. He sat up, slipping from the sheet. It was early, but the heat was already penetrating the barrack. She'd come back with him after the opening of the arts and crafts show.

Turned out that Ray's idea was a great success, gave everyone something to do and look forward to. Maybe no one had paid any attention to Isamu, but he'd been right about art. He was also right that most of the crafts presented, from the bonsai to the delicately carved and painted birds, were made by the clever hands of issei. Then there were Jack's drawings of daily life and Ray's infinite duplications of the outcrop. Isamu contributed his ironwood and plaster sculptures, modernist biomorphisms formed from desert. He noticed them looking his work over with sideway glances, curious but trying to ignore it. He knew they didn't understand. He tried to be nisei about it, that is, to move around the exhibits as if it was their idea, and he knew it was their idea after all. They were naturally communal in that sense, while he was probably what Ray told him, an individualist, an arrogant prick. He couldn't help himself. Within their ranks, the nisei had hierarchies, and he could only find himself at the top.

He thought Yuriko had moved with him in a passionate dance. True, she was a dancer, but when it was complete or maybe just finished, she sobbed miserably, and he held her until she fell asleep. In the morning, he stared at her sleeping head on the pillow, the sweet serenity in the glowing oval of her young face; it was unbearable, and he turned away.

Toshio started writing what Yuriko was calling a dance play. There was a narrator and a story; this was Toshio's part, and Yuriko worked on the choreography. Isamu suggested that they modernize a Noh play, that the narrator would intone the story accompanied by musicians and a masked dance. Better yet, he thought they should stage it outdoors by the light of the stars and moon and a bonfire. He got to work with Ray and Jack, building the set. Ray painted the backdrop; predictably, it was a version of rock outcrop. Then he designed a giant scrolling storyboard that Jack transformed into rooms and gardens and landscapes.

They went out and scavenged for the props. Jack dug out a cactus tree and managed to get a wheelbarrow to haul it back. They spent an entire evening pulling thorns from Jack's arms and legs. *Buddy,* Toshio said, *you turned into cactus.*

They collected small boulders, ironwood, branches of mesquite, adobe bricks. And Yuriko got a small troupe of willing dancers, young and old, male and female.

Ray, who turned out to be good with fabric, designed the costumes.

And finally, they got Bucky out of the tin saucer and back in shape enough to play interpretive guitar. Ray shook his head. *Bucky plays it different every time.*

Doesn't matter, Toshio said. *I wrote it that way.*

Yuriko found some kid with enough rhythm to tap a drum to her instructions.

Isamu watched the rehearsals. He watched Yuriko freeze and crumble. He'd jump up wanting to save her, watching her cower into a tight ball shaking on the floor. The first time the dancers saw it they didn't know what happened, but eventually they just did what she did, freeze and crumble, their bodies closed into tight angry fists. It became part of the choreography.

On the night of their performance, they set the bonfire before the stage. Everyone glowed in that haunting wavering light. Yuriko and her dancers froze and crumbled around the scavenged desert, Ray's rock outcrop beyond and Jack's panels of daily life scrolling by. Toshio's voice narrated over the beats of the drum and Bucky's variable guitar.

Isamu watched a small lost boy in brown overalls emerge in that weird landscape and wanted desperately to run to the stage to embrace him. The boy appeared, then disappeared. Isamu felt his eyes gush uncontrollably, tears running down his cheeks, embarrassed that he could not stop crying.

SEPTEMBER

Masatoshi arrived later, expelled from some place in Montana. He came over to Block 5 looking for Isamu because he'd seen the ironwood sculptures. *I can tell you also work in stone. Well, thing is, I work in stone.* Turned out Masatoshi was a bona fide stonecutter. *I work in quarries. At least I did until this. What we need to do is to find you some stone. Granite, marble. Out here, over there in those rocky hills.* He pointed to Ray's outcrop.

They all got in the truck and took a route west, crossing the bridge over the river, then driving for about an hour. You could drive for hours and never find the end of this desert. Isamu knew that Toshio still looked for the boy out there. *There should have been a fence to stop him.* He kept saying this. There was nowhere to go, so there were no fences. The boy went nowhere. But then, this desert was not nowhere.

Masatoshi knew this desert, knew where the rocks were. Sure enough, a garden of rocks pushed through the blazing landscape. *Monzogranite,* Masatoshi announced. *A hundred million years old. Under the earth, the plates collide, see, and molten rock gets pushed up.* He pressed his knuckles together, then raised his fists. *Then there's erosion by water and wind, and these dikes*—he pointed to the crevices between the rocks—*these dikes lace throughout. It's like some giant placed these rocks to form a stone castle. But it's all natural.*

Ray had his pin-hole camera and set it up on one rock to capture the image of another rock. Isamu followed Masatoshi into the rocks, wondering if Ray had finally moved to another subject, but then he'd probably trammel that subject until it too was unforgettable. Jack sat next to Ray's box and drew whatever it was the camera wanted to capture. Toshio found a spot and wrote haiku notes. Bucky climbed up to a high place and plucked his guitar, and Yuriko hugged and danced around the boulders. It had to be a scorching 110 degrees or more. Except for Bucky's plucking, the heat created a silent stillness among them. Jack walked backward until he could draw the whole tableau.

Masatoshi pointed to a boulder. *That one,* he said. He secured a rope around it, knotting a kind of net basket, and it took all seven of them to haul it onto the truck.

On the way back, Toshio asked Masatoshi about Montana, but Isamu noticed he clammed up. Yuriko noticed, too, patted him on the hand, said, *You don't have to say anything.*

Masatoshi said, *Out here, maybe it's safe, but over there, the walls have ears. You can't trust anyone.*

You can trust us, Toshio said. *We're all in this together.*

That's what you think, but everyone's got their reasons. He stopped talking, and everyone was quiet. Then he said in a low voice, *There's a plan you know, to kill us. They talk about letting us go, resettle out there. But it's got to be a ruse to make us think we're safe. Don't believe what you hear. And keep this information to yourself.*

Who told you this? Toshio asked.

No one in particular. I just know.

OCTOBER

Jack asked, *When do you leave?*

What? Isamu turned from chiseling.

Could you just let me know?

No plans. Isamu brushed off the questions, but Isamu had entered voluntarily and he could leave voluntarily. In all the plans for engineering a democracy through the practice of art, there was also the plan to leave it all behind. To create a miracle in the desert and to leave it there like a beautiful and perfect sculpture.

Isamu asked Jack, *What's the problem with going to school and being with kids your own age?*

They scare me. I feel like they'll tear me apart, bore a hole into my body.

What do you mean?

I feel their eyes on me. They can destroy me by just looking.

You know that's not true, right?

Sure, but it doesn't matter.

What about me? What about Toshio and Ray?

You're different.

No, we're not.

Isamu went to see Ray in the hospital. His arm was in a cast and his head bandaged. His left eye bulged under a great purple stain running down his face. *It's cracked,* he said pointing with his good arm, *but that's nothing new. Good thing I passed out, or they'd have finished me for sure.*

They?

You know who. You need to leave before they get you too.

Why?

Ray tried to sit up. *You really don't get it do you? You said so yourself. It's all surreal. They don't understand about pretending.*

Pretending what?

To be free.

After the drive in the desert out to the rocks with Masatoshi, Toshio retreated again into his garden. Isamu walked over to find him sitting on a bench in the stone path among a lot of dead flowers. Dead marigolds, dead mums, dead irises, dead delphiniums, dead freesia, dead roses, even dead sunflowers. Toshio looked up. *Heat stroke.* He pointed to the sun. *Wrong season to plant. Here, it'll always be the wrong season. Heck, what was I thinking? Wrong flowers too.* He laughed.

Isamu thought it was good he could laugh, but he changed the subject anyway. *You heard about Ray?*

Toshio bowed his head. *Yeah.*

Time to leave, he announced.

Yeah, it's time.

I'll be back.

Nah, don't come back.

No really, I'll be back.

No, you won't. Here. Toshio pulled a book from a sack. *It's our magazine, fresh off the press. My story in there and some drawings by Jack to go with it.*

Congratulations, Isamu said. He flipped through the mimeo pages and found Toshio's story. He paused at Jack's drawing. There he was chiseling, the soft features of a boy emerging from monzogranite.

He just walked away. No fences. He knew that at some point, Jack stopped following him.

VIOLET: War Hysteria

If men define situations as real, they are real in their consequences

—*The Child in America,*
W. I. Thomas and Dorothy Swaine Thomas, 1928

女は男より忙しく雑然人住ふかきつばた

Onna wa otoko yori isogashiku
zatsuzen hito sumau kakitsubata

Women are busier than men
people living in disarray and there are Irises

—Violet Kazue de Cristoforo, 1997

1943

Violet leans into the makeshift crib, a crate enhanced by pieces of misshapen lumber that Shigeru has hammered together. Unlike her crib in Jerome, it is a crude thing, but they come to a stripped barrack in Tule. When a previous family leaves, those who remain haul off anything useful or pretty—curtains, tables and chairs, cots, butsudan—and take it all to their places to settle in for the duration. Even pry away slats from the flimsy walls. It is like that manure-filthy horse stall back in Fresno. That's where this child emerges from her sickly body into an orange crate just like this crate. In the cooking heat. Is that a year ago already? From there to swampy tick-infested Jerome, and now another ugly barrack.

When she arrives here with the children, she sinks onto the dirty floor planks, clinging to the baby, and suppresses a scream. *Kaa-chan,* Reiko whimpers, reaching for her mother's attention, but Kenji runs away. Shigeru dumps their bundles next to her, lifting a cloud of angry dust. She quickly covers the baby's face, sneering at the man's back. Is this her fault? She could cry to get his pity, but she is done crying. Now where is he? Locked up in the stockade. A prison within a prison.

Hana has just come by, advising her through the wood slats that that white girl is on her way; Hana's heard her at the laundry asking about Violet, casually in a disinterested way. But these inquiries are never disinterested. And Hana is always interested. Never tell Hana anything, that's for sure.

The baby is nursed and satisfied, but Violet grabs her from sleep, whips open the door, and confronts the white girl with a crying child. Make her go away. Go away. So you want to see the rumors yourself? Violet's an abandoned mother with three children and two elderly in-laws. The man's in the stockade. Left her with his dying mother. Cancer. She blocks the threshold. The white girl is not a girl, but that's what they say instead of spinster. What a pity. The white spinster is so tall that, standing two steps down in the dirt, she is still eye-to-eye with the diminutive Violet. How old is she? Thirty? Violet's twenty-six. What can any white girl know about sacrifice? Violet's face turns cherubic as her baby's, in full smile, yet her body's poised in an aggressive standoff. She holds Kimi proudly.

Rosalie says, *Joe, ah, Kurihara-san*—insert Japanese honorifics to smooth the way—*said I should come visit you.* That lady hefts her kid like she could throw it at her. If she threw it, would Rosalie bother to catch it? Mothers and their babies, as if having them made them better, made them women.

Certainly hasn't made them smarter. The lady doesn't know Rosalie's on her side. What side is that? She'll have to find out. Rosalie scuffs the sandy soil under her boots and tries to decide on the correct attitude that will give her access to the room inside. Coyness might work with a man, but this woman will see through her ploy. A mixture of ingratiating stupidity requesting proper instruction, this might work. Try her meager Japanese to show her honest and humble attempt, stumble with the bad words like inu and ketō, just to get a small rise or knowing wink. An insider who can be trusted. Oh, that's right: She can pretend to care about the baby, about those poor children. How old is that baby anyway? Scrawny thing looks sick. How awkward, this maternal business.

It's easier to ply the men for information, play the geisha game of wit and female intelligence, the drinking sport. She can hold her liquor, cup for cup, tit for tat, get the tongues to loosen, dangle. Negotiating danger. Yes, it's dangerous. She craves danger. The war out there. The war in here. Joe says be careful; after they stab public inu number one, the next victim will be white. Untangling the tangle of hostilities and intrigue like a game of chess, anticipating the falling pieces.

Sipping tea with the women is tiresome, but this woman doesn't seem to be just any petty gossip. What a miserable household. How many times has she been displaced, scant belongings shed each time? To lose everything except her pride. And nonetheless, the place is spotless, the sign of a woman's world in control. So like her own mother. Joe says, *Don't be fooled. She's harder than nails, like that Chinese madam what's her name?* Madame Chiang, that's the dragon lady. Violet. Kazue. Rosalie renames her Hyacinth, then Mrs. Tsuchikawa, then code-names her Mrs. Q. Her husband is the leader of the radical resegregationists, and she's not shy to say it. Mrs. Q states: *The fence-sitters need to commit to renunciation or leave. That's the only way we'll have peace in this camp. We came here to be with others like ourselves, prepared to return to Japan.* She must go toe-to-toe with this madam. Rosalie reads her: bossy, defiant, uncompliant, an opponent to keep on her side. This requires more finesse. Rosalie admits it: The lady's unpleasant, and she already dislikes her, but that should not matter.

1944

Kameyo sits on the hospital cot. The aide combs her hair back and places a hat on her head. She's so nicely dressed she could be going to church. She shuts her eyes tightly and moans, palms together. *Namu amida butsu. Namu amida butsu.* Footsteps. She looks up. *Baioretto coming?* Useless aide can't speak Japanese, one of those loyals raised improperly. But the aide responds, *Kazue-san? Shimpai shinai de kudasai. Sugu kimasuyo.* Kazue is late. Why is she late? Kameyo won't go away for treatments. It's useless. Everyone dies from cancer. She will stay here and wait for Shigeru to return.

All these years, she has never been very strong, never well. After Shigeru is born, no more children come; Gohei never complains. When Shigeru is twelve, Gohei decides they'll go to California. From that time, all they do is work, save every penny for Shigeru's sake. Shigeru loves to read, to write poetry. Writes for the *Shin Sekai* newspaper. Teaches Japanese language. Such a smart son. And a dreamer. Gets his degree at Fresno Tech. He can go away to get another degree. Go to Berkeley or Stanford. But she doesn't want Shigeru to leave, is relieved when Gohei takes their money to Hiroshima and buys property. For their future. They are forbidden to buy land in America. Gohei says if they buy land in Japan, it will be there when they return. He doesn't gamble with his money like others. When others lose their money on rice or potatoes, she thinks yes, my Gohei knows best. She is married to a smart and honest man.

Is it fate? Kazue comes to live with the Stuarts, a schoolgirl. Gohei manages their vineyard. Kazue joins the haiku club; that's where she and Shigeru meet. Immediately Kameyo has her eye on her. Polite manners, speaking proper Japanese. And from her ken, Hiroshima. Such a pretty girl. She tells Shigeru it is time to grow their family. He is almost thirty, not getting any younger. Gohei invests in that bookstore on Kern Street, across from Komoto's Department Store, a good location, since he knows Shigeru loves books. When the evacuation order comes, they lock the door and leave. They burn those Japanese books. The sutras too. A sacrilege she pays for. Kazue is the daughter she never had.

Where is Kazue? She removes her hat. Stupid hat. She's not going anywhere. She'll stay here. Die here. And she'll say to Kazue to promise to take care of Shigeru and her poor old husband when she's gone. Everything has been taken from him, but he is a good man. She sees the white soldiers at the door with guns. Kameyo recoils and curls into the cot. So it's true, they are here to take her away to kill her. Kazue marches past them fiercely. Oh, such a relief. *Kazue-san, ucha, kokoni nokoru to kimetakee. Nanimo uchi o naosen. Ucha, byooin ni nagoo isugita. Ucha, yakkaimono jakee. Chiryoo nanka kikan. Kazue-san, I've decided to stay. Nothing will cure me. I've been in the hospital too long. I am a nuisance. What good are treatments? Aitsura ni korosaretoonai. Jakee, kokode shinashite tsukaasai. Tsurete ikare toonai. Kokode, anta to issho ni oritai. Aitsura ni korosaretoonai. Don't let them kill me. Let me die here. I want to stay with you. Don't let them kill me.*

1942

Tamie looks around the room. It's a far better situation than Bob, the previous researcher, ever had; what is Rosalie complaining about? She taps her shoe on the linoleum. Who has the luxury of linoleum in camp? And this nice furniture they've shipped in from that defunct hotel in San Francisco. A real bed.

She has a memory of seeing this white girl around Berkeley. Rosalie's one of Dr. Kroeber's students, but being a girl, even with her size and height, she has to work extra hard. But not as hard as she, Tamie, being Japanese. Dr. Lowie is kinder and more supportive; that is lucky..

X is leaning forward in his chair, putting on his sympathetic face, the one he usually has for her. So irritating. Why is he being sympathetic to this ketō girl? She's telling them about her depression. Says she's gained thirty pounds. Imagine. Tamie's only lost weight. Who could gain weight in this heat? This awful food. It's either food poisoning or nothing but cabbage. She's allergic to cabbage. She can feel sweat dribbling over the rash on her back. She shifts against the chair, refuses the urge to grip nails into her flesh. Reminds herself: She's heading the project here. She's hired X. She's this white student's superior. The white girl might be older but only an undergraduate. Draw attention back to the project. What would Dorothy say? Stay focused. Forget that it's 110 degrees and climbing, this horrid rash engulfing her body, fear of discovery in her gut, over her skin, rising and waning.

Rosalie doesn't have to hide or pretend; she's an inu in plain sight. But for Tamie, just sitting here is risky. The walls have ears. X, being issei, is impervious to her fears. Involving X in the project has been a godsend; he's intimately involved in the politics, enjoys influencing and maneuvering outcomes. A paragon of confidence. Since he's become her chief informant, Dorothy's correspondence has turned to praise. A relief to receive praise. Dorothy's scorn is now on this white girl.

Still she can't bear the parochialism of this prison. Hawaii was never like this. She didn't have to come here, but it's research, a degree at the end of the war. That's the carrot. Oh, if she never sees a Jap face again. She's self-hating and a misanthrope, but this is a necessary characteristic for a researcher, to have the distance and objectivity to view the hypocritical actions of men with equanimity.

Rosalie says she's read their reports. X and she have read her reports as well. That's the way Dorothy cross-checks their work. It's a subtle form of intimidation, forces competition among them. She shouldn't bear a grudge toward Rosalie, but it's impossible not to. Isn't Tamie smarter? She'll be the first to get her doctorate. She's an insider participant, but not insider enough to get the information Dorothy requires. That's where X comes in. She's a failure. Just like this girl. Both failures. Fodder for Dorothy's project. But if the white girl fails, she goes back to her white world. For her, there's no escape.

A tear dribbles down Rosalie's face. How annoying. It's for X, she thinks. If she were here alone, the girl would never cry. She wants to pull X out of there. X is *her* assistant. Tamie stands, apologizing that she's out of time, feigning concern, but filled with her own personal misery and the terrible desire to flee.

1945

Violet's arm curves behind and under the bump-bump of her baby Kimi hugging her back; her other hand grips the little toddler Reiko, short legs tripping, dust rising. *Hurry. Hurry.* They need to catch up to that man. See his tall figure striding away toward Castle Rock. *Mr. Collins!* she shrieks. Yes, she's shrieking like a madwoman. When he turns, he must see their tiny chasing figures but also most poignantly her wild eyes. Even when he stops in the road, she continues her run, heavy with the burden of baby and dragging toddler. The man's face is rugged and drawn, his figure like a mirage rising in the dusty August heat.

She hallucinates it's Mr. Stuart. Yes, he's come for them. Ted and Antoinette Stuart, her respectable adopted family, he a lawyer for the Bank of Italy and the Santa Fe Railroad. She plays tennis, speaks French, wears pretty dresses, graduates with honors from Roosevelt High School. She remembers the day in the garden, picking violets into a bouquet; she looks up at Antoinette waving from the window. Antoinette names her Violet, the daughter she never had. The cook and the gardener are French; to them, she is Violette. Better than, what do they say? Kazooy. Those years a momentary idyll, but then she marries, becomes Kazue Matsuda, and the Stuarts move away. There are two weddings, the one with Father Bryson and the other with the priest Reverend Shigefuji at the Buddhist Temple. She's written to the Stuarts, but no more. What is there to say? That she's returning to Japan? Was she ever really a Stuart? An American girl?

Kameyo also thinks she's the daughter she never had. Kameyo wants a Japanese daughter. Violet's panting, her heartbeat frantic. She's come from the hospital where Kameyo is dying. Why is she running after this white man? First Shigeru and now her kid brother is in the stockade. Even worse, in the bullpen, corralled like an animal. Tokio hasn't done anything wrong. He's sent to stop a fight. They broke a baseball bat on Kobayashi's head, then blamed her brother. Beat Tokio's face pulpy, broken teeth busting through lips. His handsome face unrecognizable. Is this justice? Tokio is a runner, a star on the track team. He can get an athletic scholarship to college. In the stockade, they'll kill him. Can't Mr. Collins help her? Isn't he here because he believes in justice? The Stuarts are lawyers, judges; they would know this is wrong. Where are they? Why has she been abandoned? Her mother-in-law is dying. Her older brother Tatsuo may die fighting in the Pacific. Fighting for their side. What does it matter which side? Whose fault is it that Tokio is on the other side, has joined the priest Kai and his kendo group? Sokoku Kenkyu Seinen-dan. He isn't really like this. A true American boy, but if you put a kid in prison, what do you expect? Walking around with that polished stick. Breaking up parties, pulling kids out of bed to exercise at dawn, shaving his head, training for the war. Her husband's been sent away to Santa Fe. Who is left to keep these angry youth from exploding? How will it end? It's been over a year. Tokio's threatening to go on a hunger strike.

Baby Kimi starts to cry. Little Reiko cries too. She will never again cry, but something inside bursts. A raging choral tantrum. Tokio doesn't deserve to be locked up. If he wants to return to Japan, let him go. *Just don't throw us out there to the dogs.* She begs the white lawyer. Pleads. Grovels, embarrassingly. *Give us back our freedom. Give us back our freedom.*

1943

Rosalie steps from her barrack room toward the toilets. She's tipsy from bootleg sake, a song limerick twirling in her head. She doesn't see the upturned spout of the oil can before it runs like a dagger into her calf. She limps into the camp hospital, blood running over her shoes. When she sees Dr. Noguchi, her stomach clenches. Word is he hates ketō. It's the recurring story in Tule. The doctor declares himself a no-no, but his son-in-law declares yes-yes. His grandson, a boy of nine, stands between. With no rights in this country, the boy he's raised from birth is turned over to the citizen father, by the doctor's standards a good-for-nothing nisei who took off when his daughter died in childbirth. Every day he remembers his lost grandson. Every day his bitterness concentrates into the tincture of hate. She scoots onto the operating table, pulls back her skirt, exposing the bloody gash, the soft knoll of her knee and white thigh. The doctor peers over his spectacles at the leg with academic interest, then tugs her skirt back down over the bloody mess, remarking curtly, *It will wash.* As if in answer, the nurse steps forward and brushes a wash of iodine over the cut.

She thinks about her conversation with young Satoshi. Pulled out of San Francisco State and thrown into camp, he makes up his mind. Renunciate. Become a full-blooded Japanese. Speak Japanese. Think Japanese. Act Japanese. Certainly he is boasting. Two hundred seinen, ten of whom pledge to die under his command, ready to attack a dozen inu. He says there's a hit list. Such an uprising will bring in the army and separate once and for all the true Japanese from the weak—fence-sitters and undecideds. The plans are in place; he only awaits the signal. She takes her Royal portable to his barrack, copies everything: his minutes from their secret meetings, his pledge to hunger strike, his personal diary filled with obscenities. She types, interspersing their conversations with denunciations of British imperialism and lessons in bushido. He admires her bravery in slipping by the administration to record their resistance. Because of her writing, when the time comes, Japan will know the courage of their convictions. She must not worry. He will protect her. Where is Satoshi now?

The doctor takes a thick needle and jabs her wounded skin. The nurse flinches, but she holds the doctor's eyes steadily. Japanese, she reminds herself, have contempt for cowardice. She risks the loss of herself to become Japanese, to become invisible. Secretly she despises the nurse who flinches. She thinks an understanding passes between the doctor and herself. At the news of the death of public inu number one, she feels what he feels, that the conspiring inu who stole from the co-op coffers has gotten what he deserves. A knife to his throat. The doctor tugs at the needle, but it doesn't give. He asks, *Does it pain?* She replies no, and in fact she feels nothing.

Satoshi has confessed he does not love his wife. He prefers strong, spirited women like her, not meek and docile. She thinks about Mrs. Q. Would Satoshi prefer Mrs. Q? The doctor motions to the nurse, who threads a proper needle. The doctor begins to stitch the cut, drawing together torn skin.

The resegregationists seem to be splitting into factions. Bald heads versus longhairs. Bōzu versus yogore. *Dai nippon teikoku banzai!* Satoshi, hairless, appears stalwart, his earnest face naked, unmasked. To this vulnerable face she validates the edicts of bushidō. She says the samurai code of ethics requires sacrifice. She thinks Japanese understand oblique references. But what has bushidō got to do with love?

The doctor grabs the stubborn needle with pliers and yanks it out. The needle has achieved a kind of numbness in the area. *Does it pain?* the doctor asks again. She feels nothing. Stoically, she stands. She thanks the doctor, bows, and takes her leave.

1945

Dorothy takes quick puffs from a mentholated cigarette. Her keen eyes pierce through smoke. It's the young men who irritate her the most. They condescend to hide their arrogance, but she knows they are stewing in their discontent. Frank, Morton, Jimmy—they all complain about the need for a theoretical basis for this study. But how can she have theory before she has facts? She sends them out in the field to find evidence and to experience, and all they do is complain that they can't find whatever it is if they don't know what it is. She needs them to be her unprejudiced eyes and ears, as if she herself were physically out there. Here is an historic event that has never occurred before. The situation is continuously in flux. She has an opportunity to record a critical moment, a moment of extreme change, to accompany these people into forced migration from both urban and rural locations to collective confinement. If she is able to assess the problems during this process, she can then create a theoretical basis to predict other migratory situations, for example, forced migration patterns that are inevitably arising on the European front.

She looks over at W.I., who's snoring in his easy chair under a bunch of reports. Everyone else in the original research group, all the men, are now enlisted into the war effort. She's left alone, as if her work on the home front is confined to the kitchen rather than in the academy. When W.I. awakes, he'll want dinner, a glass of wine. She puts out her cigarette and returns to her typewriter, typing furiously.

Morton especially is sure to get himself into trouble, playing the liberal card, pointing fingers at politicians and big wig ag farmers in California. Rein him in. This project is war material. Make this absolutely clear. It's essential to keep the project objective, based in science, statistical quantitative evidence, factually verified reportage. The WRA has their sociological unit, but what good is it? Set up too late in the game. They've obviously failed miserably, have not anticipated the consequences of this registration. Now there is no way to fix it. She arrives to study a mistake. Plus, she needs to protect her insider informants. They are all running scared. She removes them to the outside, to Chicago, one by one. Charlie. Frank. Jimmie. Tamie, who shows so much promise but in the end with nothing to show. Who's left? X. Praise the lord for X. And Rosalie, her white hope. That girl who's gone native. She pulls her out too. The vicissitudes of the academy. Few women survive. She returns to her typing. Writes to Tamie: *Your negativism has a been a source of distress and unquestionably disruptive to the morale of your co-workers.*

W.I. snorts himself awake, grabs the reports scattered across his chest, and sits up. How old he's become. She watches him pinch out the Bull Durham and roll up a nice wad. He lights up and resumes reading. She lights up, too, takes a long draw. After all these years, she knows what he thinks: Go with the oral histories. Find out what the people are thinking and saying now before it is lost in fictitious memory. She thinks: People don't respond to situations based on objectivity but based on meanings that are subjective to their own experiences. The meaning of being Japanese is subjective. Those questions, that damned questionnaire, are meaningless, but the consequences of interpreting them, choosing yes or no, shape the future. The choices are the differential behaviors. The results are the differential analyses. The statistics will support the migratory choices: to stay, to leave, to return.

1945

Violet returns from the co-op with the package she's ordered: five yards of white cotton cloth. Her father-in-law Gohei is sitting on the cot hugging the box, staring into space, same as when she left him an hour ago. She feels Kameyo's slight hand in hers, how it slips into another world while waiting to touch her only son, Shigeru, who never comes. Now ashes in that box. Gohei will take Kameyo home to Hiroshima, bury her properly with her kin, honor her years of sacrifice, honor her devotion to hotokesama. He is sixty-two this year. Everything they work for, their house, the bookstore, their savings, has disappeared. His son is already on his way back to Japan. Violet promises to join Gohei, bring his grandchildren, but he must leave before. No reason to stay. Take Kameyo home. He has property, land, and houses in Hiroshima. They can find another life, a comfortable life, off the rental of his properties. He is, after all, a rich man in Japan.

Shigeru writes to his father from prison in Santa Fe. It has to be in English, and Kazue translates, but everything is censored. What meaning can the letter have? How many letters has she written to tell Shigeru about his parents, how many letters to plead with prison authorities to release his son so that he can see his mother before she dies?

Her brother Tokio has renounced citizenship and left for Santa Fe, too, a confirmation of his true spirit. It's a badge of honor. She thinks, some who renounce and leave with him are only leaving to avoid the draft. Or they are forced to renounce so their parents can stay in confinement. If the government has put them here for their safety, let it keep them safe. They won't leave to get killed out there. Government says they are free to go. What kind of poison freedom is this? They have nothing to return to, no business, no farm, no way to live. How can the government hand them twenty-five bucks and kick them out? They declare for repatriation, for renunciation, in order to stay. They can change their minds later. Kazue smirks. Change their minds. This man Gohei and his son won't do that, are firm in their convictions from the very beginning. They are Japanese. They have always been Japanese.

She carefully opens the package, separating the brown paper from the white cloth. Gohei removes his shirt, his aging body still vigorous from constant labor, and begins with one end of the cloth, wrapping it around his bare waist, then places Kameyo's box of ashes on his belly and commands Kazue to continue wrapping, winding around and around, then ripping the ends to secure the box tightly to his body, pregnant with death. He is not separated from Kameyo. They will journey home together.

1946

Shika turns to see a woman she does not recognize. But the woman also does not recognize Shika, her scarred face, frizzled pieces of hair straggling from her burned bald head. Her eyes wander over the woman's face, observes its corruption into horror. The voice stifled midair.

A fuzzy image floats across her horizon. A wild rooster or perhaps a stray pig disappears into the cane. The voices of her children. Two boys and the girl. They chase each other in the soft rain. She taps her belly, another child on the way. She returns to her task, pressing pieces of a sleeve together under the clack-clacking of the Singer needle. A fine dress for Mrs. Stuart. Mr. Stuart arrives on the Big Island with silk from San Francisco and the latest designs from Paris. Shika copies them carefully. Her work is impeccable. She is constantly busy, sewing clothing for laborers and managers—farming hakama, muumuu, shirts, pants, elegant gowns. She's come to

Hawaii with her husband, Katsuichi. They've hired him to teach school, teach Japanese to the children on the Yamagita Plantation in Hakalau. She catches glimpses of the sugar baron Klaus Spreckels when he visits his attorney, her boss, Mr. Stuart. She fits many dresses to Antoinette Stuart's pretty figure. Her life is not the grimy toil of cane labor; she's a step above, and her husband is educated and respected. To the big house, she brings little Kazue and Antoinette dotes on her pretty little Japanese doll.

The strange woman calls her Mother. She's Kazue. Kazue. There are no words. Only sorrow.

Katsuichi is not well. He can no longer teach. They leave Hakalau. Katsuichi comes home to Hiroshima to die. A widow alone in Hiroshima with four children to raise, Shika sends each child away. First is Kazue, fourteen. Antoinette Stuart has never forgetten her Japanese doll, calls her back to Fresno like a pretty dress. Tatsuo is next. Then Tokio. One by one, they leave. One day, Kazue returns to Hiroshima with her little son and daughter; they live together for a brief happy time, but then they are gone again.

War comes. The bomb.

She wants Kazue to know it is she inside this wrecked body, behind this grotesque disfigured face. She weeps, apologizing again and again. She is still here inside this dead body.

1981

Violet pours water from a bamboo ladle over the tombstone; her mother's name slowly darkens and clarifies under the cool flow. She presses palms together and prays, the tiny smoky vein of incense slipping into summer air. After many years, Tokio has made this stone monument. Once long ago, they say Tatsuo came in uniform to visit. That was long before Tokio placed this proper stone. After Tatsuo leaves to enlist in Sacramento, she never sees him again. Never. She and Tokio are on the wrong side, a great shame to him. They are dead to Tatsuo's memory. She removes an envelope thick with fine paper, Tokio's testimony of his days in Tule, in the stockade, the bullpen, his broken face, the hunger strike, his renunciation. If Tatsuo reads this, what will he understand? She has come from Tokio's house in Nagasaki, where she's urged him to write. She will translate and present his condemnation to the congressional wartime commission in December. She shows the precious envelope to Shika's stone. She removes a second piece of folded rice paper upon which she brushes a haiku to her mother.

She lights a match at one corner. The poem flutters, gold into ashes. Her children's faces stir there.

Once again, she is huddled wretchedly with her three children on a cement block, the bombed-out remains of the Hiroshima station. They are renunciants as she promised, following Gohei and Shigeru to Hiroshima. She wraps their shivering bodies in newspaper, whimpering in the cold until morning. She finds Gohei, a miserable old man living in a house with relatives and ten children. They press four more hungry bodies into this crowded house. They live on potato leaves. Everything he owns is lost. Koreans, living in his properties, refuse to leave. He sells his land for nothing when MacArthur declares he can only keep it if he farms it. She asks about Shigeru, and Gohei turns away.

She turns from her mother's stone, winds her way out of the little cemetery. She lost her citizenship when she followed her husband to Japan. Shigeru has taken another wife, started a new family. Gohei says simply, *You are no longer married to Shigeru. You are not my daughter-in-law. You must leave.* She was always Kameyo's choice, not his. Now she is betrayed by this old man who expunges her children from his koseki. She alone must save them.

She can speak and write English. A renunciant, the Americans send her away, so she finds work with the British. Every penny she saves to send Kenji back home to California. Antoinette Stuart answers her letter, finds a nice family in Marysville. Then she sends Reiko to Fresno, to Judge Hoffman's house. The old solution for her mother, Shika, is also her solution. The Catholic services are the go-between. To save the children. But Kenji runs away. They call him a thief. And Reiko is sent away. They blame her for almost drowning a baby. When the angry letters arrive, she runs to the American consulate. She's not an American; they cannot help her. She cannot return to America. What happens to children lost to America, she can never really know. She believes she sent them away to be Americans. They believe nothing. They resent the last child born on an orange crate in a horse stall, the only one they believe she truly saves, saves for God. But when she finally recovers American citizenship and returns, the last child, Kimi, must be left behind in Japan. Years pass. Another rupture complete.

She returns from the cemetery to her aunt's house. There at the table, cushioned and sipping cold barley tea, she sees a young woman, half her age, half her features. Kimi. This is the manipulation of her aunt. A gesture with good intentions, to bring the daughter back to the mother. She sees herself in shock, then a cold mask, every emotion contained in shadow. To her daughter she is a stranger. What is righteous cannot be undone. They sip tea in silence.

1988

Rosalie parts the curtains only slightly and peers into the street. The car is still there parked in front of her house. She knows the news, sees it on CBS on August 10, 1988, the president flanked by all those nicely dressed niseis, signing the redress. That is several weeks ago. She sees the rounded bubble of the woman's white hair, hands gripping the steering wheel, eyes staring into shaded street. Violet's driven from D.C. to Saint Louis, maybe eight hundred miles, two days perhaps, maybe three. In her seventies, driving alone across the country. When Rosalie is seventy, she could have done it, but not anymore. Old age comes faster these days. Murray's gone, but he checks in. He feels guilty, as he should. He did that video interview of her to set things straight. Little good it will do if that woman is still out there in her car. If she calls Murray, he'll come over and shoo the lady away, stop her constant harassment and accusations. Dorothy and X are dead; only Rosalie's alive to be blamed.

It's true that Mrs. Q is Mrs. Tsuchikawa is Hyacinth is Kazue is Violet, the woman in the car. Her field notes don't lie: ardent lady segregationist. Even in hindsight, she cannot say she was just a recordkeeper sent into the field without direction, a student researcher taking notes, but eventually she can develop a methodology, a corrective for failure. She cannot say that she did this work so that the truth could be known as history when history makes the government accountable, forty-six years later. Neither can she say that she recorded the right actions of Japanese nationalists. She can hold no opinions about who is right or wrong, who is loyal or disloyal. Trust is a sympathetic ear. And yet to learn anything, she must be neutral, even as neutrality is impossible. A sympathetic ear may hear with the torn heart of a stranger bound by another set of rules. She is made superior simply by being researcher, impartial observer, who must see without the prejudicial lens of her own culture and experience. Yet even a robot must be programmed to ask the questions. The reports are made. Dorothy and the one they call X, make sense of them, write the story. She is a footnote. But so many years ago, only she is there to know. Too naive, too immature to understand. She risks becoming Japanese to know. Risks becoming

German. The most alive time in her life, when every moment matters, when the consequences are life and death.

Joe writes to her in August 1945 after the bombing to speak of his horror and anger. She cannot respond. There are no words. Twenty thousand will never pay off that woman. What the government did to her and to her people can never be repaid. She steps away from the window. The sheer curtains hide her crooked silhouette. She places her hands on unsteady thighs and bows deeply.

JOE: Forty-seven Yes-No Boys

The basic Japanese sense of makoto is . . . a plus sign added on to giri. "Giri plus makoto" is contrasted with "merely giri," and means "giri as an example for ages eternal." . . .

Usage in the Japanese Relocation Camps during the war was exactly parallel to that in *The Forty-Seven Ronin,* and it shows clearly how far the logic is extended and how opposite to American usage the meaning can become. The stock accusation of the pro-Japan Issei . . . against the pro-United States Nisei . . . was that they lacked makoto. What the Issei were saying was that these Nisei did not have that quality of the soul which made the Japanese Spirit . . . "stick." The Issei did not mean at all that their children's pro-Americanism was hypocritical. Far from it, for the accusations of insincerity were only the more convinced when the Nisei volunteered for the United States Army and it was quite apparent to anybody that their support of their adopted country was prompted by genuine enthusiasm.

A basic meaning of 'sincerity' as the Japanese use it, is that it is the zeal to follow the "road" mapped out by the Japanese code and the Japanese Spirit.

—Ruth Benedict, *The Chrysanthemum and the Sword,* 1946

風さそふ 花よりもなほ 我はまた 春の名残を いかにとやせん

Kaze sasou hana yorimo nao ware wa mata haru no nagori o ikanitoyasen

Even more than cherry blossoms
scattered by the breeze
memories of the passing spring
bring unbearable regrets

winds scatter
blossoms
unwilling yet
to leave spring

—Asano Naganori death poem,
The Forty-Seven Ronin / Genroku Chūshingura, 1941*

* First translation from film, director Kenji Mizoguchi; second translation by author.

1 JOSEPH "JOE" YOSHISUKE KURIHARA

I was born in a little village of Hanamaulu, Kauai, on first day of January 1895. At the age of two, my parents moved to Honolulu, the capital of the Hawaiian Archipelago. We, the boys of conglomerated races, were brought up under the careful guidance of American teachers, strictly following the principle of American democracy. Let it be white, black, brown, or yellow, we were all treated alike. This glorious Paradise of the Pacific was the true melting pot of human races. . . .

[M]y American friends . . . no doubt must have wondered why I had renounced my citizenship. This decision was not that of today or that of yesterday. It dates back to the day when General DeWitt had ordered Evacuation. It was confirmed when he flatly refused to listen even to the voices of the former World War Veterans and it was doubly confirmed as I entered Manzanar. We who already had proven our loyalty by serving in the last World War should have been spared. The veterans have asked for special consideration but their requests were denied. They too had to evacuate like the rest of the Japanese people, as if they're aliens.

I did not expect this of the Army. When the Western Defense Command assumed the responsibilities of the West Coast, I expected at least the Niseis would be allowed to remain. But to General DeWitt, we're all alike. "Jap is a Jap. Once a Jap, always a Jap." . . .

What is there for us to be ashamed of being a Jap? To be born a Jap is the greatest blessing God had bestowed on us; to be a Jap is the greatest pride we can enjoy in life; and to die as Jap under the protection of the Japanese Flag which has weathered through many national storms without a defeat for 2600 years is the greatest honor a man can ever hope to cherish . . .

I, in the name of the Nisei proclaim ourselves Japs, 100 per cent Japs, now, tomorrow, and forever.

Tenno Hei Ka Banzai Banzai! Banzai!
Dai Nippon Teikoku Banzai! Banzai Banzai!
Zai Ryu Dobo Banzai! Banzai! Banzai!*

frail seedlings
nurse tenderly
water regularly
never excessively†

---

* Essay, JERS.

† Poems assembled from Toshio Kawamoto and Joseph Y. Kurihara, *Bonsai-Saikei: The Art of Miniature Trees, Gardens, and Landscapes* (Nippon Saikei, 1963).

2 TOKUTARO "TOKIE" SLOCUM

The side that I present to you is one of a veteran's viewpoint. I served as sergeant major in Three Hundred and Twenty-Eighth Infantry in the same regiment with Sergeant York, of Tennessee; I am department chairman of a naturalization and citizenship commission for the Veterans of Foreign Wars of California . . . I am a member of the department of public relations committee for the American Legion, and I am chairman for the anti-Axis committee, which is the only war cabinet ever existing in Little Tokio . . . practically every member of my committee of the anti-Axis committee of the Japanese American Citizens League of the Southern District Council has cooperated to the best of his ability at his own expense, time, and energy, by exposing what they term to be "subversive activity" here in our part of California. We really have.

Not only that, but if you will kindly investigate you will find that the anti-Axis committee has also cooperated faithfully, sincerely, and diligently with the United States Naval Intelligence and the United States Army Intelligence . . .

I happened to be born in Japan . . . my citizenship was given to me by a special act of Congress . . . back in 1935, there was a bill called "Nye-Lee bill" . . . Yes, sir; we got that bill through and I benefited, Koreans, Chinese, and Japanese, a bunch of them about 1,000 of them benefited. Consequently, having fought for the country and then having to fight again for my citizenship, I appreciate the meaning of citizenship.

I also think that the Japanese Association itself is a very undesirable element . . . please bear this in mind: That is the element that I fought. And it gave me great satisfaction on the night when war was declared and I was summoned by the Naval Intelligence and the F.B.I., to go over the top with them, lead them to their lair, to arrest the leaders. It is so, sir, that there did exist such influence in our midst against which I really did fight tooth and toenail, and by golly they don't like me. I don't care. They are in a concentration zone now . . . However, right along I have contended that the majority of Americans of Japanese ancestry are really good Americans . . .*

as soon as strong
pliant branches trained
wiring will be awkward

* Tolan Committee Testimony, "Testimony of Tokie Slocum, Togo Tanaka, Sam Minami, Fred Tayama, and Joseph Shinoda, Members of the United Citizens Federation," National Defense Migration, pp. 11703–11723.

3 SABURO KIDO

IN THIS SOLEMN HOUR WE PLEDGE OUR FULLEST COOPERATION TO YOU MR. PRESIDENT, AND TO OUR COUNTRY . . . NOW THAT JAPAN HAS INSTITUTED THIS ATTACK ON OUR LAND, WE ARE READY AND PREPARED TO EXTEND EVERY EFFORT TO REPEL THIS INVASION WITH OUR FELLOW AMERICANS.

Signed,
President of the Japanese American Citizens League*

pinch away new shoots
healthy though kept stunted
three years
three inches

* Telegram to President Franklin Delano Roosevelt, December 7, 1941; Bill Hosokawa, *JACL: In Quest of Justice* (San Francisco, 1982), pp. 130–131.

4 MASARU "FRED" TAYAMA

Every man is either friend or foe. We shall investigate and turn over to the authorities all who by word or act consort with the enemies. We must and will mobilize our maximum energies to facilitate America's war program. We must not play into enemy hands.*

On the evening of Saturday, December 5 [1942], Fred was met in the shower room . . . followed home . . . and a group . . . attacked him and beat him severely. Approximately a half dozen men participated in the beating. All of them wore their Government Issue blue pea-jackets with collars up, their black leather winter caps which covered their ears and a portion of their faces and fastened under their chins, and thick, heavy goggles which are used extensively by Manzanar residents as a protection against the dust. Fred was taken to the hospital on Saturday evening, where it was found that he was not critically damaged. The incident would probably have passed as just another in the growing series of acts of mob violence. But early the next morning of Sunday, December 6, several suspects were whisked from Manzanar and lodged in the County Jail at Independence . . . there was a widespread satisfaction over the fact that Fred had finally got what was coming to him.†

graft goyo matsu
with smaller needles
onto the vigorous
kuro matsu

* Statement on behalf of the Japanese American Citizens League, Anti-Axis Committee of the Southern District Council, *LA Daily News*, December 15, 1941.
† Grodzins Report, Manzanar Shooting, JERS, January 10, 1943.

5 HARRY YOSHIO UENO

. . . December 5th. About 9:00, somebody knock on my door because I have got to get up 5:00. So I go to bed early, you know. Then I opened the door. I see the assistant chief of police. The chief of police is Gilkey and assistant is Williams. He came over and said, "Harry, I want to talk to you in the police station. Change your clothes and come." So, "Okay, just a minute." I had a nightgown and everything. So I changed my clothes and they had about three jeep full of Japanese policemen and assistant chief of police there. So they took me down to the police station. They asked me where I had been tonight, my movement that night. Then I told them I went to the Block 13. They had a PTA movie meeting, you know, the Parent Teacher Association, and I have my children going to school. So I belong to PTA and I look at how much people attend the movie. So I look in the—walk down the Block 13 and walk back. I have to get up early, so I went to bed [at] 8:00. Then he said—Fred and whole family came into the police station. He said Fred's wife recognized you. "You are the one that beat him." I don't know his wife. I never met her. So they said—the jail was regular barrack like ordinary where we live. Half is jail and right in the middle is the chief of police office there. The FBI came in. They questioned the people in there. Then about one-third of the building is waiting room for the policemen, you know, the people visit there. So they asked me where I had been and so on. Then about—we sit there and then the chief of police came over. We talk all the questions where I had been and that is all, nothing else. We sitting there from 9:00 to about 12:00, three hours, nothing else.

Then about 12:00, Ned Campbell came over with his car. He is driving and the chief of police came in and put the handcuffs on me. Then put in the back seat. I sit with the chief of police and Campbell drove, and he is driving to the north. I turned to the chief of police and, "I don't know where you are going to take me to, but please tell me where I am going to be to my family." Instead he answered—Campbell hear that and said, "No, Harry, where you are going, nobody knows where you are going. I won't tell nobody, and you will be there for a long time."*

prune roots
when transplanting
dislodge soil
with chopsticks

---

* Online Archive of California: REgenerations Oral History Project: Rebuilding Japanese American Families, Communities, and Civil Rights in the Resettlement Era: San Jose Region: Volume IV, Wendy Ng, interviewer, January 23, 1998, and May 9, 1998, pp. 485–486.

6 KARL GOZO YONEDA

On December 7 we found ourselves at Fort Snelling, Minnesota . . . That same day the local newspaper headline read: "Manzanar Riot."

. . . The Black Dragons, angered at our enlistment into the MIS, wanted to get "even" with some of the pro-democratic forces in camp. On the night of December 5, several persons broke into Fred's quarters . . . beat him so severely that he required hospitalization. They even invaded the hospital looking to "finish" Fred. The camp police arrested and jailed Harry, a Kibei cook, as one of the suspected assailants.

The next day . . . Elaine heard about the attack and went to the Administration Office to see if they had received Tommy's pass to return to Military Area No. 1. There she saw a crowd and heard Joe, speaking from a truck in Japanese, saying the name "Karl" a couple of times. A member of the office staff, Mr. Chester, who understood Japanese, went and told Elaine, "They are demanding the immediate release of Harry. They are in an ugly mood. Joe was saying that Karl ran away from them to hide in the Army, but Karl's son is still in here so they can still 'get him.'"

On December 7 at 4:30 A.M. Elaine, becoming more anxious for Tommy's safety as well as her own, dressed Tommy up as a girl and started running towards the Administration Office, unaware that martial law had been declared. An MP suddenly stopped them, pointing a bayoneted rifle at Elaine's chest.*

. . . Karl is one of those rare individuals who is of Japanese descent, but is open and avowed in his Communist sympathies and anything but in sympathy with the present militaristic regime in Japan. Karl is the San Francisco representative of the Japanese language newspaper Doho, *an allegedly communist inspired publication, the editorial policy of which links Germany, Italy, and Japan as the Fascist forces which this country is dedicated to overcome.*†

One of my Caucasian GI escorts hoisted a loudspeaker up about ten feet into the foliage of a teak tree facing the enemy line located behind a bamboo grove five hundred yards away. The broadcast went as follows:

"You brave Japanese Imperial soldiers! We are far away from our loved ones. We share your hardships. Let us relax and listen to Japanese music."

---

* Karl Yoneda, *Ganbatte: Sixty-year Struggle of a Kibei Worker* (Asian American Studies Center, UCLA, 1983), pp. 148–149.

† FBI Director J. Edgar Hoover memo to Assistant Attorney General Wendell Berge, April 23, 1942; Yoneda, *Ganbatte*, pp. 156–157.

We played popular Japanese records such as 'Tokyo Melody,' 'Gion Ballad,' 'Okesa of Sado,' and 'Follow the Shadow.' Then we continued with the real message:

'Since childhood you have known the old Japanese proverb, "To die is easy; to live is hard." Yet already in this war, thousands of your comrades have died like insects who have jumped into flames. They have been annihilated on Attu Island and the Marshall Islands and here in Northern Burma seventy-five hundred of your comrades have already been killed or have died of hardships.

'Those who truly understand loyalty to the Emperor—those who understand filial piety and love of the real Japan, those who have pity for their parents and love for their wives and children—they must not die!'"*

essential material
good moss
bright in color
fine in texture

---

* Yoneda, *Ganbatte*, pp. 156–157.

7 GEORGE TOSHIO KURATOMI

But even in Japan I will run into a lot of difficulties. I am radical in my thoughts. I was a most ardent New Dealer until 1933.*

I sized George up as an intellectual with a rather strange type of personality, I am not sure just what it was. He had factors in his personality which were not just Japanese or which were characteristic of the group of the evacuees. He was a type who I think missed a normal family relationship in his early life. He was away from his parents and made his own way from a very early stage. He became very much interested in politics and social problems and that sort of thing out in Los Angeles. He was also active in the Buddhist church there. He told me that most of his contacts were with Caucasians prior to evacuation. He had become very much interested in the American form of Government; thought it was the best in the world and so on. And it was for that reason that he had been so disillusioned because of evacuation. Registration, he thought, was the last straw. That was not a major issue but it was the last straw in a long line of things. He objected to registration because it questioned something which he didn't think should be questioned. It questioned his loyalty and he thought there should have been no question of his loyalty on the basis of his past record. It was symbolic to him of the last step in his break with America, and to him it seemed that he must plan for the future not only of himself but of his descendants, and it seemed to him that they had no future in America.†

WHEREFOR, the applicant demands that a writ of habeas corpus or an order to show cause issue herein directing and commanding the respondent to produce the body of applicant before this Court at a time to be specified therein and to show cause, if any he has, why he has arrested, imprisoned and detains the applicant and then and there do what this Court shall order concerning the detention of applicant, and that the applicant be ordered discharged from imprisonment and detention in the aforesaid "The Stockade."‡

sift soil
through large
medium
and fine mesh

---

* JERS Field Notes, February 13, 1945.

† Report by Edgar C. McVoy, Chief, Analysis & Procedure Section, WRA, Jerome, CSU Japanese American History Digitization Project, Densho Digital Repository.

‡ Application for Writ of Habeas Corpus, August 1944, Wayne M. Collins Papers, 1918–19, Stockade Cases, Box 21, Folder 3.

8 ERNEST KINZO WAKAYAMA

*. . . forty-five-year-old World War I veteran and the pre- World War II secretary of the San Pedro Fishermen's Union. He had been living in Block 36 in Manzanar and working as a volunteer carpenter for only three months prior to the Manzanar Riot, having been transferred there from the Santa Anita Assembly Center in connection with a disturbance concerning the camouflage net factory at Santa Anita. He, along with ten others, was indicted on federal charges and held for trial in Los Angeles, though after two months the government dropped the suit.**

Later he went to Tule Lake camp and agitated those Hoshi Dan. I met him one time. Kurihara said, "Oh, there's a big shot from Santa Anita. He's in here." I met him. He was a big talker but there was nothing behind it. I couldn't trust him. I never paid any attention. He was in Tule Lake and a friend of mine said, "Why don't you go to see him?" I said, "No, he's not my friend. I couldn't trust him." So I never went to see him in Tule Lake.†

I interviewed him during the summer of 1957 in Hakata, Japan. At which time he stated to me that he was rudely awakened about 3 or 4 in the morning. The FBI came to his quarters with a pistol brandishing, and the officer that accompanied the FBI compelled him to renounce . . . He told the Justice Department official that he will only sign the renunciation document under protest. The officer stated to him that he may do so. Consequently, Kinzo signed the renunciation document under protest. This means that the document so obtained would not be valid, and was obtained by duress.‡

in a grove
focus on the main tree
the others giving
depth

---

* Harry Y. Ueno interview, by Sue Kunitomi Embrey, Arthur A. Hansen, Betty Kulberg Mitson, Japanese American Oral History Project at California State University, Fullerton, October 30, 1976, p. 41.

† Ueno interview, note 66, Board of Review reports (December 1942–January 1943), Collection 122, JARP-UCLA.

‡ Tex Nakamura interview; Michi Weglyn, *Years of Infamy: The Untold Story of America's Concentration Camps* (William Morrow, 1976), p. 243.

9 JIRO ONUMA

Jiro was nineteen years old when he boarded the Shinyo Maru *steamship in Yokohama, Japan, headed for San Francisco in 1923, just before US federal law prohibited Japanese immigration . . . I have been enamored with the life and legacy of this gay immigrant bachelor. I was fascinated by his collection of male physique magazines and delighted by his fondness for unique homoerotic kitsch, especially his postcard of a matador donning a bronze erect penis, which could be detached and used as a necktie pin. Jiro was also clearly obsessed with Earle Liederman, a professional muscle man who ran a popular mail-order bodybuilding school throughout the 1920s and 1930s.*

One image shows Jiro posing with other inmate workers of Block 3 Mess Hall at Topaz. In the sweltering summer heat of central Utah, where temperatures could reach up to 120 degrees . . . his coworkers were gathered together between the Block 3 Mess Hall building on the left and the communal toilets and laundry building on the right. Jiro, age thirty-nine, sits on the far right of the front row among the other inmate cooks, servers, bus boys, dishwashers, and KP workers. On the back of the photograph, Jiro inscribed the date July 21, 1943, along with the names of the other nineteen men in the group portrait.

. . . He performed mess hall duties for fourteen months, forty-four hours a week, for sixteen dollars a month, or approximately nine cents an hour.

*. . . by the time the Block 3 photograph was taken, the federal government had already classified seventeen out of twenty of the men in the image as enemy aliens, dissidents, or disloyals.**

see the trunk rise
base to top
without obstruction
branches extending

* Tina Takemoto, "Looking for Jiro Onuma: A Queer Meditation on the Incarceration of Japanese Americans during World War II," *GLQ: A Journal of Lesbian and Gay Studies*, 20, no. 3 (Duke University Press, 2014), pp. 241–275.

10 SADAO ARA

*Sadao of Block 83, 4-H, Family No. 23871, age 46 . . . is a perfect gentleman, liked by everyone he meets. I will vouch for this man against any number of others in your care. The reason he worries is because he is a member of Hoshi Dan—into which, like many others was high pressured into joining it. Such disgraceful gangsterism method was and is most openly employed in the Manzanar district, engulfing him to as one of the victims. He wants to get out, sincerely regretting over it.**

seen from above
branches extend
balanced
in all directions

* Joseph Kurihara, essay, JERS.

11 REV. SHINJO NAGATOMI

Persons who swear allegiance to the United States, pretending to be US citizens while appearing Japanese may be invaluable to both sides for a while, but such deception may not continue. Their true nature revealed, excluded by both Americans and Japanese, such persons can neither stay in America nor go to Japan. They will lose their home and country.

Young Buddhists, even if you deceive others, you cannot deceive yourselves. You cannot deceive Buddha who sees all. And you cannot ignore the consequences.

It's said the mother lion drops her three-day-old cub from a cliff to test its physical strength. The young today are cubs at the bottom of a cliff. Before bearing a grudge against the mother, awaken to the fact that you are being tested. To reach the mountaintop, stand with perseverance and walk the thorny path. Do not lose your spirit from exhaustion. Hold strong belief and the attitude of a great mountain.*

do not be fooled
by thick foliage
a tree without balance
is not beautiful

---

* *Manzanar Bussei Guide 1943*. BANC MSS 67/14 c, folder O2.782, JERS, trans. Yuki Obayashi.

12 TOM SATOSHI YOSHIYAMA

After the most serious consideration we have finally decided that the only weapon and the only solution to let known our sincerity to all that we are not a trouble maker such as the W.R.A. has branded us we plan to undergo another hunger strike. . . Some of the numerous grievances are:

1. Imprisoned for over eight months without the filing of charges or the granting of a hearing or trial of any kind.
2. No proof or evidence substantiating our guilt.
3. Living a world of infamy for no reasons whatsoever.
4. During the entire time we have been in the Stockade we have been denied all visiting privileges from our wives, children, fiancées, or anyone else.
5. I was denied visits from my fiancée who I was scheduled to marry the day after my arrest on November 13th.
6. Children born since our incarceration, but to even see their wives were denied.
7. Third degree methods used on many of us.
8. Censorship of mails, including that coming from outside the Center.
9. Since July 2, we were not permitted to receive cigarettes, toilet articles, and our daily needs.
10. Beaver board erected for no reason whatsoever since July 2nd. Solitary confinement cannot be any worse.
11. Constant abusive words from the attending Internal Security Staff.
12. No medical or first aid facilities. Service to the base hospital denied.
13. Denied the constitutional right to counsel. Denial of due process of law to all of us.
14. In connection with the interview which we had with Mr. Ernest Besig of the American Civil Liberties Union, all right of privacy was denied to us.

Tonight, July 18, we had our last meal consisting of rice, two slices of balony fried and a vegetable soup. All unnecessary belongings were packed and labeled, otherwise I will be too weak from starvation to do anything. Took my shower and am now waiting for the day we shall all be released from here either to the colony or to the Base Hospital from exhaustion.*

young trees
full with vitality
nip the sprouts
force the trunk
in time
rugged with age

* Diary, JERS.

13 TOM KOBAYASHI

It was on November 4th,. 1943, as I recall, that the Tule Lake Food Warehouse Disturbances occurred. Tom, a Japanese American on security patrol, discovered several WRA Caucasian personnel stealing food from the Internee Food Warehouse during the night and loading the food on their own truck which was parked alongside the warehouse. Tom, who had the authority of a warden, remonstrated with the WRA personnel because they were taking the internees' food without authorization—they were actually stealing the internees' food. Tom was attacked by the Caucasian WRA personnel and a scuffle ensued.

Tom was brought in . . . told to hold up his arms . . , but he refused. He refused and said, "Why do I need to do that? What? Who do you think you are?" He was hit by a baseball bat. Tom was a big guy like a wrestler . . . the blood gushed out and the baseball bat actually broke in two. I was a witness to this brutal attack and remember it very vividly.

*I was not able to do anything to help Tom. There were more than ten Caucasian WRA personnel there, but none of them even tried to give him aid. Not only that, the Caucasian who was responsible for this savage attack even boasted of his act by showing off the broken bat to the other personnel and laughing.**

fruit trees
in rainy season
dispose overgrown branches
retain those bearing blossoms

* Tokio Yamane, CWRIC testimony and Densho Digital Archive.

14 KOJI TODOROGI

*The other person taken into custody with me as a result of the warehouse incident was Koji. We were asked to go to the warehouse and calm down the people there. We were running in the dark. About six or seven foreigners suddenly came out and came toward us. We didn't do anything. I didn't realize at the moment that they were all armed. We were not. There's no way that we were going toward them. They suddenly came out in front of us in the dark. No headlights. It was pitch dark. We were hit with their big fists in an instant. We got beaten up. We were both taken to the office. Our noses were bleeding, and we were covered with blood. They said, "You are the troublemakers. You started the disturbance." We were repeatedly kicked and beaten. I believe his father was a Buddhist priest who, as an intellectual, was taken into custody by the FBI at the outbreak of the war and sent to one of the Justice Department camps. Koji was a quiet fellow of small stature, and not the pugnacious type to get involved in demonstrations and disturbances. The last I heard of him is that he committed suicide soon after his return to Japan because he never got over his horrible experiences in the American concentration camps. At this time, we were all 18 to 21 years of age, very young, idealistic and naive. What a tragedy to have the internment experience make such a shamble of our lives!**

pruning is done
with the future in mind
picture the tree
in five years

* Tokio Yamane, CWRIC testimony and Densho Digital Archive.

15 TOKIO YAMANE

From about 9 that evening until daybreak, we were forced to stand with our backs against the office wall with our hands over our heads and we were continuously kicked and abused as we were ordered to confess to being the instigators of the disturbance. We denied these accusations but our protestations of innocence were completely ignored by our tormentors. The beating continued all night long and at daybreak the three of us were turned over to the Military Police and we were thrown into the stockade for confinement. It was during this night of horror that I was so severely beaten about the face that my teeth punctured my lower lip, resulting in permanent facial disfigurement.

As the days and months went by, our relatives and the internees made repeated efforts to have us released from the "bull pen," but their efforts were unrewarded and our pleas for justice and a fair trial went unheeded . . . our hopes faded and we realized that we would be spending another Christmas and New Year in the "bull pen," and since we had no alternative, we decided to go on a hunger strike until we were released or until we died . . .

In February 1945, I was sent to the Santa Fe Internment Camp for enemy aliens. I was told Japan lost the war there . . . After a while, officers from the Department of Justice came and asked me, "You expressed your intention to go back to Japan and renounce your U.S. citizenship. Is that correct?" I and other members of the youth organization were handed a paper to sign. There were no explanations or instructions. We were simply told to sign the paper. This was a document renouncing our U.S. citizenship. I signed it because by now I had become convinced that the United States would not honor its obligation to grant me the rights of a native-born American citizen guaranteed to me by the U.S. Constitution and the Bill of Rights.

On November 30th, 1945, I was transported to Japan with others like myself, leaving from Portland, Oregon, on a ship carrying such personalities as the former Japanese Ambassador to Germany, the Honorable Baron Oshima. And to date, the thought lingers on in my mind—were we pawns of war to be exchanged for American prisoners?*

never prune
out of season
safest in early spring
when trees are full
of vigor

* Tokio Yamane, CWRIC testimony and Densho Digital Archive.

16 TATSUO YAMANE

*Tatsuo was born in Hawaii and attended grammar school in Japan, where he acquired excellent Japanese reading and writing skills. He later finished his high school education in Fresno, California. During his military service he was a Japanese interrogator for the Military Intelligence Service. He served in the Asiatic-Pacific Theatre in New Guinea and Morotai Island in Indonesia.**

curved ugly
goyo matsu
straddles rock
manipulated into
beauty

* Japanese American Military Historic Collective.

17 HEKISAMEI SHIGERU MATSUDA

秋の日暮るる建坊ケンゲキを覚え

Aki no hi kururu Ken-bo kengeki o oboe

Autumn sun setting
Ken-bo learning
Sword fighting skills

Hekisamei was born in 1906 in Iimuro Mura, Asa-gun, Hiroshima Prefecture, and remained in Japan with his mother while his father immigrated to America. When he was in his teens, his father sent for him and his mother. While staying at the Fresno Buddhist Church dormitory, he participated in many church activities, including the literary discussion group, oratorical contests, dramatic plays, golf tournaments, photography contest, and haiku writing; he prided himself as the product of the Fresno Buddhist Church Youth Leaders Group.

He became a charter member of Valley Ginsha, and while he and his family were living in Fresno, he also owned and managed the Matsuda Book Shop, taught in several Japanese language schools in the Central Valley, was a correspondent for various Japanese-American newspapers, and was in charge of Japanese theatrical performances in the Fresno area. The haiku he wrote at this time was published by the Kaiko Monthly Journal *in Japan. After hostilities broke out, he was interned initially at the Fresno Assembly Center, then at Jerome Concentration Camp, and finally at Tule Lake Segregation Center. During that time, his haiku was published by the* Utah Nippo. *In December 1944, he was sent to the Santa Fe Justice Department Camp and the following December was repatriated to Japan, where he remarried. He died in late 1970.**

to age tree twice as fast
trim all leaves
in ten years
a layman deceived

* Violet Kazue de Cristoforo, ed., *May Sky: There's Always Tomorrow; An Anthology of Japanese American Concentration Camp Kaiko Haiku* (Sun & Moon, 1997), pp. 208–209.

18 SHOICHI JAMES OKAMOTO

. . . at approximately 2:20 p.m., May 24, 1944, the shooting occurred . . . the sentry . . . cocked his gun and went around via front to the other side of the truck . . . ordered James to the back of the truck. This would have been just outside the gate. James started but hesitated an instant. At this point, to speculate on the guard's motives, with true concentration-camp psychology, the suspicion is that the guard wished to shoot him outside the gate. (Shot while trying to escape). James' hesitation is explained by this point. In the moment of hesitation, in which most say no pipes were lit and no words said, the sentry struck James sideway on the right shoulder with a rifle-butt. James raised his right arm and moved his body slightly back to ward off any further blows. While in this defensive position, the guard stepped back one pace and from a distance of four or five feet fired without warning.

There were six doctors, including the Army, four evacuees, one Caucasian Chief of Medical Staff. In spite of the doctors' effort, James died at 12:10 a.m., May 25, 1944. The autopsy was performed and following are the statement made by the doctor . . .

> *The damage was found in the region of the spleen. In the right chest area was this hole which was about one centimeter in diameter and this was a flesh wound that connected to the man's insides. There were some large rents that had been torn through the man's liver and his stomach had been shattered so that when it was first seen at the operation, it was not possible to recognize the pieces as a stomach. The portion of his liver on the left-hand side of the body as I stated before had had his internal contents pushed out through the cavity so it was sticking out and draped on the outside of his body, and this particular material was covered with a sticky contents, a portion of which we recognized as spaghetti.**

red crushed soil
from Kanto
drains well
is clean and airy

* "Report of the Investigation Committee," July 3, 1944, Tule Lake, Newell, California.

19 TASAKU HITOMI

*Tasaku Hitomi, a businessman from Sacramento who I had met at Lordsburg, was seriously injured when he was mistaken for his brother and assaulted with a hammer. While these stories surprised me, I was truly shocked when a newspaper cable reported that someone had murdered Yaozo, his brother, four days after the attack. The perpetrator was never found. It was a messy and complicated affair, and both internees and the authorities were responsible for the tragic outcome.**

create jin
peel bark to expose cambrium
as if withered
naturally

* Yasutaro Soga, *Life Behind Barbed Wire: The WWII Internment Memoirs of a Hawaiian Issei* (University of Hawaii Press, 2008), p. 154.

20 YAOZO HITOMI

Co-op General Manager Slain by Mysterious Assassin: Officials Offer Resignations

Victim of an attack by an unidentified assailant, Yaozo Hitomi, 44-year-old general manager of the Tule Lake Cooperative Enterprises, was found knifed to death Sunday night near his residence at 3514-A.

He was found by his niece . . . lying against the porch of his neighbor's apartment with a stab wound through the throat, which apparently was administered with a long-bladed knife. He was dead when removed to the base hospital.

Prior to evacuation the victim had lived in Sacramento where he was working as an agent for Sunlight Insurance Company. He is survived by his wife . . . and three children . . . all residing in this center.

As a result of this slaying, an emergency Cooperative Board of Directors' meeting was called Monday morning; at which time all 17 members of the board resolved to tender their resignations collectively.

Subsequently, the following officials of the Cooperative tendered their resignations which were approved and accepted by the Board of Directors . . .

*Canteens were reopened yesterday as the result of a meeting between the Board of Directors and canteen and factory managers on the same day.**

telltale scars
inflicted by storm and snow
lightning and fire

* *Newell Star,* 1, no. 19 (July 6, 1944), p. 1.

21 RICHARD SHIGEAKI NISHIMOTO

My friends tell me that I have the appearance of a Nisei and act like one, yet my thoughts and reactions are typically those of intelligent Isseis.

I began to hear grumbling and complaints here and there in Japanese . . . "How do they expect us to work without any drinking water around." . . . "Who do they think we are? Hell, we're no slaves. We don't have to work, if we don't want to." . . . "It's too hot. No use working! We're only getting six cents an hour anyway." I breathed ominous, ugly air. Some men were leaving the field already for home . . . They were not like the Isseis I had known before the evacuation. The Isseis I had known were all industrious, diligent, obedient and courteous people. These men were not like them. They were suspicious, ill-humored, discourteous, irritable people. I calculated that they were under severe strain and in abnormal state of mind resulting from the evacuation, as they had not fully conceived the meaning of the war and had not adjusted themselves to the new environment . . . I knew that they thought of me as a white-man's "stooge." . . . my thought, "my past experiences of managing men in an orchard aren't quite enough to cope with the special situation. Something more must be figured. Here was a priceless chance to utilize my understanding and knowledge of Isseis."

. . . I decided on the following procedures: to show respect and treat them as my superiors. Never to show cockiness or discourtesy. Never to be pedantic. Always to be willing to consult them as if their advices are needed and valued. To increase faith and trust in Democracy. To help them forget unhappy experiences and unfortunate losses resulted from the evacuation. To increase the spirit of cooperation among themselves and the community. To equalize by some lawful method on the field the wage differential. (These men were to receive $12.00 a month.)*

slender pot holds an entire garden
as frames the picture
match and harmonize

* Lane Ryo Hirabayashi, ed., *Inside an American Concentration Camp: Japanese American Resistance at Poston* (University of Arizona Press, 1995), pp. 42, 43–47.

22 GORDON KIYOSHI HIRABAYASHI

. . . shortly after that the curfew orders were imposed, which included all "enemy aliens," German, Italian and Japanese aliens, plus other persons of Japanese ancestry, that's me. And it's interesting, I never was included as a citizen. That is, they didn't say "citizens of Japanese ancestry are also included," they always referred to me as a "non-alien." If you look at the definition of "alien" as being a "non-citizen," a "non-alien" is a kind of a double negative. And they used that euphemism throughout the war. I, like any other normal American, trained to obey laws that were issued by the government or in the name of the government, I complied with the curfew. And I lived in a small dormitory right next to the campus, University of Washington, YMCA dormitory. This was partly international students from the Philippines, from Canada and so on, along with the out-of-town American students, and I was one of about twelve, thirteen people who lived there. So it was a small, very closely-knit group. And when we went out to the library or to the coffee shop on the Avenue, everybody acted as my volunteer timekeeper and they'd say, "Hey, it's five minutes to eight, Gordon." And I'd gather up my stuff and dash home. Usually the others stayed on, if it's the library or coffee shop, whatever they were doing . . . But finally, towards the end of the week, it dawned on me, why I should be dashing back and my friends not? And that if I'm an American, what am I doing this for? And so I said, "Well, if I'm an American, I'm gonna act like one," and I turned around and went back.*

attach u-bolt vise
over time
straighten trunk

* Interview, October 25, 1983, Steven Okazaki Collection, Densho Digital Archive.

23 JAMES AKIRA HIRABAYASHI

. . . what I remember mostly about the Pinedale Assembly Center was that we couldn't, we didn't have any money, no way of earning money at first, and so we had to beg money from our parents, whatever little they had. And I remember my mother giving me fifty cents to go and buy something at the canteen. Then soon we had the opportunity to find work in the camp so that I remember my first job was washing dishes for eight dollars a month. And the rest of the time we sort of ran around in gangs. Because of my very strict Christian upbringing, of course, we weren't allowed to smoke or drink or anything else. We weren't even allowed to play cards because cards was connected to gambling and things like that. So I didn't learn how to play cards until I went into camp. Learned how to play rummy and pinochle and things like that. Then it got so that I was not going home except at night. Now, the barracks in Pinedale, the walls went up only to the rafters. And there was no ceiling so you could hear all the other families right down the entire length of the barracks. And I depended upon that to keep my mother from reprimanding me whenever I got into trouble. So I would just come in late at night whenever I felt like coming back home to sleep. You had to do that because that's the only place you could sleep. And then one time, my mother figured that I was getting out of control, so without further adieu, she gave me hell and all the neighbors heard, but that was the way it was. And she was trying to maintain her control.

. . . after about three months or so in the assembly center, we got back onto the train and were shipped up to Tule Lake, California, where the permanent camp was being set up. And there I just remember fooling around a lot in gangs.

. . . at night, what we would do is just for entertainment was to hassle the girls and we knew that they would have to go to the bathroom in the evening. So that what we'd do is get some black gum and we'd chew gum and we'd blacken out some of our teeth. And we'd put towels under our sweaters to make us look like real husky hoodlums and wear a hat and we'd go creeping around the corner and scare the girls. We did things like that to entertain ourselves.*

scissors to prune branches
pincette to extract weeds
peeler to create jin
wires to twist branches
tie tree to rock

---

* Interview, October 2, 1992, Emiko and Chizuko Omori Collection, Densho Digital Archive.

24 MINORU YASUI

. . . this was not a sudden decision . . . all kinds of rumors and all kinds of conditions prevailed up and down the West Coast. As a consequence, I did discuss this with the various attorneys who were prominent in constitutional law. I did discuss it with members of the FBI, particularly those who went to law school with me, and I did it deliberately after having consulted with many of the other Japanese Americans. What we were looking for, really, was an ideal case. A young ex-GI who had been honorably discharged, married with a couple of kids, because we wanted to create sympathy. But at that time, knowing the uncertainties, I could scarcely blame anyone for refusing to go ahead and deliberately violate the law. And it seemed to me that someone had to do it, and the ultimate choice became, since nobody else would do it, I did.

. . . I was in my office on the 28th day of March, which is a Saturday evening. Waited 'til 8 o'clock, Rei . . . was my secretary. . . we had Rei call the police, the FBI, to notify them that there was a Japanese person in violation of curfew walking up and down Third Avenue . . . I walked and walked from eight o'clock . . . I walked for over three hours, and during that period, I got tired of walking up and down Third Avenue. So I did approach a police officer, and being a smart aleck and being an attorney, I pulled out the proclamation pointing out that it was in violation of a military proclamation, I had my birth certificate with me, and I proved that I was a person of Japanese ancestry. Asked the officer to arrest me, and the officer says, "Look, you'll get in trouble. Go on, run along home." And that certainly didn't serve my purposes, so I went down to the Second Avenue police station and talked to the sergeant and explained what I wanted done. And the sergeant obliged me and he threw me into the drunk tank. So that's how the case began at 11:20 p.m., 28th day of March, 1942.

. . . I didn't ask the JACL for any support or help . . . so far as the JACL officially is concerned, they took the position that no test case should be started back in 1942, that they reserved the right to test the legality of evacuation at a later time. As a lawyer, I can tell you that unless you protest the time that the injury is done, you've waived your right to protest.*

along the beach
trees bend naturally
toward water
reflected light

* Interview, October 23, 1983, Steven Okazaki Collection, Densho Digital Archive.

25 FRED T. KOREMATSU

. . . I was with my girlfriend, she was Caucasian. And it was Sunday morning, and we were in a car up on the hill looking down at the Bay Area, we were deciding what to do, you know. It was a nice Sunday morning, the sun was shining, it was nice, and if we should go on a picnic or what, you know, that day. And then this came out on the radio about the Pearl Harbor attack. And it was quite a shock to me, you know, just couldn't believe it.

I was, I was twenty-one then, and I had, when you were that age, you have a girlfriend and all that, you know, just like anybody else. And she was more important to me than anything else, too, at that time, at that age. So we didn't know what to do. And in order to think clearly and so forth, I had to get away from them, and I, when the evacuation order came, I told them that I would like to leave ahead of time, you know, and maybe to go out of state before this happened. And they said if I can do it, go ahead. So I decided to leave on my own.

. . . we were thinking of all kinds of ways so that it'd be easier for me to stay and not be recognized, so that I won't have to get caught in evacuation. And I was discussing it with my girlfriend, and we were looking through the Sunday magazine section of the paper, and she pulled out an article regarding the plastic surgery, how they improve the face and so forth. And she says, "Hey, look at this." And I looked at it and read it, and she says, "Do you think it would work?" And I said, "I don't know." "Well," she says, "shall we look into it?" I said, "We haven't got anything to lose," so we decided to try it. So I went to see the doctor, it was in San Francisco, and he said that he can, said he can do pretty good work on me. But actually, I had a broken nose from playing football and then never had it fixed. And what he did was he just fixed my nose, you know, and whatever little thing he can do, but actually, he didn't do what he said he was gonna do, he just took my money, that's what it was, actually. Because everyone recognized me in camp when I went there, they knew who I was and so forth, so there wasn't anything, change, except I didn't have a broken nose anymore.*

in mountains and plains
trees bend to lowland

* Interview, November 15, 1983, Steven Okazaki Collection, Densho Digital Archive.

26 JOHN KOZO OKADA

. . . my brother John went to Nebraska—Lincoln, Nebraska. He started going to school. And after the first year, he volunteered, when they were taking volunteers, and he became an interpreter. He went to Camp Savage in Minnesota, I think it was. And my brother Charlie volunteered. And so he went with 442nd, went to Europe. And then my oldest, the one that was killed, he stayed in the army, and he was transferred to the 442nd.

. . . I think when the book came out that his generation, you know, were just starting to establish themselves. And I guess we couldn't picture someone who went to jail as being heroic in nature. Even though it was a matter of going to jail because of a matter of principle. I guess it was real hard to see to them, you know.

*. . . When I read it, I knew that many in the community that served in the military in the U.S. forces would not be very sympathetic to it. But I think my family's very proud that he could publish a book. At least for me personally, it's a hell of a role model. I'm grateful for that.**

mizutani ishi
hollow rock
holds water

* Interview with Frank S. Okada, August 16–17, 1990, Smithsonian Archives of American Art.

27 YOSHITAKI ROBERT "CHARLIE" OKADA

. . . a backlash of hatred directed towards families of the volunteers . . . The animosity got so intolerable that our family had to leave camp on work release. It must have been quite a terrible ordeal living side by side in such close quarters, eating in the same mess hall three times a day, using the same laundry facilities and rest rooms—all the while being shunned. The people in camp, I feel, should have been more supportive.*

dokutsu ishi
cave-like cavity
a man within

* "What Price Glory!" in *And Then There Were Eight: The Men of the I Company, 442nd Regimental Combat Team,* ed. Edward Yamasaki (Honolulu: Item Chapter, 442nd Veterans Club 2003), p. 253; *John Okada: The Life and Rediscovered Work of No-No Boy,* ed. Frank Abe, Greg Robinson, and Floyd Cheung (University of Washington Press, 2018), p. 46.

28 HAJIME JIM AKUTSU

I lost my citizenship—given 4-C. That was the biggest thing, 4-C, okay? . . . we were classified once 4-C. 1-A to 4-C. And you were put in camp, and then again, before the segregation—you know, when you got that question 27 and 28—you were given classification again, you were given the 4-C, okay? . . . Enemy alien, not obligated for military service . . . And I thought that here, here we are in camp, and there, they called for the volunteers, then also called, they're reinstating, you know, the selective service. And I just couldn't see myself going along with that knowing what I did know. That we as a—what shall I say—evacuee, have no obligation for military service, and that was the main point. The main point was that I am an alien, okay? Therefore I did not have any obligation . . .

I believe that my mother suffered because of the stand I took . . . she got ostracized. Got cut away from the Issei community. And the last thing that happened was, she was told to not come to church anymore. So she told me, "I can't even go to church." And it was shortly thereafter, she took her life. Not the way it was written in *No-No Boy.**

iwa large rock
white strata along base
excellent for beach scene

* Interview, August 28, 1993, Frank Abe Collection, Densho Digital Archives.

29 NOBU KAJIWARA

. . . I know this will shock you. I have volunteered to join the armed forces and will be part of the combat unit . . . A unit coming up spontaneously and not of duress (as in draft) will get far better publicity. Publicity organized and of the right kind, will be in favor of all Japanese sincerely wishing to remain in the U.S. And it is only by such positive action that the country will open up decent jobs for a decent living. Sounds idealist—I'd be the first to say that such a reformation of the American public opinion will not come about overnight. It'll take years but just consider the position of you and me and the rest of the nisei if no action were taken. I don't like the set up any more than you do and there is the further discomforting thought that I may never come back. But to be honest with myself and to keep what self respect I do have . . .*

jagged rocks
on sea coast
smooth-faced
in streams

* Letter excerpt, March 1943, Karen Tei Yamashita, *Letters to Memory* (Coffee House, 2017).

30 WILLIAM KUNPEI "BILL" HOSOKAWA

Sometimes when his father was angered by the lad's indolence or disobedience, he was threatened with the punishment of being sent "back to Japan" to live with the grandparents he had never met. He assumed his grandparents were kindly people; nonetheless the threat of being shipped off to Japan was frightening enough to cause him to improve his behavior . . .

Two other guidelines, held up frequently by his parents, helped to govern his deportment. One was *Hito ni warawareru*—you will be laughed at by others. The other, *Sonna koto wo shitara haji wo kaku*—such actions will cause disgrace. This deference to the opinions of his peers led to a certain conformity of behavior until one day he staged a quiet personal teen-age rebellion and said: "To hell with what others think of me; I'll live my own life." Perhaps that was the day he completed his Americanization . . .

He was, thus, a creature of two worlds. He approached manhood with an American heart and mind and a Japanese face. He was steeped in the American culture but cognizant of an alien heritage as well. It was a situation fraught with complications in a society which was not quite ready for him. And so there were times, following particularly abrasive experiences, when he asked himself difficult questions: *What am I? Where am I going? What is my destiny? What can I do to claim my rightful place in this, my beloved native land?*

But before he could find answers to these and many equally provocative questions, he was engulfed in a cataclysmic war that, as surely as the nuclear bombs that ended it, destroyed the comfortable, frustrating, secure, shaky, promising, dead-end world in which he had grown up.*

moss covered rocks
in time
blend into land

* Bill Hosokawa, *Nisei: The Quiet Americans* (William Morrow, 1969), pp. xiv–xv, xvi–xvii.

31 MIKE MASARU MASAOKA

Some of my friends, and some who are not my friends, also call me Moses . . . They say that like the Biblical prophet, I have led my people on a long journey through the wilderness of discrimination and travail. They say I have led them within sight of the promised land of justice for all and social and economic equality in our native America, but that we will not reach it within my lifetime.

The Japanese American Creed

I am proud that I am an American citizen of Japanese ancestry, for my very background makes me appreciate more fully the wonderful advantages of this nation. I believe in her institutions, ideals, and traditions; I glory in her heritage; I boast of her history; I trust in her future. She has granted me liberties and opportunities such as no individual enjoys in this world today. She has given me an education befitting kings. She has entrusted me to build a home, to earn a livelihood, to worship, think, speak, and act as I please—as a free man equal to every other man.*

". . . With any policy of evacuation definitely arising from reasons of military necessity and national safety, we are in complete agreement. As American citizens, we cannot and should not take any other stand. But, also, as American citizens believing in the integrity of our citizenship, we feel that any evacuation enforced on grounds violating that integrity should be opposed.

"If, in the judgment of military and federal authorities, evacuation of Japanese residents from the West Coast is a primary step toward assuring the safety of this nation, we will have no hesitation in complying with the necessities implicit in that judgment. But if, on the other hand, such evacuation is primarily a measure whose surface urgency cloaks the desires of political or other pressure groups who want us to leave merely for motives of self-interest, we feel that we have every right to protest and to defend equitable judgment in our merits as American citizens."†

slanting trees
discovered on steep hillsides
where winds blow
strongly all year

---

* Mike Masaoka with Bill Hosokawa, *They Call Me Moses Masaoka: An American Saga* (William Morrow, 1987), p. 50.

† Statement to Tolan Committee; see Hosokawa, *Nisei*, pp. 290, 291.

32 BEN FRANK MASAOKA

The army organized Japanese Americans into the 442nd Regimental Combat Team, which fought as shock troops in eight major campaigns in Italy and France. Although the 442nd never numbered more than 3,000 men at any time, it won 18,143 individual decorations, including 9,486 Purple Hearts, and it suffered 680 dead . . .

*Five of us . . . boys were in uniform, and we too paid a price. My next oldest brother, Ben Frank, died in action on a frozen French battlefield. Ike came home 100 percent disabled from combat wounds. Tad was left with a permanent limp. All five of us started with the 442nd, but Iwao Henry, the second youngest, went into the paratroops—the infantry must have been too tame for him. All of us had something to prove, and it might be called our right to share the American dream.**

twisted trunks
discovered along the seashore
cliffside

* Masaoka, *They Call Me Moses Masaoka*, p. 23.

33 JOE GRANT MASAOKA

*Only Joe Grant, the oldest and by then thirty-four years old, was not in uniform. He had told me he would volunteer if I urged him to, but I felt it was important that at least one of us remain to look after Mother. So he had gone to work for JACL to fight for democracy on the home front.**

left to fate
rocks are worthless
paired to trees
assume a place on earth

* Masaoka, *They Call Me Moses Masaoka*, p. 138.

34 ROBERT KIYOSHI OKAMOTO

Kiyoshi was a very taciturn gentleman . . . I hardly, we ever, hardly ever saw him smile. Very serious. Right, he was very serious. He didn't joke much. Every now and then he would come out with a pretty salty type of joke, and he would laugh at it himself, you know, but I can picture him and, the best I can describe him would be as a real crusty old miner, you know, prospector type. He was lean and almost skinny, you might say. And he didn't like people doubting him or refuting what he had to say. That would make him shut up. He would get sullen . . . he was temperamental. But, as I said before, he was very brilliant in his writing. His speeches weren't that great, but especially he can tend to get pretty, pretty salty sometimes . . . he would go on his spiel about the Constitution, you know. So he got up and talked about the Constitution, that we were denied due process. We didn't know—I had never even heard of "due process" at that point . . . that our Constitution, all our Bill of Rights things were violated, and that the Nisei should think about that before they answer these "yes" and "no" questions . . . So after talking to him and discussing everything, we figured, gee, this fellow really knows his Constitution and it's something that we would really like to get together with him, and maybe we can start something with this. And that's how we got to know him, and we organized it into the Fair Play Committee. Up to that point he was the Fair Play Committee of One . . .

*He was a loner, and people that didn't like him, you know, like the administration and the JACL people, would call him a rabble-rouser, you know, or words to that effect, because, well, you know, when people stand on street corners and make speeches, why, that's how they tend to look at him. And he would tend to be a little like that, you know. Whoever, people would listen, he would start talking to them about the rights that were violated. Which was true, you know. There was nothing screwed up about him talking like that. It's just I guess the way he presented it that . . . well, he was very uncompromising on that.**

to imitate nature
observe carefully
expose her concealed
beauty

* Interview with Frank Emi, Frank Abe Collection, Densho Digital Archive, February 23, 1993.

35 FRANK SEISHI EMI

The Fair Play Committee was started in 1943 about the time when the No-No and Yes-Yes answer . . . It was really actually started with an older gentleman, Kiyoshi Okamoto, who was a Hawaiian Nisei and was going around camp whenever he could gather a group of people, he would start talking to them about the constitution, bill of rights, and how everything was denied to us. We would go to different blocks of the camp and hold these big public mass meetings and tell them why we thought this was wrong that the draft should be applied to the people in all these camps . . . especially after we were subjected, kicked out of our home, put in camps, all our rights taken away, and not they want us to serve in the army just as if we were free on outside . . . finally the FBI took the . . . draft resistors that received their notices and didn't report . . . some of those resistors had physical ailments that they never would have passed the physical but they still resisted anyway in principle. So they got tried and there was 63 in the first trial, 63 people.

Like as I said before I was married and had two kids so I wasn't even subject to the draft. Neither was seven of the most active members of Fair Play committee, were indicted under the conspiracy charge . . . aiding and abetting and counseling of others to resist the draft. That was the charge. And of the seven only three were actively subject to the draft . . . two of the gentlemen were over draft age. And one was an Issei who was not a citizen so wasn't even subject to the draft. But he was indicted with us because he offered translation of our English books into Japanese . . .*

cultivate patience
through practice
training for human
tolerance

* Oral history interview, November 8, 2004, Cal State University, Northridge, Oviatt Library.

36 JAMES "JIMMIE" MATSUMOTO OMURA

*The question has been raised . . . why a responsible Nisei writer and editorialist would run the risk of tarnishing his good name and reputation by supporting a militant faction behind barbed wires. Furthermore, the leaders of the Fair Play Committee were unknown to the editor. The answer lies somewhere in the arena of a person's conscience . . . the actual issue was much greater than the mere refusal to knuckle down to army demands. It raised the very large question as to the propriety of the government to demand adherence to Selective Service requirements after having violated basic constitutional rights without any correlative rectification of wrongs so inflicted. The irony was the betrayal of the victims by their ethnic leadership into believing the false credo that "quiet" submission would be regarded by the government as evidence of loyalty to the United States and thus their treatment would be "reciprocally" rewarded.**

It is doubtlessly rather difficult for Caucasian Americans to properly comprehend and believe in what we say. Our citizenship has even been attacked as an evil cloak under which we expect immunity for the nefarious purpose of conspiring to destroy the American life.

I would like to ask the Committee: Has the Gestapo come to America? Have we not risen in righteous anger at Hitler's mistreatment of the Jews? Then, is it not incongruous that citizen Americans of Japanese descent should be similarly mistreated and persecuted?†

men leave their names
trees leave their frames

* *Nisei Naysayer: The Memoir of Military Japanese American Journalist Jimmie Omura*, ed. Arthur A. Hansen (Stanford University Press, 2018), pp. 175, 189–190.

† *Nisei Naysayer*, addendum to Tolan Hearings, pp. 139–140.

37 BUDDY KAZUMARO UNO

My family, my brothers, are dumb Americans. They are stupid enough to believe there is such a thing as equality for a race or creed in the United States.*

Uno spoke perfect American. In fact he had trouble with his Japanese, which he spoke with an American accent. This made him suspect among the Japanese. But there was little need for that. He was, and still is, a loyal Japanese subject; also bitterly anti-American because he says, "I was treated like a yellow skibby and not an American citizen, although my education was as good as any other American's. So I decided, the hell with the United States. I'd go to Japan where my knowledge of the States would be appreciated." And it was. Uno was obviously a privileged character in the Japanese Army Press Bureau. From those of his stories which I read I think he was a more factually accurate reporter than most Japanese, probably because of his American training. However, he could be just as screwy as all the rest when it came to hay-wire type of propaganda they try to peddle as emotional come-on.†

create depth and distance
optical illusions
reveal nature's
truth

* Bill Hosokawa, "From the Frying Pan," *Pacific Citizen*, April 8, 1944, p. 5.
† Royal Arch Gunnison, *So Sorry, No Peace* (Viking Press, 1944), pp. 113–114.

38 HOWARD UNO

We wish to inform you that the Jap officer—our brother—is a traitor to the American way of life under which he has enjoyed the benefits of education and freedom. We have pledged the destruction of him and all those like him.*

. . . Howard was in the Philippines as an American at that time. He was with Merrill's Marauders, and they had gone to the Philippines. They happened to go to this camp where they had all the POWs and, lo and behold, he saw his own brother behind barbed wires there. You can imagine the emotional upheaval that he went through. He hollered at Buddy. He said, "Buddy, do you know who I am?" And Buddy said, "Sure, you're Howard, you're my brother. How come you're here? What are you doing way over on this side of the world?" He said, "I'm in an American uniform." It was just one of those very, very tragic times when they saw each other with a fence between them, you know.

Howard had promised Buddy that he would be back the next day, and he couldn't go back. He was to bring him some personal provisions like shaving outfits, some soap, and stuff like that. He had a lot of work that had to be done on the ship that they were on, and he went back to his ship. He was directing the crane operator who was loading and unloading things from the dock into the ship and vice versa. The crane operator made a mistake and, instead of moving the crane a particular way, it swung toward my brother. My brother fell down into the hold of the ship which was about eight floors down. His body was totally crushed, and he was unconscious with two broken legs, two broken arms, and a broken back. That put an end to his seeing Buddy.†

scale mountain cliff
risk death
sheer luck
naturally stunted tree

* Hosokawa, "From the Frying Pan."

† Amy Uno Ishii, interviewed by Betty Mitson and Kristen Mitchell, July 9, 1973, and July 20, 1973, *Japanese American World War II Evacuation Oral History Project, Part I: Internees,* ed. Arthur A. Hansen (K. G. Saur, 1994), pp. 39–87.

39 HITOSHI "MOE" YONEMURA

Italy is a colorful and charming country—and the people are quite friendly. The war has left a horrible mark on most Italian towns, and the victims as always are poor children. They are everywhere around begging food. If I could have ever forgiven Hitler, Mussolini and Tojo for their avarice and greed, I can never now forgive them for what they have done to these children and the millions like them throughout the world.

Our situation forces us to keep moving at all times, and at each step we dig in. Boy, I am really in shape for that WPA shovel job when I get back. The other day I had just started to dig when Jerry started to zero in with his heavy stuff. Boy Buck, you should have seen me! I looked like an eager gopher looking for a Chinese friend in the most direct route! But in spite of all my frantic antics, part of me (guess what part) still stood out in the open waving in the breeze. No kidding, Buck, I still wonder if I had been wounded there if I would have been granted the Purple Heart?

Oh, but I've learned so well that this war is no picnic. Isn't it hideous? Casualties here mean so much, ever so much more than mere figures in a newspaper. Jerry is a tough and tenacious foe and a treacherous one. The boys have been and are magnificent! I've seen them under all conditions and each time they've been beyond reproach. Anybody up here has the utmost respect for our units, and that includes the enemy! I'm a little disillusioned at times when I read of further discriminatory remarks and actions at home, when boys are so gallantly fighting and dying here. What more can we do to prove our good faith? What's wrong with the world, Buck? Here we are fighting for democracy abroad—you and I, and those who aren't fighting at all—and many who weren't even born Americans, are trying to kick me out of my country, and are trying to kill the democracy we are dying for!*

exquisite shade
mellowed beauty
shibui

---

* Letter, JERS.

40 BEN KUROKI

[T]here were numerous reasons that I wanted to fly on B-29s . . . I was in Denver, tried to share a taxi with a man . . . of course wearing my uniform with all my ribbons, and slammed the door in my face and said, "I won't ride with no lousy Jap." My best friend and high school classmate, Gordy Jorgensen, was killed in the Solomon Islands by the Japanese enemy. And even when I was there in Santa Monica, my squadron friend Ed Bates came back about the same time I did so they put me in the same room together. Ed Bates' brother was also killed in the Pacific. And I told him that if I ever got over to the Pacific, the first zero I get was going to be for his brother. And there were . . . there were also the 442nd was beginning to do well in Italy. And I heard reports that, "Well, they're doing great because they're not fighting against the Japs." And somehow I just wanted to prove that it didn't make any difference to me whether I was fighting against the Japanese enemy or the Germans . . .

I was going to Heart Mountain and Minidoka and Topaz. And I think that there's been some misunderstandings about that. But they never gave me any, didn't tell me or give me any instructions . . . but the JACL had nothing to do with me . . . I was really quite shocked when I approached Heart Mountain and came up to the, to the gate and saw these armed guards and they were all wearing the same uniform I was wearing. And inside, behind the barbed wire, were all these, my own people, so to speak. Most of them, as you know, they were American citizens. It was really quite a shock. I never did get over that . . . I was asked to speak, I guess, to this Fair Play Committee group. And I'd been warned that they were quite militant and that they were concerned for my safety so they were going to put on some extra guards . . . I guess I would say that everything was okay except at one time I made the statement that if they thought Japan was going to win the war, they're crazy. I said that they were going to get bombed off the map. And I heard some hissing and booing at that time. And that was probably the most, well, the only real thing that stood out in my memory of what happened.

I was asked to speak during the church service. It was quite an experience, too. Until the war I wasn't that much of a religious man but boy, once you see that anti-aircraft shell bursting all around you, you know, God, every time it exploded there was black smoke and there were times you get out there it was so heavy you could walk on that stuff. And terrified, you sit there with two fifty-caliber machine guns and you're just helpless; you can't do a damn thing. You can't fight back cause those anti-aircraft shells, those 88mm German shells are coming up there in the tons. [Imitates noise of explosions] You feel the plane move this way and that and you sit there and go, "Oh God, let's get the hell out of here." Oh man, I'm telling you . . . oh, I don't know how I ever made it. I had a good pilot. And they said, "God is your co-pilot." Well, I had a heck of a good co-pilot, too.*

rope, pick, knife, chisel, spade, crowbar
nursing, pruning, shaping
many years
to safe removal

* Interview, January 31, 1998, Frank Abe Collection, Densho Digital Archives.

41 DANIEL K. INOUYE

And even as I cocked my arm to throw, he fired and his rifle grenade smashed into my right elbow and exploded and all but tore my arm off. I looked at it, stunned and unbelieving. It dangled there by a few bloody shreds of tissue, my grenade still clenched in a fist that suddenly didn't belong to me any more . . .

"Get back!" I screamed, and swung around to pry the grenade out of that dead fist with my left hand. Then I had it free and I turned to throw and the German was reloading his rifle. But this time I beat him. My grenade blew up in his face and I stumbled to my feet, closing on the bunker, firing my tommy gun left-handed, the useless right arm slapping red and wet against my side. . . .

"But I cannot help wondering," I said, "whether the people of Hawaii will not think it strange that the only weapon in the Republican arsenal is to label as communists men so recently returned from defending liberty on the firing lines in Italy and France. Let me speak for those of us who didn't come back . . . when I say that we bitterly resent having our loyalty and patriotism questioned by cynical political hacks who lack the courage to debate the real issues in this campaign."

I had never before called attention to my disability . . . But at that moment, blinded with fury, coldly aware that I was engaging in a bit of demagoguery, I held up my empty right sleeve and shook it: "I gave this arm to fight fascists. If my country wants the other one to fight communists, it can have it." . . .

Let me quote from the *Congressional Record:* "The House was very still. It was about to witness the swearing in, not only of the first Congressman from Hawaii, but the first American of Japanese descent to serve in either House of Congress.

"'Raise your right hand and repeat after me,' intoned Speaker Rayburn.

"The hush deepened as the young Congressman raised not his right hand but his left, and he repeated the oath of office."*

tree growing at elevation 6000
bring down gradually
over years
habituate at 4000, then 2000

---

* Daniel K. Inouye, *Journey to Washington* (Prentice-Hall, 1967), pp. 152, 248–249. *Congressional Record*, 1963.

42 HOICHI KUBO

*[S]ome Japanese soldiers had a large group of civilians in the cave, holding them hostage."I'm going in!" Hoichi told Lt. Roger Pear. Giving the officer his .45 pistol, the Maui native slid down a rope into the cave. He talked to the civilians, and began herding them out. A Japanese sergeant interrupted him, saying "You're a spy!" "I am an American!" Hoichi shouted. "My grandfathers fought with the 5th and 6th Divisions! I am here to take out the non-combatants." His opponent was taken aback on learning the Hoichi descended from fighting men of Hiroshima and Kumamoto . . . the Japanese soldiers questioned . . . how he, with Japanese blood, could serve in the army of the United States. He quoted a dictum from their own schoolbooks. Nearly 800 years before, in Japan, Shigemori Taira was urged by his father to lead forces against an Imperial faction. His quandary resulted in an oft-quoted palindrome . . . "If I am filial, I cannot serve the Emperor. If I serve the Emperor, I cannot be filial." . . . the Japanese soldiers in the cave, and all Nisei in Uniform were bound by the same centuries-old precept—that a man's loyalty goes to the higher authority. Taira disregarded his father. Nisei opted for their native land.**

growing freely
vigorous branch near top
nourishment runs to
the thickening trunk
before sprouting season
cut this branch

---

* Joseph D. Harrington, *Yankee Samurai: The Secret Role of Nisei in America's Pacific Victory* (Pettigrew Enterprises, 1979), pp. 209–210.

43 SADAO S. MUNEMORI

[A]n assistant squad leader of Co. A, 100th Battalion, he died in action on April 5, 1945, near Seravezza, Italy. His citation reads:

*"When his unit was pinned down by grazing fire from the enemy's strong mountain defense and command of the squad devolved on him with the wounding of its regular leader, he made frontal, one-man attacks through direct fire and knocked out two machine guns with grenades. Withdrawing under murderous fire and shower of grenades from other enemy emplacements, he had nearly reached a shell crater occupied by two of his men when an unexploded grenade bounced off his helmet and rolled toward his helpless comrades. He arose into the withering fire, dived for the missile, and smothered its blast with his body. By his swift, supremely heroic action, Private Munemori saved two of his men at the cost of his own life and did much to clear the path for his company's victorious advance."**

potted landscape
stones blend with trees
beauty and joy

* Medal of Honor awarded posthumously, March 13, 1946; Hosokawa *Nisei*, pp. 412–413.

44 KENJI KENNY YASUI

CBI now has its own Sergeant York... Kenny is about five feet two and weighs scarcely more than 120 pounds. And this Baby York of CBI is a Nisei...

Under the veil of protective secrecy, however, the stubborn, sturdy fighting Niseis grew to the stature of heroes. They became exceedingly popular, earned the admiration and personal friendship of every private and general with whom they came in contact. The secrecy was officially lifted a few days ago. Now we can tell their story.

The case of Sergeant Yasui, who captured 16 Japanese at the Irrawaddy River, is only one of the many bright spots the Niseis are writing into modern American military history...

It happened on the Irrawaddy River, during our mopping up operations after the collapse of organized resistance. A group of about 17 Japanese were isolated on an island. There was a call for volunteers to capture the Japs. Kenny Yasui and three non-Nisei Americans stepped out, stripped and swam over. Little Kenny took charge.

The Japs hid in the underbrush. None was seen. Then California-born Kenny Yasui yelled into the bush in the Japanese he learned while a student of Waseda University, Tokyo. He ordered the enemy to come out to surrender. The hidden men in the bush must have been stupefied to hear their native tongue. Instantly, a Nip sergeant appeared, looked amazed at the little naked man who said he was Japanese colonel working with the Americans and ordered him to show the hiding places of his comrades. The Jap was impressed and bewildered, terribly so. He took Kenny around on an inspection tour and out of many foxholes jumped many a Nip, fully armed, 20 rounds of ammunition in each man's belt. Kenny Yasui asked for their arms, ordered them to line up. In that second, a Jap officer sprang from the thicket, threw a hand grenade to blow up Yasui and himself. Yasui jumped into a foxhole and the Japanese officer into the other world. Then Kenny took his sword. While all this happened, a couple of recalcitrant Japanese soldiers were killed by the other Americans, but 13 prisoners waited shamefacedly for the orders of the little olive-skinned "colonel." Kenny remembered the close order drills he had to take while he was at Kibei in Tokyo. And he gave them the words:

"Kio tsuke! Hidari muke hidari! Mae susume."

The drill over, Yasui solved the problem of getting the party across the Irrawaddy by having the prisoners swim, pushing a raft against the swift cur-

*rent. And on the raft sat Kenny with the sword in his hand and two of the weaker prisoners at his side.**

cherished scene
indelibly imprinted
sanctuary of memory

* S/Sgt. Edgar Laytha, "Nisei," *CBI Roundup*, 3, no. 1, reg no. L5015, Delhi, Thursday, September 14, 1944 (CBI: China Burma India Theater).

45 TETSUJIRO "TEX" NAKAMURA

I talked to Mr. Collins, and he came up to Tule Lake for me, and we started getting a group of people, tell 'em what to do. So what we did was, from each block, we received a representative, and trying to relay the information of what we were planning to do with trying to file suit in San Francisco. And from each block, we nominated a committeeman that would take, relay all this information. And we finally organized a group, that was November 13, 1945, we filed a class action suit in San Francisco, U.S. District Court, one thousand people . . .

Yeah, well, see, ACLU wanted to get into, involved in the case . . . they blamed somebody within the camp, not the government . . . Mr. Collins figured that none of these people should be deported, none of these people . . . because it was the government that forced us to evacuate. And after we were evacuated into camp, the government was supposed to protect all these people. If there's any discernments like that, the government should pick those people up and incarcerate them. So they, once you make a mistake like that, the evacuation, then they keep on making mistakes constantly, and forcing people to do things against government . . . the ACLU in New York and Los Angeles . . . was appeasing . . . the government, to save the face of the government. Mr. Collins said, no, the government should not be appeased at all. They're the ones to be blamed for everything that took place. And a lot of them were in Japan, too, they went back to Japan, fifteen hundred people went back to Japan.*

in spring and autumn
place outdoors
sun and breeze plentiful
dew at night

---

* Interview, September 24, 2009, Densho Digital Archive.

46 EDWARD KINTOKU IGE

November 22, 1947

Dear Mr. Collins:

Please include my name in the equity suit. My wife . . . has been acknowledged during her stay in Tule Lake and has come to join me.

Will you please take my wife and my request in a special manner? I realize the cost of special favor. My parents, sisters and brother are all residents of Hawaii of present and request me to return as soon as possible. They desire me to return to take control of a business that demands my attention.

Is there any means of entering United States soon? I am ready to leave here at a moments notice. I will gladly volunteer for the U.S. Army if I am given the privilege to do so. Moreover I am willing to pay a lawyer's fee, bond, etc that may not be permissible for an average renunciant.

In as much as I do not possess Japanese citizenship I am much confronted with peculiar problems.

I do not know to what nation I am a national of, but have faith in my motherland America!

Yours very truly,

c/o Maj. H. Suzuki
291 Hisagi Zushi Cho
Yokosuka Shii, Japan*

life made bearable
prolonged by
natural beauty

* Letter, November 22, 1947, Wayne M. Collins Papers 1918–1974, Online Archive of California.

47 EDWARD TAKESHI MIYAKAWA

[B]y the time I leave Tule Lake, I have developed 4 or 5 psychosomatic illnesses. I became a bed wetter at 8 years old. I developed a fear of the dark that I never had before . . . I developed an obsession with matches, and I would steal matches and I almost started a major fire in Tule Lake. Because I got this obsession and I would get coals and I started this fire next to this barrack and all of the sudden this whole barrack almost started bursting into flame, and people started shouting, "Fire, Fire!" and I ran away and so then I lost my appetite, and I was a very skinny kid, and I stopped eating the food. And so my mother became very worried because she couldn't make me eat and I got even skinnier . . .

Ken, along with some older boys, started picking on me, and they made my life miserable. And I remember being in these barracks and then I'd look out the window and there were half a dozen guys standing outside of my barrack apartment waiting for me to come out. And we would play a game like "kick the can" and they would—I would be the guarder of the can and they would make sure I could never be anything but the guarder of the tin can. I just remember that, and I'd be sitting there trying to guard the can and they would distract me to one place, and they would kick this can and then the game wouldn't end until it got dark . . .

And then, they would blind fold me . . . have me walk with them and say "hey, follow me" and just kind of force me. And then I would step into this hole . . . I pulled my foot out and it was filled with flour and urine . . .

[A]nother time, they would take me and put me on this wooden horse, it's just a 2 by 4 with wooden legs . . . I'll never forget this story: "Take the blind fold off!" And I'd take it off and I'd be in the women's latrine. Well that's not a big deal, but when you're a 7 year old, I was just infuriated! I'd come out and I'd throw a rock and hit Ken in the stomach and he'd come up to me and threaten to kill me . . .*

rock garden
focal point
all directions
radiating harmony

---

* Oral history interview, August 18, 2007, Elizabeth Uhlig, interviewer, Oregon State University, Japanese-American Association of Lane County.

MINÉ: Citizen

There is another wild looking thing who has been to Europe on an art scholarship, and she is doing a lot of sketches so that there should be quite a bit of material available for future studies of this mess.

—Charles Kikuchi, *The Kikuchi Diary*, 1942

Frank marched purposefully with his wooden tripod, rucksack of supplies on his back. Miné trudged behind holding the giant Graflex Super D like a big baby. *Thing weighs a ton,* she complained.

Not far at all. We're here, Frank announced, approaching a gathering of rocks, the centerpiece a gigantic slab propped up by the tumble of others. Frank set the tripod down, took the Graflex from Miné and set it down gently in a bed of dry grass.

Miné leaned into a nearby boulder, sipped water from her canteen, but Frank trotted up to the big rock, ran his fingers over the glyphs. She was thirty; he was sixty-seven, but he was like his nickname, a billy goat, seemed not to need water, pranced over the rocks and uneven terrain. *Are you supposed to touch them?* she asked. *I mean, if I painted something a thousand years ago, I don't know if I would want you putting your dingy fingers on it.*

Twelve thousand years, he corrected. *Probably shouldn't,* he agreed, *but feel it, right here. Not this one, but this.* He pointed at a spiral form. *There's a ghost here, emanating.*

She pressed her index to the middle of the spiral and thought she felt a tingling. *How do you know which one to touch?*

Joe says one direction is good, other is not. Frank twisted his finger in the air to the right and to the left.

Oh, thanks for warning me.

Joe says it's a whirlwind, one of those twisters you see out there raising dust, a spiritual presence.

You keep talking about Joe. He's Paiute, right?

Belongs to the land. So do we, we just don't know it.

When am I ever going to meet him?

One of these days, when he wants to, he'll show up. By and by . . .

In the meantime, I've got you.

That's right. Frank nodded. *You've got me, an old white man.*

No offense but you're pretty smart for a white man, not to mention spry.

Frank chuckled. *Joe said the same thing.*

She passed Frank the canteen. *So, tell me more.*

Frank took a good gulp. He broke a branch from a nearby cedar, pulled off the smaller branches, and pointed his stick like the rock face was a giant blackboard. *It's easier if you isolate the glyphs into symbols like, you know, your kanji.*

You know I can't read kanji, Miné grumbled.

But if you could, Frank posited, *I bet you've got a kanji for rainbow.*

No idea, Miné shrugged. *Ask Jim, he's the linguist. All I know is the kanji for dog, but that's only because I read Jim's article. You want dog?* She grabbed his stick and drew the character in the dirt. *And here's my kanji for rainbow.* She drew three arching lines.

Oh amazing. Your Mongolian origins. Frank smiled. He pointed to the rainbow glyph, the same arching lines on the rock.

I don't know, Frank, kinda obvious.

But take a look at the figure beneath the rainbow.

Yeah, okay.

Actually, boy or youth. Rainbow youth.

How do you know it's boy? Why not man? Old man?

It's the rainbow! Frank threw up his hands in excitement. *I'll tell you a story. One day I was hiking with Joe, and I was trying to figure out his age, which I found out he really doesn't know, but I thought if he could compare it to my age, we'd figure it out, but he said, "Frank you stand under rainbow." I was confused, so he explained: "Man under rainbow always boy. Live forever."*

Miné mused, *A glyph for immortality.*

Maybe.

Or a man in the rainbow of his life.

I like that, Miné. I like that. Frank looked for the sun and scanned the desert landscape. *Sunlight is perfect.* He adjusted the tripod feet beneath the Graflex, read the settings on his light meter, back and forth, camera to meter.

Miné got her sketchbook out from the rucksack and found a rocky seat behind Frank. *How long have you been studying petroglyphs?*

Been awhile, before I met Joe, maybe a decade, then studying with Joe, another decade. Trekking up and down Utah, Nevada, Arizona, every chance I get. There's more to it than you think. Archaeology, geology, the lay of the land. Got to learn the old ways. Only the old-timers like Joe know that, but as Joe says, some things not for white man. You got to go back in time, read old accounts, diaries. Learn Spanish to read the padres who came through back in the seventeen hundreds. Anything written, I read it.

Impressive.

If I could spend all my time studying this world, that's what I'd do. Take the advice of an old man. Follow your passion because life happens.

Like this war. I was in France when it started.

You went there to study art?

Well, yes, but really to study people, the Europeans. Does that make sense?

You might be an anthropologist.

I don't think so. I don't really like people. I'd prefer to be alone. Just me and my art.

I'm guessing you don't have to like people to be an anthropologist.

You mean to study people, you turn them into subjects.

To draw people, you turn them into subjects.

Frank, do you like people?

I like them very much.

Miné smirked. *I like them sometimes. I need to leave soon. They're driving me crazy.*

Ha.

I like you. She tapped her pencil on her sketchbook, then held it up for a quick look. *Have you thought about this? I'm sketching you photographing petroglyphs. I,* she pointed to herself, *am a camera.*

Yeah, they ought to liberate you and cameras, but from what I know, you see better and more than, he pointed to his Graflex, *this camera. No one with a precious camera would be recording what you see. I say keep sketching. That last cover you did for your magazine, TREK. That wasn't just a sketch. It was an entire story.*

Miné shrugged, her pencil dashing about adroitly over paper. *Folks look at my work and think it's a bunch of cartoons.*

What's the matter with cartoons? I draw them all the time.

Obata had all his students outside painting landscapes. Barracks and barbed wire at sunset, like romantic paintings.

Miné, if I were in your place, I'd go outside and paint too. We need landscapes, need nature, especially living in barracks inside barbed wire. It's not what they paint; it's what they feel. Confinement is painful. It needs space and an outlet. Mr. Obata had the right idea.

Yeah, and look where that got him.

I miss Mr. Obata. He is a very fine man. I hope he got his eyesight back. Terrible shame. If he were here now. He sees the big picture. That's his vision.

Miné nodded. *I get it. Then there's Ansel's landscape photography. Same difference.* She paused and huffed, *You know, I'm a real artist.*

Never said you weren't.

Once I see something, it doesn't leave my mind.

Photographic memory?

I don't think so, but if I don't draw it, it stays here. She pointed to her head. *Sometimes my head hurts.*

Drawing takes every bit of your concentration, I suppose.

No, my head hurts if I don't draw. If I can draw, the world disappears. Okay, makes no sense. Her voice cracked. *I need to get out of that hellhole.* She pointed over the boulder. *Away from those people. The only way they disappear is if I draw them. Over and over again.* Her voice trailed off.

Frank looked back at Miné. *Are you trying to make me disappear?*

It's not like that. It's about being inside my head. Quarantined in my own space. My mom was an artist, but she gave it all up to wash our dirty socks. I'm never doing that. Never. Miné got up and gesticulated. *Frank, you're pointing that camera in the wrong direction.*

Frank looked around and scanned the wide expanse of desert.

Miné pointed. *Over there. Do you see him?*

What? Frank squinted.

I think it's a little boy. In brown overalls.

Desert playing tricks. Coyote snuck into the brush.

They scrutinized the snowy mountain peaks beyond, clouds billowing. *You're right, but I'm not Ansel. This here,* Frank pointed at the glyphs, *is a human mystery. Someone left it here for others to decipher.*

You think so?

Maybe not. He removed his hat and fanned the air. *But, I think these glyphs are like mnemonics, you know, patterns to hold memory. That's language. You've got to read through them, not from, not superficially, I mean. From twelve thousand years, wisdom comes to us.*

Maybe they were just scribbling, cartooning like me. She gestured over her pad. *Glyphing.*

Right. And this slab of rock looked like a perfect surface.

Miné pointed. *That smooth empty edge at the bottom. I could add a few figures of my own. You know, as a twentieth-century primitivist. Hey, I'm capable of doing an entire mural!* Miné stood up, waving her pencil.

You stay away! Frank yelled, his arms flinging out in mock defense.

Okay. Okay. Don't get too excited.

They both laughed, their howls echoing, then sucked into dry landscape.

Miné returned to her drawing. *Frank, thanks for bringing me out here. Others don't get this chance.*

Well, maybe I should have asked Mr. Obata instead. At least he'd be looking out in the right direction. Frank pointed behind him.

Miné picked a small gray stone from the sandy soil and threw it at Frank.

Hey, watch it. I'm old and scarred, but this Graflex—Frank picked up the piece of Miné's stone that bounced off his trousers and examined it. *What do you know,* he murmured.

What? Miné turned the page of her sketchbook.

This is a trilobite, Elrathia kingii. *Very fine fossil specimen. Released from its stratum. Wonder what it's doing here.*

She got up to look at the ancient water bug. The size of a silver dollar in Frank's palm.

Three-and-a-half billion years old, this little bugger.

Billion? Sorry I threw it.

Oh, if it's lasted that long, it will last a lot longer. This is a special find. Usually you find these up over there, around Antelope Springs. Split open the slate and voila! See this hole? I bet this was on a necklace. Joe says they used to go look for them to ward off bullets.

She made a quick sketch.

Here. Frank placed the fossil in Miné's hands, folded her fingers around it. *You keep this. Make a necklace. Keep you safe.* He repeated, *Keep you safe.*

She nodded and carefully shoved the trilobite deep into her pocket.

Frank returned to his camera settings, and Miné returned to sketching Frank with his Graflex, the expanse and mystery of petroglyphs a great canvas backdrop containing his wry figure, a crooked shadow in dust and rock. They worked in silence, the swirling of small whirlwinds spinning in the cool air. They did not speak again.

CHARLIE: Resettlement

botchan (坊っちゃん)
noun: young master; son of a good family; title of the novel by Natsume Soseki; sometimes interpreted by nisei to mean spoiled son

boochie
slang: nisei-speak derivative of botchan, referring to nisei generally

If I remember correctly, I began my story with the words "I am an American." I insist I am an American. But am I? What is an American anyhow? Archibald MacLeish says it's "a strange thing." I'll say it is!

—Louis Adamic, "A Young American with a Japanese Face,"
From Many Lands, 1940

Wednesday, December 23, 1942

Last night, my team sold no JACL memberships in block 39. Tonight, we only sold three. We were wondering what was wrong when we found out that some rumor is sweeping that block. Some Issei and Kibei are going around and telling the parents that they should not let their children join because if they do the boys would all be taken by the draft. This is due to the recent stand the National JACL made on Selective Service as a part of our civil rights. Three more young Nisei came to us with the story that their parents wanted them to withdraw. I really laid it down to them. I told them that the Nisei had been under parental influence too long, and if they really believed in democracy, they would have the guts to take a firm stand now. I told them that serving in the Army was part of our civil rights, and we had to fight for these principles. I told them that they had to think about the future, and if they intended to stay in this country, they should go "all out" on a stand for America.

This guy Charlie who comes around, he doesn't recognize me but I know he ran with my neech and the Yamato Garage Gang before he got into State and Cal, snuck into Chinatown to chase skirts and pocket money. Now he's one of those jackals who press you with the boochie religion.

A bunch of us have a friendly round of poker going. When we hear the knock, it's a scramble to hide the coins. Think it's a raid, but then he's no warden, comes in trying to get us to sign up. If he sits down at our table, he'll wipe us out. I know from my brother—Charlie is good at the table. We pretend to play on, look at him above the cards while he tries to sell us on membership.

Yosh speaks up and says, "My pop says okay to the Kibei club, but not the JACL. He says you want me to enlist. I'll get stuck in the front line, and they'll pick us off like pigs."

"Yeah," Hiro says, "what's the use of making the Issei get mad at us? They went through the same things we'll face after the war. Okay, I'm American, but the Ketō will never accept us. If they hadn't evacuated me, I'd be willing to sacrifice anything."

Then Kats says, "Folks say the JACL sold us down the line. You're the reason why we're here. Is that true? Why would we join the very club that locked us up?"

Charlie argues that we needed to grow up and take responsibility for our own decisions. I got to agree, but then I only got my mom, and she stopped trying to tell me anything a long time ago.

Tak don't say nothing, but when the guy leaves, he says that Charlie is one of those college guys who got a job with admin. Works in the welfare department doling out money to the poor.

I say, "Hey, what money? I'm poor."

Yosh slaps his hand down and says, "You gonna be poorer, that's for sure."

Nobu plans to send Mitsumori, the ex-serviceman, down to block 39 to talk with some of the Issei who most seriously object to the JACL.

There're rumors going around about the strike in Poston. Dai Nippon Banzai and all that. Kats hears it from the other Kibei. Meanwhile, Kats says there's another rumor about taking boochies to train for military intelligence. My nihongo is only good for talking to Ma, but Kats says, "You'd better think twice. They'll make you study Japanese so you have to spy. The U.S. don't know anything about Japanese military installations, their naval strength or movements. The Nisei got yellow faces so that they can be shipped behind Japanese lines to get all the dope. But if you get caught, you lose your head. You will be nothing but a stool pigeon."

Yosh says, "All they want Nisei for is to instruct the hakujin soldiers so they can conquer those islands. If they get any prisoners, they can use us to act as interpreters, but that means you'll be in a camp again but no girls around. And hell, you can't beat the Kibei. You have to know a lot of Japanese. Damn Kibei get all the breaks." He shoves Kats-the-Kibei. "And it's because of you guys being Japanesy that we got stuck in camp in the first place."

Kats says, "What you got to blame me for?"

Nobu is thinking of asking for a Rec Hall for the J.A.C.L., since the Kibei group were given one. Believes that we will hit the 1000 membership. Next Monday evening he and Ken will go to Canal before the teachers, and he asked me to come along. He feels that something is going to stir up soon. Nobu feels that we may as well go all the way, and if the Kibei want a riot, it is up to them.

Like Charlie, we live on the Butte side where most of the Tulare folks are. Canal is Turlock. You'd think we'd all get along fine being mostly bumpkin farming folks, but it's not like that. Butte's more American. Canal leans Japanese. There's a secret Issei-Kibei club with about 500 and a young Buddhist Club and Kibei Club.

Kibei rule over in Canal, but they're not all the same. Just because a guy spends time in the old country doesn't mean he's all for Japan. Some Kibei hate Japan, and I figure they must know what they're talking about.

Then there's Nisei who never been, but since evac, they turn Japanese. Like Tak. He thinks he's going back to Japan, but he's not going back because he's never been. He tells me the other day when he gets to Japan, he'll look up my brother and fight for the rising sun. Hell, then you hear the old Issei with nothing to show for their lives, talking about wanting to be buried in Japan.

Mr. Eto is having a tough time getting proper food. He has had diabetes for the past seven years. At the present time, he has to take an injection every day. The hospital has been giving him a certificate to get a special diet at the mess hall, but they just cannot give him the stuff which he needs. Eto has to eat a lot of meat, eggs, and cream, which are practically unobtainable. Therefore, the man has to spend his own money at the canteen to get other foods. He has only $300 to his name. This is in the bank at Fowler. He said that if the government needed this money, they could freeze it and use it. But he wanted to save it for Relocation, so we granted him an allowance of $9.00. The man tried to work but the doctors advised him against it.

Other day, another high-tone college-type comes around on a bicycle. I walk up to see this guy on the stoop talking to my mom. She understands English, but when it's appropriate not to, she doesn't. I can see that it's not appropriate today because he's struggling even though his nihongo is good enough. He tells me my kid brother hasn't been going to school. He says, "It's important that students keep a strong interest in school." He pauses then adds, "despite the present circumstances." I agree with the guy and say I'll talk to Ken. He gets back on his bike and spins away, and Ma mutters, "Urusai." I find out later that this boochie Okuno works with Charlie in the welfare department on juvenile delinquency. Hell, I guess that's us, my brothers and me, and once upon a time, Charlie too, even though only I know it.

The camouflage net project seems to have received a big boost today. It was announced that from now on, the workers would get to keep all profits above the 1000 square feet per day. This means that they will not have to work for the other people in camp after their quota is reached. Now, if they have 1500 square feet per day over a period of a month, they will be able to get about $90.00 clear. This new plan will greatly raise the income of the net workers. The move has been necessary in order to get more of the Nisei out there. Recruiting has been very slow. There is no doubt that a lot of the fellows and girls will now be going out there. The net workers will now become the most favored group at this time.

> I get curious about where Ken goes when he doesn't go to school, so I follow him out one day. I figure he could be shoplifting from the canteen or tossing dice, usual stuff. I follow him to Block 51, what they're calling the red-light district Yoshiwara. Holy Christ, he's peeping through a hole in the tar paper. I grab him by the collar and pull him away. I got to say these whores are hags, but it's what's available in camp. If he were peeping with a gang of kids, that's one thing, but a lone peeper? I threaten to show him into the door of camp Yoshiwara, stuff his face into those low-hanging fruit. He tries to yank away, and I say he better go to school, or I'll bust his face. He runs off. When he's around the block, I can finally have my laugh.

When I came home and found a package from Mr. Ikeda, I was extremely angry. At first, I thought that it may have been a bribe on his part. Then I stopped to think of his past actions, and I realized that this gift was an expression on his part of an independent attitude. Made him feel good to show me that he still had money left which he could spend as he pleased. His motives were of the best. I felt that I could not accept the gift, since it may set a bad precedent. Miura has already received about seventeen pounds of candy from his former clients at Tulare. I did not want these people to start feeling obligated. Okuno thought that the man would feel insulted if I took the gift back. He said that it was customary for the Japanese to show appreciation by gifts. However, I felt that I could return the gift and at the same time could get Mr. Ikeda to realize that I appreciated his sentiments.

When I went over to his house, only his wife was present. I was able to make her understand why I returned the gift. She kept thanking me over and over for my kindness, and I kept telling her that she should thank the government.

I know Charlie was just a kid, maybe nine years old, when he gets kicked out by his old man and put up in the Salvation Army home somewhere out there in Salinas, probably begging door-to-door contributions. Maybe his pop thinks he's a bastard, since his picture bride was a beauty. Hell, my little mom must have been a beauty too. When Charlie comes back ten years later, he joins up with my brother and the Yamatos. If you get out of Japantown, why come back? But he comes back. Hell, no place else to go. I hear my brother say Charlie's smart to the street but dumb about Jap town. Has to be reeducated. After a stint, he gets away from the gang life and on to the college route. Now he's back in camp Jap town like everybody else, living with his mom, three sisters, a kid brother and his sister's kid. All crowded into one lousy barrack. They have to leave his pop in the hospital back in California. Probably die there. So now Charlie's busting his butt to be big neech of the household. What ma calls oyakōkō. If I got kicked out for ten years, would I come back? Jesus, no. Prodigal helluva son story.

The following is confidential material which I had not intended to enter into this record. It took me quite a while to decide on it. It is now 2:30 A.M. Here goes.

As I was coming home this evening, I had a premonition that somebody was following me. Immediately my mind flashed to other incidents. My natural reaction was that some of the Kibei we had talked to in our section had not liked it as I did not pull any punches when I told them where the Nisei stood. Then I figured that it was my nerves. I have been feeling periodically depressed in the past few days, and I thought that the thing was getting me down, jittery and neurotic. But I walked faster and kept looking behind without seeing anybody. The feeling persisted, so I ducked in Nobu's house to tell him about our snags tonight in the drive.

I get to know Tak at Turlock. His brother tried to enlist, got turned down and then tried to kill himself. It's Tak who finds him strung up and gets him down, saves him. They send the brother ahead here to Gila, but when the rest of the family gets here, the brother stops talking to the family. And everybody talks behind their backs.

Tak says his pop is 69 years old and has a slip from the doctor saying he's not strong enough to work, but he still wants to work. He won't take a handout. He's too proud. Says he just wants some cash for ciga-

> rettes, but I bet they're down to their last pennies. They could use the brother's help, but he left to do beet work, and I bet he'll enlist first chance, if they ever open service again to the boochies.
>
> Tak could work on the net crew, but he won't because they're making those nets for the war, and he won't support that. He tries in lumber, but there's no lumber left to work with. He tries with the firefighters, but he starts a fight, and they throw him out. Then he finds out that his pop got desperate and got a clothing order and $5.00 from Welfare Charlie. After all, his mom could use a dress. Holy Jesus, she's all in patches. To make things worse, Tak's pop gets Charlie a gift to thank him for his trouble. Japanese-style, you know. Tak gets hysterical, blaming Charlie, blaming Ketō-America.

It was around 9:45 when I came out and started for home. I could still feel that there was something in the air, and then I figured that it was an overworking of my imagination. But it wasn't. As I crossed the road towards the lot, I suddenly heard a voice say, "That's the one!" Suddenly, two figures were upon me. A great fear filled me, and I started to swing and kick desperately. I received a couple of blows on the back, and one fellow was trying to get some sort of wrestling hold on my arm. I thought he was going to try and break it, so in fear and desperation, I lunged forward and broke loose. I started to run, and one of the fellows yelled something in Japanese. I ran all the way across the empty lot towards the net project. The two fellows chased me for about 100 yards, and then they turned around and ran back. I was plenty shaken up.

It happened so fast that I could not possibly identify either of the two. They were wearing the black mackinaws which everyone has. The words they said in English did not sound like a Kibei. I couldn't be sure. A great rage filled me after I saw them running the other way, and I felt like I could kill the dirty sons-of-bitches. I walked around a bit in order to calm down. I did not intend to tell the family about it as it would cause them unnecessary worry.

I just can't figure out why the attack. I was not hurt, but they looked like they meant business. I don't know what the motives are. It may be the JACL activity; it may be the clothing issue; it may be the fact that I don't speak Japanese; it may have been a mistake; it may have been any number of causes.

I decided not to report the matter to Williamson because I did not think the fellows could be caught anyway. And if it did get out, it may scare many Nisei out of the JACL. This is not time for us to lose our "guts." We have to fight like Nobu thinks.

> Tak and Kats get into an argument. Tak starts yelling about how he didn't give a damn about his American citizenship. About how he's for Japan and Japan's going to win. "America treats us like dogs and now it wants us to help beat the Japanese people." First chance he gets, he's renouncing his citizenship and going to Japan.
>
> Kats laughs at him, says he's staying right here until the war is over and then maybe he's going back to Japan, depending. Kats is Kibei, can go both ways. Tak argues that Kats needs to choose a side. Kats yells, "Banzai! Banzai!" and starts marching around like a wooden soldier.
>
> Tak gets up, grabs Kats and pushes him to the floor. They start pounding each other, but Kats keeps yelling *banzai* and laughing like a madman. We finally pull the guys apart, and Tak storms out. We haven't seen him again.

My mind was a confusion when I got home. I tried to act natural. I felt desperately in need to somebody to talk to, but I did not want to tell the family of the incident. I was scared and worried as hell that somebody might try something on them someday. I had the most lonesome feeling, and my mind was in turmoil. I was so upset and nervous. I tried to control myself. Went over to Bette and stuck my hand on her back casually. She was cross about it. Did the same with Emiko, and she was touchy. So I sat down and started to write. My mind was flashing with all sorts of things. I did not know what to think.

It was almost 10:20, so I went into the next room to turn off the radio and Mom and the rest got angry. Mom swore at me. This humiliated me and filled me with rage. I went into the room and turned on the radio full blast. I don't know what made me do it. Mom was stubborn. Alice came in and tried to turn it off, but I wouldn't let her. Mom went out to the latrine, but she was still stubborn, and I was still stubborn. Emiko started to yell about how Miyako couldn't sleep. She was also very angry. Almost in tears. She turned the radio off. I turned it on. This happened four times. Finally, she just yanked the wires right out of the radio. I was furious, and I don't know what made me do it, but I slapped her. Emiko got into hysterics. Bette sat up in bed and kept saying, "What's the matter with you anyway?"

One always feels sorry when it's too late. I don't know what possessed me. I worry about them, and yet I do a thing like that. I felt like a dam about to burst. Mom came back, and she didn't know what had been going on. Apologies are never enough. I've never been so disturbed so much before. I don't know what to think or do. Emiko was the innocent bystander. I did wrong her. But apologies won't clear that up.

The events in the past few weeks have been accumulating. I try to be calm about things but it is hard. Those bastards that hit me from behind threw a terrific scare into me. But I can't scare out now. We have to fight for certain principles, and no God-dammed yellow Kibei is going to intimidate me. At the same time, I feel uneasy about the family. Nothing must happen to them. I just have to run the risk. For the first time in years an emotional upheaval overcame me. I told Alice what had happened. She kept saying that I shouldn't have taken it out on the family. I know that, but the damage is done now.

> Yosh says his mom heard that twenty families came in from Phoenix and another fifteen from New Mexico. They were out there free to be free, but they came knocking at the barbed wire saying they needed in. I tell him that rumor is a bunch of bull.
>
> "Nah," Yosh says, "don't you see? My mom says this proves if we go out there, there's no work. We'll starve or get killed. This resettlement talk is like throwing us to the wolves."
>
> I say, "I've been out there digging up sugar beets. No wolves out there, but you think it's easy digging sugar beets? You bet it isn't. There's work out there, but who wants to work beets if you can sit around here and gamble? Only reason I got to get out is to pay my damn debts."

I went outside and walked around for two hours in the cold night air. I almost froze. I couldn't make up my mind on whether to tell Williamson about the matter. I don't think there is any deliberate plan of action against the JACL. Nobu or Harry and the rest would be ganged first. I am an innocuous member. It must have been something I said to some Kibei or Nisei down in the block 39 or 40 section. I can't figure it out. If the dogs would only come out into the open.

And the family mess. What should I do about that? Heroics is no answer. I'm angry one minute at those fellows and depressed about the family. Guess I need to take a rest and forget everything until next year. Deep inside of me

I feel a hurt worse than a wounded animal. I think that I would go crazy if I were alone in camp without the family to add the normal touch. I begin to hate all things Japanesy even more. I'm anti-social. I must have a mean streak. Jesus, I sure put myself into the doghouse all around. And I try so hard to have everybody in the family like me. I don't want to be a stranger. It almost drives me nuts not to be able to talk to them. Bette is about the only one who seems interested. Now she is angry. And Emiko will never forget this. Alice seems to have some understanding of what has been bothering me. I feel like I am going to pieces. Maybe tomorrow the great calm will come. What a life!

> The boochies say they want to go out, but I bet they're not too anxious about it. I'd say that many of us are happy here. What does Charlie know? He's a city slicker. If you come from the farm, you had to work a lot harder for almost nothing. Now I work a few days and get enough, hand over most of it to Ma. Who wants to think about resettlement? If you think about it, we have no future. Maybe those kids in high school. They don't know anything else and want to get out of here. I know the feeling, but I've been out there, and I got no illusions.

Thursday, December 24, 1942

All quiet today on the family front. Guess they have forgotten already. I felt pretty low today, the day before Xmas and things were certainly quiet.

I was busy most of the day getting the clothing grants to the people so that they could have them before the holidays. They did not come from Bennett's office by 10:30 so I went after them. They were laying on the desk, and the secretary had forgotten to bring them over. I sorted the whole batch out by blocks and gave some to Okuno to deliver.

I took Mrs. Yamauchi's order for $5.99 to her and as usual she started to complain that $5.00 was not enough for two dresses, and she said that she would sell the clothing order and use the money to buy her own dress. I figured it out that she was a proud person, and she wanted me to be sure to recognize that the condition was not due to her own faults. She complained a lot just to justify her own feeling on the matter.

Ran into Helen for the first time in weeks, and she was busy as ever. They have to worry about the installation of stoves now. She said that some of those mothers with new babies were really suffering, so we decided to write a letter from the welfare office to the engineering department. The stoves are being put in, but no oil yet.

> We got a baseball team going and got the cooks in the block to support it. This is just strategic because then we can hang out in the mess hall to get some better food from time to time. If I slip Ich some bootleg, he dishes up some fried rice and steak and gives me the inside scoop. Anyway, he's cooking it and telling me the latest.
>
> Turns out Kawakami gets a permit to join his relatives in Poston and left yesterday. Trouble is that he leaves his wife behind. So, she goes looking for him. Hell, Kawakami has another woman in Poston, and he's got plans to take her out and resettle in Denver.

One of the cases I visited today was the Noguchi family. The mother and father have both been ill, and the son is in a critical condition from an attack of meningitis. They have spent most of their money up for various items related to their health. They only have about $20 left in cash. This is their total assets aside from the clothes and things that they have in their rooms. They have two sons in the Army, both sergeants. The father was almost in tears because he had to apply for cash assistance. I told him that this was a right of his, and he should not feel this way, especially since he had given two sons to the service.

The Misano family also were having a hard time. There are eleven children and the mother here. Alice is the oldest, and she is only twenty. The youngest child was born just before evacuation. The father has been interned. He leased a hotel in Stockton, and he was picked up for his activities in the various Japan organizations. Only two children were working, and they only got the jobs recently. All of the children were in need of shoes and sweaters, and the mother said that they would have a sad Christmas because she had no money for presents. I took Alice up to see Tuttle, and he rushed the order through so that the girl was able to get shoes and sweaters this afternoon just before the canteen closed.

> Everyone says the L.A. chapter is corrupt. And take for instance the Oxnard chapter. I don't know where that is, but I do know Izzy Otoni. Kats says Izzy collects funds for Oxnard, then doesn't turn in the money to national headquarters, so no one gets their cards. Stashes

the money in some bank. What're we giving up our cash for anyway? A membership card and some newspaper?

I talked to LeBarron today, and he had great plans for his public relations department. Said that the experiment in this camp would be used for the future when vast numbers of people are resettled on the large government reclamation areas such as Grand Coulee. He thought that this would be the only way to resettle many of the soldiers returning from the war. LeBarron also plans to expand the Japanese section here to include world news as he says that a lot of the unrest here has been caused by misinformation. His immediate purpose is to try to enlighten public opinion on the outside. He is getting a good foothold on the paper here. He promises them a printing press.

I check out Charlie whose been going over to see Mary who has a two-year-old kid. I know her story: came away from Seattle to divorce her Issei husband. He did nothing but gamble and beat her up. Younger brother quits school to support her, but then he leaves for Army intelligence. Now she's got nothing and no relatives. Welfare Charlie's supposed to help her out, but it's a problem because I figure she needs to get married. Charlie better leave camp before he gets roped in.

I had lunch with Ken and told him about the incident last night. I told him that I wanted it kept quiet. He thought that I should report the matter to Williamson, so I went over to see him. It won't get any results since I could give little identifying information.

Williamson was in the process of dictating a letter suggesting that the disloyal elements be segregated from the loyal. He has taken a sort of Gallup poll in the community to find out what the criticisms toward the JACL are. Williamson wants to be fair in this matter and not favor any one organization too much.

He suggested that I stay home for a couple of evenings before continuing with the drive. Since it is the holiday season, I was not intending to go out there anyway. I asked Williamson to keep the whole thing quiet since news about it going out would only tend to scare some of the more timid Nisei.

Ma tells me she was in the laundry, and all these ladies are crying. Turns out there's a rumor that their sons were hypnotized into enlisting. I tell her I'm not going to get hypnotized. No way I'm enlisting.

Every block is having a Xmas party this evening. Our mess hall has been all decorated up with a tree and all. They are singing and having entertainment tonight. All of the women in the block made the decorations. Miyako is going to do a recitation. I didn't go as I was not in the mood. Alice stayed home also as she has a cold.

The administration offices allowed the personnel to quit at 3:00 this afternoon.

Friday, December 25, 1942 CHRISTMAS

Today was Christmas, and things were quiet. Last night, we went caroling until 1:30 a.m. About 500 young people were walking around at one time. We visited every block and ended up out by 59 where we had a bonfire. Afterwards, Emiko and Bette went to take a shower. We had expected to sleep late, but Miyako came in about 8:00 and woke us up. She couldn't wait to open up her gifts. We were able to get to breakfast on time because it was served late. After breakfast, Tom and I went to take a shower. The house was cleaned up, and then we proceeded to open up the piles and piles of gifts which were stacked up on the rugs on the floor. Everybody was cheerful and excited about the various packages. Emiko passed them out because she had wrapped most of them and knew what they contained. Everybody has been enjoying their gifts all day. I got some books from Mariko, but I passed the time reading the funny books which Miyako and Tom received as part of their presents.

Toshi, Albert, and Joe were over so I served the fellows some Xmas spirits. We had papers and string thrown all over the floor.

It rained today, and the wind also blew hard so that it was almost impossible to go out. All I could do was to put my wool sweater on and stay around the house. Bette, Emiko and Alice gave it to me for my present. Also received packages and packages of cigarettes—enough to last me a month or so. Time Magazine subscription, stationery, and other things were also in my Xmas pile.

Lunch was served at 2:30 p.m. We had beef bouillon, fruit cocktail, roast turkey with dressing, sweet potato, peas, biscuits, apple, orange, pie and coffee. No dinner was served tonight. Instead, they passed out some rice balls. We had plenty of leftovers to bring home after we had stuffed ourselves.

Most of the events which had been scheduled for today were cancelled because of the wind and rain. In spite of the present situation, we had a very normal Xmas. The radio gave us the proper holiday atmosphere. Miyako went to bed early. She exhausted herself running around the house playing with her friends and showing off her presents. Tom has been throwing those darts at a target all afternoon, but he only made one bull's eye.

> Being, my Ma says, Buddhists, we're not much for Xmas, but I get Ken a couple of comic books and some fabric for Ma to make herself a dress. She says it's too gay for her age and looks at me sad-funny, like she knows I gamble. It's windy and rainy out. We got our new stove, but nobody wants to cuddle-up cosy, even when Ma went to town to hide the defects of living in this hellhole. Ken splits to find his baby gang. I know they go pick pockets in the bathhouse. Easy pickings when the guy's naked in the shower. Ma goes off to her ladies' gossip group to make arts and crafts. I head out to find Yosh or any of the team for a round of poker.

Yesterday, somebody walked into our house and stole $5.00 out of my wallet and one pack of gum. Probably some little kids whose parents can't give them money to spend at the canteen. We haven't been locking our house at all but will do so hereafter since there is a minor epidemic of stealing going on now, especially in the shower rooms.

> I got myself a date for the Christmas dance. We got to talking about getting out of here. Seems like you got to get this question out of the way in order to date a girl since maybe her folks are on one side or the other. I keep my options open. I don't commit to anything. Hell, it's just one date. But this girl says she doesn't want to get out and do the resettlement thing. Says she wants to have as much fun now while she can. "They are only trying to shove us out now because they are short of workers. We go out and work, and then after that, they'll shut us up again. Why worry about something you can't do anything about?" I like her perspective about having fun now. Might be like my old country girlfriends in Frisco, sweet and lonesome. Maybe I can get her into bed.

Mom is still trying to finish up some knitting which she was doing. She had hoped to get the article completed and sent off before today. Alice is knitting socks. She started to make a dress but got distracted.

Now that Xmas is over, Emiko will have time on her hands. She really put a lot of effort into it, and if it were not for her, we would not be enjoying it so much. She either made or sent for most of the things. She hopped into bed about 7:00, and she is now reading a magazine and munching on two turkey sandwiches, a piece of apple pie, an orange, and an apple. If this is not enough, she has some candy to eat.

Bette is just sitting on her bed. She says that she wishes that she were in Vallejo so that she could go visiting her friends.

Most of the evening we just talked about things in general. I really enjoyed the day. At least we were able to have a good family atmosphere for the day. Some of the people who came over remarked that our place was fixed up just like a real home.

Saturday, December 26, 1942

It got cold again this morning. The wind kept us in. Kimi and I decided that we would not work this morning so I slept. Everybody else in this house also stayed in bed. We did not get up until around noon time. It feels good to just lay around and take it easy. Emiko was restless and bored. She has always been used to a lot of activity. The Christmas preparation has been keeping her occupied up to now. Her new friends—Nancy and Mary—came over this afternoon so Emiko taught them how to dance. Emiko is going to sing at one of the dances going on here on New Year's Eve. The three plan to go into the camouflage net work either next Monday or after the first.

I spent most of the afternoon reading one of the books I got for Christmas. In the evening, we all went to the movies in the amphitheater. The wind was biting cold. I think I am catching a cold as I don't feel so well.

> Ma came back from Jun Noguchi's funeral. He died a few days ago, and his two brothers got here just in time. Helluva time. Ma says that Mr. Noguchi didn't really die from valley fever or meningitis like they're saying. The real cause is all the badmouthing going around about him as councilman in Tulare. People blame him for everything. When he gets to camp, he and his family are forced to move four times because people bully him constantly. She says he was unconscious, but he keeps saying, "I didn't do anything to hurt people. I didn't do anything." He dies saying this. His last words. I tell her you can't die from bad words, and she snaps, "Yes, you can."

Sunday, December 27, 1942

Things are very, very quiet yet. Nothing much happens except that small groups go visiting. Each block is beginning to prepare for the New Year's Day. They really go in for that Japanese custom of making mochi. This is a special kind of rice which is pounded up. Everybody turns out to help. They have a fire pit built out by the laundry in which this rice is pounded after being steamed. All of the men take turns. The women put flour on it so that it will not get sticky. Little cakes are made of these. The people put them on the mantle as it is supposed to represent good luck.

Japanese customs persist to a stronger degree in this community chiefly because of the large rural element here. Even the Nisei taking part in the making of mochi were all jabbering in Japanese. The people here do not miss the lack of a Christmas tree, but it is unthinkable for them to be without the mochi.

> Holiday time I get to reminiscing about Frisco days. Even during curfew, at least we are free. Go over to Chinatown after 8 and fool around, pick up girls, hang out in the bowling alleys or play pool and pinball. We'd go to a Chinese bar and nightclub and drink. Whore houses are closed by then, but we try to pick up whores on the street and take them to one of those cheap hotels. If we can't pick up a girl, we sleep in the room or go play some dice. By six in the morning, it's safe again to go back to Jap town. I'll be all fagged out, so sleep all morning, then go over to the Jap employment agency. Try to get a job or just play pool.

I did not feel so well so went to bed this afternoon. Two planes just zoomed over the roof and gave everybody a scare. Blackie's hair stood on end as it roared past. Emiko turned white and shook a little. She had her friends over this afternoon and they just gossiped. Bette went to a basketball game, and Alice went off with some of her friends.

Tom made a lot of noise with his friends. He got three of them crowded into the dogbox, and then he blocked the opening up so they could not get out.

Monday, December 28, 1942

One of those things which is a problem for every young girl came up today for Bette. She wanted to go to the New Year's dance. I thought that she was too young to go to those big dances, but I told her that she would have to make her decision herself. At Tanforan she ran around a lot, and it would be very easy for her to do the same thing here because she is so popular. Bette pulled me over to one side as I got home to ask me if I would say "yes" or "no." I told her that this would be up to her, although it was my personal opinion that she should not get started yet because of her school. Bette still wanted me to give a definite answer, but I told her that I could not do this. She was very disappointed. She had the boy come over this evening, and she wanted to know if it would be all right if he asked Mom. When he did come, Mom almost said "yes," but she decided that Bette should wait a while longer before attending the "grown up dances." I wasn't home at the time, but Mom said that Bette took it fairly gracefully.

Under ordinary conditions, there would be no objections, but in this camp, it would be too simple for her to plunge into a complete social life to the exclusion of everything else. Bette is too young to see this yet, although she has some idea. She would not have brought the matter up except that Emiko is going so that she feels she must go also. But Emiko is two years older. At the present time, Bette has a much better social life than Emiko in her high school group, and it is just as well that she remain in this crowd.

I appreciate the fact that Bette does come to me to see what I think, but it puts me in a tough spot. I suppose I could easily slide away from the responsibility, but I don't because I feel that Bette has a lot of possibilities that need encouragement. At times, there is bound to be resentment when she feels that things are not going completely her own way. I would certainly hate to be a parent. I weaken too easily. If Mom had not given a negative answer, I probably would have given in anyway. And that would not have been so good for Bette. She has plenty of high school activities and dances so it is not necessary for her to do everything that Emiko does. The whole situation was handled pretty tactfully all around so it was only to be a passing event, leaving no deep scars. Mom let Bette give the final answer to the boy, so "face" was saved for her, and she will not feel tied down. Bette certainly has more freedom than most Nisei girls around here, except those who are considered "wild."

I go out with Kats to work on the firebreak crew. Kats says to join up since the crew is run by some Kibei who knows how to treat his workers. But hanging around with the Issei on the crew, the story is the other way around. The Issei say they trained this Kibei to show them respect. In the beginning he acted like he's the boss, but now they fixed him.

I covered half the block this evening and got only two memberships. The vigorous Issei-Kibei propaganda has swung the indifferent mass of Nisei to their point of view temporarily, although not to the point of them being disloyal. They are following the path of least resistance and do not hold principles so strong that they would be willing to actively oppose the Fascist forces of this camp. If they continue to be indifferent and escapists, their cause is lost. Who will fight for them, if they are not willing to fight for themselves? I feel sorry for them. They have not given the matter enough thought, and they need another terrific jolt to make them come to their senses. In this respect, they are just like most Americans who still don't realize that we are fighting an all-out war.

> Working the firebreak, we run into a Mexican worker who says, "You must be having a lot of fun in there with all those whores running around." Everyone laughs. He says he'll get us a bottle if we get him a Jap whore. He's serious. I think about the hags in Block 51. I figure maybe I could sneak him in and get a bottle out of him.
>
> But this Issei hears this talk and comes over. "It's that camp newspaper that spreads this nonsense, and people like him on the outside think we're all gamblers with whores running all over the place. We Japanese are a proud people, and this is an insult!"

Landward will be on leave for a week so that our office was crowded all day with people making inquiries about leaves and transfers. The whole matter of getting leave permits are quite a mess. Some of the people have been waiting for the past four months without any definite answer from the W.R.A.

Our Social Service department is getting more organized daily, although there is a lot of catching up to do on old cases. Tuttle leaves me alone to make my own decision so that I feel that I am making headway. I have to eat my words and admit that I am enjoying the work actually. It gives me a chance to get a good cross section of the public pulse and at the same time do something worthwhile.

> It's one year since Pearl Harbor. Helluva a thing to get blamed for. Over at the post office, I see Ken and his baby gang playing around. Someone watered the so-called lawns, still just seed bed and mud. The boys are making mud bombs. Ken yells, "You're a Jap, and I'm

> Doolittle in a P38. Bombs away!" He lets go of a glob of mud in another kid's face. The mud-faced kid cries and runs home. My kid Ken Doolittle smacks another kid who runs off too, then keeps yelling "Bombs away!" and bombs the side of the post office. I'm about to go grab him when the postman comes out yelling, "Baka baka!"

Went down to see if I could get the JACL drive over with, but everybody went to the wedding. Sachi Egami and H. Mittwer are getting hitched. Emiko and Alice went to act as usherettes. Sachi is having a very simple wedding without all the elaborate Japanese ceremonies.

> We live next to old Mr. Nishi. Ma feels sorry for him. He's 75. Got no relatives. Story is about five years ago, he has an auto accident, lost his intestines and empties his poop through a tube from his stomach. Just lays in bed all day in a room with nothing in it except for a cardboard box of his clothing. He's got no money, so Ma brings him things, apples, some tobacco, newspapers. Nishi used to be in the Navy. Then he works as a cook in some L.A. hotel, makes 300 a month. He spends all his money on hospital bills. He should see a doctor but won't. Sometimes I hear him yelling at Ma to scare her away, but she never scares. She knows he's just afraid she'll tell others he's sick like this. If it's quiet in there, Ma worries he's dead. Welfare Charlie comes around, but what's the use?

Stopped in to talk with Harry Kamiya. No wonder people consider him so rich. He said that he cleared $120,000 last year in the Santa Maria valley. He specialized in those red peppers. The price zoomed up after the foreign markets were cut off and none could be imported. Harry had over 400 acres of the stuff, and he made a tremendous profit. The peppers are used by such companies as Swifts and Armours. Harry said all of the Japanese farmers in Santa Maria valley hit it rich for the past two years. At the time of evacuation, the Caucasian operators who took the farms over hit it rich since the crops were harvested, but he doubted if they could make money on vegetables next year because they did not have the skill or experience.

"Farming is a terrific gamble. One bad year may wipe you out completely. I hit it rich for a couple of years, but I could not quit. It gets in your blood because it is such a gamble."

Harry said that there were about fifty Japanese families that hit it rich before evacuation so that they were well off. "Big companies like Minami and the Guadeloupe Produce made as much as a half million clear. I figure that I would have made around $300,000 this year if I were back there. I hired mostly Filipinos and Mexican laborers as they were better to deal with."

Most of the Japanese along the coastal valleys made comfortable profits because they leased the land and operated for only about three or four years before moving on. The soil gets worn out fast. The reason why they did not buy more land was because the initial out-put was too high, and a lot of those farmers did not intend to stay here. They made a pile and then returned to Japan. This made it bad for those of us who intended to stay. That is why those Japanese lived in such shacks. They did not want to invest money in a permanent home. But they all bought good cars to show off their wealth.

Charlie's got to toe the boochie line over resettlement, but I figure most of the Issei are like my mom. They'd rather stay in camp. Ma works all her life and for what? Pop leaves us. Takes my brother with him. Jesus, who knows where they are? Back in Japan? If so, my neech must be lugging a gun to kill Chinese somewhere. Good thing Ma is smart, gets us out of farm work and starts that candy store. But that's all gone. She's got something in the bank, but that's got to be gone by the time we get out, if we ever get out.

However, most Japanese farmers did not make so much. They were in the interior, and they bought 15 or 20 acres in their children's name and just settled down to make a living. When the children grew up, they were dissatisfied with the drab country life. They wanted more of the American life, so they drifted to the city. But there were no jobs there. Some of the parents sacrificed to send their children through school in the hopes that America would give more to their children. But those ended up by working for small Japanese employers at small wages or else they returned to the farm in great discouragement. That is why the majority of the famers are poor. They never made much, and they worked hard.

I hear a good piece of gossip that some Issei killed himself and his wife because she was having an affair with a Kibei. They say the Kibei ran away to the beet fields.

Ken U. believed that the net work was the best thing for the Nisei because it was real work. He thought that the project jobs were bad because they were not real jobs, and there is a tendency for them to take things easy. After the war, they will have to work hard and it is very important that morale is kept up.

Nobu was a little worried about his job. He has been putting all his time into the JACL work. He wanted to work with LeBarron in the publicity department, but turned it down when he found out that LeBarron planned to emphasize Japanese culture. LeBarron believes that the Issei have to be reached first. But who is going to separate Culture from Nationalism? Playing up to the Issei will not solve anything. Granted that Democracy has not been fulfilled for them.

The prime emphasis should be placed on the Nisei. There is plenty of educational work to be done right there. The Nisei should be given the straight facts and not be treated in a patronizing manner. They don't have enough Caucasian contacts as it is, and teaching Japanese culture to the Issei would only give them more influence.

> On the outside, I work how many different jobs? Delivery, stockboy, janitor, gardening, fish market. We're just a bunch of sad bastards, pushed around, never get a chance at the better jobs. Wasn't like I don't try. College Charlie can't judge us. I go to junior college and do time with NYA training to be a welder, but they cancel my tests because we're Japs.

Bette says that the Pilgrim's Forum is going to discuss "Should We Learn Japanese in a W.R.A camp?" Bette is the only one who will take the negative point. They were all shocked she said, "Why imitate the Japs any longer? I wish I were Chinese." Bette did this deliberately because she believes that the high school crowd is too Japanesy. Some of her friends believe that they should learn Japanese because their parents have told them that they will need it if they are sent to Japan after the war. No wonder the kids are getting disillusioned. And it would make things worse by teaching Japanese culture.

The W.R.A. should have made two camps—separate one for those who want to go back to Japan. I may be bigoted about the matter, but I can only see it from the point of view of the Nisei future in this country. Any sign of the opposite philosophy is a threat to us. I respect the Issei and Kibei opinions, but I certainly would oppose them when they start to give their propaganda to the young Nisei who are in a most difficult period right now. This is wartime, and Japanese culture is too closely connected with Japanese nationalism.

> I'm sitting bench during the last baseball game. Hell, I played football in high school. Anyway, this old guy Shibota sits there smoking. He tells me he was a vet, but he's staying out of the ex-servicemen's club. I don't know they have a club for that, but I guess they got clubs for everything. Nothing else to do here but join clubs. Shibota tells me those ex-vets are a bunch of selfish hypocrites looking out for themselves. He's from Hawaii, never been to Japan, fights in the war, slaves for thirty years, never breaks a single law, and what does that get him? You'd think they'd exempt him from evacuation. Says, "Dumb Nisei think they should show their loyalty and join the Army," but, look at him. "White people think we are all treacherous Japs. Treat us like dogs. Go around praying to a white God for victory. Buddhism is a better religion. Japan wasn't treated right, so she was forced to start a war. Japan will teach the U.S. a lesson. If it weren't for Japan taking a stand, no colored people in the world could hold up their heads."

Nobu was supposed to talk to the Hawaiian Club this evening. They have 90 members, but only about 15 turned up so they asked Nobu to come back next Tuesday. Nobu believes that if they are talked to man-to-man, they would join the JACL as they are pro-America. But they are the rowdy type, and they go in groups and gangs. He feels that this group could give the Kibei a good battle if they asked for one since the Hawaii boys are independent and not controlled by any first generation. Most of them are single fellows. He is going to press the point that there are 5000 Hawaiian Nisei at Camp McCoy who have given the Nisei group a lot of good publicity.

> The other day a plane roars overhead. It's so loud that Ma drops her laundry. She thinks it's going to bomb us. She crouches in the dirt, then gets mad because she's got to pick up our dirty clothing. She's picking up the laundry and finds an envelope. Tossed out the plane like a Christmas card. She gives it to me to read, and I pass it on, and someone passes it on like a chain letter. Ends up with the

block manager who hands it to Charlie. Bunch of nonsense signed by some Chinese. But that was bull too because no Chinese is named Sumosso. Anybody spent time in Chinatown knows they are all Wong and Chin. And hell, what Chinese flies a plane? Outside, ketō think we're a bunch of dumb spies.

TO THE TEMPORARY RESTRICTED: from a foe, yet a friend

Phoenix, Arizona December 28, 1942

To Our Contemporary Japanese People:

Ever since the ancestors of men began to settle down and cultivate the land, war has always been a crime. It has always been a burden to the participants regardless which side loses. For nobody has ever won a war.

Most unfortunately, China and United States should take the pain to fight their Japanese neighbors who should have shared peace and happiness with the others. This, of course, did not happen out of one single reason. The reasons are so very many that it will take a year to narrate them all.

The only reason which I am to complain here is that the Japanese people have BEEN MISLED TO THINK THAT THEY ARE THE ONLY RACE FIT TO BE THE MASTER OF Asia, and what is worse is that some of them think of all the other races merely fit to be slaves. Here I am not taking you as a whole, as I am using the third person when I complain. I certainly believe as well as hoping that few of you think that way. We came from much of a same race. Your ancestors introduced the using of our language. Your houses and homes were built after our old artistic style. You learnt to roast tea and raise silkworms. You copied everything which provided our everyday life.

But then you turned to imitate the western science. We on the continent admired your progress and your industriousness. We began to send our students to your country and wished that you would help us in gaining new ideas. But besides following the western industrialistic development, your militarists and capitalists began to follow the imperialistic maneuvers to prey upon the Chinese people.

A man might have graduated from the best college in the country, yet he has no right to despise his old school teacher who once taught him to spell the simplest words or adding five and three, nor has he the right to scorn the limited knowledge in the head of his tutors in the high school even if he has attained the degree of a Ph.D.

We have rejoiced at the thought that at least there is one country in Asia, one yellow race with which we can boast that we are not inferior. But alas, you would not even accept us as your equal. Since there can be friends in another race so can there be foes in the same Mongolian blood. It is really a tragedy. Could we not live side by side in peace? Could we not share the limited resources left us by our ancestors? Must we kill and fight before we can be satisfied? We have always admired your brightness shown in the last century. It is a shame that your militarists should spoil the good reknown by killing and slaughtering.

Let us see how you live in the peaceful canyons of Arizona. I must say that the Americans are more liberal than the Japanese agents in all parts of China. I do not wish to hurt your feelings by telling you the sad stories. I have seen enough of that.

For you at present, it might serve to think that it is the land in which you live that sustains you. Be loyal and true to her and her communities. You prosper as they all prosper, and you will not profit by their fall.

I am,
your Chinese Contemporary

SUMMOSO

A MERRY CHRISTMAS TO YOU ALL

December 29, 1942

Last night, I had a funny dream which may be termed "wish fulfillment" by a psychologist. I dreamt that Bette and I decided that we wanted to get out of camp so we decided to walk to Phoenix. Bette was dressed in jeans, and she carried a half-dozen oranges (California brand) in a paper bag. I wore the black mackinaw jacket. We walked out to the edge of camp and slipped through the barbed wire fence. Every time we saw a mounted warden, we hid behind one of those huge cactus trees. As the day wore on, it got hotter and hotter. The sage brush scratched on our legs, and the snakes made us jump. As night came on, we suddenly realized that we were lost. Nothing but flat desert country before us for miles and miles. But in the distance, we saw some low foothills which I thought were in the direction of Phoenix—Northeast. Bette wanted to go in an opposite direction. So, we ate an orange and argued. Finally, we decided to go towards the hills in the morning. I lit a fire with my cigarette lighter, and we could not sleep much because of the cold. Once in a while, a fox or some desert animal would come near.

The second day was worse. We walked and walked. By this time, we got scared. There was no water around, and we only had one orange left. That night we slept soundly. The third day we ate the last orange. I lost my cigarette lighter, so we were almost frozen that night. The following day was horrible. We suffered from thirst, and our feet became swollen. I had to cut the shoes so that our feet could expand out. We saw all sorts of mirages, but the water holes never materialized. Walk . . . walk . . . walk . . . Soon we were staggering along, and all looked lost. Our shoes got big holes in them from walking around. I tried to get water from a cactus plant, but nothing came out. Our tongues were so swollen we could no longer talk. Just about the time that we were ready to drop, an old Indian came riding along. We tried to attract his attention, but he did not turn. He went further and further away. Just about when we had given up hope, he turned and saw us. He came galloping up. After reviving a bit, he told us that he was a blood brother. He wanted to know which tribe we came from. We told him that we were evacuees from Sacaton. The Indian was very surprised, and he asked where we were going. We told him that we were on the way to Phoenix. This amazed him. He told us that we were in Mexico, 250 miles to the south. And the final blow was the fact that the U.S. highway was only 100 yards to the left of us. We had walked along it for 100 miles.

Some Dream ???????

Mr. Mori is another of Ma's charity cases. He used to be a rich labor-gang contractor. He's the guy who helps her out when Pops and Neech leaves, sets her up with the candy shop. But he gets in an auto accident. Same as old man Nishi. Steering wheel crushes his chest. Hasn't worked a day since. Then just before we get evacuated, he gets knocked in the head and robbed of $93. Loses his memory and wanders around after curfew until he gets thrown in the can. Next day, he's fined $10, and they evacuate him. He can remember the $93 but not much else. Tells Ma he's going to give it all to her. I tell her it's $83, and she gives me her baka slap. If Ma doesn't go and sit with him with a cup of tea after dinner, he'll up and get lost, wander around camp all night.

The oil stoves were put in the other day so that the room is much warmer now. The stoves are very good. They are new, and the design is very modern. In a few more days the whole camp will be fixed up. Instead of appreciating this, they grumble that it is about time. The people who said that the government would never give us the stoves are quiet now. In a few days, they will renew the cry once more. This time it will be for the linoleum.

Someone says you can buy chickens from the Indians. Someone else says it's prohibited because live chickens in camp will be unsanitary. Anyone who's lived on a farm would say that chickens and eggs are a good idea. Ma used to make chicken and eggs over rice dish. If I tell her I miss her oyakodon, she smiles her sad smile.

The family is harmonized once more. There were no arguments today. Tom has found a gang of friends and he also goes to the Boy Scouts once a week. He is still scattering wood all over the place with intentions of making various articles. They are rarely completed.

Miyako plays with dolls all day long with her friends. They put mud pies all over the steps today and left a big mess of empty tin cans all over the yard. Our lawn still has not been planted as they have not come around with the seeds. The ground is getting very hard once more so maybe we should have let Tom plant his vegetable garden after all.

There's an old professor gent other side of our block. One day, I turn the corner and see him yelling at his son. Woody. I know the boochie, but we never talk. Everyone kowtows to the old man who gets nice packages of chocolates and tea from his white friends. Wife shuffles back and forth with his dinner. Hell, he's never entered the mess hall. From what I figure, Woody wants to marry this girl, but the old man's against it. She must be a nice country girl. They elope out of camp. Now the professor spends all his time writing and reading in his shack, pretending it never happened.

Emiko signed up for the camouflage net project today, and she will go to work in a week or so. She is pretty busy with her friends now. Bette also keeps active with her friends who came to visit this afternoon. They ate all of the chocolates up. There is no school until the 4th. Alice is getting things slowly ready as she expects to get a leave permit soon to go to her job in Chicago. Mom knits away all day long and keeps busy mending Miyako's and Tom's clothes. Everyone is waiting for Pop to come, but they have not sent us any word yet. It takes such a long time to get the clearances through.

Blackie is sick now. She coughs all the time. The dust around here has probably made her sick. Emiko just had to put her box by the stove so that Blackie could keep warm. If I insist upon carrying out the promise of putting the dog outside at nights at the first of the year, I will be called all sorts of mean names. Guess I will have to postpone it for a while, unless I want to get scalped. The weather is not so bad now that the stoves are in. During the afternoon it gets into the 80s, and I have to wear a T-shirt. The mornings and evenings are cold.

I go over to the hobby show with Ma and Ken. Ma wants to show us the flowers she made out of paper and silk. There's a lot of polished ironwood stuff. They say there was a real sculptor living in Poston, but he left. Couldn't take the heat and bad food. None of his work in this show. Lots of paintings on the walls. Ken's glued to one. I go over to see what it is. Some painting of two Jap planes shooting down American planes.

The Okamoto family is badly off. The father died four years ago, leaving this wife with six children. The older is a 19-year-old girl. The father was a farm laborer, and he did not leave them any money. Up to the time of the evacuation, the oldest girl worked as a school girl, and she supported the family on $30 a month, which she made during the summer. The whole family went out to work in fruit picking. They do not have a cent now. The oldest girl is the only one working, and the others are all in school. I suggested to the girl that she investigate the net project as this would be one way she could make a little extra money. She will give it a trial. In all of my cases, I suggest that they go work on the net project. The Okamoto family do not know what they are going to do after the war. They don't have anything to go back to. They do not see any future. In fact, this is a case where their living standards are much higher in camp. They were in poverty before, but they would never apply for relief "because that would disgrace all of us."

> When I get hungry, I go over to see Ich in the kitchen. He lives in the bachelors' barrack. Bunch of old farm workers. Never saved anything. Hang out with nothing to do. One of the old guys, Sakai, pulls out his pockets. What's he got? 7.50 bucks to his name. Same for the rest of them. Sakai comes to America to study sent by the Jap government, but he gives it up. Ends up following the harvests. Says his buddies who came over with him are back in Japan, high mucky-mucks. He's got one old copy of a Japanese newspaper and reads it over and over. Hell, I don't read no papers, but they need to start printing stuff in Japanese so at least the news changes for these guys.
>
> There's another old Issei whose got a swollen jaw. Jesus, jaw's bulging. Tooth's infected, but he can't trust the dentists in here. Says he got to get out to Phoenix, have a white dentist extract it. Meanwhile, he's spending his last miserly hoard on medicine some witch is brewing in her barracks. What's he gonna do anyway since I heard admin won't pay for teeth and glasses.
>
> You get old in here. Reading isn't an option. Neither is eating.

This gives some picture of the poorer Japanese. They worked hard all their lives, and they never had time to be treacherous. They are just simple people trying to make a living, but they were caught up in the web of circumstance, spent their last few dollars on medicines, and now are pictured as spies. Most of the people here are poor, law-abiding persons who never had much of a chance. From these personal frustrations (not their fault) they have clung to the only thing they can have—Japanese citizenship—and they surely should not be condemned for that. But I would hate to see this poison of bitterness spread to their children who have a long, but uncertain, future ahead of them.

Wednesday, December 30, 1942

In the afternoon, Tuttle had the staff come over from Canal, and we held a joint staff meeting. Tuttle is beginning an in-service training class for Okuno, Shizu Abe, and Mrs. Hosoru. He said that I would not have to attend, but I might as well as there is still a lot I can learn, and it will be a good review. Tuttle plans to lecture on Wednesday and Friday afternoon for 1½ hours each time. And a half-day off per week will be allowed for study. He is basing the course on four classes he took at the University of Chicago. It will deal with case work, child welfare problems, and juvenile delinquency. I'm supposed to take Tuesday afternoon off for study. This means that three afternoons per week will be taken up.

We have been trying to get clearance on the matter of false teeth and glasses. The hospital won't pay for them. One boy broke his glasses while working in the mess hall. I tried to get the W.R.A. to replace them, but each department passed the buck. I could have given him the $7.75 on a welfare basis, but Tuttle said it was a legal problem and sent him to Terry. Terry sent him to Landward and so it goes. Tuttle wants to wait until the W.R.A. makes policy in Washington, but Bennett should be able to "OK" it. The hospital has a large surplus fund that it should use. When it comes to a matter of teeth, the people can't wait until a policy is made like they did on clothing.

I ask Kats about Tak. I think Tak must be somewhere sulking, but Kats says he joined some young Buddhist group, and they got a plot to start a riot to get kicked out and put in a segregation camp. They also got a blacklist going of inu they want to beat up.

Kats says Nisei are a bunch of selfish boochies who want everything for themselves. They don't think about all of the Japanese in camp. Kibei are different, aren't looking for favors. He figures Tak's a typical Nisei who can only see in one direction or the opposite. Black and white vision. "Now he's going the Japanese way, but he could easily go American. Matter of pride."

"Hey," I say, "I'm Nisei. I don't think either way."

"Don't be so sure. You'll be tested."

This evening I went down to finish up the 28 Block. Fay and I went to one section, while Florence and Albert went to the other end. In the whole block, we got four memberships, and they got two. Reception down there is still very cool.

Fay and I stopped to talk with the Sumida sisters for about an hour. They are different from most girls around here. There is an intellectual atmosphere about their place. Alice and another sister are planning to go out to college next month. All three attended UC. We talked about resettlement and the future of the Nisei. They pumped me so much that I had to do most of the talking. They were good Americans and outspoken so we got along swell. They said that they had never been among the Japanese much which may explain their friendly feeling towards strangers.

> Charlie comes around, but he's got no time for poker. Like always, he's got the same old boochie pitch, but then he pumps us for news. We tell him we hear, over Canal-side, they beat up Tada with ironwood clubs. Tada's against the gambling rings corrupting his six kids. So he reports them to the admin. Consequently, U.S. Marshalls come and make arrests. Gambling guys get back at Tada. First, word is Tada is killed, but they just bust his wrist and the watch on it. Then they say the Issei who beat up Tada get lynched, but probably the FBI just take them. Charlie says it's nonsense, but I figure there's always at least two stories depending which side tells it and who wants to hear it.

The people of the block pounded their mochi today. We got 70 of them. The things are very heavy. Alice sent about 5 to Mariko, and it cost 25 cents in postage.

Emiko will probably be busy most of the night on her new dress. I gave her the material for Xmas, and Emiko wants to get it finished in time for the dance tomorrow. She got several more presents today including a box of chocolates. Yum.

I have a terrific headache and a cold so that I can't concentrate much tonight. Fine way to end up the year. Makes me feel lousy.

> Ma comes home with some mochi. Then the Kibei Club comes around with more. The Kibei Club writes in Japanese on the mochi. I ask about the writing, and they translate the kanji: "Good Luck" and "Celebrate the 2600 anniversary of the Japanese Empire." Holy Jesus. It's the year of the sheep. They say sheep means peace. I say we are the sheep.

Thursday, December 31, 1942 NEW YEAR'S EVE

Only a few more hours until the New Year. I'm just passing a little time before I go out for the evening. I should feel gay and happy, but I'm not. The next year doesn't look so optimistic for all of us all over the world. It's only the beginning of the second round. Maybe I worry too much, but it's not easy to force these things from my mind. Tonight, we are all supposed to be gay and force all of those hollow dull pains out of consciousness. Quite a difference from last year when we were free to do as we please. Most of the Nisei stayed home one year ago. War had just broken out. But this year, there are many dances and parties in camp. It's a release. New Year's is the big holiday for these people here.

Emiko is still working like mad on her dress. She will just make the dead-line. Mom had to pitch in so that she could finish up on time. Bette has one of her friends over for the evening.

Each block is having a block party for the stay-at-homes, and there will be a big wiener roast. Forty pounds of weenies, plus buns were distributed.

Emiko is singing at the dance tonight so she is pretty excited. She will make a hit when she starts twinkling those eyes of hers. When I look at Bette, I feel sort of guilty. We have asked her not to go to dances for a while yet because she is so young. I know that she is deeply disappointed and wants to go, but she is taking it like a good sport.

> We can't have New Years without the mochi. Personally, I don't go for it. It's a sticky lump with no taste, but that's me. If it brings good luck and money, okay, but if you ask me, we lost our luck and money. Can't be the same as before. Old days, Ma goes all out with the food. Spends days cooking. Big red lobster. Sushi. Sashimi. Shoyu root dishes. Noodles. Those sweet beans. Red and green gelatin. Eat all day for three days.

3:00 A.M.

It's 1943 now! All in all, it was a quiet evening around here. Around midnight, there was a little noise, and we had the New Year's spirit. Went to a party and ate and ate. Most everybody reminisced about how different it was on the outside. Didn't even have a drop of liquor to drink.

Mom cleaned the house up after we left. She said that this was a Japanese custom—to start the New Year with a clean slate.

My plans for the evening did not follow through. The girl I was going to take suddenly got sick at the last moment. I did not go to the dance. Around midnight, I went over and had something to eat and then went back to the party. The New Year's Eve spirit just was not there. The dances were well attended, but they did not get noisy like on the outside.

Today also makes it eight months since we were evacuated. A lot of changes have occurred in that time. Complete readjustments have not been made. In most likelihood, our most trying period is ahead. This looks like the year which will determine the outcome of the war. As for these camps, the resettlement program will really get underway. Here's hoping there will be a lot of opportunities.

Good-bye 1942! Hello 1943!

Note:
Diary entries are excerpted from Charles Kikuchi diary entries, Gila River, Japanese Evacuation and Resettlement Project, Bancroft Library, University of California, Berkeley.

Other entries are fictionalized stories garnered from Kikuchi diary entries and from "CH-31: Errand Boy," *The Salvage: Japanese American Evacuation and Resettlement*, Dorothy Swaine Thomas with the assistance of Charles Kikuchi and James Sakoda (University of California Press, 1952), pp. 264–297.

RICHARD: X

We would be missing a very big opportunity if we failed to study the Japanese in these Camps at some length before they dispersed . . . These people, gathered as they now are in these communities, afford a means of sampling opinion and studying their customs and habits in a way we have never before had possible. We could find out what they are thinking about and we might very well influence their thinking in the right direction before they are again distributed in communities.

I am aware that such a suggestion may provoke a charge that we have no right to treat these people as "guinea pigs." . . .

—John J. McCloy, letter to Alexander Meiklejohn, 1942

Nandabakayaro in direct translation means, "What? This foolish servant" . . . There are two common inflections . . . One denotes a high excited emotional pitch or a fight mood . . . translated as, "God damn it!" and "You, bastard!" The other inflection denotes a mood mingled with ridicule . . . "Hell with you! or "You sap!" . . .

The phrase, *shima nagashi ni suru* is translated directly as "to let one drift to an island," meaning "to send one to a distant prison" or "to send one to a distant place." As the phrase contains a little of the punitive intent and betrayal, I thought appropriate to translate into "to sell one down the river." . . .

I translated *hakujin ni peko-peko suru* mildly into "to apple polish" although it has a vulgar tone.

—Richard Shigeaki Nishimoto,
Inside an American Concentration Camp, 1995

STATEMENT OF UNITED STATES CITIZEN OF JAPANESE ANCESTRY

1. .... (Surname) .... (English given name) .... (Japanese given name)

(a) Alias ....

X. His alias. X turned the key, pulled open the door on what he called his broom closet. It was larger than that, an old basement dispensary that he'd turned into his storage room, his personal cell. He reached for the string and pulled; the overhead bulb blinked on. He tossed his newspaper on the cot, sank into the thin spongy edge of the old mattress, gripped the scratch of the woolen blanket. The cot, the mattress, the blanket. He sneered to himself. The reverend at Oakland West Tenth had said, *Sure take it away. Hostel's closed and no need for them now. If you can use it. And here, take a blanket. Certified Army.* He smiled. *Sent from Topaz. Bona fide camp. You feeling nostalgic?* The reverend was a kidder, kept things light, but he wouldn't have joked if he thought X needed it. X's story was that he got a night job in a hotel and could use a cot at the place to nap. *You don't have to be awake all night? No, I got an alarm clock, wake up, do the rounds, go back to nap or read. Mostly get my writing done.*

That was his excuse. Did the room smell? Of course it did. Musty and sour. He lit up a cigarette, took a long draw. There, smoke up the mildew. He tried to be fastidious, but what did it matter? Books and papers in piles and boxes stacked along the walls up to the ceiling, in suitcases and trunks, under the cot. He stood up, walked down the hall to the tank and filled the kettle with water from the faucet, walked back and set it on the hot plate. He had snaked an extension cord from a hallway outlet for the hot plate and desk lamp, both propped on stacks of books next to the cot. He gripped the cig between his teeth, puffed, and shook loose leaves from a small canister into a mug. X poured hot water, watched the leaves swirl and dip.

2. Local selective service board .... (Number)

.... (City) .... (County) .... (State)

Cheeko had come up from L.A., said *Papa, your work here is done. Time to come home.* Home, X thought. He had the room on Geary in J-town, rented it from the fish store folks. One of the sons and his family lived upstairs. Their two boys running up and down, making a ruckus. But that wasn't why he escaped to the broom closet. There was the necessary night job and the quiet but maybe also the comfort of being next to the work. He looked around at the boxes of notebooks, stacks of books and manuscripts. In an earthquake, he'd have to get out quick or be buried in it. Slowly he removed everything into this closet, made the studio apartment on Geary spare and respectable, put up some paintings and set a bonsai on the windowsill, made it look nice for Cheeko, so she wouldn't go back and talk about her pathetic father.

3. Date of birth .... **Place of birth** ....

The leaves spread wings in the hot water. He watched them settle and steep into warm green, flicked the ash from his cigarette, punched it into the tray with the rest of the herd, then sipped. He was born in Tokyo, Japan, on August 23, 1904, into a samurai family, the meaning of which, a half-century later, now eluded him. It meant that he was educated, that he should have succeeded because of his station in society. What did it mean now? He struck a match, lit the end of another Lucky Strike.

4. Present address .... (Street) (City) (State)

His father left him behind in Tokyo. He was raised by grandparents. No one ever spoke about his mother as if she never existed, and he didn't know his father until he arrived in San Francisco at the age of seventeen. He hadn't been in the bustling city but a few days, when he was sent to Colusa, into the rural heartland of the old Gold Rush, sixty miles north of Sacramento, put to work digging ditches around 2,500 acres of rice. He'd never known labor of any kind and was ridiculed for his soft upbringing. Didn't know his father had sent word to toughen him up, turn him from privileged botchan to man. A test of manhood, but for X, a bitter welcome to a strange land.

5. Last two addresses at which you lived 3 months or more (exclude residence at relocation center and at assembly center):

.... **From** .... **To** ....

.... **From** .... **To** ....

Cheeko was their emissary, the one who maybe missed him or more likely felt responsible.

She said he should stop smoking. Suggested cutting down. Five a day, then three, then one. Not a pack, not a chain. She was right. Lately he felt a heaviness in his chest, huffed up stairs. He stood up and walked into the corridor, back and forth. Up there on the floors above, old men were snoring or humping whores. He knew the place back from the old days when migrant laborers came in from the valley to spend their cash on booze, poker, and women. It wasn't a dump then, actually rather posh. Up until and during college, he'd stayed here himself when it was inconvenient to be at home. After all he'd got his comeuppance in Colusa with those laborers. He arrived fresh off the boat, as they say, and never really knew a home until he married. How soon did that dream fade away? He stood in the doorway of his broom closet, filled with the detritus of research, thousands of pages of statistics and documentary note-taking apropos three years of confinement.

He puffed donuts into the exhaustive archive. He could throw in this cigarette and light it all up like a giant candle.

6. Sex .... Height .... Weight ....

When the executive order was issued, X was living in Gardena, a rural town south of L.A., where around 2,000 Japanese families settled to raise strawberries and flowers. By then, he was married with two daughters, living in a comfortable house, and running a retail grocery business, selling Japanese vegetables to white folks. He remembered conversations with clients and neighbors, talking about the coming war. X read everything, English and Japanese newsprint, compared the news and thought he could predict the future, but no one wanted to listen to his warnings. Considered him a crackpot. Then, two days after Pearl Harbor, his landlord ordered them evicted, said he didn't want his property burned down because he rented to Japs. X closed his business, stored their stuff, and moved in with his wife's family in East L.A. The Gardena folks all went to Tulare, but X's family was sent directly to Poston in June 1942. Their new residence: Block 43, Barrack 2, Apartment C.

7. Are you a registered voter? .... Year first registered ....

Where? .... Party ....

Arriving at Poston, everyone vied for some position in the new hierarchy. When they were spread out in farming towns and even social ghettos, they could pretend they were not all the same, lived without the intense scrutiny of these close quarters, the failed upkeep of social niceties and attitudes of class, the lapse into crudity, the uncouth manners of common laborers. X, like the others, looked for work appropriate to his status and education, but it was they, the BSR, Bureau of Sociological Research, who searched him out. After all, he was educated at Stanford and bilingual. Leighton, the Commander, was a naval psychiatrist and sociologist charged to run the bureau, set up an office to research, evaluate, and assess Japanese evacuees and make recommendations to the camp administrators. X was needed in this effort. The Commander plucked his researchers from the lay nisei internees themselves; he would conduct classes on research methods, teach these novices the ropes. How to achieve their objectives in a humanitarian and democratic way. Bunch of bull, but X didn't discount his place in trying to alleviate the pain. *Write me your autobiography,* the Commander requested. *Tell me about yourself. Tell me what you're made of. We'll get you situated appropriately.*

8. Marital status .... Citizenship of wife .... Race of wife ....

What did he write in that autobiography for the Commander? That his father died in 1930 from bronchial pneumonia, and the following year, he married a nisei girl in San Francisco, brought her home to the outskirts of Los Angeles, a town called Gardena. He wrote to the commander psychiatrist that he *took the fatal step with eyes wide open, that every woman wants to believe that her husband was deeply and blindly in love when he married her. Let it go as so. Why should we disillusion anyone?* And finished by declaring, *I was happy ever after, still happily married in 1942, eleven years after the Lohengrin's march.* X played the Commander. The story of his life was a fractured fairytale.

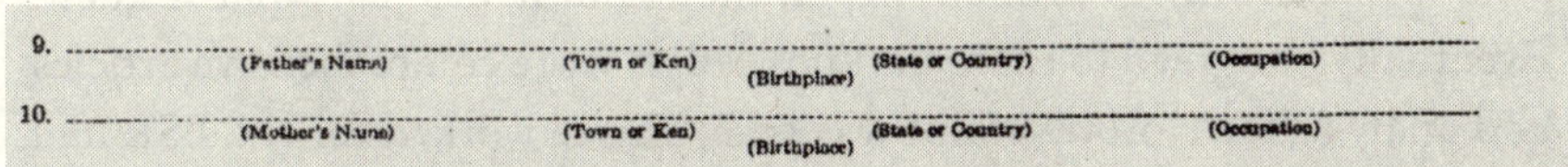
9. .... (Father's Name) (Town or Ken) (Birthplace) (State or Country) (Occupation)
10. .... (Mother's Name) (Town or Ken) (Birthplace) (State or Country) (Occupation)

His wife reminded him that he'd met Tamie in Los Angeles. She was the kid sister of Hisako, his wife's friend at UCLA. Tamie and Hisako had been over to the house in Gardena. He thought he remembered, but she'd made no particular impression at the time. But what was she doing at Poston? She could have returned home to Hawaii, didn't have to get caught up in this evacuation. She came with the Santa Anita bunch. How did she end up there? Even joined another family. She seemed to be inserting herself into everything, showing up for meetings. He was a block manager, so he noticed her. He saw her taking notes. When he got the chance, he followed her. Thought she must be a snitch. He tracked her into the BSR, into Ed's very office. Ed, the Commander's assistant. He had to laugh. They were both working for the same bureau. Takes one to know one.

In items 11 and 12, you need not list relatives other than your parents, your children, your brothers and sisters. For each person give name; relationship to you (such as father); citizenship; complete address; occupation.

11. Relatives in the United States (if in military service, indicate whether a selectee or volunteer):

(a) .... (Name) (Relationship to you) (Citizenship)

.... (Complete address) (Occupation) (Volunteer or selectee)

(b) .... (Name) (Relationship to you) (Citizenship)

.... (Complete address) (Occupation) (Volunteer or selectee)

(c) .... (Name) (Relationship to you) (Citizenship)

.... (Complete address) (Occupation) (Volunteer or selectee)

DSS Form 304A (1-23-43) *(If additional space is necessary, attach sheets)* 16—32065-1

It was Tamie who gave X his alias. Or rather, X chose his alias, and Tamie agreed to only refer to him as X. That was the agreement. No one should know, or he would lose his effectiveness, put his public position into question. That's why he quit the BSR. It wasn't for him, that desk job. He preferred his involvement in actual camp politics, the opportunity to influence people and events.

He found satisfaction in his ability to negotiate deals, manipulate various sides into the compromise he supported. Only X, an educated bilingual issei, could play both sides with such finesse. What did Spicer call it? Applied anthropology. It was Tamie who realized his obvious talents, pleaded with him to work for her, for Dorothy. At first he said no, but to placate her he tossed her a lengthy analysis he'd written for Leighton but never turned in. A paper on gambling. Tamie read it and asked if she could send it to Dorothy. A brilliant paper, they said. It was just what X knew. Eventually he agreed to share his knowledge, write comprehensive articles and analysis for Dorothy. So it was true, Tamie worked for the BSR *and* for Dorothy's project at Cal. A double agent. That was why she was so busy being a busybody.

12. Relatives in Japan (see instruction above item 11):

.... (Name) (Relationship to you) (Citizenship)

.... (Complete address) (Occupation)

.... (Name) (Relationship to you) (Citizenship)

.... (Complete address) (Occupation)

In Tokyo, X was a schoolboy, elementary school from ages six to twelve, then middle school at the American Episcopalian Rikkyo. When he finished in 1921, his father sent for him. He was seventeen. After the rice fields it was Lowell High School, San Francisco, and in 1929 he graduated with a BA in Engineering from Stanford University. In less than a decade, he perfected his English skills, spoke and wrote with clarity and ease. Within the Japanese community, folks thought he was a nisei, maybe a kibei, but with the sophistication of an educated issei. When he got into Stanford, he thought this was his chance, and he put every effort into it, worked summers in Vacaville picking fruit, made this money to support his schooling. At Stanford, he lived in the Japanese House, got a reputation for political savvy, organized support for Hoover for president. He discovered he was good at this, enjoyed working behind the scenes, thrived at being the man behind the curtains, learned his Machiavelli pulling strings.

13. Education:

Name	*Place*	*Years of attendance*
(Kindergarten)		From ______ to ______
(Grade school)		From ______ to ______
(Japanese language school)		From ______ to ______
(High school)		From ______ to ______
(Junior college, college, or university)		From ______ to ______

(Type of military training, such as R. O. T. C. or Gunji Kyoren) (Where and when)

(Other schooling) (Years of attendance)

Before he could return to L.A. with Cheeko, he had to clear out this broom closet. Dorothy was gone to Chicago. Otherwise, he could dump it in her old office at Cal. He needed to write to her. He was long finished going through Rosalie's Tule research. Rosalie even collected those pro-Jap mimeos she couldn't read. But X read them. He pulled the book from a pile. *The Spoilage*. That was his idea, wasn't it? The trilogy. In the end, Rosalie dug herself into that mess, got close to those hoshidan no-nos. They thought she was a German ally or something. He laughed. He and Tamie had gone to Gila to see Rosalie just after she'd arrived, a greenhorn out of Cal. She was a weepy mess, and they had to prop her up in a hundred-degree heat and offer her some water. Dorothy was really hard on Rosalie, though not as hard as on Tamie. Turned out Rosalie had potential. Who was it who described Rosalie as a stevedore? She was physically big and finally bold. He sifted through every page of Rosalie's detailed revelations, deciphered the factions, tried to make sense of political manipulations and power dynamics. If he'd been there at Tule instead of Rosalie, he'd have understood it better, but then he might have been killed like Yaozo. He had to figure it all out from her notes, piece it together from a white girl's perspective. That was why Dorothy brought him in. X was the real deal. Without his cultural knowledge, there would have been no book, no thesis.

14. Foreign travel (give dates, where, how, for whom, with whom, and reasons therefor):

Graduating from Stanford, all the white guys got the jobs, their lousy standing regardless. X was the superior student, but he was turned away. Same for all the other Japanese grads. Humiliated and in debt for $400, he said to hell with engineering. Predictably he got thrown back into work with the Japanese, managing farm laborers, then selling insurance policies to Japanese businesses. The business of insurance introduced X to the judicial system, since companies and individuals sued for or disclaimed compensation. In those days, he brushed shoulders with the likes of Jerry Giesler who represented the Hollywood crowd. X got a job as a junior rep and went to court as an interpreter. That's when he worked with Sammy, a brilliant young Jewish barrister, who taught him the trade, how to assess the character of jurors, manipulate the narrative, the material and witnesses, frame rebuttals to win their cases. As interpreter, he also learned how to finesse his translations with appropriate connotations. X wasn't lying; he was introducing the subtleties of the language, the stuff behind the words, the cultural meanings that couldn't be known by direct translation.

15. Employment (give employers' names and kind of business, addresses, and dates from 1935 to date):

Tamie's paranoia became a problem. If he had tracked her, there were probably others as well, she was sure of it. It didn't help that she couldn't eat camp food, but then who liked cabbage and mutton? She was growing thinner each day and ravaged by heat rash covering her torso, thighs, and underarms, any sweating surface. She complained, *I've turned into a red sausage.* X denied this to her face, but it was rather the case. The Arizona desert was a sauna. There was no escape. She was trapped, imagined specters, agonized over the smallest inconsistencies, saw them as signs of conspiracies brewing. Suspected by the FBI, she must be under surveillance. Her notes could be confiscated. Maybe they opened her reports sent by U.S. Post, used her information to arrest dissidents. Within camp, she was on the black list, a suspected inu. There were death treats. About all this, she wasn't really wrong. They beat up that Korean FBI agent. And then Nishimura at Poston, and when the attackers were picked up, it pretty much started the riot. X saw her brilliant mind cracking. It was a matter of time. She spread her anxiety to everyone. Dorothy lost patience because she began to hear complaints about Tamie from others. It did not help that Dorothy had the others read Tamie's work to correct or reconfirm its contents. Tamie took it to mean that her work and veracity were under attack. Well, everyone read everyone's work, Dorothy's way of promoting competition, not necessarily teamwork. Finally, Tamie could not trust anyone except X and depended on X to produce the information that kept her work afloat. Only X had access to the inner circle of issei and kibei men, could navigate their political and social relationships. It was, after all, second-class as it was, a man's world. X knew this, and tried to accommodate, but his identity was not covert to Dorothy, who knew who was really producing the work. Dorothy began to correspondence directly with X.

16. Religion .... Membership in religious groups ....

....

Did X love Tamie? His wife accused him, and he tried to reassure her that it was only a friendship. Finally, he had to tell his wife what he was doing, even though he had kept it a secret. He was X, working undercover. But by the time he confessed his professional relationship with Tamie, his wife already did not trust him. Tamie had written to Dorothy saying she would rather have a relationship with a hippopotamus than with X. He laughed about this because it was probably true. Tamie was only interested in her research. But despite everything, there was something there between them, an intellectual understanding, and Tamie polished his ego with her perceptive and inquisitive mind. He enjoyed her company, their collaboration. The research made him feel necessary and alive. He could utilize his leadership skills and also write about it. He felt proud of his tireless and devoted work in camp, and he knew these were, ironically, the most productive, most useful, years of his life. But he watched that mind of Tamie's go batty, and he, even he, in the end, betrayed her. Maybe it was finally her outspoken disgust of other Japs. She hated them, would be happy never to have anything to do with them again. In the islands, it was different.

These mainland Japs were parochial, simple-minded. Of course, she was angry and frustrated, but wasn't he a Jap? He quipped to Ed at the BSR that if they were concerned with neutralizing Tamie, he, X, had finally accomplished that.

17. Membership in organizations (clubs, societies, associations, etc.). Give name, kind of organization, and dates of membership.

____

____

Was it Jimmy or was it Tom who came up with that paper arguing against Dorothy's methodology? These guys were students at Cal, pre-anointed for this work, thought they knew everything. They said there had to be a thesis or hypothesis. This was how science worked. They couldn't operate without the scientific method. But Jimmy and Tom were nisei, the very subjects of the research, and who were they to criticize the directors, Dorothy and her preeminent husband? A possible scientific method: if, then. If you corralled 18,000 Japanese into a camp, then—. Maybe it was his Stanford degree, but X was unimpressed. It turned out Dorothy wanted numbers, and Dr. W.I. wanted stories. They wanted to gather the material, allow people to define their own truths, their own field of perception, turn the numbers into percentages, organize the data and compare. Until X came along they had no vision except to separate the Japanese into issei, kibei, nisei. Then it was no-no and yes-yes. But finally, it was about resettlement, who would resettle, who refused. The hypothetical question of removal and resettlement, how a refugee population might be accommodated after war. But were displaced Europeans the same as displaced Japanese? Were Japanese in America the same as Japanese in Japan? Refugees might embrace safety, but what about the incarcerated expelled into hostile territory? Defeated people might bend to peace, but the violated citizen?

18. Knowledge of foreign languages (put check mark (✓) in proper squares):

(a) Japanese	Good	Fair	Poor	(b) Other______ (Specify)	Good	Fair	Poor
Reading	☐	☐	☐	Reading	☐	☐	☐
Writing	☐	☐	☐	Writing	☐	☐	☐
Speaking	☐	☐	☐	Speaking	☐	☐	☐

A rat scurried along the wall in the corridor. X grimaced. After he discovered the nest, a bed of shredded books and documents and rat poop, he laced arsenic in food scraps, found the lot of them dead. Whose shredded research was that? Tamie's? Before she left Poston, she dumped on X her notebooks and pages and pages of typed analysis. *This is your problem now.* He still had the arsenic. Kept it in a rusty tea can. Got it from Chinatown. They never said it was arsenic, had a Chinese name for it. Of course, it worked on rats.

19. Sports and hobbies ....

....

....

When had he seen Tamie last? She came to that coffee place on Telegraph. It was just after she put the final period on her dissertation. After the war, she was there at Cal for only a year. Proof of her brilliance was that she finished an entirely different project, fieldwork and all, in that short period. A comparative linguistic study of Athabaskan folklore. At the time, he was working for Dorothy, writing *The Spoilage*. Tamie tried to avoid him, must have taken pains to skirt around the social sciences. To her, that old Jap project was anathema. But it was impossible not to cross paths. He might see her jump from a cubby in the library and run with books and papers in the other direction. Did she know he had left his family back in L.A.? He was too busy with the project, put all his energies into writing, editing, cross-referencing the data. He kept his mind with the work to avoid a deep sense of loss, to justify his sacrifice. When they met that last time, Tamie was even radiant. She had finally finished, a pedigreed scholar. He was just a layman, but a published layman. He never had much respect for the so-called scholars he met in the field that was camp, their arrogance over theories that attempted to explain, seemed to speculate about what really happened. He understood how they might interpret events and hope to predict them based on their research. This was social science and human engineering. Wasn't he trained as an engineer? From the mechanical of machinery to the mechanics of human society. He too believed that it was possible to figure out social and cultural structures, that he had achieved the same level of expertise but had, more significantly, known it in practice. Sitting at that table with a cup of black coffee, Tamie looked tiny to him, the same petite woman he knew in camp, but without the mental instability that had marked her in those days. *I wanted you to know, I'm not mad anymore. And, in case anyone is in doubt*—she pushed forward her dissertation manuscript. She smiled, and he congratulated her. She still called him X.

20. List five references, other than relatives or former employers, giving address, occupation, and number of years known:

(Name)	(Complete address)	(Occupation)	(Years known)

Peepo stopped talking to him. She was most hurt by camp, an adolescent going through changes, and he hadn't helped. She stood by her mother, as she should have. It was in camp, wasn't it, that his wife whispered to him that Peepo got her period. He remembered something churned inside of him, an anger that she had to be inside a prison and not free to embrace this change. He was an issei, an enemy alien. His wife, his daughters—they were legitimate citizens, born in America. He should have gone alone, taken the heat, but they'd come together as a family, and he'd failed them. He thought he was working for the greater good, the larger community. It was his prerogative as a man. The women and girls just came along. It was more complicated than that. Tamie taught him that.

Women were the foundation of everything, took on the burden of events made by men. He was responsible and failed. In the end, his wife and daughters hated him. He lost them to the war.

21. Have you ever been convicted by a court of a criminal offense (other than a minor traffic violation)? ....

Offense	*When*	*What court*	*Sentence*

After he met Tamie that last time, he heard she had signed up with SCAP to work in Tokyo for the Occupation. She leaned forward over her dissertation and asked him if he didn't want to do the same. It was a kind of invitation. He wasn't sure. The Jacobus manuscript was on his desk. It was a mess. Disjointed, repetitive writing, not by one scholar but a committee of three. Three disparate essays to work into one book. It was a challenge. Jacobus,

Chick, the principal author was blind, but he was brilliant, plain brilliant. It was because of Chick that X thought that mess could become a book. And he was fool enough to take it on. He told Dorothy that he did the work altruistically, rather as if he had joined a cause. Get the research and the truth into print. Straighten out misconceptions about the Japanese. Make a contribution to science. But he was really bucking for a job. He lit up another cigarette and stared into the corridor from his broom closet. He'd needed a job. Of necessity, he'd do anything: gardener, nursery, laundry, but sociology was his passion. Even though Chick said he'd recommend him, X was too old to go back to school, to get a degree. He'd paid his dues. Smart as or smarter than these Ph.D.s whose work he was sent in to fix. In the end, they all abandoned him.

What was Tamie implying anyway? Maybe nothing. He was too old to decipher such things. He could join her there later. Join her? What did that mean? He lit another cigarette. X was a fool.

22. Give details on any foreign investments.

(a) Accounts in foreign banks. Amount, $..........................

Bank .... **Date account opened** ....

(b) Investments in foreign companies. Amount, $..........................

Company.................................... **Date acquired** ....

(c) Do you have a safe-deposit box in a foreign country?

What country? .... **Date acquired** ....

Contents ....

Before Chick's manuscript, there was Morton's. Dorothy and Chuck were Morton's doctoral advisors, but they hated their protégé's political version of the internment. They sent X in to fix it and, for a while, the revised manuscript became X's version. It could have been X's next book. What was the problem? X puffed the cig to remember. Oh right. The California political machine (Morton's thesis) versus the unconstitutional overreach of military necessity (Chick's argument). X had championed Chick's version, but if he thought it over today, both were complicit in his confinement. Dorothy and Chuck couldn't get Morton to agree to change his ideas, threatened a lawsuit, but he bucked off his old mentors and arranged publication with the University of Chicago. *Americans Betrayed.* To hell with California. That was back in 1948. After that, there was part two, *The Salvage*. Charlie and Jimmy got their names attached to that book but as assistants. Of all the Cal kids who worked on the project, X knew Dorothy and W.I. preferred Charlie, the least arrogant and the best storyteller. They sent him to Chicago to tell the resettlement story. Still, in the end, only X got listed as author of any part of the trilogy.

28. List contributions you have made to any society, organization, or club:

Organization	*Place*	*Amount*	*Date*

X pulled down a box. It was heavy enough to make him gasp, then sneeze from the dust. He set it down next to the cot. He should start this process somewhere. He should have marked the boxes. He'd have to open them one by one, but what was the point? What would he do with them? Ship them to Cheeko? Why save this stuff, precious only to him, to his ego, to all those lost years? Now that Dorothy was in Chicago, W.I. dead, and Tamie in Tokyo, what did it matter? He'd finished his work with Chick, and Dorothy concluded that this publication had put Morton's book *in the shade*. Mission accomplished. As Cheeko had said, *Papa, your work is done here.* He needed to go on to another phase in his life. The war was over; the camps closed; the study finished. He opened the box and pulled out the manuscript on top. It was his book-length study, the history and analysis of the economic baseline of Japanese Americans in 1940, at the very turn of their lives. He looked at the date of his manuscript. 1948. He'd written it in preparation for and as the basis for the book *The Salvage*. Under the manuscript, there was a copy of his letter to Dorothy, dated March 5, 1952. He read it over. He wrote to Dorothy that this work was based on a 25 percent sampling, that the sources were unique and constituted almost the complete census data of the Japanese minority group at the time. He thought about Tamie's dissertation. Dorothy never responded, never asked for the manuscript, never considered that it, like Chick's book, should be published or recognized, never read the thing. X dumped the papers back into the box in a puff of degrading cellulose and dust.

24. List magazines and newspapers to which you have subscribed or have customarily read:

Spoilage. Salvage. Residue. Poetic, wasn't it? X thought about Chick's trilogy: *Genesis. Exodus. Leviticus.* More lyrical, certainly biblical, and respectable. That was the sort of transformation that their history deserved. *Spoilage* was for those Japanese who renounced American citizenship; *Salvage* for those who were loyal; *Residue* for those who got left behind and couldn't make up their minds. But *Genesis* was for the military impetus for the evacuation; *Exodus* for the execution of the evacuation itself; *Leviticus* for the final judgment, the failure of the Supreme Court in its commitment to the Constitution. X worked with these structural inventions, trichotomies to organize thinking. For *Spoilage,* X got an author credit. For Chick's tome, he got his name in the acknowledgments, was listed as an advisor, but was never paid. It had been months of tedious work, often sentence by sentence, an excruciating headache to edit, revise, to fact-check meticulously. Demographic statistics and secondary sources had to be corrected. Inaccurate quotations and dogmatic statements. Exasperated, X abandoned the niceties of tact and let Chick and his coauthors know their stupid mistakes to which they quipped, *What next, Mr. Moto?* But then, seeing all their corrected faux-pas, ingratiated themselves to Master X. In the end, three bona fide academic authors got the credit for three disorganized essays that somehow X united into one book. He'd written Dorothy that he'd done this work because he believed in it, but who believed in X?

25. To the best of your knowledge, was your birth ever registered with any Japanese governmental agency for the purpose of establishing a claim to Japanese citizenship? ....

(a) If so registered, have you applied for cancelation of such registration? .... (Yes or no)

When? .... Where? ....

Nisei were cocky. That's what issei thought. X knew what issei thought because he was an issei himself, but also because he worked with them. He knew issei to be inherently gentle but extremely proud. They worked with a sense of purpose and self-worth and demanded respect. They were suspicious of being exploited and sneered at overbearing attitudes and arrogance. They thought nisei thought they were better because they were close to the ketō, but look how they sold their fathers down the river. Young punks acting important. Issei called them *nisei bigshots*. But what nisei had that issei didn't was citizenship. When Dorothy pulled strings to get him a lectureship in Japanese Studies at Michigan, he wrote to say he wasn't qualified. This was a lie. His excuse was that the passage of the McCarran-Walter Act made it possible for him to apply for citizenship, as if. X never applied. He'd held the stigma of being Japanese for too long. It was pride. What did it matter now?

26. Have you ever applied for repatriation to Japan? ....

In camp, X might have been an issei bigshot, but he was too clever to show his hand. He was politically moderate, and in camp, he manipulated processes and strategized events toward a moderate outcome. X smiled to himself; he had neutralized that pro-Japan radical Okamoto on several occasions. Where was Okamoto now? Probably back in Japan struggling to survive, using his lousy English to work for the Occupation. But how was X any better off? No man is free of complicity. X had been a native insider-informant. In the end, he helped to define what happened in camp, and he would take the blame for his information, his definitions.

27. Are you willing to serve in the armed forces of the United States on combat duty, wherever ordered? ....

Tamie, Jimmy, Tom, Charlie, all gone on to other prospects, X remained in camp and literally on the project, the last man standing. X followed these events: on January 28, 1943, the right to military service for Japanese American citizens was restored; on the following day, January 29, the registration program was announced; on February 3, the administration of registration and the loyalty questionnaire began; and on July 15, the segregation of interned Japanese based on answers to the loyalty questionnaire was announced. Those offering negative answers to questions 27 and 28 were forced to move to the designated segregation prison at Tule Lake. Had X foreseen these edicts? Certainly he had described and analyzed those events—the riots, beatings, deaths, internal conflicts—that led to the applied consequences, led to segregation of the *disloyal* from the *loyal*. He knew these designations were complicated if not meaningless, but his analysis was after the fact. On-site, he witnessed events and eventualities, his research done in secret. After all, wasn't he X? His research did not have any real effective influence on this past history, or did it? X groaned, agony charging through his chest.

28. Will you swear unqualified allegiance to the United States of America and faithfully defend the United States from any or all attack by foreign or domestic forces, and forswear any form of allegiance or obedience to the Japanese emperor, or any other foreign government, power, or organization? ....

X examined the dregs of his tea, sipped its bitter remains. He snuffed out his last cigarette, lay down on the cot. From that horizontal perspective, he could peruse years of research, towering precariously, closing in. He promised Cheeko he'd get ready to leave. She pressed back on his inertia. He'd told her he needed time to get his affairs in order. He meant: empty the broom closet. The dingy string dangled above; he reached to pull it. Light flickered to dark. X closed his eyes, concentrated on the yellow afterglow of the bulb against lidded red, the warm pulse of blood slipping into black.

NOTE.—Any person who knowingly and wilfully falsifies or conceals a material fact or makes a false or fraudulent statement or representation in any matter within the jurisdiction of any department or agency of the United States is liable to a fine of not more than $10,000 or 10 years' imprisonment, or both.

U. S. GOVERNMENT PRINTING OFFICE 16—32808—1

(Local Board Date Stamp With Code)

Form Approved
Budget Bureau No. 33-R046-43

STATEMENT OF UNITED STATES CITIZEN OF JAPANESE ANCESTRY

1. ________ (Surname) ________ (English given name) ________ (Japanese given name)
   (a) Alias ________
2. Local selective service board ________ (Number)
   ________ (City) ________ (County) ________ (State)
3. Date of birth ________ Place of birth ________
4. Present address ________ (Street) ________ (City) ________ (State)
5. Last two addresses at which you lived 3 months or more (exclude residence at relocation center and at assembly center):
   ________ From ________ To ________
   ________ From ________ To ________
6. Sex ________ Height ________ Weight ________
7. Are you a registered voter? ________ Year first registered ________
   Where? ________ Party ________
8. Marital status ________ Citizenship of wife ________ Race of wife ________
9. ________ (Father's Name) ________ (Town or Ken) (Birthplace) ________ (State or Country) ________ (Occupation)
10. ________ (Mother's Name) ________ (Town or Ken) (Birthplace) ________ (State or Country) ________ (Occupation)

In items 11 and 12, you need not list relatives other than your parents, your children, your brothers and sisters. For each person give name; relationship to you (such as father); citizenship; complete address; occupation.

11. Relatives in the United States (if in military service, indicate whether a selectee or volunteer):
   (a) ________ (Name) ________ (Relationship to you) ________ (Citizenship)
   ________ (Complete address) ________ (Occupation) ________ (Volunteer or selectee)
   (b) ________ (Name) ________ (Relationship to you) ________ (Citizenship)
   ________ (Complete address) ________ (Occupation) ________ (Volunteer or selectee)
   (c) ________ (Name) ________ (Relationship to you) ________ (Citizenship)
   ________ (Complete address) ________ (Occupation) ________ (Volunteer or selectee)

DSS Form 304A
(1-23-43)

(If additional space is necessary, attach sheets)

16—33063-1

12. Relatives in Japan (see instruction above item 11):

(Name) (Relationship to you) (Citizenship)

(Complete address) (Occupation)

(Name) (Relationship to you) (Citizenship)

(Complete address) (Occupation)

13. Education:

Name	*Place*	*Years of attendance*
(Kindergarten)		From ...... to ......
(Grade school)		From ...... to ......
(Japanese language school)		From ...... to ......
(High school)		From ...... to ......
(Junior college, college, or university)		From ...... to ......

(Type of military training, such as R. O. T. C. or Gunji Kyoren) (Where and when)

(Other schooling) (Years of attendance)

14. Foreign travel (give dates, where, how, for whom, with whom, and reasons therefor):

15. Employment (give employers' names and kind of business, addresses, and dates from 1935 to date):

16. Religion ...... Membership in religious groups ......

17. Membership in organizations (clubs, societies, associations, etc.). Give name, kind of organization, and dates of membership.

16—62355-1

18. Knowledge of foreign languages (put check mark (✓) in proper squares):

(a) Japanese

	Good	Fair	Poor
Reading	☐	☐	☐
Writing	☐	☐	☐
Speaking	☐	☐	☐

(b) Other................ (Specify)

	Good	Fair	Poor
Reading	☐	☐	☐
Writing	☐	☐	☐
Speaking	☐	☐	☐

19. Sports and hobbies ....

20. List five references, other than relatives or former employers, giving address, occupation, and number of years known:

(Name) (Complete address) (Occupation) (Years known)

21. Have you ever been convicted by a court of a criminal offense (other than a minor traffic violation)? ....

Offense	*When*	*What court*	*Sentence*

22. Give details on any foreign investments.

(a) Accounts in foreign banks. Amount, $....................

Bank .... Date account opened ....

(b) Investments in foreign companies. Amount, $....................

Company.................................. Date acquired ....

(c) Do you have a safe-deposit box in a foreign country?

What country? .... Date acquired ....

Contents ....

10—[illegible]-1

23. List contributions you have made to any society, organization, or club:

Organization	*Place*	*Amount*	*Date*

24. List magazines and newspapers to which you have subscribed or have customarily read:

25. To the best of your knowledge, was your birth ever registered with any Japanese governmental agency for the purpose of establishing a claim to Japanese citizenship? ....

(a) If so registered, have you applied for cancelation of such registration? .... (Yes or no)

When? .... **Where?** ....

26. Have you ever applied for repatriation to Japan? ....

27. Are you willing to serve in the armed forces of the United States on combat duty, wherever ordered? ....

28. Will you swear unqualified allegiance to the United States of America and faithfully defend the United States from any or all attack by foreign or domestic forces, and forswear any form of allegiance or obedience to the Japanese emperor, or any other foreign government, power, or organization? ....

.... (Date) .... (Signature)

NOTE.—Any person who knowingly and wilfully falsifies or conceals a material fact or makes a false or fraudulent statement or representation in any matter within the jurisdiction of any department or agency of the United States is liable to a fine of not more than $10,000 or 10 years' imprisonment, or both.

U. S. GOVERNMENT PRINTING OFFICE 16—32865-1

JIMMY: Origami Checkerboard

What the Sam Hill does non-alien mean?

—Kay Sakai Nakao, Bainbridge Island, Washington*

* https://www.nichibei.org/2022/02/minidoka-survivors-on-u-s-governments-violation-of-americans-civil-rights/.

February 19, 1945

Camp population: 7,770 (83% of peak population)

Dillon Myer, WRA Director visit

Gymnasium speech (irony: exactly 3 years to date of EO 9066)

In attendance: 1,500

Announced camp closure date set for November 1, 1945

In no uncertain terms, camp will close

Make plans to leave, take advantage of WRA resources to find housing and jobs on the outside

Words stern and benevolent, even congratulatory, like graduation

Get new lives (again) (his job is over)

Employment Division already renamed Relocation Division in fall 1943

Their charge: interview family heads; discuss future plans; put out weekly bulletins; provide information on job, housing, positive updates on adjusting to the outside.

But numbers show folks aren't budging.

All camps statistics

Issei: 85% "un-relocated"

Nisei: 67% "un-relocated"

J sat down with Father K, straddling a bench pew in the empty barrack serving as a church. He ran his fingers over the grid precisely carved into the polished grain of a go board. *Where did you get this?*

Found it. Abandoned in a boiler room over in block 23, the school block. School is closing down.

Pretty soon, summer vacation forever. J picked up the board and examined the gnarled feet, polished to a dark slick burnish.

Father K nodded. *Greasewood. The board itself must be from a packing crate. You'd never know.*

How about the stones?

Couldn't find any.

Pennies?

And nickels. Father K held up two bulging socks. *Co-op coffers. I'm rich.*

Not Sunday offering?

See anyone left going to church? Father K poured out the coppers. *Pennies are black.*

Suits me.

March 20, 1945

Arguments against leaving for Midwest/East since closure announced: too many unknowns, why hazard new troubles and setbacks; wait for West Coast to open

But now that West Coast open, argument is it's not safe there

J followed Father K around as he made his visits, sometimes to the hospital to see a sick parishioner. Stood around pretending to be some kind of acolyte and listened.

Father K, we are really scared. They say we have to leave, but we've heard from people who returned to California. They were shot at.

Another spoke up, *The G family, remember them? Their business was taken over. All their stored things stolen or trashed. We heard this from the sister-in-law.*

Father K sympathized, and J took mental notes.

We leased a farm, but we buried everything there. Can you imagine going back and trying to dig things up? They'd shoot us for sure.

Father K suggested, *Perhaps it's best to first go to a big city, Seattle, for example.*

We have small children. We're not going to be the first to leave to get killed out there.

April 14, 1945

Mostly Issei left in camp

Children on outside working/struggling: don't want to be a burden; food and rent are free in camp

Sons in military: waiting

Bachelors (including Kibei): running boiler rooms, mess halls, bizarre rumor Japan is winning the war

J started the board with his penny. He had a strategic sweet spot he liked to play first, and he thought he had a plan that day. Father K forced a yawn, as if he'd already noticed that recurring play. J smiled and said, *So what's the news? Any Japanese battleships headed for California?*

Father K shook his head. *Mr. Y has a shortwave radio and reports to the others that there are ships sailing into our ports now. He says that there are Japanese troops camped three hours from here. Can you imagine?*

J laughed. *Does his radio even work?*

Probably no batteries, Father K said.

Three hours, huh. J pondered, *What do you figure? Yakima, Washington? If I were the Japanese, I'd take Las Vegas.* J made his move and continued, *If only Shibs were here.*

Shibs?

Guy who went to Cal with me. He was studying rumor construction.

You can study that?

Sure. Other day, I heard this woman talking to her friend. Ne, he imitated the lady, *we don't want to make any moves that show our disloyalty to Japan. Ne, we registered yes-yes, but that was because they said we could stay in camp, wouldn't be forced to leave. In the first place, we don't have anywhere to go. There are plenty of people who registered yes-yes who are loyal to Japan. It's just a piece of paper, deshoo.*

May 23, 1945

Memorial Service (4th ceremony) in gymnasium

War dead: 12

This camp: Highest number of war casualties, feeling punished; government distrust amplified

Military volunteers: 300 (25% of enlistment total of all camps)

Draft resistors: 33 (serving prison sentences at McNeil Island since September 1944)

J left his barrack and walked with his notebook over to the church. Father K was sitting on the stoop with a cup of tea.

Have a seat, Father K offered. *What's on your mind?*

I'm writing a report. Do you remember when the exchange happened? After

the questionnaire, there was the switch. Here are the numbers. No-no segregants numbering 335 from here were switched for 1,520 Tuleans.

Father K nodded. *That's when you arrived with the old Tuleans transfers, yes-yes loyalists. You displaced by five times the no-nos who left; there was no room to house all of you. You all had to sleep in the mess halls on cots.* He stood up and pointed to the board. *Come on in. We need to finish our game.*

Tule Lake was a dark and hostile place. Personally, for me to come here, to Minidoka, was a relief. But Tuleans had a more volatile experience, didn't trust anyone.

I remember, they couldn't go along with the rules, questioned the admin, said we were cozying up to authority. said we were submissive. They bonded with the dissatisfied complainers here.

That's when the territories got switched around, see? J sat down and pointed to the empty space surrounded by his pennies. *Now that everyone here in Minidoka is yes-yes, we have a redistribution of yes-yes conciliatory and yes-yes antagonistic.*

Yes-yes-yes and yes-yes-no.

Readjustment of leadership.

Why is it so hard to get along?

I don't know. I guess that's what I'm studying. That's the problem.

We aren't your guinea pigs, you know.

I have a confession to make, J said.

I'm not that kind of father.

I know.

Let's say it's as a friend to a friend.

Father K made his move on the board.

I'm supposed to be recording the social structure of this place. It's part of a larger study. I say it's my dissertation, but it's a bigger project.

That's why you get those envelopes from Berkeley. You need to be careful.

I've been doing this since the beginning of the war. My buddies working with me, Charlie and Shibs, got scared, left for Chicago. Not me. I stuck it out. J looked around and smirked. *Nobody left to call me inu.*

Are you?

No, just an observer.

But you are also an evacuee, a prisoner, just like all of us.

I am, but studying it has given me some distance from it all.

You didn't have to stay.

I don't have to stay at all. I'm just here to see it through to the very end. To see what happens. How it turns out. J looked around at the empty barracks. *Why are you still here?*

Same as you. Father K looked up. *See it through to the very end. It's my job, and it's a bloody Sam-Hill mess. They corralled us into a reservation and turned these people into sheep. Now they want to kick out the sheep.*

You will have to shepherd them out, J retorted softly.

Father K sneered. *Are you studying me?*

J looked down at the board and pointed, *No, but you'd better study that atari.*

June 1, 1945

High School Commencement

Graduating Seniors: 101

All schools will close permanently

J tried to pick up his capture of nickels, fumbled with the coins in disgust. *There's got to be stones left around somewhere.*

Father K's fingers pushed to correct the line of coins. *Maybe, if we went to Blocks 14 or 30, see if the canteens left anything behind.*

Boiler rooms are a better bet.

How about the fire station?

From that day on, they took to roaming through the empty blocks. Occasionally they'd find someone, a mother hanging up clothes in Block 16.

Father K asked the woman, *Your water still running?*

No, I had to go all the way to Block 22 to wash, then carry this back.

Wet clothing is so heavy, Father K said sympathetically.

I found a wheelbarrow.

J asked, *Block 22? Wasn't that where they had the tofu factory?*

No more tofu, the woman sighed. *The family left a while ago, took all the equipment with them.*

Maybe they can start up their business again on the outside, Father K said positively.

They looked around. J observed, *No water, so of course your mess hall closed too.*

The woman nodded.

Anything left?

Go on in. Don't think there's much. If there's anything, help yourself. Could be some canned tomatoes, you know? Be careful of the rats.

When they went to search, there were no rats except an origami rat, seated squarely on a cutting board.

Ha, exclaimed J. *It's folded from a loyalty questionnaire.*

July 8, 1945

Spanish Consul visit

> Spain is "neutral party" designated to intercede for Japanese nationals, but consul says no official word from Japan regarding status
>
> A lot of talk about abandonment.
>
> Some have started to realize it's time to leave.

Father K put down the first penny. *I'm black today,* he announced with confidence.

J smiled. *Today I beat your brains.*

Father K nodded. *You're a smart kid. What did you study in school?*

Psychology.

So that's your dissertation?

Not exactly. It's mixed, I think. Social psychology.

What's that?

I figure sociologists want to know how society is structured. I'm more interested in how people behave inside the structure.

They put down the first pennies and nickels in quick succession. Then J said, *Take this board, for instance. This is society. But the stones, individuals, they can move in any direction.*

Not any direction.

That's right. It depends. That's behavior constricted by the rules of engagement, by the borders and territories we create.

And within the board.

Yes, within the board.

Fewer liberties at the border, Father K observed.

Okay, J pointed at the board, *so this is my dissertation.*

But this is a game.

I know. Maybe, our game here didn't have to go this way. J gestured around them.

Maybe, Father K mused. *God works in strange ways.*

August 1, 1945

Administrative notice no. 289

Procedures outlined for camp eviction

Statistics

March: 500 relocated
April: fewer than March
May: 725
Summer: fewer than May

Today: less than half of 7,770 left

Closure of mess halls

March: 2
April: 1
July: 3
August: 11 (planned)

Total closures: 17 = 1/2 of camp food services (of 36 blocks)

Co-op liquidation

Remaining merchandise reduced to 10%

Talk of consolidating blocks, but project director believes in psychological impact of isolating last families in empty blocks to encourage relocation

Since there were no longer rugs or furniture to hide them, occasionally J and Father K found a trap door that led to a hiding place under the barracks. In one cubby entrance, the carved characters: デマ苦しいの家.

Dema-kurushii, read J out loud. *Democracy?*

House of painful hoax, but sounds like democracy. Pun.

J picked up a folded questionnaire. *The origami guy has already been here.*

Looks like a jellyfish, don't you think? Father K mused. *How about this one? A beetle?*

Cockroach, J decided in disgust. *I thought we were looking for stones.*

August 15, 1945

Japan surrenders

Outspoken pro-Japan fellow returned from harvesting beets in Boise

Singing a different tune

Every day, J and Father K met and walked. After they investigated a block as thoroughly as they thought necessary, they moved on to the next. It was a process. They were serious scavengers. They targeted some mess halls and barracks with greater scrutiny.

That barrack there, they had a gambling thing going.

I think a group of prostitutes lived there.

What do you know about prostitutes?

Prostitutes are God's children.

That one there, must have been a tunnel underneath leading to another barrack. They say there are cellars full of stored sake.

I doubt anything's left. Drank it all before they left.

And every now and then, in what Father K called the Sam-Hill crevices, they'd find another strange animal, the telltale folded form.

Scorpion?

This one's an alligator.

In one block, they visited the Buddhist temple and its remaining priest. The majority of the Christian churches and their pastors had left to open hostels for relocating internees, but most of the intransigents seemed to be Buddhists. So, like Father K, the priest also remained. Before finally leaving, folks brought the priest little gifts of farewell or shared the last of their meager food. *Have you seen these?* The priest pointed to two paper figures on his altar.

As a matter of fact, we have. J picked them up. *What are they?*

Not sure. This one, I think, is a nautilus, prehistoric.

Oh, this is an octopus. It's very clever, extremely detailed. The folder is a master.

Father K nodded. *They seem to be scattered here and there.*

J said, *Things that survive.*

The priest said, *Such intricate and precise work. I found the nautilus in the latrine. A little girl gave me the octopus before she left with her family.*

September 19, 1945

WRA 3-day eviction notices starting to be issued

"Recalcitrants" = inmates who refuse to make plans to leave

Their game was interrupted by the U family. They came to bring some blankets, furniture, and toys, wondering if the church would be interested in distributing them to anyone in need. *We know the camp is closing, but it seems such a shame to just leave this behind only to get pillaged.*

Father K smiled, said nothing, had them put their belongings along the wall with a pile of other donations. *So what is your leave date?* he asked.

We're going to wait until we get our three-day notice, said Mr. U.

Mrs. U chimed in, *Of course, we are prepared to leave, but we won't leave until we get that notice.*

Why? J was curious.

Mr. U said, *Because a three-day notice proves that we were forced to leave, that we didn't try to relocate willingly, that we continued to be prisoners until the very end. There'll be no question of our loyalty to Japan.*

Besides, said Mrs. U, *they say if you are forced out, they come with a car and take you to the train station.* Then she added with some disdain, *Did you hear that Mr. Y left yesterday?*

J perked up. *Mr. Y who has the shortwave radio?*

Yes, he didn't even wait for a three-day notice. He just packed and left with his family. And he was the one saying we should wait for the Japanese troops to liberate us.

By the time J went to see the project director, it wasn't an issue anymore. That is, there was no one left to observe his movements and create unwanted rumors. He could just be there in that office because he was one more recalcitrant still hanging around. By this time, the old project director had left to run food and agriculture in Germany, and his assistant WR had taken over. WR used to be the irrigation man; now he was the guy turning off the water.

At WR's office, J would run into E, the last outside community analyst analyzing the situation, still trying figure out how to get people to leave.

WR and E were about to pull the big camp map off the wall. Unlike the other camps, theirs wasn't a rectangular grid, but a sprawling half-moon of barrack blocks across the barren landscape. WR had some idea that they'd plant the map flat on a folding table and push around checker pieces to track block closure and the movement of inmates, like it was a war game.

J put up his hands. *No, don't take it down. Don't bother. There's an easier way.* He drew on a large piece of butcher paper. It was a map in his mind, but obvious only to himself. *See,* he broke down the abstraction. *There are thirty-six blocks.*

Hey, interrupted E. *There are forty-four blocks. Here, see. Block 44 is the last block.*

No, the north side is odd numbers, the south side even; see the gaps? There's not a full set of forty-four blocks, only thirty-six. Makes it easy. You can make up a grid like this. Six times six. Give me that ruler there. He drew the grid out.

E looked on in awe and said to WR, *J has the mind of a goddamn machine. I tell you, I throw him stats, and he comes up with the diagrams,* he pointed to J's head, *right out of that thick brain.*

When it was done, the map on the table was a rectangular grid of thirty-six, six by six, twelve barracks each. J looked up. *Now where are those checkers?*

E took apart the checkerboard sets and tossed in the plastic pieces.

Red is for recalcitrants with no plans to leave. Black is for those with a date to relocate.

They leaned over the table.

WR pointed. *Block 29, over by the onions. See that? One family left digging onions and anything else left in the earth for soup. And over there, 44 at the end, out in the sticks. We turned off the lights, water, no coal for heat, everything. Nothing doing.* WR slapped down the red checker. *Goddamn it! Out there, one last fool of an old man.*

October 1, 1945

Inmate count: 1,482

Inmate employment halted (mess halls and boiler rooms run by volunteers)

Food

warehouse has been cleared
orders of fresh food and vegetables stopped
field food collection abandoned
Poultry farm and pig sty closed (animals sold or slaughtered)
Menu is monotonous—eggs, macaroni, beans, eggs, macaroni, beans

Water

shut down in blocks (shower curtains/latrine dividers removed)

J and E argued with WR. *Your methods aren't working.*

WR grumbled, *What's their problem? Why won't they leave? They've been complaining that we imprisoned them, taken away their rights, and sent their sons to war. And now, they are free to leave. The door is open. Just leave!*

J threw up his hands. And go where? Do what? Live how? These people have lost everything, and you want them to leave and go where?

E said, *Think about it. We've created a kind of socialism inside here. Everyone gets paid about the same, regardless of the work they do, and regardless, they all get the same food, the same lodging, the same prison. Why work? Or why work too much? Some of these people, issei especially, never had a free day in their lives. All of a sudden, they can sit back, take English classes, practice sumi-e and haiku, polish wood, play go, hanafuda, gamble. It's not everyone, but maybe some think they'll wait the war out, see who comes out on top, then make their decision then.*

J said, *Hey, I wouldn't sugarcoat it like that.*

October 15, 1945

Inmate count: 390

Father K noticed, *You're quiet today. Usually, you have a problem buzzing in your mind.*

J shuffled some pennies in the palm of his hand. *And I force you to listen.*

Yes, I admit I don't understand everything, but I have to think about it.

You want something to think about?

Sure.

But I get the feeling you don't approve.

Approve?

Well, I like to think about systems or models. This camp is an experiment. If you can step aside, you can see it just as an enclosed space with people thrown in. How can or should it be organized?

Social engineering.

Yes, social engineering. E, for example, was hired to figure out if how best to engineer this camp as a social experiment.

And you were sent in to study if it worked.

That's what you can't approve of.

No, I guess not. We, your subjects inside, are not just pawns in a game. We have lost our lives, lost our possibilities. It will take many years to leave this tragedy behind. It is a great injustice.

Yes, I believe that, too, but I also think that it can be like a mathematical problem. That is the only way I can stand to be here.

What do you mean?

This go board, this game is mathematics. Every movement on this board, every stone placed creates infinite possibilities. Liberty at every cross-point. When I imagine those possibilities, I can imagine my freedom.

October 18, 1945

Inmate count: 0

J drove with E to the train depot at Shoshone. E said, *They finally caught him.*

Caught who?

Mr. H. The old guy who's been hiding out in Block 44. First, he hid under the barrack, so they boarded up his place, figured they could just ship out his stuff later.

I've seen the signs. They're only in English.

Oh, guess they didn't think of that.

Most of this residue is issei.

Yeah, English signs were stupid. Well, you know he's been a moving target. E looked significantly at J. *No, literally. WR figured Mr. H would just leave. No secure fences. No soldier mans those towers. Why didn't he just leave?*

There're hunters out there. He'd become open game. Hey, J interjected, *you still pushing around the checkers on that grid?*

Not me. WR. He had that one red checker left. It was driving him crazy.

Yeah, Mr. H. He'd get a report sighting him in Block 1, then back in Block 44. Set fire to a barrack in Block 21.

21 is near the fire station.

Yeah, convenient.

He's not stupid, just a prankster.

Turned the water back on in Block 16.

Oh, that's nice of him. That lady in 16 was having to lug her wet wash back and forth.

Then, get this, you know that guy with a shortwave radio? He couldn't hear a goddamn thing, but then suddenly he gets a scratchy signal. Someone hooked up a wire on his roof.

Mr. H?

Yeah, so we suspect.

Then, you know that party over in 29? Those guys got really drunk. Say they were celebrating Japan's victory. When they vacated, they discovered six empty jugs. Six jugs of homebrewed sake! Where'd they get that?

Mr. H? You can't blame him for everything.

Well, he's been stealing stuff, that's for sure.

More like scavenging seems to me. Hey, you missing a stack of loyalty questionnaires?

Those old things? Tossed them long ago. E sniffed and continued, *But what really pickled WR is that he'd come into his office and find his map all screwed up, all the black checkers red, stuff like that.*

You or I could have done that.

E looked at J. *You didn't.*

I didn't.

At the depot, J watched the last folks boarding the train. He calculated: the last 390, but out of 390, how many families, how many bachelors, how many nisei, kibei, issei, and their ages? Probably E had those stats. He wasn't going to try to count them now.

He waved down Father K and ran up to him. *I'll see you in Seattle.*

Look me up. You know where to find me. I'm going to miss our games.

J nodded. *Me too.*

Miss our walks and conversations. Any last thoughts?

J paused, then asked, *What do you think would be the most successful outcome of all of this?*

Father K laughed. *What sort of question is that? It was a disaster. A real test of one's faith. I suppose we can hope for peace.*

I guess my thinking isn't so lofty. J pulled his fingers through his hair. *They're going to say we were loyal or disloyal. Black or white stones. Whether or not we became Americans.*

Ha, Father K chortled. *Sam-Hill nonsense.* He turned to board the train.

On the curb outside the depot, J saw an elderly man sitting. *Are you Mr. H?*

The man nodded.

What are you doing here?

I don't know. They brought me here.

J pointed to the envelope under the man's arm. *There's a train ticket in there, some cash, some documents, a letter of introduction, I think.*

Is that right?

Yes. Can I help you get on that train? It's the last train out. Where are your things?

Back there. The man pointed south.

We'll have them sent to you. Do you have family?

Yes, my wife and daughter. They left a long time ago. They wanted their freedom. That's fine with me.

The man stood up and walked with J, boarded the train obediently.

J escorted the man to his seat, then noticed his coat pockets bulging on both sides.

Oh. Mr. H pulled a cloth bag from each pocket. *I almost forgot. These are for you.*

J descended the train. Hefting the bags, he realized they were go stones. He turned and jumped back into the train, running toward the old man's seat, but Mr. H was nowhere.

Sam-Hill. J thought of Father K's curse, stared at the thing left behind in the seat's dipped leather. Was that the man's ticket? No, his folded release document, now nothing but an origami turtle.

October 23, 1945

Camp officially closed

WR had closed the gate with a padlock. It was a dumb formality; most of the fence had been torn down, posts used for furniture or firewood. J jumped the perimeter and walked into the old admin office. It wasn't even locked, and pretty much everything was still there, boxed for storage. The potbelly stove was cold. J rubbed his hands together and stared at his map. Through windowpanes, October light flooded the room, casting focused squares of cold light over the 6-by-6 grid, dappled with the last red and black checkers. J swept the sheet from under the plastic disks, scattering them to the floor. Carefully, he made the first fold at the center. Found the ruler to score the fold sharply. Then, fold by fold.

1		
1	2	3
4	5	6
7	8	9
10	11	12

2		
1	2	3
4	5	6
7	8	9
10	11	12

3		
1	2	3
4	5	6
7	8	9
10	11	12

4		
1	2	3
4	5	6
7	8	9
10	11	12

5		
1	2	3
4	5	6
7	8	9
10	11	12

6		
1	2	3
4	5	6
7	8	9
10	11	12

7		
1	2	3
4	5	6
7	8	9
10	11	12

8		
1	2	3
4	5	6
7	8	9
10	11	12

10		
1	2	3
4	5	6
7	8	9
10	11	12

12		
1	2	3
4	5	6
7	8	9
10	11	12

13		
1	2	3
4	5	6
7	8	9
10	11	12

14		
1	2	3
4	5	6
7	8	9
10	11	12

15		
1	2	3
4	5	6
7	8	9
10	11	12

16		
1	2	3
4	5	6
7	8	9
10	11	12

17		
1	2	3
4	5	6
7	8	9
10	11	12

19		
1	2	3
4	5	6
7	8	9
10	11	12

21		
1	2	3
4	5	6
7	8	9
10	11	12

22		
1	2	3
4	5	6
7	8	9
10	11	12

23		
1	2	3
4	5	6
7	8	9
10	11	12

24		
1	2	3
4	5	6
7	8	9
10	11	12

26		
1	2	3
4	5	6
7	8	9
10	11	12

28		
1	2	3
4	5	6
7	8	9
10	11	12

29		
1	2	3
4	5	6
7	8	9
10	11	12

30		
1	2	3
4	5	6
7	8	9
10	11	12

31		
1	2	3
4	5	6
7	8	9
10	11	12

32		
1	2	3
4	5	6
7	8	9
10	11	12

34		
1	2	3
4	5	6
7	8	9
10	11	12

35		
1	2	3
4	5	6
7	8	9
10	11	12

36		
1	2	3
4	5	6
7	8	9
10	11	12

37		
1	2	3
4	5	6
7	8	9
10	11	12

38		
1	2	3
4	5	6
7	8	9
10	11	12

39		
1	2	3
4	5	6
7	8	9
10	11	12

40		
1	2	3
4	5	6
7	8	9
10	11	12

41		
1	2	3
4	5	6
7	8	9
10	11	12

42		
1	2	3
4	5	6
7	8	9
10	11	12

44		
1	2	3
4	5	6
7	8	9
10	11	12

BOX 3
RESIDUE

3.1 Harry Kitano
1944–1945 Midwest J.C. Higginbotham
Jazz passing / assimilation / integration / acculturation

3.2 Robert Hashima
1945–1952 Japan Benedict, Hearn, Soseki, Fleming, Dazai, Kusama
Occupation & Cold War applied anthropology

3.3 Nobuya Tsuchida
1955–1964 Harlem Yuri Kochiyama & Malcolm X
Black Nationalism & Peace coalitions / intersections

3.4 Michi Nishiura Weglyn
1968–1976 San Francisco / New York Wayne Collins
Renunciation & Resistance archives, truth & justice

3.5 James & Gordon Hirabayashi
1968–1969   San Francisco   Esther Schmoe
Civil Disobedience   sociology x anthropology x ethnic studies

3.6 Dana Takagi
1974–1980   Berkeley   Wendy Yoshimura, Paul & Mary Ann Takagi
Radical Criminology, Prison Abolition   eugenics & deviance; prisons & courts

3.7 Aiko & Jack Herzig-Yoshinaga
1980–1988   Washington, D.C.   Peter Irons
Civil Liberties & Reparations   history & law

3.8 Michael Omi
1986–1988   Hawaii   Lois-Ann Yamanaka
Settler Colonialism   racial formation

3.9 Emiko Omori & Bruce Yonemoto
1999–2014   Borders   Chris Marker
Black Lives Matters & Immigration   memory & mental health

3.10 Yuki Okinaga Hayakawa Llewellyn
2022   Manzanar   Lee, Miyatake, Kitagaki, Fujihata
Museums & Memorials   photography & AR

HARRY: Enryo Syndrome

What did I do to be so black and blue?

—Fats Waller, Harry Brooks, Andy Razaf, 1929

Going to sprout my wings and fly right over that fence,
'Cause staying in here don't make no sense . . .
Ask the Count and Jimmy to wail these blues,
Dream on, baby; ain't nothing left to lose.

—*Buddhahead Blues,* Ernest Michio Matsunaga, Santa Anita, 1942

I don't know why we're here. I don't know where we're going, but I'm sure that things will work out.

—Harry Kitano, Topaz, 1944

How you doing, man? That's how Harry always greeted me. He'd open the case, peer in, observe me in pieces—bell, slide, mouthpiece. He was extra careful with my slide, checked the lock, then placed my bell in the receiver, set my mouthpiece, lubed my slides. Took a soft cloth and polished me shiny. Then hefted me in his left grip, pinky gripping my slide, and pulled me to his chest. *How you doing, man? How you doing today?* Even then, I was old and beat up, cheap acquisition from the San Francisco Japanese Boys Association Boy Scouts Bugle Corp, Troop 12, but I was precious. Understand?

We've been places together. Folks expect to hear how I got stashed with socks into a duffel, a couple of ties, and underwear, next to a phonograph player and a 78 platter of Count Basie's "One O'Clock Jump." Kid was fifteen, and that was all he could carry. We got shipped off to Santa Anita to play for a combo NorCal/SoCal dance band called Starlight Serenaders, then to the Utah desert to join the Topaz Tooters. That's the story folks want me to tell, but when you are fifteen and change happens, you don't understand tragedy. Social catastrophe. Things could have been different, but shikataganai. When you're fifteen and the world changes, you got to step outside the change and see who you can become. You think maybe this is your chance. And that's when my story begins.

FIRST: MILWAUKEE

It was April 4, 1944. By this time, Harry was almost eighteen. What was left of his family in camp—it was a big family, mind you, Harry being the youngest—walked us to the gate. Was there a girlfriend? Maybe there was, but she was long gone to Tule. We caught a ride by truck with a bunch of farmhands to the Delta depot. Stood there alone on that little platform, a government indefinite leave permit with a letter from the WRA, and a little short of fifty bucks—twenty-five from the government and the rest that Harry'd saved and the family managed to scrounge up. The train pulled up, incoming from L.A., a load of soldiers coming or going. Harry lugged me in one hand, a suitcase in the other, hefted us up into the train. In the aisle, at the end of the car, he balked, searching for where to sit. No one paid him no mind. He was harmless, and they, government issue, young as they were, had already become old and war-weary. At his age, poor kid, he could've been going in the same direction. He looked out the window, caught sight of the Great Salt Lake, and saw Utah go away.

Harry kept my mouthpiece in his coat pocket. He pulled me out, pressed in his embouchure; pulling his lips into his cheeks, we practiced a soft buzz up and down the scales. Salt Lake to Denver, Denver to Omaha. Government issue unloaded and loaded there. Then Omaha to Chicago, Chicago to Milwaukee. Over the jagged Rockies and Great Plains, cities spilling into flatlands, flatlands spilling into cornlands, the sheer buzz of crops, backing into the backside of factories, smokestacks, the pillage of the land in and out. From Milwaukee, it was a farther train ride thirty miles up, hugging Lake Michigan, its big blue body in a state of defrost, the stuff of spring sprouting, landing finally at lakeside Port Washington.

If there were nothing but Mormons in Utah, in Wisconsin there were nothing but Germans. It was not lost on Harry that these Germans seemed to pose no threat to no one. All things being unequal, Harry and I stepped over the threshold of a farmhouse owned by a German family and took a room. *Japan,* the farmer said over dinner, *is a great country, and you are a great people. Time will tell.* Harry nodded, not because he agreed but because the farmer's wife proffered a generous second heaping of mashed potatoes. To get seconds in camp, he'd had to run to another mess hall in another block. Post dinner, the farmer asked, *What instrument do you carry in that case?* He was delighted that I was a trombone and left the room to get his clarinet. And just like that, the table was cleared, and the daughter appeared with a zither, the wife with an accordion. Harry and I played Oktoberfest polkas for the rest of the night.

Turned out the WRA contract sent Harry from dairy farm to dairy farm to build corn silos in exchange for room and board and nominal pay. He was day labor. Pretty soon it became apparent that there were thousands of dairy farms with corn silos spread all over the state, and they all needed more corn in more silos to feed the cows that provided milk to feed the thirsty nation still at war. You didn't really need any experience to do this work. Harry had chosen it instead of farming, then wondered at his choice. All those dairy cows mooing and chomping on corn feed from long troughs. Waking with the stink of their piling dung every morning. Some silo engineer manager type came with his work team and barked orders to tear down the old silo, dig the ditch, mix concrete, lay foundation, construct the new thing in metal pieces from a kind of humongous kit. It was hard painful labor. Harry was, after all, a city boy.

Music should be a respite, but we learned that playing German polkas was a rarity, maybe a no-no. The farmer's daughter explained, *You made my father very happy. But you see, my brother is in a POW camp somewhere, maybe*

Poland, still behind the line. We shouldn't take chances. So instead, in the evenings, she turned on the radio. It was Lawrence Welk, broadcasting from the Chicago Trianon, Bing Crosby singing "Don't Fence Me In." Harry's mouth formed the embouchure, and we played along in his mind.

By the time Harry was on his third dairy farm, he was made of tougher stuff and had some friends. Got to talking with some guy on the crew who perused *DownBeat* during breaks. *Hey, Woody Herman's back at the Riverside this weekend. He's the band that plays the blues.* From then on, after every payday, Harry headed to the city to spend his hard-won cash club-hopping on Walnut Street. The black-and-tan world opened its doors, and Harry walked right into the high life, lowlife, gangsters, hustlers and con men, ladies of the night, artistes, the drunken, addicted, worn and torn, witness to the wail and travail, and all the while the war out there our constant rhythm. Club to club, Lindy Hop to jitterbug, swing was swinging. On the cusp of life, prison wires rusting behind, this was something else. Harry fingered my mouthpiece. If only, if only we could just get up and blow.

SECOND: MINNEAPOLIS

Harry borrowed *DownBeat,* answered an ad for a trombonist, gave notice, and bid the German dairy farmers and their satisfied cows goodbye. We headed for the Twin Cities where Tiny Little ran a ragtime band that moved in the direction of swing, depending on his audience. Tiny tried us out but soon gave Harry two weeks' notice, and sent us on to other possibilities.

He was never going back to build silos for Holsteins. Harry sent a quick letter to his big sister in Chicago. He could use some cash to buy a new jacket, since he was going need it to play, if he could play. Plus, in Minnesota the snow came earlier. They say it could get down to twenty below. Was he whining? She wrote back with a word to her little bro, something about practicing gaman, like Mama and Pop would expect, tucked in some cash, plus the address of a friend of a friend in Minneapolis. Anyway, all Harry would have had to do was to look around because, after Camp Shelby in Mississippi, Fort Snelling just south of the Cities was the biggest second home to soldiers of the nisei persuasion. This was a kind of well-known secret. To all six thousand of them. Harry found a room, and we even played a couple of gigs at the local YWCA, set up to send nisei off to the second and last front of the war, the Pacific. One draftee, a trumpet player, admitted, *Two thousand kanji, man; the white guys are better at it. But,* he pointed, *I got the ear, you see.* And for a while, it was just like home, or rather camp, playing Tommy Dorsey's sentimental journeys.

THIRD: OMAHA

But the dream would not yet be deferred. We were wanted, this time by a wannabe Glenn Miller band with a big brass section, and we most definitely wanted to be. Next stop Omaha. In those days, musicians went and stopped where the trains went and stopped. If they'd been a Negro band, they'd have played on the north side at Dreamland. Being all white, except for Harry, who was now surname Lee and presumably Chinese, we played at the Music Box for the engineers who were building B-29s and for the pilots flying them out of Offutt. "Chattanooga Choo Choo." We got to sing those bombers off the runway and into the clear blue skies.

In Omaha the steaks were big, one-pounders dripping juice, flapping off the plate. One of the guys across the table leaned in and said confidentially but loudly, as if he were gifting good news to the big band, *We are bombing the hell out of the Japs. You heard it here.*

Harry pretended to be occupied with his steak knife, savoring horseradish on sirloin.

The guy continued, *LeMay's dropping these M47s in streams at five thousand feet. At that altitude, you could probably see the people burning. Hell, I heard we practically incinerated the entire city of Tokyo.*

Harry concentrated on the potato stuffed with sour cream and chives. The piano player said, *Hey, Harry, you sure got an appetite. I got this lemon meringue pie for dessert.* He pushed it forward. *You're a growing boy.*

Nah. I'm fine. Harry picked up the napkin and wiped his mouth.

Up for grabs, his bandmate nudged.

Harry hesitated and the guy across interrupted. "I got room. Hand her over."

Harry thought he'd lost his manners back in camp, and grimaced inside about how restraint didn't work with Americans. He watched the pie glide over the table.

The drummer chimed in, *Hey, I heard Harry practicing "India." Plays it with the mute, don't you know. Not bad. Why don't we give him the solo?*

And just like that, they started introducing Harry and me, a kind of explanation for having a Chinese in an all-white band: *Ladies and Gentlemen! Today, direct from India, our own Harry Lee, playing "Song of India."* In fact, we were a big hit, night after night. Harry became a popular vaudeville schtick, under a turban, working my slide and muted bell like we were teasing a cobra.

FOURTH: KANSAS CITY

On the train, guy called Cosmos took a seat next to Harry. Cosmos was first trombone, though not much older than Harry, maybe a couple of years. To be nonchalant, Harry looked out the window.

Tell me something, Cosmo started in. *Why'd you pick up the trombone?*

Don't know. Why did you?

Cosmos shrugged. *When they were passing out the instruments, that's the one I got.*

Same here. Harry shifted awkwardly, but he wanted to keep his cool. He offered, *I think I kept at it because it slides.*

Not an easy instrument, requires more than muscle memory. Requires an ear to make it sing.

Yeah, I guess I enjoy the challenge.

Don't lie to me, Cosmos cajoled. *You play it because Dorsey and Miller play it.*

What's wrong with that?

Nothing wrong. You want to be like them, up there, leading.

Harry bristled. Maybe. Why not? What's wrong with that?

Nothing. Nothing. You know—his voice quieted. He looked around at the guys sleeping in the rows before and beyond. *You don't have to solo "India," if you don't want to. Ask for a different solo.*

It's okay, Harry said.

Cosmos said, *Nikolai Rimsky-Korsakov.*

What?

Rimsky-Korsakov, the Russian. He wrote the original song.

Harry swallowed his sigh. Were we going to have to sit next this smart-ass the whole way to Kansas City?

Cosmos continued, *Originally, it was the opera,* Sadko. *"Song of the Indian Guest."*

Oh yeah?

Look, I'm not trying to be a jerk. I had to play it in the symphony orchestra.

Yeah?

Yeah. Cave of jewels. Sea of pearls. Phoenix with the face of a maiden. And a song to make you forget. That's the song, basically.

And I play it every night.

And you play it every night.

To forget.

To forget. Cosmos smiled widely.

Harry sort of blushed. *I'm new. I finally got a contract to play, and I want to finish this gig. I got an obligation, and I got to stick it out. You might not believe it, but I'm having a good time. I'm doing what I dreamed of. I'm free.*

They both looked out the window, the train trundling through farmland. Cosmos nodded. *I hear you.*

Hours later, we pulled into Kansas City, home of Count Basie. Harry still had it with him, the only 78 rpm he'd managed to bring out of San Francisco, "One O'Clock Jump."

We played a venue on Twelfth Street. Harry had heard all the stories about the Paris of the Plains, railroad hub, den of old speakeasies, where Prohibition never really was, and therefore everything else flourished. Even so, at the outset, we found it pretty sedate. But when our set was done, Cosmos motioned to Harry.

Where're we going?

Lose the others. Come on. Didn't you say you're free?

We followed Cosmos to Eighteenth and Vine, and everything changed. The real music began after hours. It was all about the riff. Could we improvise a solo in the chaos that was not chaos but everybody doing-their-thing collective hearing? Could we join a counterpart, tail, or control? It was fierce and wild. Mean and ruthless. Bellicose and intuitive. Joyful and hilarious. It took all our courage and determination to stay in the game, get beat up, and come back fighting. Harry followed Cosmos's feints and gut punches. We knew it was a test and we could not fail. Before this, Harry thought he knew, but he knew nothing. And it wasn't really about knowing. It was about feeling, this unexplainable epiphany, and this was the only way to get it. And we had to do it together. And did we have the chops?

When it was done, we sauntered back to the hotel, day breaking. Harry was exhausted, but he had to ask. *How did we get in there?*

What do you mean?

Harry was silent. Then, *Remember, I'm the guy you send in to solo "India."*

Hey, don't put that on me.

Harry scrutinized Cosmos, who looked away.

I just know the culture.

Culture?

It's not about race, you know. It's a culture.

Harry thought about this. He pointed back down the street. *But, what was that?*

Don't know. It's what it is, if we go there.

Where is that?

You tell me.

FIFTH: ST. LOUIS

Now, who has not made a version of the "Saint Louis Blues"? Harry and I were about to make one of our own.

Saint Louie was smack-dab in the center, between New Orleans and Chicago, between D.C. and San Francisco. Story was that riverboats traveled up and down the Mississippi with the music. How many got their chops playing "Dixie" continuously for traveling dancers? It was an era long gone, but it left its mark indelibly. We weren't going to be there long, but it would be long enough to don a turban to play "Song of India" or whatever pleased the dancing crowd at Casa Loma or the New Lindy or Cinderella, stationary extensions of the old floating dance halls.

And long enough to slip away after hours with Cosmos to catch George Hudson at Club Plantation. Cosmos walked in casually, Harry at his coattails, took a table. Cosmos leaned in and said, *Try the spaghetti and meatballs, like Mama makes.*

Harry looked around. It was not lost on him that on stage Hudson and his band were all Negro and the audience all white. We'd been playing with and to all whites all along.

Their plates arrived with a gracious follow-up. *Parmesan?*

Harry stared at the cheesy snow and Cosmos said, *Tony's the owner.* He said it like he knew him, with a lilt. *Scarpelli.*

Harry shrugged.

Let's just say they are a family of some persuasion.

Cosmos seemed to settle in comfortably, ignored the glances from patrons at another table. *Don't worry, Harry. Italians are friendly. Seems like you are an honorary white boy.* Cosmos twirled pasta at the end of his fork.

Harry stiffened.

Do you know the thirty-six-thirty parallel, what they call the Missouri Compromise?

Harry snorted back. *Another history lesson, Professor?*

What did they teach you? Cosmos growled. *Above that parallel, no slavery, but even though it's above, Missouri is the compromise. It's like that stage over there. That's the dividing line. We go through the front door, but Hudson and his boys go through the back. And right here,* he pointed to the table, *is the home of Dred Scott, condemned to be a slave forever.*

Harry bristled. *Are you proud of that?*

No. Just saying. Cosmos looked at his watch and got up.

Hey. Harry waved his fork. *I'm not done. And there's another set.*

Let's go. We have no time for this. Billy Eckstine is where it's at. Down the street, over at the Riviera.

Harry rushed after. He stopped on the sidewalk and thought about leaving the guy, going back to the hotel to sleep his anger off, but Cosmos nodded at him with his customary friendliness. *Come on, Harry. You got to see this.*

What the hell. Harry obeyed.

A little less than two miles down Delmar was the other nightclub. Though the band looked about the same as at Plantation, the clientele was most definitely Negro. Settling down at this table, Harry asked, *And now, what are you? An honorary black boy?*

Touché. Sorry back there.

From across the floor came a big voice. *Jimmie! What you doing here?*

Cosmos looked up and away, but the man with the voice proceeded to their table. *Jimmie! Is that you? How long it's been? You were just a kid. Look at you now. How's the folks? You still playing?*

Cosmos got up and received the man's embrace.

I thought you got diverted with the others to Chicago to play band for the Navy.

Nah, Cosmos said. *Got flat feet.*

Don't blow with your feet.

They laughed.

The man looked at Harry and asked, *You gonna introduce us?*

Cosmos cleared his throat. *This is Harry Lee. Harry, this is my uncle Jordan.*

Harry shook the man's hand. He was tall, handsome like Cosmos, the same build, but heavier and shades darker.

Were you going to leave town before you came to pay your respects?

We're just here for a split second. On the road, you know.

Where you playing?

Nothing special. Lindy Hop dances. It's a job. We came over here to hear what's special.

Jordan shook his head at the stage. *I don't know about these dudes. They're experimenting.*

Cosmos's usual bravado had disappeared, but he asserted, *I like it.*

I'm old-fashioned. Look here. He reached into his breast pocket. *Just happened to have two tickets to the Kiel Auditorium. You around?*

Cosmos eyed the dates. *Yes, sir.*

Now that—Jordan pointed at the tickets—*that's the real thing.*

Harry watched Jordan saunter away, greet other tables, work the room. Then he turned to query Cosmos who'd turned his body to the stage, concentrating hard on the sax player.

Harry didn't know how Cosmos arranged it, but somehow he found two trombone replacements for their night at the Kiel. Uncle Jordan had bequeathed them two orchestra tickets to see the Duke. *Black, Brown and Beige.* Harry couldn't believe it. It was a sit-down benefit concert for the YWCA. A jazz symphony. Highfalutin. At intermission, Harry practically floated into the lobby. Was he dreaming? A white-haired Japanese couple moved toward him, smiling. They could have been his mom and pop, prim and well dressed. What were they doing here in Saint Louis? *Papa.* The woman prodded her husband. *Don't you remember? Motoji-san no ko.*

Haa, the man murmured, bowed slightly, and put out his hand. *I'm Obata,* he said.

Harry perked up. *Mr. Obata,* he exclaimed. *This is my friend Cosmos. But, what are you doing here?*

I'm an Ellington fan.

I mean, in Saint Louis.

Mrs. Obata said, *Our younger son is going to school at Washington U. Are you also there?*

Architecture, her husband added. *What school are you?*

No, no. I'm—Harry jammed his hand into his pocket, fingered my mouthpiece for security. He nodded at Cosmos, who completed the sentence.

We're on the road, sir, playing with a band.

Papa, he's a very talented musician. Mrs. Obata smiled almost tearfully, and continued, *Your parents are still in Topaz?*

They are.

Mr. Obata smiled encouragement. *Hopefully, the war will end soon, and we can all go home.*

Cosmos backed away respectfully.

Later, Cosmos and Harry swapped draws on a reefer and laughed. *I guess we're even.*

I guess so.

I always knew, you know. Cosmos held his breath and released.

Knew?

You were Japanese. Did I really fool you?

Well, you could be a dark Italian. Harry puffed. *To be polite.*

Sicilian. Puts people off. They think mafia. Just a step up, but white, you know. My maternal granddaddy really was from the old country. Settled in New Orleans, played the trumpet at Mardi Gras. My brother is a dark dude, but I got the light side of the stick. Got to cross over, as they say. I go by my granddaddy's name, Cosimo. But, you know—Cosmos extended his arms dramatically, like a maestro toward the stratosphere. He laughed. *Guess I owe you.*

Owe me nothing. Way I figure, like my people'd say—Harry felt a stupid giggle swell in his belly like a revelation—*our mutual obligations cancel each other out. You are free.*

Free, indeed.

SIXTH: INDIANAPOLIS

Cosmos announced, *Harry, you'll be happy to know that you will be playing your song in India-no-place, a real tribute. My hometown, Indianapolis, as it turns out.* He looked at Harry seriously. *Nobody needs to know that this is my town. You understand?*

Keep our invisibility visible.

Understood. But how about a home-cooked meal?

Harry tried to remember family meals. His folks had run a four-story hotel in Chinatown. It was a single-residency place with shared bathrooms. Their family of nine crammed into four narrow rooms on the ground floor, living with and serving the guests—migrant and sojourner laborers, out-of-towners, tourists, couples of assignation, traveling salesmen, but mostly Negro bachelors living on welfare. Mama cooked on a small stove next to a hotel sink. Dining was Japanese-style on the floor, elbow to elbow on cushions around low tables. In those days, Pops had his place at the head, but for everyone else it was whoever got there first. After that, Harry'd spent three years running with his crew from mess hall to mess hall, trying to beef up. Never did. He was a skinny dude.

Stepping into Cosmos's home was a revelation. Living room. Library.

Dining room. Lace tablecloth, silver platters, crystal glasses. Cosmos's father presided at the head of the table, sliced the roast. His mother served the gravy and sides, and his brothers and sisters all sat obediently, displaying perfect table manners. A guest was present, and it was Harry. He entered an old interior world, stilted yet safe—gracious elegance, patriarchal authority, ritual, and propriety.

Cosmos introduced his father as *Doctor.* The doctor had trained in Chicago and returned to serve the local community. His wife was a manager for the Madam C.J. Walker manufacturing line of hair-styling products. She asked Harry, *Now, where are you from? Your family?*

Cosmos interrupted, *Mama—*

But Harry said, *They're in Utah. We're originally from San Francisco, but with the war, we were relocated.*

The doctor said, *I know all about it. A great injustice. Your people are imprisoned, and meanwhile, you have a segregated unit over there in Italy.* He paused and looked at his son. *Your generation bears a heavy responsibility.* Then he turned to Harry. *If this war goes on much longer—*

I haven't been called yet, replied Harry.

Cosmos offered, *If we keep on moving, they can't find you.*

His mother smiled, then pursed her lips. *James*—she called Cosmos by his real name—*is attracted to the nomadic life of a traveling musician.*

The doctor intoned, *This is all right for a while, but eventually you'll have to settle down, get a proper education.*

Harry looked at his plate uncomfortably.

Cosmos clarified, *They're not talking about you, Harry. They're talking about me.*

The Avenue, son, the doctor interjected, *is not the cakewalk it used to be. Lost its old respectability. You can't hang out there forever.*

Mother poured water for Harry. *James got his training in high school, at Crispus Attucks. Reads and composes. Did he tell you he used to play with the symphony orchestra?*

Cosmos looked at Harry almost helplessly. *I was light enough to pass, so I got the position. But that's not what I wanted to play.*

But his mother persisted. *Do you know, Harry, James was a first-year medical student, top of his class?*

Harry smiled. *He's way smarter than me. Better trombone player too. I would say the best.*

Cosmos groaned. *Why don't we talk about Harry?* He looked at his younger brother and said, *Louis, ask Harry a question, why don't you?*

Louis thought for a moment. *I heard about the Japanese. They're the enemy.*

Harry reddened. *I'm American. Born and raised here. I've never been to Japan. I'm not the enemy.*

So why'd you let them take you away?

When it happened, I was your age. You go where your family goes, right?

I guess so.

Harry met Louis's quizzical face. It was an innocent question. Suddenly he was filled with shame and contempt. He really didn't know how to answer to that question.

The doctor had excused himself. He was in his library listening to music. The sound from the phonograph seeped across the house, Armstrong wailing, *What did I do to be so black and blue.* Harry caught the scat in his throat. *Waz waz buz waz giz wa joz wa ze yesss—*

SEVENTH: CHICAGO

Finally we arrived in Chicago, birthplace of Benny Goodman, the really big hub, country's middle navel. Two of Harry's sisters had relocated to Clark and Division, the reinvented Japantown of the Midwest. We found them crowded into a single room in an apartment house run by an enterprising Japanese named Matsunaga. Harry's big sister smirked. *How do you like it, Harry?*

Second big sister added, *We'd show you around, but this is it.* She waved her arms.

Big sister #1 declared, *From Clay Street to Clark Street.*

It was call-and-response.

Sister #2: *Just like old times.*

Sister #1: *We could cram five beds in here easily.*

Sister #1: *You are welcome to stay.*

Harry said, *Only if I get the bed next to the door.* He remembered their barrack. Sister #1 sneaking in late, in the dark, climbing over their sleeping bodies, stocking feet stepping on his head.

Sister #2 pointed out the window to the street below. *Down there, you have to navigate a lot of vice.*

#1 qualified, *By vice, she means pimps and whores.*

#2 added, *We don't go out at night.*

#1: *Can you believe it?*

#2: *Our Chinatown was classier than that.* She wagged her finger at the street.

#1: *Mama and Papa are better off in camp.*
#2: *We got free to come to this?*
Harry laughed. *Well, I can't complain.*
#1: *You starved for Chinameshi?*
Sure.
#2: *Down the street, there's a place.*
#1: *They call it Hiraribaa.* She emphasized the *baa.*
What's that?
#2: *Gila River Bar. Get it? Hira Ri Bar.*
#1: *We're never going to shake those damn camps.*

Cosmos met up with Harry at the Gila River on Clark. He tried the katsu plate on rice with gravy. *This is good,* he crooned.

My people food, Harry said. *The secret is shoyu.* He hoisted the little bottle in the air.

Cosmos said, *Harry, I'm confessing now. This is my last stop.*

Chicago?

Maybe. I'll figure it out. Moving out from here. Southside. Harlem. Play for real, you know.

Not going home to Indianapolis? What do the folks say?

My family thinks I was gifted with this face, so I can go anywhere, do anything I want. It's not true.

A blessing in disguise.

Truth is, down deep, I think they hate me.

They don't. We all just hate ourselves. That's the problem.

You psychoanalyzing me? I didn't ask for this.

Neither did I. Hey, think about it. Maybe your folks are right. You got that chance.

What I want is not what they want.

That's another problem. My sisters are badgering me about college, too, you know.

They looked around at the diner crowd. Old bachelors nursing beers or swapping cups of sake. A nisei soldier in uniform sitting with family, maybe a last dinner send-off. He'd probably already been to see the issei parents still in camp.

Harry said, *I had a friend in school. We blew together. I heard he's out there playing with Lionel, really doing it. I don't think I've got it, not like that. My sister might be right. How do you do it?*

Truth is, I work at it, memorize everything, so it looks like it's sucked out of the air. That's what they want, want to believe it just comes out of your belly. It's easier to be white because they don't expect so much. If you're black, it's got to be in your genes, and if your genes don't show, they fire you.

If it's genes, you got no excuses, Harry said. *But you're the man who taught me it wasn't about race. You said, it's a culture.*

That's the conundrum.

Yeah. Harry poured the hot sake from the ceramic pot. He toasted. *You got no excuses.*

The last night Harry and Cosmos shared the stage, it was another one of those indistinguishable downtown hotel dance halls filled with white swingers. Harry's sisters were invited and sat at a table near the front of the stage. Cosmos went over to greet them. They said, *We were stopped at the door, but we said we were Harry Lee's sisters. Now we're Chinese.* They giggled.

Harry heard the story backstage and rolled his eyes.

Cosmos said, *You know the story? There's always a challenger out there, says he's better than you. Maybe it was Satchmo who said, Tell him if he ain't Gabriel, don't bother.*

I ain't Gabriel.

Don't matter. You gonna take me on, rise to the occasion? Last chance.

Let's do this.

And just like every other night, the bandmaster announced, *From India, our very own Harry Lee!*

This time, Harry got up, moaned the tune like always, an octave lower, coaxing the cobra with my slide, but then we kept on moaning and then diverging and taking the Russian's tune away maybe to Moscow, then to New Orleans, to Kansas City, to Harlem, to San Francisco and on to Topaz. Somewhere around Kansas City, he pulled the mute from my bell like a plug from a drain, and the water whirled free, a wild deflecting Coriolis. And then Cosmos stood up and bleated his bone into the melody that became the mire, and the sounds wailed around in a dreamscape that reshaped the subaltern world, and our two trombones fought and battled, cried and confessed, contrapuntal and bellicose, bitter and sweet.

The couples on the dance floor stopped dancing, stood out there confused. Some drifted away in disgust. Others just hugged each other, stared and listened, shocked or entranced. We had tamed the cobra good and finally.

End of the night, predictably, we were fired.

Somewhere near Clark and Division, Cosmos tipped his hat to Harry, said, *Give me your phone number, if you ever get one. Maybe we'll be in touch.* And we walked our separate ways.

I didn't see Harry much after that. Just every once in a while. Eventually we made it back to San Francisco. Played some gigs. Harry got a degree in sociology, then psychology, at Cal Berkeley. If he came around, I'd be there, and like I said, he'd greet me as usual. *How you doing, man?*

ROBERT: Kiku & Katana

A soldier whose business is murder as a fine art, a diplomat whose calling is based on deception and secretiveness, a politician whose very life consists in compromises with his conscience, a business man whose aim is personal profit within the limits allowed by a lenient law—such maybe excused if they set patriotic devotion above common everyday decency and perform services as spies . . . Not so the scientist. The very essence of his life is the service of truth.

—Franz Boas, Letter to *The Nation*, December 20, 1919

[I]t is according to the dictate of time and fate that we have resolved to pave the way for a grand peace for all the generations to come by enduring the unendurable and suffering what is insufferable.

—Hirohito, radio broadcast, 15th day of the 8th month of the 20th year of Shōwa (1945)

Not you
Not you
It was not you
We were waiting for

—Dazai Osamu, *Dry Leaves in Spring*, 1946

You only live twice:
Once when you were born,
And once when you look death in the face.

—James Bond, after Bashō, *You Only Live Twice*, Ian Fleming, 1964

Now Ruth be Benedict
whenever she got bored,
she put away the chrysanthemum
and did it with the sword

—limerick, author unknown

Robert turned the pages of the dossier, capturing its contents in mental pictures. He paused on her photograph, the official one on the dust jacket of her book. She liked those blouses frontally lace-frilled. He smiled at the thought: a big white chrysanthemum over her bosom. He meant no disrespect and imagined her stern demeanor curling into a gentle smile. She would understand his joke. She looked matronly, fiery white hair swept back into that French bun. She was aging, but in a divine way. The photograph was not flattering, did no justice to the beautiful, elegant woman he knew.

Across the desk, K sat back in his chair and puffed languidly. *You know her, of course.*

Yes, sir, I worked as her assistant in D.C.

She's gone missing. Last seen—K snuffed out his cigarette. *Well, frankly, hard to say. Hiroshima? There are conflicting reports.*

Sir, I wasn't aware she was in Japan.

She hasn't contacted you?

No, sir. She might not know I am here too.

Your last contact with her?

Just a letter, sent in the States, at the time of the bombing, back in August forty-five. Robert recalled the letter, her careful handwriting and precise words. *Dignity and virtue in defeat.* She'd addressed him: *Bob.*

K turned to a stack of papers, indicating the meeting was at an end. *Go find her.*

Sir?

Avoid an incident. No headlines. K sneered. *"Prominent anthropologist kidnapped." "Suicide." "Murdered." "Cavorts with the left." "Apologist for Soviets." "Saves the Emperor." None of that nonsense. I don't care. Just get her out of Japan.*

Mission impossible, Robert remarked, under his breath.

What?

Nothing, sir.

K rose, stood to his full height, which was not that tall but taller than Robert. *Look, I know your kind. Goddamned lucky to be born in America. Got something to prove? Well, prove it.*

Robert turned and walked out, a voice in his head speaking, *Ya boss, Sakini say you drive a haarudo deelu.* What the hell, giving him a dumb job like this to find a dame. Okay, not just any dame, his former boss. And what could he expect, anyway? They only listened when what he said supported their own ideas. He'd seen it firsthand. The anti-commie China intelligence sector won out over his Japan side. If you could speak Japanese, they sent you to Siberia, well, Okinawa. Didn't want any pro-Japan prejudices to seep into deep policy. Pro-Japan? When was he ever pro-Japan? He'd revealed the underbelly of that society to make it possible to undermine and conquer. And now, with his face, he couldn't pretend not to know, to hide his linguistic skills.

She, on the other hand, hadn't treated him with any preconceptions. Based on his interpretive expertise, she'd published his ideas, and even thanked him publicly. She'd put an *on* on him all right. Maybe she was in trouble. Like K ordered, he just had to find her and get her back to Columbia.

DISAPPEARANCE

What was she doing in Japan? She'd never been, that was true. Finally, it was time to see the place for herself. Test the truth of theory. Turn patterns into reality. If he were her, where would he go? He walked out onto the Ginza, then headed for the station, took the train toward Shinagawa. It was a wild stab in the dark, but if he could start anywhere, he'd start at the temple, Sengaku-ji, pay respects to the forty-seven.

He stumbled on the path between tombstones, cherry blossoms flitting in soft swirls, the scent of incense wafting. The voices of schoolchildren beyond. A monk sweeping the stone path. A figure in kimono moved along the great stone embankment. He thought he saw the back of her head, that French bun of hers. Stupidly he called out. *Doctor? Professor?* Then finally, *Sensei!* The figure turned momentarily, the powdered face angular and provocatively masculine, then scurried away in a shuffle of cloaked silk. A kabuki actor? He ran down the stairs toward the temple, but she was gone. He pranced to the gate, searching down the street and through traffic. He was losing his wits. He checked his watch. He was supposed to meet Tiger.

Tiger was at the bar, alternately talking up the bar mama and staring glumly into his Suntory on ice. *Robert-san, you're late.*

You didn't have to wait.

Tiger nodded to mama, who poured whiskey for Robert.

Got me doing goddamn police work.

I wouldn't take this business too lightly.

Yeah, an important asset. She's a tourist, for god's sake. If she wants to get lost, she gets lost.

She's not lost. Tiger looked forward and said, out of the side of his mouth, *Those guys, in the corner.*

Your ninjas, Robert smirked.

Not mine. They're, Tiger emphasized, *not too smart. We can just switch hats.*

Are you kidding?

No, give me your hat. I know how to act like a Japanese American. Bataa kusai.

Fuck you.

Go take a pee, then leave by the back door. Tiger nodded at mama, who smiled graciously.

Robert shrugged. *Just to humor you.* He left his hat on the bar. *Need to take that piss anyway.*

He could hear Tiger thanking mama in Japanese with an American accent. *Idiot,* he muttered. He sauntered out the back and around the alley to the front. Thought he'd get Tiger to go for ramen or something, keep drinking till the wee hours. In the street, he found four men scattered on the ground in different angles of defeat and bloody pain, two running past him and the last holdout trying to avoid Tiger's kick-punch, turn, and fling routine. Robert grabbed the holdout, flung him into one the of stone lions guarding the bar. *Need some help?*

You took your goddamn time.

I thought you were joking.

There's a train leaving in an hour. Take that one or any one headed for the backside of Japan. Just get out of here.

Where am I going?

Izumo. Don't you know? The sound of sirens broke their bruised twilight. Tiger handed Robert a ticket and slip of paper. *Go, now!*

At Izumo, Robert headed with scattered pilgrims through the torii toward the shrine and looked up at the gigantic straw rope twisting beneath its eves. The thing was unnerving, must weigh several tons. He moved into darker recesses and pulled Tiger's slip of paper from his pocket, inscribed with the kanji 八雲. Yakumo. He chuckled. No doubt for Lafcadio. Code word? Tiger's dumb spy joke. He supposed the contact would find him anyway. He walked the immense grounds toward the mountains, toward the safety and danger of shadows, gravel paths leading to small shrines, leading to nowhere. He knew he was being watched. The Japanese had eyes in the back of their heads. Be patient, he thought. The day went on like that. He bought an ema, one of those wood plaques, took out a pen, wrote: *Ruth, where are you*? and strung up the wood talisman with hundreds of others. Couldn't hurt. Again, he thought, *Think like her, in patterns.*

Lafcadio had lived up the coast in Matsue. Why not? He took the local electric, skirting Lake Shinji, chugging stop by stop to the castle. The house was preserved in the old samurai district, on the north side just outside the moat. These spring days were cool, but he was in a sweat, walking from the station. He observed the cloistered wood-and-tiled wall surrounding the house in irritation. He was tired. Hungry. From the house emerged a figure in kimono, that same strange woman of the French bun. This time he said, *Lafcadio-san?* The figure continued away. *Hearn-sensei?* He watched the pigeon-toed gait slacken, then hasten. Exasperated he called, demanded, *Yakumo.*

She turned, feigning curiosity. *You've been following me.*

He stared at her undefined white-powdered androgyny, confounded.

I am not what you think. She looked away. *You must be tired, hungry. Please,* she ushered him to walk ahead. *There's a ryokan a short distance from here. An old samurai house, converted.*

Robert groaned. He wanted to kill Tiger, but he walked forward, glancing back at each crossroad for direction from Yakumo, who pigeontoed behind. Damn nuisance. And yet.

There were all the amenities of the ryokan—bath, massage, yukata, ten-course dinner in a private tatami room overlooking the garden, and Yakumo, who came in and out in an apron, sleeves tied back, kneeling to serve the dishes, pouring tea and sake. Cup after cup. He drank, bemused at his descent into antiquity. But then he spoke. *Will you stop?*

Yakumo looked confused.

He sat up straight. *Cut the crap. You speak perfect English.*

And perfect Japanese as well.

So do I. He barked. *The disguise is unnecessary. I mean you're obvious. Where is she? Have you disguised her too?*

Yakumo pursed her lips. *The person who is disguised, Robert-san, is you.* This time she poured him a glass of whiskey on ice, took a sip herself, then handed it to him coyly.

He looked into the garden, floral at this time of year, the clatter of the bamboo cup on stone, spilling water into the koi pond. Alcohol rocked his brain, a boat floating out to sea. Yakumo seemed to be speaking in Zen koans. The nonsense about one hand clapping, that sort of mind puzzle. Her lips opined, *Ephemeral. Impermanent. Transient. Vanishing.* Life is a dream. The next morning, Robert woke naked, the warm impression of Yakumo lingering, moist and sweet. She was gone.

On the pillow she'd left the book *Botchan.* A maple leaf marked the page.

It was that same page he'd had to dissect for Ruth, about a debt of one-and-a-half sen for a dish of fruit ice. He remembered muddling over it sentence by sentence, pulling apart the meaning of obligation, differentiated between superiors, equals, inferiors. Rising from the bedding, his sensations were tortured yet fulfilled. Did it matter, the terms of their exchange? He packed the book with his belongings, left for the station, and plotted a train and ferry route to the southern islands.

When he arrived in Suyematsu, he took out the *Botchan* like it was a travel guide and asked about the inn, Yamashiroya. Turned out there was a Yamashiroya. Maybe she was right. Fiction is truth. The innkeeper even turned out to be erudite, speaking English with a British accent. *You will, I hope, enjoy the simplicity of our life here, as compared to your no doubt Dickensian existence in Tokyo.*

Dickensian? It's us, the Americans, who now occupy Tokyo.

Indeed. My observations are dated, but they are of movements, not time.

Obviously you've traveled.

And returned. Tea? Our local brew. He poured from a distance to create a performative cascade and to cool the pot's contents as it spilled into porcelain. *You have missed her.*

Excuse me?

A very elegant and pleasant American woman. I am fond of such intelligent women. They are much less arrogant than your gentlemen, present company not included. He eyed Robert, assessing his discomfort while enacting an ingratiating intimacy. *I believe you understand my meaning. On the one hand, pure white inherited arrogance; on the other, the copycat yellow fop. We, however, are liminal in these matters.*

Robert shifted on the cushion and sipped the tea bitterly. *Speak for yourself.*

The innkeeper continued as if oblivious. *We enjoyed many intense arguments, or rather, shall I say, riveting conversations.*

Where did she go?

She taught me a very interesting idea, that we are a culture of shame, whereas the West is of the persuasion of guilt. A perfect binary. East and West so succinctly defined. What do you think of that?

Robert closed his eyes, experiencing a momentary mind-plummet, a mind previously vacated, vacuumed clean. Was it his fault? He feigned, *I have no idea. That woman, she's my friend, and I need to find her.*

We also had an enlightening conversation on "The Lady of Shalott," *with whom I surmise your friend identifies. Living in a high tower of mirrors, condemned to weave beautiful silk patterns, until one day the mirrored figure of her lover is insufficient. Finally looking at his real knightly figure passing breaks her spell, and she dies.*

Robert saw the innkeeper's brows bounce. *Robert-san.* His voice changed. *You must leave now. There is a passage through the bath to the street. You will find my rickshaw. Go now, quietly but quickly.*

Robert slid open the bath doors and, surprising a flurry of women, young and old, in various stages of soap, shampoo, and soaking, ran through naked bodies and steam. Outside, the appointed rickshaw was waiting, the runner's face hidden under a straw hat. He jumped on, and they sped away at a magnificent trot. Robert looked back, and sure enough they were being chased by a bunch of rickshaws. His rickshaw swerved into a side street and out another. Sometimes the clever runner slipped into an alley, and they watched the others charge by, only to find themselves followed when they emerged. They were going in circles. The village was a touristic labyrinth, villagers scattering, fish and tofu peddlers, baskets of daikon and cherries, mothers with children tied to their backs, old men playing go and drinking tea, farmers planting rice. Along the cliffside road, one last rickshaw managed to keep up. Side by side, they raced like chariots. The rider spit a knife into Robert's seat, but, closing in, Robert managed to grab the enemy runner by his collar and pull him down into the road. The rickshaw, having lost its running engine, plummeted off the cliff. They charged down the hill to the seaside dock. A boat was waiting. Robert got off and faced his able runner, drenched in sweat, his kimono pasted but open to his incredibly muscular chest. The man pulled off his straw hat and heaved vomit into the sea.

Tiger!

Goddamn you, Robert. Tiger sputtered, but looking up, they saw the team of rickshaws still approaching. *Get in!* He loosed the rope and shoved the boat forward.

Robert yelled, *This boat better have a real engine.*

What do you know about real engines, you goddamned pansy.

They sped away.

Where are we going?

We found her. She's captive on Hashima. They call it suicide island.

Tiger's ninja met them at sea, their innocuous fishing boats tossing out nets and pulling up nets of copious catch. The plan was that Tiger and the ninja army would scale the fortress walls, but Robert would approach through the front door.

What's the front door to an island? Robert quipped.

Tiger sneered. *You're the decoy. You figure it out.*

Robert pointed at the ominous island, a gigantic tanker emerging from the ocean. *What is that place?*

It's actually the entrance to an abandoned coal mine. Hundreds of Chinese and Korean coolies are buried in its bowels beneath the sea, died producing raw material for the empire. Industrial gravesite.

Why can't we just bomb the hell out of it?

Spoken like a true American, but I don't do that anymore. After I survived the Tokkatai, I promised never to fly another plane..

Just my luck, I got a failed kamikaze for a sidekick.

Don't complain. I just might save your life again.

Robert was left to commandeer the motor boat around the island the size of Alcatraz until he found a dock, where armed guards with swords stood at attention. When he arrived, they actually bowed and greeted him. *Otsukaresama deshita.*

It's a goddamned tourist trap, he murmured.

A steel door made to appear like an antique screen papered in gold leaf and festooned in chrysanthemums slid open. In the dark portico, holding a paper lantern, there again was Yakumo.

Robert-san, we have been waiting for you. She led him through the tunnel to an elevator that emerged at the top within a lush garden. *You will follow that path.* She indicated stone steps. *And,* she warned, *do not stop to smell or touch the plants.* She put her finger to her lips, a warning.

He wandered through a bamboo forest, then lush almost suffocating vegetation that opened into an exotic fusion of the Japanese and the tropical. He knew enough botany to know that it was all poison. *An acquired taste,* he thought. In one direction, he saw a fortress tower; in the other, a teahouse situated on a promontory overlooking the sea. The emperor of this garden was seated there. He expected to see her as well, but the man sat alone, an ugly white cat in his lap.

The emperor spoke. *Robert-san. Please, have a seat.* He stroked the cat. *Wagahai,* he introduced the feline. *I hope you aren't allergic. I can prevent you from eating from my garden; allergies, however, are another problem.* As if it understood, Wagahai hopped off the emperor's lap and slouched away into the shadows. *Of course, eating poison fruit might be your choice. Westerners be-*

lieve in choosing knowledge, eating apples, for example. Can you imagine, calling this paradise suicide island? Do you not agree that knowledge is suicide?

Where is she?

Somewhere writing poetry, I suspect. I have told her that poetry will not absolve her of her sins. She came here, I believe, to save me, and failed.

Save you?

I am an empty vessel. There was never anything to save. On the other hand, mankind clings to this desire for death.

I didn't come here to discuss philosophy.

Didn't you? After all, you are chasing a phantom, which you yourself have let loose. They say that I am the enemy, pursuing world domination. Let me be very clear: World domination as endgame is always a foil.

Tiger walked up from the garden holding Wagahai, limp over his arm. *I found this dead cat,* he announced. *I think this killed it.* He held up a half-eaten fugu. *Tasty but venomous.*

The emperor rose in horror. Tiger's ninja jumped from trees and out of bushes, over the fortress walls, encountered their counterparts and fought hand to hand, sword to sword, knife to knife. Tiger yelled to Robert. *Go, find her!*

Robert ran toward the tower and scrambled up its spiral staircase, round and round and round. At the top, curtains flapped into the sea breeze. And from that pinnacle, in a dizzy frenzy, he could see Tiger below, lying twisted in a deep pool of blood.

OCCUPATION

Returning to Tokyo, Robert turned the key and stepped into his apartment. They called it a mansion, but it was just an apartment, in a building with a view of the skyline, and if it were clear, you might see Fuji between the buildings. Normally it was a mess, but it had been tidied up. The dishes in the sink were gone. The bedding stored. The trash removed. He set his suitcase down and pulled the pistol from its holster. He could hear water splashing from the tub. He kicked open the door. A woman was cuddled deep in hot water in the square of the tub. She looked at him with disdain. *You know, it's polite to knock before you enter.*

He closed the door, and she emerged in his yukata, her blonde wet hair splashing water on the floor. *You don't have any towels.*

Japanese don't use large towels, just that narrow thing you've got in your hand. You're getting the floors all wet.

She wrapped the narrow towel around her hair and investigated the rooms. *I thought Americans in Japan lived with more privilege. Is it because—*

I'm a nisei? Or I don't have towels.

I was going to say race prejudice is an evil that perpetuates inequality.

Let's just say I'm not at liberty to live like an American.

It's inconvenient?

It's always convenient to be an American.

I mean in Japan.

No, it's always convenient to be an American, he repeated.

I know who you are. What you are, Robert.

Then why are you asking such a dumb question?

I'm sorry, we haven't met properly. I'm Anne. She untied the woven belt at her waist and let the yukata slip to the floor.

He pretended to be unfazed and asked, *What's your story?*

Do you speak French?

No.

Too bad. You won't understand my story. Tu n'es pas mon premier. Mon primeir était chinois. J'avais quinze ans, sur un ferry traversant le Mékong. Mon deuxième, Eiji, un architect d'Hiroshima. You are from Hiroshima, isn't that so?

He didn't reply. He was only educated there. Well, he thought, force-educated from the age of ten. A cultural half-breed. His folks, everyone, all dead.

Like me, you are an orphan. We make good spies.

Why should I trust you?

Don't worry. I'm not interested in your race. Only your culture. The finesse and intricacies of your rituals, the patterns you perform without thinking.

What the hell, he kissed her.

You and I are broken people, fragments of a lost past. Spies like us are necessary to put the puzzle back together again.

There will be missing pieces.

The important thing is to imagine what is not there.

Maybe it happened. Maybe not. Goddamn wet dream. He sat in the same bar staring at the same mama, sitting in the same seat. But Tiger wasn't there looking over his shoulder. The first glass of Suntory was for Tiger. The second for himself. And the third and so forth.

They came in and sat on either side, Osamu to the right, Stormy to the left. Stormy jiggled the ice in his glass. *K says you need to come in from the cold.*

It's summer, if you haven't noticed. I hate this heat. I hate this place.

Then, you should go home.

Where is home?

Stormy sank into the bar on his elbow. *Ever tell you about my pop? Smoked a cigar, had one of those mustaches, wore a sombrero, spoke Mexican, drank Mexican beer and tequila, but he was Japanese through and through. Used to get drunk and tell stories about Pancho Villa, how he and his buddies were sent in by General Pershing to kill the old bandito.*

Viva la revolución! Robert toasted the air.

When we got sent to camp, Pop was enraged, said he'd sacrificed for the U.S. of A. and they couldn't do that to us.

Yeah, but they did.

I always thought he was just making it up, but he could recount every detail, down to Villa's nose hair. He wasn't lying. Thing is, just like my pop, nobody will believe what we're doing here, and they're never going to know.

And given the chance, they'll put us in camp again.

Right. End of story.

Tell K I'm not coming in. I'm going to find her.

Dead or alive?

Dead or alive. They're using her.

To fuck with us?

Osamu lifted his head from the bar, and the two nisei deigned to acknowledge him.

Where'd he come from? Robert sniffed.

I am ninja. Disappear. Appear. Osamu ordered a Coke, pointed his glass at Robert's, and said, *That stuff will kill your liver. You should try opium.*

Maybe I will.

I have a contact. Crybaby, you. Osamu pointed at Robert. *You need to get laid.*

Maybe I have.

Stormy swiveled back into the conversation. *Look, Robert, forget her. Help me out with my thing. It's real, not imaginary. There's this old zaibatsu cat tied up with pre-indoctrinated kamikaze turned black market yakuza. I'm in there like a trained dog. They're going to stage a strike to rile up the commies. It's twofold, I figure: one, force a bigger war at the DMZ, and two, use the chaos to create distraction to slip out a shipment. Way I figure, they're working both sides, selling guns to everyone.*

Osamu snarled. *It must be an inside job. Black market. Guns and missiles, either American or Russian. Swapping spit.* He puckered his lips. *Kiss kiss.*

Robert quipped, *He's a cynical bitch.* He stood up to leave, grabbing Osamu's arm. *But*—he turned to Stormy—*I'll take him over you.*

Stormy lifted his glass. *Same difference.*

Osamu slumped into the seat next to the window. Then he opened the window and shouted to a peddler with a cart, ordered two bowls of noodles and pulled them into the train. He handed a bowl and chopsticks to Robert. *You need a holiday.*

Robert didn't ask where they were going, didn't care. Slurped the noodles and drained the broth.

Osamu looked up from his bowl and asked, *So how was she?*

She?

Miss Singleton. Anne.

Crissake!

She's a friend, you know. She reads my work. I read her poetry. Smoke and mirrors, I think. That's the spy stuff. Then wind and water. If I could psychoanalyze it, I say it's a feminine desire for freedom, about which, incidentally, I myself have written.

You turned her into one of your Japanese characters?

No, she turned herself into a Japanese character. Do you think the desire for freedom is exclusive to Westerners?

They changed trains at Atami, and from there got on and off the local trains to the end of the peninsula. At every stop, Osamu knew a bar, a brothel, all lousy with artists and writers of his ilk, dissident intellectuals, impoverished aristocrats, bohemian dandies, dissolute, lost, weary, opinionated, and eager to tell Robert the truth

Robert-san, we are no longer a culture of war. We have reinvented ourselves as a culture of peace. We had to self-destruct to do so, but ka-boom!

Osamu unskewered a mushroom from his teppan stick and dumped it into Robert's drink.

Or

Robert-san, de-mo-ku-ra-shi has failed. The true path—justice, purity, love—to rid us of the old Japan is through the people. Those who hinder societal progress must die.

Osamu agreed. *It's true. My life is insignificant. Useless, but*—he rose drunkenly. *I will entertain you.* He danced. They clapped and sang.

Or

Robert-san, some have nostalgia for war. Others for peace. But this nostalgia

is corrupted by beauty. Beautiful war. Beautiful peace. No one really believes in either any longer. Both signify death.

Osamu pulled out his pipe, lit it. A spark, then fumes wafting.

Or

Robert-san, we went to war for economic reasons. An island with no resources, cut off from all means to a modern industrial revolution. A little island country with nothing but guts. Like England. Of course, it was okay for them to colonize the world. Then, when it is all said and done, all they want to talk about is our guts, and we spilled them all over this archipelago. Now we eat our guts because that's who we've become. Fucking nonsense.

Osamu puffed languidly.

Or

Robert-san, they say we are a modern society delegated by a feudal system of duty and obligation. What do you think?

Osamu stretched out on the tatami, soon asleep and snoring.

Or

Robert-san, my family was not samurai. But you think we are all samurai. Japanese culture equals bushido. If you want us to be samurai, we can be samurai. You can turn us into anything you want. But everything, everyone has a price. These days, who is not taking bribes? Getting rich off our defeat? What is the difference? Co-prosperity or Pax Americana? Fascism or McCarthyism? To be clear, Robert-san, world domination as endgame is always a foil.

Robert grabbed Osamu and jerked him up. They wobbled out, clinging to each other, laughing, euphoric hysteria. It went on and on, station to station, bar to bar, house to house, increasingly inebriated, then depressed, an ignominious descent into a dissipated hell.

Finally, they were dumped in the sand and slept until the tide washed in. They awoke, their bodies swishing like dead fish in spume and tangled seaweed. Flotsam. Jetsam.

Stormy arrived steering a convertible Buick, wheel on the left side. It was too big for the roads, but it was the only car he could requisition. Somewhere on the way back to Tokyo, head flopped back into his own vomit, Robert opened one eye to see in the rearview Stormy's indifferent eyes behind aviators.

Robert felt the cold towel on his forehead. She was there again. *These little towels are actually very versatile.* She said this as if it were a notation in a dissertation. He pulled the towel away and saw her smile.

Stormy and Osamu were out on the balcony smoking. Stormy with a cigarette and Osamu with his pipe. They looked on in amusement. Osamu said, *I should have gotten really drunk. He gets all the attention.*

Stormy remarked, *Not very good at pretending.*

An intellectual romp with the underbelly of society. What we have become? Osamu shook his head, twirled his pipe at Robert. *Crybaby.*

Stormy said more positively, *So, gentlemen, we made contact.*

Robert lifted his head and groaned. *We did?*

Osamu proffered his pipe. *It was that guy. He likes to say his family is not samurai. My family comes from royalty. Pure blood. That's why I'm no good. But he's still got a chip on his shoulder. You wouldn't know it, but he's a dangerous genius.*

I don't remember.

I myself am just a genius.

Obviously.

He runs an underground subway system.

Stormy snubbed out his cigarette. *We're going to blow it up.*

Another labyrinth, this time beneath the streets. Decked out in workers' suits and goggles, they slipped through a sewage portal. *This is not the underbelly I'm used to,* Osamu grumbled.

Stormy returned, *Same difference.*

Robert looked down the long tunnel and thought he saw a figure, pulled up his forehead to catch a glimpse with his headlamp. The eyes of a cat?

Stormy motioned. *This way.* Like he'd said, he was in like a trained dog, sniffed his way to the abandoned platform. *Just wait.* He looked at his watch. *It should be here on time.* When the train arrived, the doors parted and henchmen all dressed just like them in suits and goggles stood waiting, nodded them in.

The thought passed through Robert's mind, as if she were speaking amiably into his ear. *Uniforms are important to belonging.*

They marched through the moving train, pressing the bombs in their appointed hiding places. Arriving at the caboose, the last henchman got curious. "Hold on," he yelled. "Who are you guys?" It wasn't easy fighting in those suits. It was knives and guns and hand-to-hand. Inside the train, outside the train, on top of the train, men crawling all over the speeding convoy like giant gutter roaches, jammed between cars and doors, blood splattering over dank tunnel walls. Robert ran after Stormy, knocking off the guys in his wake, Osama knocking off the rest. At the very end of the train, Stormy yelled, *Jump!* Robert jumped. They sat in the tracks like two broken twigs, caught sight of Osamu at the end of the caboose with the bomb timer in his hands. Billowing flames and smoke ignited the dark tunnel.

On the platform, he saw a figure running up stairs, away. *Anne!* He yelled. Then he recognized the French bun at the back of her head, hairpins flying, white hair cascading.

REINVENTION

Stormy downed a tequila shot followed by beer. *Kirin,* he surmised, looking at his glass. *It will have to do.*

Robert had the same. It was the same mama and the same bar. *I'd take a puff of opium for Osamu, but I lost his contact.*

Most of the time, he was only pretending. Stormy downed another shot.

I thought he was a high-functioning addict.

Aren't we all?

I saw her.

Give it up, Robert. I'm done with this. I'm going home to become an honest Christian. Make the world a better place.

Here's to your future, toasted Robert.

To yours. Stormy set down his glass, tipped his hat, and walked away.

A woman with a bob, perfectly cut bangs, slipped onto Stormy's emptied stool. *Robert-san, you don't remember me?*

Please refresh my memory.

I'm a friend of Osamu.

To be honest, I can't remember anything I've ever done in his company.

We can start again. I am Yayoi.

Osamu is dead.

Yes. She pulled an object from her sleeve. *I have his pipe.*

He took the pipe and examined it.

It's not what it seems. Here. She pointed to a tiny microphone. *I designed it myself. It can also afford you some pleasure.*

You're one of his artist friends.

I am. I believe you will require my expertise.

Yayoi accompanied Robert on the Shinkansen to Hiroshima. She made him sit on the left side and nudged him from sleep to view Fuji blip past.

During the trip, she pulled out pre-sewn cloth pieces of what looked like misshapen tubes. She had an entire bag of them. She stuffed them with cotton batting and sewed each one shut. She pointed one at Robert. *What do you think this is?*

Robert shrugged. He didn't want to admit that it looked like a penis. *I hope that's not your idea of a weapon.*

But it is. She flipped it into a bag with others. *Don't worry. I have something useful for your mission. It fits in your pocket.*

The train seemed to squeeze silently into Hiroshima. He hadn't returned until that moment, hadn't cared to see it or whatever it had become ever again. But it was his last chance to find her.

Yayoi adjusted her backpack, stuffed but in fact very light. She tucked a small package into a pocket hidden in his jacket. *I call this little gadget Infinity. Don't use it until it's absolutely necessary.*

What does it do?

Creates infinity. Infinity will protect you. She patted his jacket and smiled. *Okonomiyaki,* she suggested. *But you are from Hiroshima, so you know. I will leave you now.*

He watched her trudge away with her squished phallus multitude and searched obediently for an okonomiyaki-ya. The station had spit him into his old haunts, but he had to reimagine the old streets, vaporized then quickly replaced by this—what did it look like to him? Chinatown.

Robert looked through the window at the hot grill, the swirling splash of egg batter, the perfectly executed and timed ritual, mesmerized by the toss of shaved fish flakes, a flutter dance in heat, their faint and delicate throe of death. His gaze moved from the skilled hands to the face of the cook. She was staring back at him. Smitten, he rushed into the shop, breathless. Pulling the cotton kerchief from her head, she spoke with sweet villainy. *Robert-san.*

She had the most ridiculous name, an Occupation holdover he assumed, Kissy, or was it Kitty? He couldn't say it, so he never did.

The next day they took a kayak into the bay, found a deserted island except for wild pigs wading in the clear aquamarine surf. They fed the pigs bananas and searched for shells. They made love in the shallows, tiny translucent fish flitting. The day after, she met him with a junk, which they sailed farther out, circling pillars of limestone in dragon formations, then set anchor and swam in and out of grottoes and caves, made more love in deep shadows. The third day, she hired a half-submerged mini-sub. It couldn't really dive, but it had a glass bottom, and it was fast. Yellow. Robert thought, *Why not?*

The fourth day never came. They witnessed everything from the tossing yellow bug. That great titan of dinosaurs emerged in a tsunami from the bay, screeching, roaring flames, torching the city. It ripped out the great torii at Utsukushima, discarding it on land, and crushed the atomic dome with one big giant leap for mankind.

My ex, Kissy gasped. *Only he can save us.*

You've got an ex?

This is his sub. He let me keep it.

Kissy's ex turned out to be Dr. Noppie. They sped off to his hideout in a dead volcano.

They found the doctor in his lab, white coat using a microscope with his good eye. The other eye was covered with an eyepatch. His hair, too jet-black to be natural, was disheveled, spiked in all directions. He continued to stare down into the scope, their presence an annoyance. *You want me to destroy that monster?* He laughed. *Why should I save your puny race?*

Because we're the same race?

Speak for yourself, Robert-san. Let's talk about you.

Let's not.

Oh let's. The doctor finally looked up, offered Robert a lab chair. *They have you chasing chimeras, don't they? But you are just a convenient bridge over which they cross with impunity. Over there.* He pointed east. *Over here.* He pointed west. *Back and forth.*

Kissy interrupted. *Noppie, we don't have much time.*

We have all the time in the world. He sneered. *That is, if I am the true enemy. Let me be very clear. World domination as endgame is always a foil.*

Robert looked at Kissy, agitated.

The doctor demurred, *Well, if you insist. My machine is a thousand times more destructive than that monster or the atomic bomb that seduced it from sleep. I've been looking for an opportunity to test it.*

It came to Robert in a slow-motion brain flash. Wasn't the first weapon the first mistake? *No, I've changed my mind.*

The doctor walked to a panel and pressed a red button. *Oh, too late. At precisely zero eight sixteen and two seconds—*

Robert grabbed Kissy's hand, walked briskly to the door, but not before reaching into his jacket pocket. He ripped out Yayoi's gadget, tossed it back.

They ran. Behind: an infinity of mirrors within mirrors exploding, a multiplying kaleidoscope reproducing itself exponentially. Tossed into a sea of pyrotechnics, he felt Kissy's body go limp, float. He saw her skin peeling from her lovely features, her keloid maidenhood revealed, sputtering electronic wiring. Her brain was an array of chips. He traced and caressed them, searching for an algorithm, but the system sank into a mercurial mire, the faintest reflection of her familiar face slipping into oblivion.

NOBUYA: Invisible Man

I phoned the UCLA Asian American studies bibliographer, a consultation about my research. In our conversation, she apologized to say she could make no promises to meet me as she was busy flying between Los Angeles and New York, collecting Yuri's archive. She explained that Yuri had suffered a stroke, was recuperating, though alone in her apartment. Her granddaughter looked in on her; her sons and daughter in California hoped she would move, but she refused to leave Harlem.

My acquaintance with Yuri had been a brief afternoon thirty-five years ago, but the bibliographer assumed that if I were in New York I could look in on her, see if she needed anything. Groceries, trip to the doctor, help around the house, mailing, accompany her to meetings. My research had nothing to do with Yuri, but something compelled me to consider reliving what was my first visit to the United States. A visit that changed my life. I didn't think she would remember me; after all, my acquaintance with her was a brief afternoon thirty-five years ago. But I discovered that Yuri wanted to remember everyone.

545 West 126th Street, Broadway and Harlem. Apartment 3-B. I knocked on the door, surprised to find it slightly ajar. *Hello? Hello?*—and entered to face a long corridor, entries and doorways to either side. Was it the same? I tried to recall. To the left, the kitchen. To the right, the living room. I set my backpack down, slipped from my shoes, and walked in stocking feet down the hall. Family photographs and political posters covered every inch of wall. I peered into an open door—next to the bed, a walker with tennis-ball feet, and huddled under the covers, the small lump of person, sleeping.

Slipping away, I continued my sleuthing. In one room, piles of papers, books, albums, posters, correspondence, manila folders, and memorabilia covered the floor and tables. The organized chaos the bibliographer had described—metal file cabinets and boxes lining the walls; in the far corner, printer and fax machine. A broom and dustpan against the wall. Why not? Moving in and around and under the stuff and furniture, I swept exposed parts of floor. From room to room, collecting a small pile of debris. Congregated trash from cans into a single plastic bag.

In the living room, an ironing board had apparently become permanent decor, for at its square end was a dial telephone and spiral notebook, every caller, time, date, and phone number carefully inscribed. I sank into the sofa, rearranging the crocheted cushions and a multitude of stuffed bears surrounding, tried to recall that room crowded with people. Had it been this small? That day, moving between Japanese and English, interpreting questions and answers—polite, tentative, respectful, curious talk, I was too overwhelmed to notice. Beneath stockinged feet, dark wood floors, burnish of use, scuff of wear.

I wandered into the kitchen. The table seemed familiar—vintage fifties, vinyl cushioned chairs styled over chrome. On its Formica top, envelopes, sheets of U.S. postage stamps, more spiral notebooks and Rolodex noted meticulously with names, addresses, and mailing dates; a letter in process with anticipating pen. No, mustn't touch anything here. The envelopes were already addressed, to person after person in such-and-such correctional facility or state prison. She was an inveterate letter writer; no one in prison should be left alone or forgotten.

Jammed over kitchen counters, the usual condiments, medicines, cereals, snacks, peanut butter and jelly, fruit, coffee maker, radio. I snatched paper towels, found a bottle of Windex under the counter, swished and wiped over and under everything. Moving to the sink, I picked up the sponge, pooped a dab of dish soap, got the water up to temperature and washed the dishes, left them clean in the dishrack. Then, I scrubbed around a pot of soup cold on the stove. Sounds from the street. Voices. Play. Inside, the silence of sleep.

If counted in every guestbook, hundreds of people of every creed and politics had been invited into this home from 1960 until that moment, had entered this home of a family of eight. They had crowded into the small kitchen and every crevice—ate, drank, played, argued, pontificated, created, strategized, plotted, spied, acted out, recovered, got on their feet, found solace, hung out, took advantage, slept, laughed, hugged, loved, wept, howled—yes, the list was even longer, but simply told, they had lived in messy revolutionary times.

I filled the kettle with water and set it on the stove to boil. Chose a mug from the rack—WORLD'S GREATEST DAD—dipped and lifted the teabag. Crossing back to the living room, mug and dust cloth in hand, I scanned the walls with framed photographs. Stopped to study a small black-and-white photo, my own name typed in the caption, followed by the parenthetical title: interpreter. I paused on the youthful faces of the Writer and the Reporter, and standing behind, taller by a full head, the man of honor on that day. I gripped the mug, hugging its warm ceramic to my chest. A tiny splash of hot tea whipped up onto my shirt; beneath, a drop of skin burned.

On the ironing board, she'd left a stack of scrapbooks, a yellow sticky note on top with my name. I set down the mug, wiped a thin film of dust from the album's cover. The subtle must of degrading paper fluttered from each page; I turned them, one by one.

I believe it best to begin with events that anticipated that day, but where to begin? Would it be August 6, 1945, at 8:15 in the morning, the date and time the atomic bomb dropped on Hiroshima? It was also the date of my own birth, a fact, as it seemed inauspicious, I did not care to share. John Hersey wrote the stories of six survivors, one of them Reverend Kiyoshi Tanimoto. The continuation is that Shigeko Niimoto came to ask Reverend Tanimoto if he would support her and a few young hibakusha women. Girls at the time of bomb, their faces and bodies disfigured, they craved common community but were uncomfortable sharing their stories with outsiders and men. Eventually their group included the twenty-five who arrived in New York City on May 9, 1955, for reconstructive and plastic surgery at Mount Sinai Hospital. How and who created the moniker, I have often wondered, but Shigeko and her companions became the Hiroshima Maidens.

Over their year-and-a-half-long stay, the young women were housed in Quaker homes with the support of philanthropists, among them Norman Cousins, editor at the *Saturday Review*. Along with the American Friends, they received support from organizations such as JICUF, the Japan International Christian University Foundation, and the New York NSO, Nisei Service Organization, largely veterans of the 442nd Regimental Combat Team. Yuri's husband, Bill, worked for the JICUF and helped found the NSO, so this was how their family became involved in supporting the maidens. In numerous letters, Yuri is thanked for her visits, for bringing Japanese food and gifts. She must have also remembered birthdays and festival days. The family Christmas newsletter the following year reported that the 442nd veterans sponsored a ball in their honor, inviting maidens to dance. THE HIROSHIMA SEQUEL: SCARS DIMINISH AS LOVE MUSHROOMS.

On May 11, 1955, Reverend Tanimoto appeared on national television, an NBC show hosted by Ralph Edwards, *This Is Your Life*. At the time, I was only nine years old in Tokyo, but years later, I watched footage of Edwards turning the pages of Tanimoto's life, from witnessing and surviving the bomb to sacrificing his life to serve his Nagaragawa congregation of Hiroshima hibakusha. Two maidens revealed in silhouette behind a gauze curtain, followed onstage by his American missionary teacher, his college friend at Emory, the copilot of the *Enola Gay* who dropped Little Boy over Hiroshima, and finally, to complete a happy picture, Tanimoto's wife and three children. Who in America had not watched this early version of reality TV? In the distance of time, I confess, witnessing Tanimoto's life as spectacle churned nausea within me, but no doubt he understood that show as part of his commitment to peace.

In 1959, Shigeko Niimoto returned from Hiroshima as the adopted daughter of Norman Cousins, and in the same year, the NSO regaled her as Queen of the 442nd at their annual dance. NO MORE HIROSHIMAS. Two years later, at Shigeko's entreating, Yuri and Bill added a ten-year-old Japanese boy to their brood of six children. Hiroshi, a burn victim receiving a series of ten reconstructive surgeries from the same doctors at Mount Sinai, lived with the family for a year. This was the year after the move from midtown to Harlem, to this more spacious apartment in the Manhattanville project.

Harlem: home to Black art and culture, the Renaissance itself, political, historic, and social center of civil rights and resistance; it was impossible not to be stirred by its activism, revolution. By 1963, Yuri had joined the Harlem Parents Committee and participated with her children in the Freedom School, just across the street and a block down. Here she read W. E. B. Du Bois and Frantz Fanon, got schooled in Black history. She befriended Freedom Rider James Peck and joined the campaign to elect African American Progressive Labor Party candidate Bill Epton to the New York State Senate. And in July, she joined CORE, the Congress of Racial Equality, to protest unfair labor practices at the Downstate Medical Center in Brooklyn, disrupting construction to force the hire of Black and Puerto Rican workers. She and her teenage son were arrested when they laid their bodies down to block construction vehicles. In August, following the March on Washington, the family boarded a train to Birmingham to visit churches, lunch counters, meeting places, the city where Martin Luther King Jr. wrote his famous letter from jail. A week after their visit in September, the 16th Street Baptist Church was bombed, killing four girls. On October 16, at the courthouse trial of Downstate protestors, Yuri met Malcolm X, an encounter and date she would never forget. In November, John F. Kennedy was assassinated in Dallas, Texas, and Malcolm X made his controversial statement that "the chickens had come home to roost." That year, the family announced they would not celebrate Christmas. In a matter of three years, Yuri and her family had fully joined their lives to the Harlem community and its movements.

Yuri's scrapbooks recorded this family history and transformation in newspaper clippings, photographs, letters, postcards, newsletters. I turned the pages of a story that preceded and made possible my visit to this home in 1964.

I stood up again to look at the photograph on the wall, wiping the glass carefully. The date: June 6, 1964. I stared at my face nearing twenty, its softness, an almost dreamy quality. I was too young to understand the significance of that day. Even much later when I discerned its meaning, I did not feel comfortable inserting myself into that story. I had been an observer; I was occupying a role, but thinking back, it was more complicated.

The Writer wore a printed shirt, the rest of us formally white-shirted in suits with thin ties. They were my sempai elders by at least ten years. My small power was that I spoke English fluently and had been in New York already one month. I saw that the Writer's brows were slightly pinched, his demeanor serious; he looked away from the camera, other images in his vision. The Reporter, on the other hand, wore a shy smile. The photographer was Yuri herself. I suppose the Reporter tried to accommodate her cajoling. I think it was a simple Kodak Brownie. She had to wind the film forward and might have even said *cheese*. But none of us showed teeth, all our thoughts held closely within captured surfaces. Now it occurred to me a kind of curated serendipity that Yuri in this apartment in Harlem made this photograph possible.

I had arrived in New York that summer on an internship at the JICUF. As I said, Yuri's husband Bill worked at JICUF, and I had just graduated from ICU, International Christian University in Tokyo, and this would be my first trip beyond Japan. That summer I lived in a dorm at Columbia, just a few blocks' walk to the foundation. My job was to translate correspondence and eventually to interpret for visitors, Japanese to English or English to Japanese, depending on the circumstances. My schedule was not fixed, and I was encouraged to explore the city, to learn the subway system, to find my way to museums and tourist attractions such as the Statue of Liberty or the Empire State Building. Eventually, I would be asked to take visitors to these sites and to explain their historic significance. I had to learn everything quickly, become an expert, as if a real New Yorker. True, my English was exceptional, and I'd even become somewhat adept at American slang and colloquialism. I admit I read a lot of comics in those days. But I'd never employed my skills outside my university, outside Japan, and there was the matter of accent. For some reason, my professors and supervisors assumed that my language competence was all that was required to navigate life in America.

Nine years had passed since the visit of the Hiroshima Maidens. This year, the Writer and the Reporter were among twenty-five chosen for the Nagasaki-Hiroshima World Peace Study Mission. On the day of the bomb, they were little boys who survived. Now they joined a mixed group of hibakusha, among them teachers, doctors, housewives, labor unionists, and students, under the leadership of Dr. Takuo Matsumoto, who was, at the time of the bomb, head of the Hiroshima Girls School. Many in the delegation wore visible signs of disfigurement; they bore their status as bomb survivors with varying degrees of defiance and quiet dignity. Proposing a global tour of 150 cities, their stated purpose was to study peace, to exchange stories, to stop the proliferation of nuclear weapons. They were the living survivors of a cautionary tale. Setting out from Tokyo in April 1964, they would cross the American continent, then go on to Europe, the Soviet Union, and China, circling the globe. The mission listed sponsorship with names such as Norman Cousins, Bertrand Russell, John D. Rockefeller IV, Reinhold Niebuhr, David Riesman, and James A. Pike.

That spring, the New York World's Fair opened in Flushing Meadows in Queens, with 140 pavilions, an international array of exhibits and restaurants, spectacular water fountains, and an amusement park. Its theme: Peace Through Understanding. It was my job to usher our guests into the fair, especially to the Japanese Pavilion, where we could see the country's return to industrial capitalism, its exhibition of space rockets, high-speed cameras, automated ships, and an Electronic Travel Brain operating over a large map of the world, then transition through a sublime garden with kimono-clad women and a demonstration of flower arranging in a traditional Japanese house. I mention this because, days later, we were invited by our organizers to also tour the World's Worst Fair, a response to that extravagant future unavailable to Harlemites. There we were guided through a rat-infested tenement house with backed-up toilets, broken windows, crumbling staircases, frayed electrical wiring, representative of impoverished and substandard living conditions right here in the U.S. of America. I understood my job was to interpret only, but I wondered what went through the minds of my Japanese charges, hibakusha whose lives had been irrevocably destroyed, for whom inhuman conditions, technology, and serenity had incomparable meanings.

I don't recall how many were in the peace delegation that day. The twenty-five had been divided into groups to take separate trips to other cities. That was how the mission would accomplish its promise to visit 150 cities. There was another interpreter, a young woman, also from ICU assigned to our group. She and I were the interpretive pair; she attending the women; I the men.

From the Harlem fair, we walked to Yuri's apartment in these Manhattanville projects, six twenty-story pinwheel-shaped buildings, public housing to replace four blocks of tenement slums, built in 1961. They were brick-faced mega-structures set in tree-lined green spaces with wide walkways. In 1964, the apartment was new, considered modern and international, more spacious than what I knew in Tokyo. We took an elevator up three floors and were greeted by Yuri and a large crowd, racially mixed, who'd organized this day for us—Harlem parents, Freedom School teachers, CORE members, Christian peace activists, Japanese American veterans. They had prepared a program of poetry and songs, and we snuggled together on the sofa and close arrangement of chairs in the living room to listen.

In the middle of this presentation, a knock was heard, and Yuri flew excitedly to the door. A tall, elegant Negro man entered, accompanied by two others. A stricken hush resounded, but then, as he bent to take Yuri's hand, the standing crowd in the hallway and kitchen surged forward, outstretched hands eager to touch, to shake the hand of Malcolm X. To be honest, I did not know who he was, but the Writer leaned toward me, nodded, and he and the Reporter rose to their feet. Ushered toward us by the ebullient Yuri, I introduced each of the mission members as he shook their hands, inevitably matching our bowing gestures.

Malcolm X took center stage and began to speak. I thought I should interpret, but the Writer held up his hand. I understood my interruptions would be rude. I would simply have to recall everything he said. I could see Yuri with a notebook, like a student, writing everything down, but I had no paper, no pad, certainly no recorder. Now I wonder at what we did not bring to that day. I recall a man with a camera, but what became of his photos? Perhaps Yuri's memory and the fuzzy photograph are our only record.

At the end of Malcolm X's speech, there were no questions, only informal chitchat and the meditative absorption of the man's presence. Well, this was probably the case because the hibakusha could only have understood isolated words. What Malcolm X imparted in his talk was our common suffering; even if they did not follow the particulars of his politics, they could understand that much. Offering questions seemed foolish, at best banal. The sensibility that transpired between us could not be translated. Each person stood apart and deferential, respecting their own agendas for lives lived, destinies ordained.

But then, Yuri intervened, recognizing me as the interpreter. *Oh,* she smiled with pleasure, *your English is impeccable.* She asked me to point out the Writer and the Reporter in our midst. *They must meet Malcolm,* she exclaimed, then gathered us together for that photograph. At that moment, awkward words were exchanged, and the Reporter, as if suddenly realizing his responsibility, asked for the record, and I translated, *How do you believe we can achieve world peace?* Malcolm answered at length about the white first world and its stranglehold on third world people of color, that if we were given our freedom, we had no need for war. The Reporter stared up intently, in awe, then listened carefully to my interpretation. The Writer stood by nodding, then talked at me as if into a recorder and said, *In the last war, Yuri was imprisoned in an internment camp in Arkansas while her husband was a soldier in Europe. Nisei like Yuri's husband and Black soldiers fought in segregated units. Now segregation has ended. In this war in Korea, for example. Is this an improvement?* Malcolm seemed impressed with this question and answered, *Just because colored people have the right to fight for democracy doesn't mean they enjoy democracy.* This was my only memory of translating anything of significance between the three men.

What this photograph showed and what it hid: deference to the other hibakusha who would not be photographed. Among Japanese the camera seemed ubiquitous, but among this group, even the Reporter refrained from taking pictures. And I did not ultimately know what he wrote about that day, although certainly he must have sent his reports back to his newspaper in Hiroshima. Similarly, I found no accounts by the Writer. Perhaps it was not so surprising. Yet, still I wondered if somewhere, surely in their journals or correspondence, they must have recorded their impressions of that day, of the yearlong travel, which was only beginning. Perhaps other events along the way occluded their trail, the road stretching forward with hope, the path left behind, like history, something that cannot be undone, only forgotten.

The women gravitated to Yuri and she to Malcolm; I have a memory of his tall benevolence among them. Perhaps their exchanges were more substantive.

Malcolm X left with his entourage, pausing at the threshold to grasp Yuri's hand, her face behind pink cat-eye glasses joyful and earnest. He bent toward her gently. *I promise from now on, I will write to you. I promise.*

We left the apartment, the group separating. The Writer, Reporter, and I headed north and east across St. Nicholas Park down 135th to the jazz club

Small's Paradise. The Reporter, who followed American sports, hoped to catch a glimpse of the owner, the basketball star Wilt Chamberlain, and the Writer wanted to hear jazz played live in Harlem. We sat down for dinner and beers.

The Reporter pulled out a letter from his wife, sent to an address in New York. She was expecting their child. He confessed his anxiety, that the baby might be born before he returned. The Writer urged him to stop worrying. I deduced that this conversation was ongoing. The Reporter stuttered, *The bomb, the radiation. We can never know.*

Stop it, the Writer snapped.

I sipped my beer timidly while the two men smoked and drank. I waited for them to ask me what Malcolm X had said, but instead the Writer settled into his beer, listened to the band onstage, slowly became voluble, reminiscing about the first time he'd heard the voice of Billie Holiday. He twirled his cigarette over the table and evaluated me; probably he was about my age then, he said. He'd saved his money to buy her record, played it over and over. He admitted he didn't know the words she sang. It was the timbre of her voice. He tried to describe it. Sweet and painful.

The Reporter added, *Shibui.*

No, the Writer said, *not so elegant. Raw.* Five years later, when he learned of her death, he was devastated.

Do you think she is here? asked the Reporter.

Maybe. We stopped to listen to the bass, thrumming his solo, demanding our quiet attention. When the band returned to full sound, the Writer said wistfully like a thwarted lover, *In those days, she lived with me in Hiroshima.*

The Reporter smiled kindly, but the Writer snorted to cover his sentimentality.

The Reporter changed the subject. I could see that, traveling cross-country in the past two months together, they had formed a relationship, the gentle, anxious Reporter mindful of the Writer's moody exterior. *Ralph Ellison*—he suggested, as if an unfinished conversation. *Mienai Ningen.*

The Writer nodded and queried me. *Have you read it? What do you think of the translation?*

I had to admit I did not know the author nor his novel. I was schooled in the American literature of Emerson, Thoreau, Melville, and Twain.

The Writer sneered. *I would like to meet Ralph Ellison. Can you arrange it?*

I ignored his condescension and turned to listen to the saxophone. After a while, I asked, *How did you find Malcolm X?*

The Writer said, *Tell me what he said.*

I felt the beer clouding my mind and struggled to remember the salient points: One, America bombed us, and we have felt the scars of war; likewise, Black people have been bombed and feel the scars of racism. Two, Japan was not colonized because Japan has no extractive resources, and because of this, Japan became strong. Three, the war in Vietnam is a struggle against American imperialism and colonialism, and we should support the Vietnamese people.

So, the Writer returned, *what do you think about that?* He turned to order another round of beers.

I hesitated but had no answer. Dumbly, I justified, I was only the interpreter.

He said with some disgust. *Isn't he correct? The atom bomb is the same as the bomb of racism. White Americans could not see our humanity, so they dropped the bomb on us. They would never have done so in Europe.*

The Reporter shook his head, the alcohol pressing on a pugnacious hidden part of his person. *The racism you speak of is also the Japanese nationalism that destroyed our country. This is mistaken thinking.*

The Writer thought about this. *Nationalism has been exchanged for other isms. Communism. Capitalism. Now we fight about which ism will win out. We are watching a bomb tossed back and forth by two sides. Ready to explode. What kind of peace can we expect?*

The Reporter shook his head. *They call it a cold war.*

The Writer smirked. *Cold war. What do they know about hot wars?*

The Reporter said, *I thought we would meet Martin Luther King. I only learned recently about Malcolm X. He is not known in Japan. They say he is against Reverend King's pacifism. I am not sure I understand his position. Today, I did not see a violent man. Is it possible to make peace with race hatred?*

The Writer spoke with frustration. *We keep asking: How we can make peace? But peace can't come until people are free. It's armed revolution or nonviolent revolution. Which do we choose?*

The Reporter said, *It is not so simple is it? That's the contradiction of our methods. How do we make peace from war?*

The Writer pouted. *Did you notice his bodyguards? Do you think they were armed?*

The Reporter looked surprised, then sheepish. He asked, *How was our visit arranged today?*

The Writer shrugged, *They,* he pointed in the air, *arrange and schedule everything.* He looked at me. *Arranged for him too.*

But perhaps today was different. The Reporter was thoughtful.

The Writer continued, *I have been thinking about Ellison's novel, the relationship of good white liberal people and colored people. Right here in Harlem. We are really here.* He perused the people and tables, waiters and entertainers, all Black except for us. *Do you remember that character? Brother Jack?*

The Reporter nodded. *Brother Jack who, finally, is really exploiting the narrator.*

The Writer puffed, pointed his cigarette. *How is our situation any different?*

What do you mean? asked the Reporter.

Sometimes I am not sure why I am here. There are times I feel I am in a circus.

What are you saying? Don't you believe in our peace mission? The Reporter's voice rose in agitation.

Of course I believe in our peace mission. Calm down.

No, you have come with the wrong attitude. I understand. We have come to the home of our former enemy, but—

The Writer inserted, *It is also the home of our saviors.*

That's not what I mean.

Then what do you mean?

The Reporter pushed himself away from the table.

The Writer said flatly, *We are invisible. Can't you see? You should go home to your wife.*

The Reporter hung his head.

You are the lucky one. I have no one to return to.

I turned away from the two men, confused by their argument. In any case, I had ceased to be there. I tried to concentrate on the wail of the saxophone.

So many years later, the historic day of Malcom's X visiting Yuri's home had for me faded, but the biting words of the Writer and the Report still crystallized as yesterday. Perhaps it was a casualty of being the interpreter, English passing through my mind—ears, mouth—as a sieve. I see now that big history encompasses little histories, overshadows and encumbers. The small matters of small individuals become invisible, pass into oblivion.

What became of these men, I don't know. I know not if they completed their mission or if they returned to Hiroshima.

In the days following our meeting in Yuri's Harlem apartment, the Peace Study Mission left New York for Europe, and Malcolm X began what would eventually become his pilgrimage to Mecca. The following year, he was assassinated at the Audubon Ballroom, his last breath cradled in Yuri's arms. After his death, with riots in Harlem and segregated cities across America, the possibility of a peaceful movement for civil rights came into question. His words were prophetic.

I turned away from the photographs and collected the scrapbooks, gently replaced them on the ironing board. I finished dusting and sweeping the rooms, scrubbed the toilet and bath, mopped the kitchen floor, shoved a soft duster with polish over dark wood floors. Finally, I unrolled my sleeves, pulled on my jacket, remembered to pull from my backpack a small bag of Japanese manju and rice crackers. This I left on the corner end of the ironing board.

Standing for a moment at the threshold of apartment 3-B, I listened for the soft silence and promise of sleep. Passing through, I pressed in the button that would lock the door, this time firmly.

MICHI: Infamy

[C]uriosity led me into exhuming documents of this extraordinary chapter in our history, which had seen the shattering of so many hearths, lives, careers—of so many hopes and dreams. Among once impounded papers, I came face to face with facts, some that left me greatly pained . . . Persuaded that the enormity of a bygone injustice has been only partially perceived, I have taken upon myself the task of piecing together what might be called the "forgotten"—or ignored—parts of the tapestry of those years.

—Michi Nishiura Weglyn, *Years of Infamy: The Untold Story of America's Concentration Camps*, 1976

Carl Stern, NBC News: Mr. Clark, does the Justice Department have the name of the man who killed Dr. Martin Luther King?

U.S. Attorney General Ramsey Clark: We have a name that we are working on . . .

Samuel Yette, *Newsweek*: Mr. Attorney General, this nation prides itself on being a nation of law. At this time we hear, even, the rumors of the possibility of concentration camps for black people. In order to maintain, as you say, order and stability, what are we going to do with respect to concentration camps and that kind of concern?

Ramsey Clark: There are no concentration camps in this country. There have never been concentration camps in this country. There will be no concentration camps in this country . . . Rumors and the fear that arises from rumors, are a great threat to us. Fear, itself, is a great threat, and people who spread false rumors about concentration camps are either ignorant of the facts or have a motive of dividing this country.

—*Meet the Press*, NBC, Sunday, April 7, 1968*

---

* Lawrence E. Spivak, producer, *Meet the Press: America's Press Conference of the Air*, National Broadcasting Company (NBC), 12, no. 14 (April 7, 1968).

And now, Athenians, I am not going to argue for my own sake, as you may think, but for yours, that you may not sin against the God by condemning me, who am his gift to you. For if you kill me, you will not easily find a successor to me, who . . . am a sort of gadfly . . . always fastening upon you, arousing and persuading and reproaching you . . . When I say that I am given to you by God, the proof of my mission is this:—if I had been like other men, I should not have neglected all my own concerns . . . coming to you individually like a father or elder brother, exhorting you to regard virtue . . . If I had gained anything . . . there would have been some sense in my doing so; but now . . . not even the impudence of my accusers dares to say that I have ever exacted or sought pay of any one . . . And I have a sufficient witness to the truth of what I say—my poverty.

—Plato, *Apology of Socrates**

---

* Plato, *Apology*, trans. Benjamin Jowett, Project Gutenberg.

MICHI: Where are we?

WAYNE: In the clouds.

MICHI: Heaven?

WAYNE: You, my dear, should be in heaven. As for me, I seriously doubt it.

MICHI: Oh I see now. We're in the archive.

WAYNE: That would be purgatory now, wouldn't it?

MICHI: I loved the archives. I've come home.

WAYNE: Here's your scrapbook.

MICHI: Over here, this manila folder. TADAYASU ABO, etc., et al., Plaintiffs v RAMSAY A CLARK, etc., et al., Defendants. The final batch of renunciants, their cause brought to an end and to justice.

WAYNE: 1968. Twenty-three years later.

MICHI: But it begins in 1944 when you defended Fred Korematsu before the Supreme Court.

WAYNE: I lost that case.

MICHI: You defended Japanese Americans who renounced their citizenship in the duress of wartime incarceration. Your legal efforts worked to recover their rights.

WAYNE: And you researched and wrote a book about it.

MICHI: I found the hard cold documents, the original stuff. Hidden in the bureaucratic desire for a paper trail. Some clerical boneheads filed them away: reports, memos, correspondence, affidavits, questionnaires, photographs, telegrams, newspapers clippings, receipts.

WAYNE: I saved everything too. A necessary evil in the pursuit of justice.

MICHI: Justice? All this makes me wonder. What is justice? Here I find the unnecessary with the incriminating, all saved and marked "confidential." You would think they'd trash it all.

WAYNE: But the record matters—never mind the reasoning. Legacy, arrogance of history, banality of evil.

MICHI: Years later, meaningless to the naked eye.

WAYNE: But evident and remarkably naked to your perceiving eye.

MICHI: Here, I find the evidence, the factual matter, the truth.

WAYNE: Ah, the truth. And now you must wonder: What is the truth?

MICHI: The truth is that American citizens were removed to concentration camps, denied the right of habeas corpus, and, under such duress, renounced their citizenship.

WAYNE: That truth was an injustice and against the Constitution.

MICHI: By what can we measure justice, if the laws are not just? On July 1, 1944, Congress passed the Denaturalization Act or Public Law 405 to allow renunciation of citizenship within the United States in time of war. Before this, such renunciation was unlawful. A new law made it lawful.

WAYNE: Men, politicians, make laws to suit their interests.

MICHI: It was the attorney general at the time, Francis Biddle, who suggested amending the Naturalization Law of 1940 to address the large numbers of incarcerated Japanese petitioning for repatriation or expatriation and deportation to Japan.

WAYNE: Repatriation and expatriation are not the same as renunciation of citizenship. Renunciation is serious business. No way in hell can it be lawful for an American to renounce citizenship in time of war while denied the right of habeas corpus.

MICHI: That is so. But, under the amended law, if citizens deemed to be disloyal to the United States renounced their citizenship, they too could be deported.

WAYNE: Damned convenient. An excuse to be rid of those resistant no-no disloyals.

MICHI: Following the passage of Public Law 405, army officers staged hearings for renunciation. They asked: *Do you want to stay or leave?* They implied that renunciation would allow the applicant to remain in camp until deported.

WAYNE: People were misled. Sham hearings without representation.

MICHI: In December 1944, WRA director Dillon Myer announced that the camps would close by the end of the following year. Citizen nisei did not want to leave their issei enemy alien parents behind in camp or, if deported, to be separated from family.

WAYNE: These people became renunciants to keep the family together. What American can't understand that?

MICHI: In January 1945, the Department of Justice sent John Burling with a team of attorneys to Tule Lake to administer individual hearings among incarcerated citizens. A total of 5,589 citizens, 5,462 of them in the Tule Lake segregation camp, renounced their citizenship.

WAYNE: Tule Lake, a segregation camp designated to imprison the disloyals. Disloyal because they'd signed "no-no" on a damned questionnaire. The leaders among them were isolated in the stockade. A prison within a prison.

MICHI: In time of war, what is loyalty? In July of 1945, President Harry Truman signed Executive Proclamation 2655 for the "Removal of Alien Enemies." Who is the enemy?

WAYNE: Inconvenient questions. Ship out the suspicious before the inevitable end of the war. In August, they dropped the atomic bomb on Hiroshima and Nagasaki. These people suffered the humiliation of a concentration camp only to be shipped out to a defeated and war-ravaged country.

MICHI: In September of 1945, Tetsujiro Nakamura, a graduate of politics from the University of California at Berkeley who also worked in the legal department at Tule Lake, organized the Tule Lake Defense Committee of one thousand renunciants seeking to rescind their declarations of renunciation.

WAYNE: Tex Nakamura contacted Ernest Besig of the Northern California ACLU for help, who then enlisted me.

MICHI: On November 1, 1945, you mailed a nineteen-page protest to Attorney General Tom Clark rejecting the idea that the renunciants possessed dual citizenship, which would make them automatically alien enemy Japanese.

WAYNE: In fact, renunciation made them stateless. And many of them were minors under the age of twenty-one. Never been to Japan; couldn't speak the language. They were victims of coercion, fraud and duress by the government and by organized pro-Japan gangs in camp.

MICHI: On November 5, 1945, you entered a class equity suit on the behalf of 987 named plaintiffs in the Southern Division of the US District Court for the Northern District of California, a Complaint to Rescind Renunciation of Nationality, to Declare Nationality, for Declaratory Judgment and for Injunction.

WAYNE: Heading the list of plaintiffs was Tadayasu Abo.

MICHI: The case entered as number 25294-S, known as *Abo v. Clark*, argued for an injunction against deporting so-called renunciants and argued that applications for renunciation be canceled and rendered null.

WAYNE: We were counting the days to forced deportation. I couldn't leave the office, day or night, for fear the government would ship these people out under my nose.

MICHI: On November 13, 1945, the deportation of Japanese American renunciants ceased when District Court Judge A. F. St. Sure issued a temporary restraining order pending suit and judgment.

WAYNE: All deportations were halted, and the Department of Justice was forced to initiate mitigation hearings to show cause for deportation of each individual.

MICHI: On November 15, 1945, repatriation ships began to sail, removing 7,100 repatriates to Japan.

WAYNE: However, involuntary deportation of renunciants was halted.

MICHI: On the week of January 4, 1946, the Justice Department commenced mitigation hearings, in which 2,280 of the 3,186 renunciants were granted a stay of deportation orders.

WAYNE: Mitigation hearings—another sham. Besides, a stay of deportation did not restore citizenship.

MICHI: Through the spring of 1946, additional plaintiffs were added to the *Abo v. Clark* suit, eventually including over 5,000 in the category "et al."

WAYNE: We included renunciants held at Department of Justice prisons: Fort Lincoln in North Dakota; at Santa Fe, New Mexico; and in Crystal City, Texas. Government didn't want to let us talk to them, but by God we found a way.

MICHI: In a letter dated August 5, 1945, sent to ACLU executive director Ernest Besig, Under Secretary of Interior Abe Fortas concluded that eighty percent of citizen renunciations were due to pressure by pro-Japanese organizations within camp.

WAYNE: I added that letter as affidavit to my brief.

MICHI: On April 15, 1946, in retaliation to the Fortas brief, the government filed a Motion to Strike.

WAYNE: And this was followed by a series of briefs and cross motions with affidavits back and forth to substantiate claims for government fairness versus accusations of government duress. They volleyed and we volleyed back.

MICHI: On February 20, 1947, Judge Louis B. Goodman replaced an aging Judge St. Sure.

WAYNE: St. Sure was the district judge in San Francisco who sentenced Fred Korematsu back in 1942. By this time, St. Sure was ill, died in '49.

MICHI: On June 30, 1947, Judge Goodman granted your habeas corpus petition.

WAYNE: This meant that the plaintiffs could not be declared enemy aliens by renunciation, making their imprisonment illegal.

MICHI: On April 29, 1948, Judge Goodman delivered his opinion on *Abo v. Clark*, declaring that group and parental pressure, fear of white hostility and deportation, and mass hysteria caused the plaintiffs to renounce their citizenship.

WAYNE: He also asserted the government's duty to admit a wrong. A tiny slap on the cheek, but nevertheless a slap.

MICHI: On September 27, 1948, Judge Goodman transformed his opinion into an "Interlocutory Order," canceling renunciations, as having been the result of duress, menace, coercion, and intimidation. He found that the plaintiffs were native-born citizens and not subject to detention or deportation.

WAYNE: However, he granted the government four months to designate "critical" individuals for whom it could introduce evidence to the contrary.

MICHI: On February 25, 1949, the government presented a "Designation of Plaintiffs," listing 3,500 individuals in twenty-two categories considered critical: Were they kibei? Hokoku leaders? Already voluntarily deported to Japan?

WAYNE: Twenty-two categories. Goddamned nonsense. But on March 23, 1949, Judge Goodman held that the lists presented had no competency, relevancy, or materiality.

MICHI: On April 12, 1949, Judge Goodman issued his Final Order, holding that the government lacked constitutional authority to detain and imprison American nisei citizens not charged with criminality, and condemned conditions at Tule Lake and government duress.

WAYNE: The plaintiffs were native-born U.S. citizens, and the government could no longer detain them.

MICHI: On April 26, 1949, the government appealed their case to the Ninth Circuit Court, declaring that, still in question and requiring further determination, was which individual renunciations were actually voluntary.

WAYNE: Goddamned Justice guys didn't want to give up.

MICHI: On August 25, 1949, Chief Justice William Denman ruled for the plaintiffs in *Murakami v. Acheson*: That plaintiffs, having renounced their citizenship not of free will and intelligent choice but because of mental fear, intimidation, and coercion by pro-Japanese factions within the camp, were to be restored to full citizenship and issued passports.

WAYNE: A. L. Wirin, ACLU attorney for the Southern California branch, in cahoots with the JACL jackals, argued that duress came from other inmate Japanese rather than the government. This was to appease the government. And, rather than restore rights to every renunciant, Wirin narrowed the court's decision to three plaintiffs, only three, who could show duress by their fellow Japanese, in effect blaming the victims for terrorizing themselves.

MICHI: On January 17, 1951, Chief Justice William Denman delivered the court opinion on *Abo v. Clark*. Of the 4,315 plaintiffs, 1,004 plaintiffs were minors, that is, under the age of twenty-one, and their renunciations were deemed unconstitutional. The remaining adult plaintiffs, having renounced after the bombing of Hiroshima and Nagasaki, were presumed to have done so for expediency.

WAYNE: Expediency? An atom bomb blew up their parental home, for Chrissake! Who wants to get deported to a radioactive, bombed-out hole in the earth? It's the principle of the thing.

MICHI: Proof to the contrary lay with the renunciants, but the government had to accept and process their individual affidavits.

WAYNE: Paperwork. Lives exchanged for paperwork.

MICHI: In October 1951, Judge Goodman ordered that individual affidavits be submitted, one by one, and if the Justice Department could show nothing in its files to contradict the written testimony, the plaintiff would be restored to citizenship.

WAYNE: Pain in the neck. We submitted, were rejected, resubmitted again and again. Had to submit ten thousand of these damned affidavits.

MICHI: On April 28, 1952, the war with Japan officially ended.

WAYNE: The question of deportation became moot. What was the point of holding these last Americans hostage to their renunciations when we were at peace with Japan? But we continued our fight.

MICHI: On February 7, 1957, Judge Goodman issued a Final Order with respect to Tadayasu Abo himself.

WAYNE: Yet Abo was only one among 3,300 plaintiffs.

MICHI: For over two decades, affidavit after affidavit was submitted to each succeeding Attorney General, eight in all. On July 4, 1967, new Justice Department regulations deemed court proceedings unnecessary, and they agreed to accept written petitions by renunciants.

WAYNE: We wore them down. From Tom Clark to his son Ramsey Clark. Started with the father, ended with the son.

MICHI: On March 6, 1968, Judge Alphonse Zirpoli ordered the Withdrawal and Dismissal of the last plaintiff in *Abo v. Clark*: Tokuji Nakamura.

WAYNE: In the end, of the 5,589 renunciation applications, 5,409 petitioned to restore their citizenship, and of those, 4,978 were restored.

MICHI: These numbers, what do they mean? What did we do, you exacting justice, and I, searching for truth?

WAYNE: A life's work.

MICHI: How did it matter? Many of these people are old or dead.

WAYNE: Now we are dead too.

MICHI: In archive heaven.

WAYNE: You might be in heaven. I'm still going to hell.

MICHI: What kind of people were we? What kind of people fight for ideas and for others?

WAYNE: Idealists. Dreamers.

MICHI: Believers.

WAYNE: Self-righteous sons of bitches.

MICHI: Why did we do this?

WAYNE: Wasn't made another way. It's stamped into my soul.

MICHI: It has been a lonely life.

WAYNE: But not without its rewards.

MICHI: The government initiated a grave injustice, but if you believe in justice, then you have to take the government to task, and using its own arguments, work to right a wrong.

WAYNE: Amen.

DEPARTMENT OF JUSTICE
WASHINGTON, D.C.

NOTICE OF APPROVAL OF RENUNCIATION OF UNITED STATES NATIONALITY

To: Hayao Chuman
(born May 24, 1913, Los Angeles, Calif.)
1604-A 1
Tule Lake Center
Newell, California

You are hereby notified that, pursuant to Section 401(1) of the Nationality Act of 1940, as Amended, and the regulations issued pursuant thereto, your renunciation of United State nationality has been approved by the Attorney General as not contrary to the interest of national defense. Accordingly you are no longer a citizen of the United States of America nor are you entitled to any of the rights and privileges of such citizenship.

Date: May 3, 1945

Herbert Wechsler
Assistant Attorney General
War Division

(finger-print
impressed in blue)

(reverse side stamped:)
received Sep 24 1945
O.S.I. AND N.S. DETENTION STATION
SANTA FE, NEW MEXICO

April 23, 1946

HONORABLE TOM CLARK,
Attorney General of the United States,
Department of Justice Building,
Washington, D. C.

Dear Sir:

On or about November 1944, I signed an application for renunciation of U.S. Nationality at the Tule Lake Center, Newell, Modoc County, California.

I hereby repudiate, withdraw, retract and revoke the said renunciation upon the following grounds and for the following reasons:

(1) The circumstances under which said renunciation form was signed by me did not constitute a fair and impartial hearing and was a denial of my constitutional guaranty of due process of law and of the equal protection of the laws;

(2) I was not a free agent at the time when and the place where said renunciation form was signed but then and there was held in duress and was the victim of fraud, menace, undue influence and mistake of fact and law;

(3) I then and there was and for a period of time prior thereto had been detained in said Tule Lake Center by official authority and was deprived of substantially all my constitutional rights, liberties, privileges and immunities as an American citizen and was treated as though I were an alien enemy and thus was discriminated against solely by reason of Japanese nationality of my ancestors;

(4) I was intimidated, coerced and compelled to sign said renunciation form by reason of the duress in which I was held by the government and the duress, fraud, menace and undue influence of groups and individuals within said Center, against which the government failed to protect me.

Because of the foregoing reasons the said renunciation was fictitious and is invalid and void.

I am not a citizen or subject of Japan and I do not and never have owed or given the country or nation any allegiance. I am not an alien enemy. I am a native American by birth and by choice. I have no dual citizenship through any act or acceptance upon my individual part.

I demand that you withdraw and set aside the said renunciation form, and the approval thereof if any approval thereof was given.

I am ready and willing to have this matter re-opened and a hearing be granted me in order to prove the said renunciation application was executed under the circumstances above-mentioned when I was not a free agent in any sense of the word but was acting under duress, menace, fraud, undue influence and mistake of fact and law.

I respectfully request your immediate consideration of this urgent matter.

Very truly yours,

Hayao Chuman
D-60-A
Alien Internment Camp
Crystal City, Texas

2-43-B-1
Alien Internment Camp
Crystal City, Texas
May 14, 1946

Mr. Wayne M. Collins
Attorney At Law
Mills Tower, 220 Bush St.
San Francisco, California

Dear Sir,

I am enclosing ten dollars to pay up my one hundred dollars as I am renunciant and I am in the case. I have a wife and two infants living at 116 E. Church St. Stockton, California. They are living with wife's parents but my wife is having quite hard time.

My wife and I want to know any possibility of my deportation or removal to Japan, because I receive my removal order May 2, 1946.

At this opportunity I like to present to you some of my camp life experiences, which caused me to be in this internment life.

1. June 26th or 27th, 1944. Midnight. Mr. Susumu Kurihara, who lived 7417-F Tule Lake, next to my apartment was attacked, and I was considered as same and I was to be attacked. Because Mr. and Mrs. Kurihara came to my apartment every night for about 4 months on account of their childless lonesomeness. From my fear I entered the Hoshi dan through friends help and also renounced my citizenship.

2. I felt I was always suspected and watched from December 1943 to January 1945.

3. From December, 1944 to January, 1945, all the lights around my apartment went off every night almost every night and I was to be attacked. I was notified of my danger two times, once was night of December 31, 1944 and other time was some time in January, 1945.

4. After I was removed to Santa Fe internment camp January 29, 1945, tried to get away from the Hoshi and Hokuku Dans (clubs) and I took individual action. This individual action, appealing for family re-union to go to some other center, was considered as a traitor to the Hoshi Dan and to Japan. I took this action to get away from the pro-Japanese group on March 6, 1945. I have presented my wife's letter to the hearing officer Feb. 19, 1946 at Santa Fe Internment Camp as evidence to prove my intention and action.

Some of the Dan found out my action and someone stole my wife's letter written after April 19, 1945. Again at May 18, 1945 when I was in the K.P. duty someone stole my application for family-re-union form to Miss Evelyn Hershey Assistant Commissioner Enemy Alien Control Philadelphia, PA.

After finding out my action and intention to get away from the Hoshi Dan everywhere I go I was stalked and followed by the many Dan people from end of March 12, 1945 to the first repatriate left Nov. 26, 1945.

My room-mate Mr. Toshio Sakaguchi, now lives at P.O. Box 1230, Honolulu Hawaii, T.H. advised me to inform the camp authority to move those Japanese into another camp. But I did not inform the authority because I must think about safety of my wife and child in Tule Lake Center.

While I am being watched and followed, my wife was given a warning from ladies for our actions and intentions and my wife faced very embarrassing situation at Tule Lake. I have presented my wife's letter as evidence to prove this to the hearing office Feb. 19, 1946.

All of these fears caused me to say or act to be in this internment life separating from my wife and children. Please trust me that I am loyal citizen of America and I'll prove it to you if the time comes. I am really praying for your health and your help.

Yours Sincerely

Masatsuji Ide

AFFIDAVIT

INSTRUCTIONS FOR THE PREPARATION OF AFFIDAVIT

This affidavit should be specifically addressed to the circumstance of your particular case and should not consist of generalities. When you are uncertain as to matters related in your affidavit write "uncertain." Where you claim that any action was taken by you as the result of fear, you should state in each instance, with the greatest possible particularity, what was feared and why. If it is claimed that the fears were caused by threats from individuals or groups of individuals, the nature of the threats, the names of the individuals making them, if known, and the time, place and occasion for the making of the threats should be given.

1. Name ________________________________ Date of Birth ________
2. If born prior of December 1, 1924 (A) Have you ever renounced Japanese nationality? __________ When __________ Where ______________
3. If born since December 1, 1924 (A) Was your name ever registered with a Japanese Consulate for the purpose of reserving your Japanese nationality? __________ If so, did you thereafter renounce your Japanese nationality? __________ When ______________ Where ______________________
4. State periods of visits to Japan and purpose of each visit: Date __________ Purpose ____
5. Give details concerning any formal education in Japan: School __________ ______________________________ Period of Attendance __________ Specify subjects studied ____________________________________
6. Have you ever made application for repatriation to Japan? __________ If so, give date, and your reasons for applying: ______________________
7. (A) Have you ever expressly indicated that you would not swear unqualified allegiance to the United States? __________

   Have you ever declined to answer when asked whether you would swear unqualified allegiance? __________ Or have you ever given a qualified answer to such question asked at War Relocation Centers? __________

   If so, give your reasons: ____________________________________

   (B) If your answer to any of the questions in (A) is affirmative, then did you ever subsequently change your mind and express your willingness to swear an unqualified allegiance or would you have been willing to do so if an opportunity had been afforded you? __________ If so, state when you changed your mind and your reasons therefor: ______________________

   (C) Did you ever indicate that you would not swear unqualified allegiance to the United States either expressly or by refusal to answer, or a qualified answer, knowing that by doing so you would be sent to the WRA Segregation Center at Tule Lake? __________ If so, give reasons: ______________
   ____

8. (A) Were you ever at any time a member of any of the following organizations:

Organization		PERIOD OF MEMBERSHIP
Black Dragon Society (Kikuryu Kai)	YES ☐ / NO ☐	
Central Japanese Association (Beikoku Chuo Nipponjin Kai)	YES ☐ / NO ☐	
Central Japanese Association of Southern California	YES ☐ / NO ☐	
Dai Nippon Butoku Kai (Military Virtue Society of Japan) or Military Art Society of Japan (Hokubei Kai)	YES ☐ / NO ☐	
Heimusha Kai, also known as Hokubei Heieki Gimusha Kai Zaibei Nihonjin, Heiyaku Gimusha Kai, and Zeibei Heimusha Kai (Japanese residing in American Military Conscripts Assoc.)	YES ☐ / NO ☐	
Hinode Kai (Imperial Japanese Reservists)	YES ☐ / NO ☐	
Hinomaru Kai (Rising Sun Flag Society—A Group of Japanese War Veterans)	YES ☐ / NO ☐	
Hokubei Zaigo Shoko Dan (North American Reserve Officers Association)	YES ☐ / NO ☐	
Japanese Association of America (Zaibei Nihonjin Kai)	YES ☐ / NO ☐	
Japanese Overseas Central Society (Kaigai Doho Chuo Kai)	YES ☐ / NO ☐	
Japanese Overseas Convention, Tokyo, Japan, 1940	YES ☐ / NO ☐	
Japanese Protective Association (Recruiting Organization)	YES ☐ / NO ☐	
Jikyoku Jin Kai (Current Affairs Association)	YES ☐ / NO ☐	
Kibei Seinen Kai (Association of U.S. citizens of Japanese Ancestry who have returned to America after studying in Japan)	YES ☐ / NO ☐	
Nanka Teikoku Gunyudan (Imperial Military Friends Group of Southern California War Veterans)	YES ☐ / NO ☐	
Nichibei Kogyo Kaisha (The Great Fujii Theater)	YES ☐ / NO ☐	
Northwest Japanese Association	YES ☐ / NO ☐	
Sakura Kai (Patriotic Society or Cherry Association—comprised of Veterans of Russo-Japanese War)	YES ☐ / NO ☐	
Shinto Temples	YES ☐ / NO ☐	
Sokoku Kai (Fatherland Society)	YES ☐ / NO ☐	
Suiko Sha (Reserve Officers Association Los Angeles)	YES ☐ / NO ☐	
Hokoku Seinen-Dan	YES ☐ / NO ☐	
Hokoku Joshi Seinen-Dan	YES ☐ / NO ☐	
Sokoku Kenkyo Seinen-Dan	YES ☐ / NO ☐	
Sokuji Kikoku Hoshi-Dan	YES ☐ / NO ☐	

(B) Give reasons for becoming a member: ______________________________
____

(C) State nature of your activity and offices you held: ____________________
____

(D) If you voluntarily discontinued membership in any of the aforementioned organizations, give approximate date and reasons for doing so: __________
____

(E) If you claim that your membership in any of the aforementioned organizations, your activities therein or your acceptance of an office was due to misunderstanding of the purpose or nature of the organization, explain fully: ____

(F) If you at any time wished to discontinue membership, activity or office and were prevented from so doing, explain fully: ______________________________
____

9. (A) When did you decide to apply for forms upon which to renounce your United States citizenship? Give reasons for so doing: ____________________
____

(B) If reasons given in answer to preceding questions differ from reasons given to officer who held renunciation hearing, give your explanation for difference: ____

(C) If you claim that your renunciation was caused by fear, you should explain fully why such fear extended from the time of the application for renunciation papers until the date of actual renunciation: ____________________________
____

(D) If the fear did not extend from the date of application to the date of approval by the Attorney General, you should state whether you made an effort to withdraw your application and if not, explain fully: ____________
____

(E) If, after approval, you requested the Attorney General to withdraw his approval of your renunciation or to cancel your renunciation, give the reasons for the delay in making such request: ______________________________
____

(F) If there are any other facts which influenced your action in renouncing your United States citizenship, state fully below or on a separate sheet if necessary. ____

10. (A) If you now are in Japan, give your reason for having returned to Japan.
____

(B) If you are in Japan, have you since you returned to Japan taken an action to resume or acquire Japanese citizenship? ____________ If you have, state nature of action taken and reasons therefor. ___________________________
____

11. (A) If you have served or are serving in the military or naval forces of the United States fill in the following: I enlisted (or was drafted) on (state the date) in the (state the Branch of Service); my Serial number is________________;

I still am in such service (answer Yes or No) __________; I was released from active duty on ________________ and received my Discharge on ________________.

(B) If at any time while in a war relocation center or since then you volunteered for military or naval service but your offer of service was rejected, state the time when and the place where you volunteered. ______________

(C) State why your offer of such service was rejected, if the reason was made known to you. ____

(D) If you were rejected for military or naval service by your Local Draft Board since your release from a war relocation center, state the reason for the rejection if known to you. ____________________________________

12. If any member of your family has served or is serving in the military or naval forces of the United States, state the relationship of such person to you, the name of such person, the branch of service and serial number of such person: ____

Signature in full of applicant ____________________________________

Subscribed and sworn to before me this __________ day of __________ 19___

This affidavit may be executed before any person authorized to administer oaths.

November 23, 1954

Dear Mr. Collins,

Would you please examine and give the comment on the enclosed Affidavit which I filled out as a sample.

I feel that I've done fairly well in answering the questions in first two pages, but the answers I've given in the last two pages seem to me inadequate.

I would also like to request you to send me a new set of affidavit form as I've spoiled all of them which were sent to me previously.

Yours truly,

Tatsumi Yamamoto
101 Oak Ave.
Redwood City, Calif.

November 30, 1954

Mr. Tatsumi Yamamoto
101 Oak Ave.
Redwood City, California

Dear Mr. Yamamoto:

I believe that the answer you have made to question 9(A) in the affidavit form is not sufficiently explicit. I suggest, therefore, that you amplify that answer on a separate sheet of paper and send it to me. You should state the names of the person who threatened you or who asked you the questions about whether or not you had applied to renounce. You should state the names of those persons, whether they were aliens, renunciants or citizens. It is necessary for you to state the names of the person or other means of identifying them and also the statements that they made to you which you believed constituted threats against you.

I suggest that you telephone me so that I can explain this matter to you in greater detail.

Very truly yours,

Wayne M. Collins

P.S. Call me in about 2 weeks & make an appointment to come to my office

[added by WMC; written in script]

PERSONAL QUESTIONNAIRE
Page 11

Re: REQUEST FOR FORMS UPON WHICH TO RENOUNCE CITIZENSHIP

64. When did you send a letter to the Attorney General or the Justice Department asking for forms upon which to renounce your citizenship? ______________
____
65. Did you send that letter to the Attorney General or to the Justice Department *before* that December 21, 1944 announcement that all the WRA Centers will be closed within a year? ______________________________
66. Did you send it *after* the announcement of January 29, 1945, that the Tule Lake Center would be kept open? ______________________________
67. Did you send the letter to the Justice Department asking for forms upon which to renounce citizenship because of any of the following fears, namely: (a) fear of separation from *alien members* of your family; (b) fear of being separated from *citizen members* of your family; (c) fear of being deported yourself because you had given negative answers to Questions Nos 27 or 28 and were considered a disloyal person; (d) fear of threat or harm to yourself or family members from gangs in the Center: (e) fear of mistreatment or physical harm from the Government or its agents? ______________________________
____
68. Did the announcement of December 21, 1944, that all the WRA Centers would be closed within a year cause you to send that letter to the Justice Department? ______________________________
69. Did you send the letter to the Justice Department asking for forms upon which to renounce your citizenship because you feared that . . . citizen members of your family would be forcibly relocated without money, a home or job in an area where people were hostile to Japanese while the war still was going on unless you renounced your citizenship? ______________
70. Did you send that letter because you believed . . . you would be interned . . . until the war ended and then be safely relocated when public hostility to Japanese died down? ______________________________
71. Did any members of your family fear or tell you that you would be forcibly relocated and run the risk of danger from hostile Caucasians unless you sent that letter and renounced your citizenship? ______________________________
72. Were any members of your family in fear of what might happen to you or to them if you did not send such a letter? ______________________________
73. Did you fear that if you did not send the letter and request forms . . . you would be separated from alien members of your family? ______________

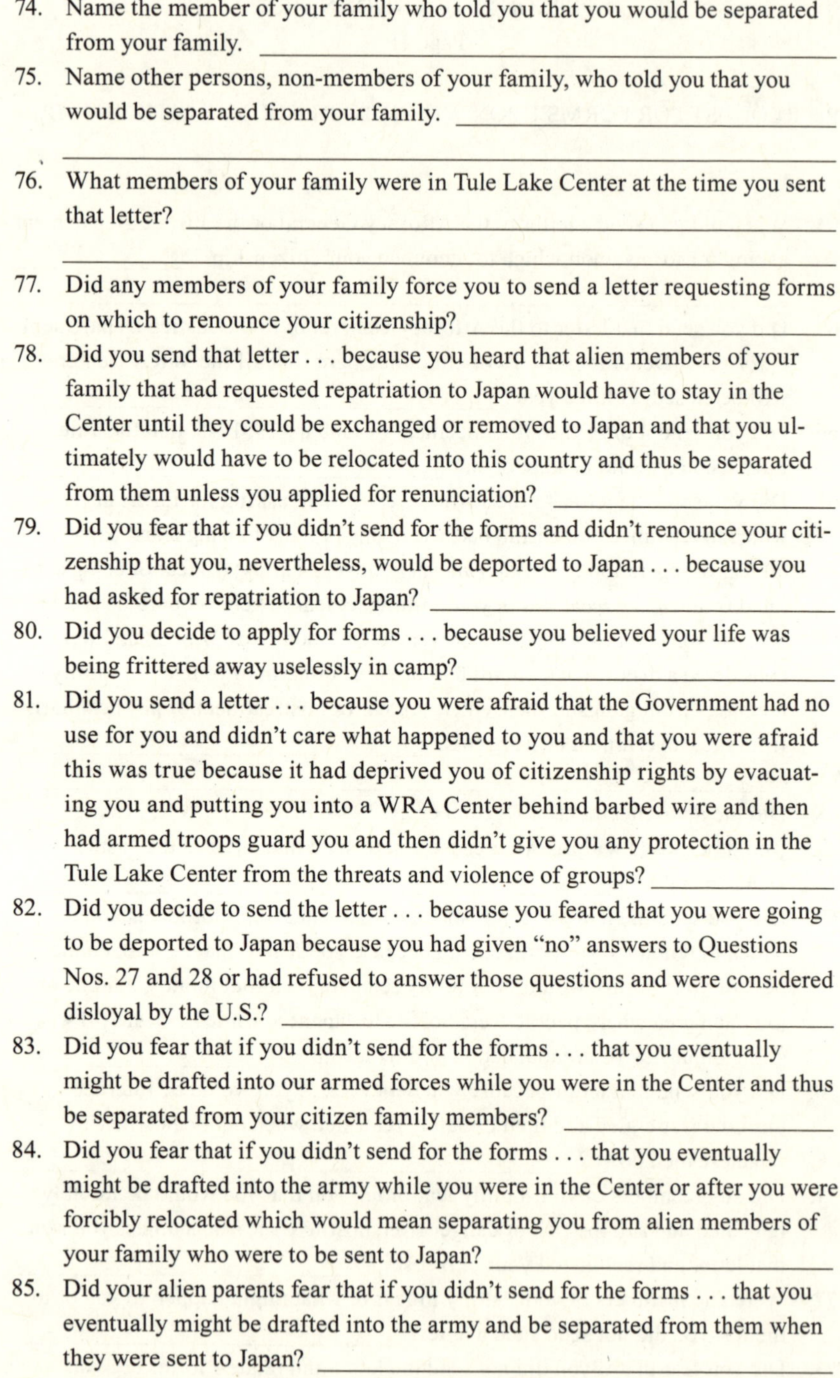

74. Name the member of your family who told you that you would be separated from your family. ________________

75. Name other persons, non-members of your family, who told you that you would be separated from your family. ________________
____

76. What members of your family were in Tule Lake Center at the time you sent that letter? ________________
____

77. Did any members of your family force you to send a letter requesting forms on which to renounce your citizenship? ________________

78. Did you send that letter . . . because you heard that alien members of your family that had requested repatriation to Japan would have to stay in the Center until they could be exchanged or removed to Japan and that you ultimately would have to be relocated into this country and thus be separated from them unless you applied for renunciation? ________________

79. Did you fear that if you didn't send for the forms and didn't renounce your citizenship that you, nevertheless, would be deported to Japan . . . because you had asked for repatriation to Japan? ________________

80. Did you decide to apply for forms . . . because you believed your life was being frittered away uselessly in camp? ________________

81. Did you send a letter . . . because you were afraid that the Government had no use for you and didn't care what happened to you and that you were afraid this was true because it had deprived you of citizenship rights by evacuating you and putting you into a WRA Center behind barbed wire and then had armed troops guard you and then didn't give you any protection in the Tule Lake Center from the threats and violence of groups? ________________

82. Did you decide to send the letter . . . because you feared that you were going to be deported to Japan because you had given "no" answers to Questions Nos. 27 and 28 or had refused to answer those questions and were considered disloyal by the U.S.? ________________

83. Did you fear that if you didn't send for the forms . . . that you eventually might be drafted into our armed forces while you were in the Center and thus be separated from your citizen family members? ________________

84. Did you fear that if you didn't send for the forms . . . that you eventually might be drafted into the army while you were in the Center or after you were forcibly relocated which would mean separating you from alien members of your family who were to be sent to Japan? ________________

85. Did your alien parents fear that if you didn't send for the forms . . . that you eventually might be drafted into the army and be separated from them when they were sent to Japan? ________________

86. Did any person or group of persons tell you or spread the rumor that if you didn't send for the forms . . . you would get in trouble with the Japanese government when you were deported to Japan? ______________
87. Name the other member of your family whom you believed would get in trouble there if you didn't renounce? ______________

____
88. If any member of your famly were in Japan at the time, did you fear that they might be punished by the Japanese government if it learned that you did not renounce your US citizenship? ______________
89. With what agents of Japan did you think you or your family member would get in trouble if you did not renounce? ______________

____
90. If anyone else told you to send that letter, name the persons who did and state whether they were Issei, Kibei or Nisei and the Blocks in which they lived or worked at Tule Lake Center. ______________

____
91. Were any groups of leaders or members of the Seinen Dan or Hoshi Dan moved away to Santa Fe before you sent in that letter? ______________
92. Were you in fear that if you didn't send for the forms and renounce your citizenship that your name would be put on the organization's black list and would be reported to the Japanese government and you would get in trouble with the Japanese government when you arrived in Japan? ______________
93. If you or any members of your family or any friends were attacked by any of the leaders or members of any of the pressure groups for not doing what the pressure group leaders wanted, state the names of the persons who were attacked, the time and place where attacked and by whom. ______________

____
94. Were you in fear of being attacked and beaten up by them or other organizations, if you did not send for the forms and renounce your citizenship?

____
96. Were you in fear that members of your family might be attacked and physically harmed, if you did not send that letter, and, if so, state what member of your family who you feared might be harmed. ______________
97. While you were in Tule were you ever called an inu, a spy, a stooge, an informer, a white Jap, a traitor, kokuzoku, or other names? ______________
98. How many persons called you or spoke to you and asked you if you had sent for the forms? ______________
99. Were any members of your family or friends attacked, beaten or threatened for not sending for the forms? ______________
100. While you were in a WRA Center, did the US Immigration Service commence any deportation proceeding against your family for a violation of any immigration law? ______________

April 22, 1958
101 Oak Avenue
Redwood City, Calif.

Dear Mr. Collins:

I was very much disappointed to hear that the Department of Justice rejected my affidavits and denied my administrative clearance. However, I was much encouraged to know that there still is a possibility of my receiving administrative clearance by preparing a new affidavit. For your continuous assistance I'm always very grateful, and I earnestly hope that this time I'll be able to get my administrative clearance. I shall appreciate it very much if you would kindly correct errors in my English so that I would be expressing myself more accurately and in more proper manner.

Following are the answers to your questions which I've written to the best of my ability:

1. What were your reasons for giving negative answers to Questions 27 and 28 of the Army-WRA registration form?

    The main reason why I gave negative answer to those questions was that at that time I had very little understanding of American language and of American way of thinking as I received most of my education in Japan. Therefore, I had to depend largely on rumors to understand what those questions were and why those questions were asked us at that time. I was especially influenced by those speeches given by Nakayama and others in which they pointed out the unjustness of the Army and the WRA to ask us such questions after they had forced us to evacuate from the West Coast unconstitutionally and after confining us in the concentration camp surrounded by barbed wire fences, guarded by armed soldiers, and completely depriving us of our freedom.

    There also was a rumor in the camp that if we answered those questions affirmatively then we would be forced to relocate as we had previously been forced to evacuate from the West Coast, and I was afraid of relocating to a new, unfamiliar place because I had not confidence of finding a job with my inadequate ability to speak English.

Besides, prior to answering those questions, my father had, in my name, applied for expatriation to Japan, and I thought that it was almost imperative for me to give negative answers to those questions if I were to expect to be allowed to enter Japan which was then dominated by militarists.

2. What were your reasons for applying for repatriation on July 23, 1942?

The living conditions in Tanforan Assembly Center were so miserable that by all means I wished to get out from there as soon as possible. It is almost unbelievable that such thing happened in the civilized country like ours, but in the excitement of war hysteria, many of us, including women and children were forced to live in horse stables, and the thought of having to stay in such a place to merely waste my time for the duration became more and more intolerable as days went by. One day a friend of mine who was able to speak English much better than I did went to the administration office and asked for the permission to leave the camp in order to continue his study outside, but was rejected for the reason of his being Kibei. From this incident I concluded that it was the policy of the WRA to confine us Kibeis in a concentration camp till the end of the war, and when I heard of Red Cross accepting our application to repatriate I thought that was the only way for us Kibeis to get out from the camp.

3. Why, during an interview by an FBI agent at Topaz on March 20, 1943, did you state that you were loyal to Japan?
4. Why, in that interview, did you state that you wished to return to that country to enter the Japanese Army and fight against this country?
5. Why, in that interview, did you further state that you would commit sabotage in this country if directed to do so by the Japanese Emperor?

I would like to answer all these three questions together because they seem to be essentially the same question to me, and I wish to avoid repeating the same explanations over and over again.

Now I deeply regret that I did not answer these questions with the help of an interpreter because, as I stated before, my ability to understand and, specially, to speak American language at that time was quite inadequate to answer accurately and in proper manner such important questions as these under such complicated situation I was in at the time. Fact being as it was, what I actually said in that interview were several "Yes's" and "No's", except saying in my broken English, that I thought it was impossible for me to commit sabotage when I was confined in the concentration camp and so heavily guarded by armed soldiers. Since I could not understand why the FBI agent was conducting such a questioning, I hoped to imply by replying that this question as well as some others made no sense because they were based on supposition. It was absolutely impossible for any one of us confined in the concentration camp surrounded by barbed wire fences and guarded by armed soldiers to commit sabotage or to enter the Japanese Army, but this FBI agent who questioned me seemed determined to make a saboteur out of me and he further asked me, menacingly, if I could commit sabotage if I were allowed to stay out of the concentration camp. By this time I got so completely sick of this sort of questioning that my only wish at that time was to get it over with as quickly as possible regardless of the consequence. I believe anyone can immediately understand what a difficult situation I was in and how I felt to undergo such questioning if he imagined himself to be in a Japanese concentration camp and had to answer this sort of questions in Japanese language. To be confined in the concentration camp and completely deprived of freedom despite my being an American citizen was bad enough to me, and I could not help feeling strong anger when I had to undergo and further tortured by such questioning which was based entirely on suspicion.

I also regret that because of my youthfulness immatureness at that time I lacked courage and wisdom to refuse to sign those statements. But at the end of this hearing I was so completely exhausted that I had no will power left to resist when I was asked to sign them. Besides, I felt that those statements could not have any legal significance because those questions were asked under supposition and also because I was at that time confined in the concentration camp and was under heavy duress.

In this concentration camp where I was in one was instantly shot to death by an armed guard merely approaching too close to the fence, and under such confinement I could not express freely what I wanted to say even if I were able to speak English fluently. My fear to speak and my inability to understand the purpose of that questioning and also my inability to answer those questions accurately and in proper manner made a saboteur out of me, but the fact that there had not been a single case of sabotage found among people of Japanese descent proves that this was merely an imaginary thing and never could have happened actually. It is my deep regret now that I wasn't at that time able to explain the fact that just before this questioning took place I worked for Mr. Rice in Clifton, Idaho, for over a month without any incident which I believe made such questioning quite unnecessary.

6. What were your reasons for being a member of the Sokuji Kikoku Hoshi Dan and why did you not resign?

I never became a member voluntarily but was forced to do so quite reluctantly by Doi in order to avoid being considered an informer by him and other members of Hoshi Dan. He was one of the leaders of Hoshi Dan in my block, and I did not want to make my life in the camp more miserable and uncomfortable by refusing to become a member and thus being suspected as an informer by him and other members of Hoshi Dan. It was quite possible that I could have been attacked by some of the radical member of Hoshi Dan if I could not give the reason which satisfied him, and I wished to avoid taking the risk of receiving such bodily harm by all means.

The reason why I did not resign was that I did not put much importance to the existence of Hoshi Dan and its activities except my passive interest to avoid being considered as an informer and being attacked by them. Since that was the only reason I gave my name as member, I did not even bother to withdraw my name from it until Tule Lake Camp was closed.

7. Why, at your renunciation hearing, did you affirm that you were

loyal to Japan and that you wished to return to that country for permanent residence?

One of the reasons why I was forced to renounce my U.S. citizenship was that I was afraid of being considered as an informer by Hoshi Dan members. And in order to renounce my citizenship, I thought it was necessary for me say that I was loyal to Japan and that I wished to return to that country for permanent residence.

8. Why, at the subsequent hearing on January 17, 1946, did you state that you renounced because you would have been called an informer if you did not do so?

When people in Tule Lake Camp started talking about renouncing U.S. citizenship, I thought it was a very foolish thing to do and I decided not to renounce my citizenship. But as days went by more and more people were forced to renounce their citizenship by Hoshi Dan leaders and they in turn urged their friends to do likewise. Doi, Kadowaki in my block and Kawasaki, Inouye were some of the Hoshi Dan leaders who finally forced me to renounce my U.S. citizenship despite my great reluctance to do so. I tried as long as possible to keep my U.S. citizenship by avoiding to talk about renunciation and even by pretending that I had already done so, but in the end when majority of the camp residents had done so the pressure was so great that it was no longer possible for me to keep on just pretending. I was afraid to be considered as an informer by Hoshi Dan members because I thought it was possible that I would be sent to Japan with them on the same boat since I had applied for expatriation.

I hope I'm not sending my answers in too late. Please examine them and give me further advice as to what to do next.

Very truly yours,

Tatsumi Yamamoto

February 26,1964

JWD:PJG
146-54-1381
93-1-1320

Cecil F. Poole, Esquire
United States Attorney
422 Post Office Building
Seventh and Mission Streets
San Francisco, California 94101

Re: Tatsumi Yamamoto
Your ref: Abo et al. v. Kennedy: Furuya et al.
v Kennedy, 25294, Cons. 25294-0, 25295, ND
California SD

Dear Mr. Poole:

This is in response to your letter of December 31, 1963, enclosing an affidavit for a determination as to whether the case of the above-named renunciant may be considered as coming within the coverage of the ruling of the Court of Appeals in the case of Acheson v. Murakami, 176 F. 24, 953, in accordance with a letter from this Department dated September 21, 1953, to Mr. Wayne M. Collins.

In accordance with your response, we have reexamined the affidavit, together with the pertinent Governmental files and you are advised that we adhere to our view as expressed in our letters of July 25, 1957, October 13, 1958 and April 14, 1960, that this subject's case may not be considered as coming within the coverage of the decision in the Murakami case.

In accordance with our letter of September 21, 1953, we attached the original and two copies of this subject's affidavit for return to Mr. Collins.

Yours very truly,

JOHN W. DOUGLAS
Assistant Attorney General
Civil Division

By:
Paul J. Grumbly
Special Litigation Counsel

Enclosures:
Original and two copies
of affidavit, dated February 5, 1960.

(Notes on folder: Processed US June 25,1957; Reject 7/25/57; Reprocessed US 2/17/60; Reject 4/4/60)

February 18, 1967

Mr. Hayao Chuman
757 West 165th Place
Gardena, California

Dear Mr. Chuman:

I wish to inform you that the Justice Department still is adamant about giving you administrative clearance in equity proceeding No 25295, Abo v deB. Katzenback and wishes the few remaining plaintiffs to be dismissed from that suit without prejudice to their rights.

For your information I wish to state that if you will file the "Application to File Petition for Naturalization", Form N. -400, which I prepared for you and sent on to you on May 6, 1964, I believe your petition for naturalization will be granted and that you will become a naturalized citizen of the U.S. That petition can be filed by you at the office of the U.S. Immigration Office in Los Angeles. It will be processed promptly by the "naturalization bureau" of that office. The charges that were brought against you by the Justice Department and the things you may have said or done in the Tule Lake Center at your renunciation hearing will not be held against you in a naturalization proceeding for you meet the requirement of being a person of good moral character necessary for naturalization and you are attached to the principles of the Constitution of the United States.

If you need any assistance in connection with your Application for naturalization Tetsujiro Nakamura, Esq., attorney at law, 124 South San Pedro Street, Room 215, Los Angeles 12, California, telephone Madison 4-47238, will be glad to assist you as I also will be.

Two other renunciants in the U.S. are to file similar applications soon and they have asked me to dismiss them from the equity proceeding No. 25294-25295. One already has been accepted and will be naturalized in the U.S. District Court in San Francisco next week. He also has requested to be dismissed from the equity suit. Five renunciants in Japan who no longer wish to return to the U.S. or to recover citizenship will also be dismissed from the suit in order to terminate the suits I heretofore filed on behalf of some 4,754 renunciants.

It will be necessary for you also to be dismissed as one of the plaintiffs in equity suit No. 25294 without prejudice, however, to you or to your rights. It is best in my opinion that the suit be dismissed since it will not harm the rights of anyone left in the suit, and it will prevent the Justice department from forcing individual trials in which it would produce evidence as to what each renunciant's conduct in the Tule Lake Center may have been and what each said at his renunciation hearing, etc. Naturalization proceedings will not go into detail as to what transpired in camp because the sole requirements are that a person applying for naturalization must be a person of good moral character and attached to the principles of the Constitution of the United States for a required period of time. You already possess the required qualifications for naturalization.

Please communicate with Tetsujiro Nakamura, Esq., for immediate assistance in bringing form N-400 up to date before it is filed at the U.S. Immigration & Naturalization Office in Los Angeles. Also please write and let me know that you have received this letter and that you are applying for naturalization so that I can dismiss you as a plaintiff in equity proceeding No. 25294.

With best wishes, I am
Sincerely yours,

Wayne M. Collins

WMC/W

March 1967

Dear Mr. Collins,

I have received your later dating Feb 18, 1967. Since I understood that the Justice Department dropped or dismissed our case a few years back, I did not know you were still working on my case. Mr. Collins, please dismiss my case and feel easy. I am, however, so grateful for your endless efforts that I will not forget what you have done for us.

As far as naturalization concerned, I am not worrying too much because I came along for twenty years without U.S. citizenship even I felt a little handycap and inconvenient. I am now fifty-three years old and I'm not sure if I will live another twenty years. Besides, I do not have any ambition to be a politician, an important leader or millionaire. I believe when I go to beside God, I do not need any country's passport. Only thing I need, is how I lived in this world. I wish this whole world will be one country and a passport or a tariff will be unnecessary thing some day. Then there be no prejudices between races or wars between countries.

Right now I'm struggling to raise my eight children to be decent and well educated. Three of my children are now going to colleges and next fall another.

I hope someday before two long, I could see you in person and express my deep appreciation.

Sincerely your renunciant,

Hayao Chuman

April 25, 1967

United States Attorney
Federal Building
450 Golden Gate Avenue
San Francisco, California 94102

Attention: Charles Elmer Collett, Esquire
Chief Assistant United States Attorney

Dear Mr. Collett:

Annexed hereto you will find original and two copies of the affidavits of the following named persons:

(1) IDE, Masatsuji, born December 25, 1912.
(2) CHUMAN, Hayao, born April 24, 1913.
(3) NAKAMOTO, Tokuji, born December 8 1916.
(4) YAMAMOTO, Tatsumi, born April 2, 1917.

Persuant to my telephone conversation with Paul J. Grumbly, Esquire, who is, I understand, in the general litigation section of the civil department of the U.S. Department of Justice in Washington, D.C., these affidavits are presented to you to forward direct to his attention for review pursuant to an agreement I entered into with the Attorney General some years ago.

Mr. Grumbly will review said files with a view to determining whether or not the Justice Department will consent to the entry of a judgment in favor of said persons cancelling their renunciations and declaring them to be U.S. citizens by birth.

I would be grateful if you would forward the affidavits to the Department of Justice to Mr. Grumbly's attention as soon as possible.

Very truly yours,

Wayne M. Collins

WMC
kt
Enclosure

June 14, 1967

Hayao Chuman
757 West 165th Place
Gardena, California

Dear Hayao:

Enclosed find a certified copy of the conclusive final copy of the final judgment which cancels your renunciation and declares you to be and at all time to have been a U.S. citizen and national and as such entitled to all the rights of citizenship.

The judgment cancels your renunciation as at the time it was made and, in consequence, it was a void renunciation from the beginning.

I am pleased that your U.S. citizenship no longer is in doubt.

With best wishes, I am
Sincerely Yours,

Wayne M. Collins

WMC/W

July 13, 1967

MR. MASATSUJI IDE
3295 Mr. Diablo Blvd.
Lafayette, California

Dear Masatsuji:

Enclosed find $200 in currency which you left at my office and intended as a gift to me but which I cannot accept.

None of the persons who were plaintiffs in the mass habeas corpus and mass equity suits contributed more than $300 to the trust funds which enabled the litigation to be carried on to completion. Many contributed nothing or very little. You contributed your full share. As the trustee of the funds heretofore raised and exhausted I could not accept from you more than your share and I am opposed to receiving gifts.

I appreciate the motive which prompted you to make the gift to me.

With best wishes to you and
your family, I am

Sincerely yours,

Wayne M. Collins

September 16, 1967

MR. & MRS WAYNE M. COLLINS
68 Presidio Avenue
San Francisco, California 94115

Dear Mr. & Mrs. Collins:

The San Francisco Chapter, Japanese American Citizen League is hosting a Pioneer Issei Banquet on Friday, October 13, 1967. The banquet's twofold purposes are: first, to honor our Issei (first generation Japanese) for their contribution toward the progress of all Japanese Americans; secondly, we wish to honor our friends such as you who were actively concerned and sympathetic with Japanese Americans before, during and immediately following our evacuation twenty-five years ago.

We would certainly appreciate your presence at this banquet. The banquet will be at the Four Seas Restaurant, 731 Grant Avenue, San Francisco. Social period will begin at 6:30 p.m. with dinner commencing at 7 p.m.

Sincerely,

Wesley T. Doi, Chairman
Banquet Committee, SF JACL
1568 Union Street
San Francisco, California 94123

R.S.V.P.
By October 1, 1967. Thank you.

October 20, 1967

Mr. Wes Doi, Chairman
Banquet Committee, SF JACL
1568 Union Street
San Francisco, California 94123

Dear Mr. Doi:

I acknowledge receipt of your letter invitation to attend the Pioneer Issei Banquet which was scheduled to take place on Friday, October 13, 1967, and convey my thanks to you personally for notifying me of that banquet. I declined the invitation for the reasons hereinafter set forth.

I must apprise you that I hold and expect to hold during my lifetime a constant hostility towards the Japanese-American Citizens League. I cannot conceive of any circumstance or reason whatever that would induce or impel me to accept an invitation that emanated from the JACL, the pronunciation of which I deem a most appropriate one for that wretched organization.

In my opinion and to my knowledge the JACL has no honor to bestow on anything or on anybody, least of all on the Issei. Because of its lame attitude and apathy during World War II toward the plight of the victims of the 1942 evacuation and also because of what it, as the self-appointed spokesman for the affected people, did to and also for what it did not do for the victims of governmental oppression, I hold no respect whatever for the JACL but I do and shall hold an intensive hostility toward it.

The Issei made no contribution whatever toward the progress of any or "all Japanese-Americans." There are no such entities as "Japanese-Americans." The hyphenated name consists of two names which are antithetical. One cannot be a Japanese and at the same time be an American. One cannot be an American and at the same time be a Japanese. Those who were born in this country are "Americans." They are not Japanese. They are not Japanese-Americans. They are not American-Japanese. There cannot be such a person as a hyphenated American. Further, I do not believe in the myth of dual citizenship or dual nationality. Such a spurious and hypothetical status is incompatible with one's allegiance to the United States.

The pioneer Issei need no honor to be bestowed on them by the JACL for their contribution to the progress of their own children, whether those native born United States citizens are Nisei, Kibei or Sansei. The arrival of the Issei in this country was a signal honor to our country and our people. Their presence here is a continuous honor to us. What they have done for this country is an honor to this country. This country owes them a debt it cannot repay.

I do not think it essential, desirable or important to honor those whom you term in your letter to be "friends" whom you state therein "were actively concerned and sympathetic with Japanese American before, during and immediately following" the wartime evacuation of 1942. That evacuation was unjustified, vicious and criminal action taken by our government against a loyal segment of our population. It was the oppression of a segment of our citizenry and resident aliens for no reason whatever, save that some of their forebears may have owed allegiance to the government of Japan while residing in that country.

The so-called "friends" to whom you refer, with few exceptions, did little, if anything, to prevent that outrage and mass incarceration of our wartime concentration camps. Few of them even protested the infliction of that indignity on the innocent evacuees. This country forever will bear shame for what it did to them. Our people bears like shame for what it allowed our governmental agents, supposedly our servants and not our masters, to do to them. Had a representative portion of our people voiced immediate protest against the evacuation and, perhaps, had the JACL, as the pretended spokesman for the affected people, mustered sufficient courage to oppose the uprooting and imprisonment of these innocents in those concentration-camp—prisons the government would have halted its criminal action against them.

I do not intend to forget or forgive the government oppressors for what was done to these innocent people under the guise of wartime military necessity. I do not intend to forget that our population at large was apathetic to the suffering it imposed on them. I do not intend to overlook the fact that the JACL was indifferent to what happened to them and that it did nothing to help them. Had the so-called "friends" genuinely done something and been quick to try to halt the outrage committed by the government there would have been no wartime concentration camps and no discrimination practiced against them on a racial basis or on any basis.

I believe that the JACL would be doing the members of our population who are of immediate or remote Japanese ancestry a service were it to disband and disperse.

Very truly yours,

Wayne M. Collins

WMC:hh

IN THE UNITED STATES DISTRICT COURT FOR THE NORTHERN DISTRICT OF CALIFORNIA, SOUTHERN DIVISION

TADAYASU ABO, etc., et al., Plaintiffs v. RAMSAY A. CLARK, etc., et al., Defendants.
Cons. No. 24294
(Nos. 25294 and 25295)

WITHDRAWAL AND DISMISSAL OF LAST OF PARTIES-PLAINTIFF WITHOUT PREJUDICE AND COURT ORDER THEREON AND STATEMENT OF COUNSEL FOR PLAINTIFFS CONCLUDING CASES

TOKUJI NAKAMOTO, born December 8, 1916, and who became one of the individually named parties-plaintiff in the above-entitled causes, hereby withdraws as a party-plaintiff from the above entitled cause and the said cause is dismissed as to him without prejudice.

Dated: February 22, 1968, at San Francisco, California.

/s/ WAYNE M. COLLINS
WAYNE M. COLLINS
1300 Mills Tower
220 Bush Street
San Francisco, California 94104

SO ORDERED:
March 6, 1968

STATEMENT OF COUNSEL FOR PLAINTIFFS CONCLUDING CASE

The signing and filling of the foregoing order disposes of the above-entitled causes as to the last of the individually named parties-plaintiff therein. This brings to a final conclusion these consolidated mass class equity proceedings instituted on November 13, 1945. The proceedings involved the determination of the basic constitutional rights and liberties of several thousand individually named parties-plaintiff and hundreds of other persons who were cast into similar predicament by the government.

Each of the plaintiffs and persons affected by these causes was a native-born citizen of the United States. Simply because each had ancestors who once were inhabitants of the country known as Japan, each, under "civilian exclusion orders" issued under authority of "executive orders", in early 1942 following the onset of World War II on December 7, 1941, was ordered excluded from our West Coast. Under military orders each first was forced to enter a temporary camp called an "Assembly Center". Thereafter, each was ordered removed from the West Coast and was confined in one of our ten wartime concentration camps termed "War Relocations Centers", two of which, strangely enough, were situated in California, namely, the Manzanar Center and the Tule Lake Center.

Thereafter, each was interned either in the Tule Lake Resegregation Center in Newell, Modoc County, California, or in an Alien Internment Camp at Bismarck, North Dakota, or at Santa Fe, New Mexico, or at Crystal City, Texas, or placed on "relaxed internment" at Seabrook Farms, Bridgeton, New Jersey. Each was scheduled for removal to Japan under a claim of color or authority of the Alien Enemy Act and on Executive Proclamation as if he or she were an "alien enemy" instead of a native-born United States citizen simply because each, while held in custody by the government and under its duress, purportedly renounced his or her citizenship. Hundreds of them were removed to Japan in late 1945 and early 1946.

The abusive treatment of these citizens was halted by the commencement of these consolidated class proceedings in equity together with companion proceedings in habeas corpus in this court. In the course of time those who had been interned were liberated from internment and returned to their homes. With few exceptions the purported renunciations of citizenship finally were ordered cancelled for having been unconstitutional and void ab initio. A majority of those who had been forcibly removed to Japan were restored to their homes in this country. The fundamental rights, liberties, privileges and immunities of these citizens now are honored. The discrimination practiced against them by the government has ceased. The episode which constituted an infamous chapter in our history has come to a close.

Dated: March 6, 1968.

/s/ WAYNE M. COLLINS

WAYNE M. COLLINS
1300 Mills Tower
220 Bush Street
San Francisco, California 94104
Telephone: 421-5827

Attorney for the Plaintiffs

Archival documents transcribed from Wayne M. Collins Papers: 1918–1974, Bancroft Library, University of California, Berkeley

JAMES: Pacifism

ON STRIKE! SHUT IT DOWN!
—San Francisco State College, 1968–69

One day it occurred to me that I should bring my brother out of the cold, that is, Canada. Gordon had been hiding up there, middle of Alberta, with his wife and kids, living a quiet life as a middle-aged professor. My motives were ulterior. Let me explain. We were not close, being eight years apart, but also because he'd spent the war years in prison, then after college went off to Lebanon and Egypt, and now Canada. He'd lived outside the U.S. for the last seventeen years. I hadn't seen or had much contact with him. One of the last times I saw Gordon was in Idaho in 1943 when the rest of our family was digging up sugar beets on sanctioned leave from Tule Lake. He came by on his way to complete his prison sentence in Arizona. When I counted, that was twenty-five years ago. We had some overlap at the University of Washington, but he ran in other crowds. We both got married, had kids. Gordon took his family to the Middle East, mine followed me on a Fulbright to Japan.

As I said, my motives were ulterior. I thought perhaps we could, after all these years, get to know each other, fill in our time apart, since, after all, we had taken similar paths into the academy, he in sociology, and I in anthropology. But more consequently, I recognized that at a critical moment in history, he had taken a stance in protest, and I was embroiled in a similar moment. They say your relationship to family and siblings, its implicit hierarchies, despite time, remains the same. In a Japanese family, the older brother is niisan; the first son chōnan, and Gordon was number one. The younger is otōto; I would always be otōto, but perhaps enough time and experience had passed so that I could finally ask for advice and dole out some of my own.

Around Christmas 1968, I sent my brother our obligatory Christmas card, enclosing a photograph of my kids, but this time adding a personal note asking if he couldn't find the time to come to San Francisco. I also included a lengthy article describing events at my college.

Just returning from sabbatical and narrowly escaping the civil war in Nigeria, I'd come home to a campus also brewing revolution. While I was in Africa, students at SFSC had formed the BSU, Black Students Union, and TWLF, Third World Liberation Front, had caused the resignation of one president, occupied the YMCA demanding the retention of history professor Juan Martinez and the admission of four hundred students of color, and, during that spring protest, incurred twenty-six arrests by police. As the fall semester began, I was appointed faculty instructor for the first lecture course in ethnic studies with African American sociologist Nathan Hare. In October, however, a young professor of English, George Mason

Murray, made incendiary remarks in a speech at our sister state college in Fresno. The board of trustees called for his resignation, and a week later the BSU and TWLF made a list of fifteen demands and initiated a strike that would continue for almost five months. Two weeks following, seven faculty members joined the strike, and by the end of November, the new president had resigned, replaced by the semanticist Sam Hayakawa. Under Hayakawa's declaration of a state of emergency, three hundred police were called in to "break up this reign of terror"; nine students were injured, thirty-one arrested. On December 11, the AFT, American Federation of Teachers, voted to join the strike, believing that an officially sanctioned strike with faculty would decrease police violence. From that moment on, I was walking Holloway with a placard, ON STRIKE!

My brother arrived after the holidays. On January 6, first day of classes, some four hundred faculty joined the picket line. I dragged him into the line. We walked and talked. Gordon pulled out the article I'd sent, and quoted from Murray's infamous speech: *We are slaves and the only way to become free is to kill all the slavemasters . . . Political power comes from the barrel of a gun. If you want campus autonomy, if the students want to run the college, and the cracker administration don't go for it, then you control it with the gun.* Gordon turned to me, eyebrows raised above his glasses, his unasked question hovering in the din of protest. *On strike! Shut it down!*

I replied, *Yes, but—*

But? Gordon grimaced alarm.

Might be metaphorically speaking.

Guns? Metaphorical?

My brother was a Quaker and a pacifist. I was neither, but we had been raised in the same family with the same values, if not Quaker, a similar Japanese version. I'd strayed from this, but in his presence I was again the same kid brother in the same family.

Gordon was kind but firm. *Perhaps,* he suggested, *rather than argue, we should air our differences, as if in a Quaker meeting?*

I replied, *Speak to God?*

Gordon grinned. *Yes.*

And so we began.

I said: *I was too young to know, but now I understand. The war changed everything. I know now that you—*

Gordon turned to me and shook his head.

I corrected myself and continued, *My brother took a principled stand and paid the price. Now I know he did it for all of us. It was wrong, illegal and racist, to send us to camp. We were prisoners, but at the time, a rebellious kid like me got freedom there. Ma couldn't reprimand me, couldn't raise her voice in those barracks with thin walls. Everyone could hear everyone's business. So, I did as I pleased. I was a smart aleck. I think I resented my brother's absence. If he'd made his own decisions, so could I. He wasn't around to set an example or give me grief. I took advantage of our situation.* I paused.

Gordon said: *It's true. The war changed everything, separated me from my family, forced me to make choices. I was young and full of idealism. Some people think I was a fool, but I had steadfast friends. The Friends. And a girl who loved me. I couldn't let her down.*

I heard a soft shudder in my brother's voice. Even on the street in public space, surrounded by the din of protest, our conversation spun cautiously intimate. I rallied us back to classroom generalities and replied: *We should have learned something from that time of change. What did we learn?*

I believe I learned to take responsibility.

I spoke again to God: *My brother was courageous, his actions brave. My lessons were less respectable. For me, it was about how to be resourceful, how to manipulate and take advantage, to cultivate cunning.*

Gordon responded: *Taking responsibility for one's beliefs is not so different. There's cunning involved, if the action is to have some greater effect. Timing and strategy. Active nonparticipation. Direct action. And training to resist violence.*

We turned the corner toward the main entrance. A larger contingent of protestors congregated there.

Gordon looked on and said: *The idea of sacrifice, giving one's life for others, for a larger cause.*

I continued: *Commitment to a greater good, to justice and an ethical conscience.*

Out of a nowhere as only we brothers understood, we both exclaimed simultaneously: *Jesus died for our sins!*

At the college entrance, the roar was loudest, drowning out our laughter. *On strike! Shut it down!*

Gordon said, *When I think about it, over there in White River, we were brought up in a small village. We were a group of farming families, all related, all Christian followers of Uchimura Kanzō.*

Mukyōkai, I remembered, *was an anti-institutional sect. No leaders. All followers. Japanese Quakers in America. We were a kind of Japanese Puritan experiment. If we hadn't lost the land and then been dragged off to camp, what would our lives have become? Maybe that's why I studied that village in Nagano not far from where our parents came. But what I studied was postwar change—land reform, technology and modernization, farm and city exchange.*

Gordon nodded. *Come to think of it, I studied rural villages in transition, too, in Canada, the Doukhobors, then in Lebanon and Egypt.*

The Doukhobors. Who were they again?

Russian peasants from the seventeenth century, persecuted for their religious beliefs, run out of the country, first to Cyprus, then Canada. They were pacifists, supported by the Friends. I studied their communities in Saskatchewan.

Now I remember, I said. *Weren't they the people who ran around naked rather than join the military?*

Yeah. Gordon chuckled.

Not a bad idea. Can you imagine? I looked around at our protest and laughed. *What about your research in Lebanon and Egypt?*

There, too, I looked at village life as the last vestiges of old traditions, hypothesized it as the holdout of social structures, conservative and fundamentalist in thought and political leaning. How would village life respond to new politics, to democracy?

And? I asked. *What did we learn?*

Gordon paused, then blurted out: *Bunch of numbers! We were there in the middle of a war! Village boys sent to fight Israelis. When they died, didn't matter that I tracked newspaper literacy or radio audience to ascertain political awareness. That was thirteen years ago, but today, you read the papers and they've started another war. Arabs against Jews. I'm supposed to be a pacifist. What kind of research can stop wars?*

Maybe we are asking the wrong questions. I watched your work in sociology, numbers as scientific proof—

I looked at Gordon who muttered, *That's a simplification.*

It is, but I thought anthropology, mapping cultural patterns, was a cut above. Now I wonder if we both got it all wrong. Who said: Sociologists study society; anthropologist study themselves? Bunch of self-centered navel-gazers.

Hasn't it all been said already? Sociology born of capitalism. Anthropology of colonialism. Social science born to fix the problem.

Born to save the problem. That's—I gestured at our marching lines up and down the street—*That's what this is all about. We've got to cut loose. We can no longer fix or save. We've got to change. You want numbers? Student population: 75.9 percent white, 5.3 percent black, 2.3 percent Mexican American, 7.9 percent Oriental, 0.5 percent Indian, 1 percent Filipino, 7.1 percent other or nothing!*

Numbers are good for something. It's true we place too much faith in scientific proof. Whether sociology is science or not is irrelevant. It's a way of seeing, a methodology. Whether I've chosen the best way I can't say.

We teach students to see.

Maybe we teach them to see what we see. We have to teach students to see with their own eyes.

Their real eyes.

Maybe it can't be taught.

Maybe. They are all out here telling us it's irrelevant. They don't want sociology or anthropology, tools of the white man.

What do they want?

Black studies. Third World liberation. Chicano studies, Asian American studies. Ethnic studies. Cultural studies. Whatever it is, can't be minority studies.

They're still subsets. You are aware of that?

Yes.

What will they do when they find out?

They're not stupid. They'll figure it out. Wait. What were the rules for our Quaker meeting?

No rules. Just speak to God. And don't interrupt.

On Strike! Shut it down! we both yelled to God.

Professor! Professor!

Gordon and I both turned. I recognized Paul, one of the student leaders of TWLF. He came up, lifted his dark shades, and shook my hand in a kind of power shake. *So good you've joined us. Means a lot.*

Paul, this is my brother Gordon.

Paul looked on Gordon somewhat aghast. *You mean, the . . . ?* He repeated my brother's full name, pausing on each syllable like it was a sacred mantra. He stuttered. *I, I. I'm so honored, sir.*

When did Paul ever call me sir?

Gordon smiled and shook Paul's hand.

Ah, ah, we're meeting tonight. Debriefing. But if you could be there, it would be an honor, sir. Paul looked at me, pleading.

Sure, I answered for Gordon. *I'll bring him over.*

Paul ran off to catch up with his contingent, and Gordon said, *What was that all about?*

You really don't know? That kid Paul knows your story. They practically preach it in the study groups. About how you refused to go to camp. How you jumped curfew, went to prison for your rights.

Gordon shrugged.

You're a hero. One of the few, if not the only. I got you over here for a reason.

Well, several, but . . . Look—I turned to Gordon—*it's time. These kids get it. Took awhile, but I got a feeling.*

Gordon said, *You know, Bayard's my old friend. How many years ago was it, he was trounced by Malcolm X in those debates? Malcolm articulated the problem. These kids are following Malcolm, not Bayard. We're has-been.*

Bayard's arguments came out weak. He used that old word, integration. Malcolm asked: Why integrate with the enemy, the man who enslaved you?

Bayard spoke the truth. A separate theocratic state is unrealistic. Preaching white hatred alienates allies in the same struggle.

I pointed at the students marching. *Have you seen their fifteen demands? Unrealistic? Found a department of Black studies, a college of Third World liberation. Turns out we*—I pointed to Gordon—*are the allies in the same struggle. I think it's time.*

But at what cost? This? Gordon tapped the article under his jacket. *Nowadays, guns are radical. Not pacifism.*

Agh. I waved the air. *Panther talk. Look out there. The police have the guns. You want a war? That's why you're needed. If you speak, they'll listen.*

I've been away too many years. I don't live here anymore. And there's work to do in Canada. I've been thinking I need to apply for Canadian citizenship, but I thought maybe there's a chance we can reverse my old court decision. It was never just about curfew. So, I've kept my U.S. passport. As time passes, who's around to remember anyway? And look what's happened? King's assassinated. Malcolm as well. And how old is Bayard? Floyd, Nevin, Mary, and Burt—the Friends. The Fellowship. We're all getting too old for this. How about Yasui? He bucked the curfew in Portland. And now he's got connections to the JACL, who never supported me. Didn't support the draft resisters, the no-nos. We all got a bum rap. Only the guys who went to war, carried a gun, they're the heroes—

Shut up! I suddenly yelled out. Maybe it was to God. I don't know.

Gordon halted.

I'm taking you to that meeting with the students tonight. You need to hear them out.

We marched along in silence for another block. We'd come full circle around the campus.

Gordon broke our silence. *What happens when this is over?*

I don't know.

We study societies, how they are built. Institutions like this are the foundations of society. They can't be broken so easily. So, this university will survive but not without change. I bet they make you dean of this new Third World college.

What? My mouth hung open.

They're using Sam; they'll use you.

They've always used us. Aren't all your articles coauthored? You do the work; they get you published.

Play by the rules. One day maybe you get autonomy. What do we call it?

Academic freedom. I shook my head.

Think about it. Dean. What will you do then?

I groaned.

Gordon continued. *Sam thought he could govern using his theories, as if semantics can solve everything. If only he got people to think correctly in order to act correctly. Look where it got him. Let that be your lesson. You are, unlike me, a pragmatist. After the idealists and self-righteous go in and tear things down, guys like you go in to build the thing. It won't be perfect, but in the future, guys like me are useless.*

We stopped at a drive-out to let honking cars pass.

Useless? Bullshit. I set the placard down and turned to Gordon. *Thanks for coming. I needed to hear this. Truth is, I'm scared. I thought I'd ease into a quiet afterlife—teaching, traveling, writing. Hey, start dating again.* I leaned into the placard stick and rubbed my aching shoulder. *But you didn't come here to tell me this.*

No, I came to tell you my marriage is over.

We crossed the street silently. *I've been worried about you.*

Got any advice for your big brother?

Mine ended awhile ago. Hard on the kids, but in the long run better. I left for Nigeria, gone two years. Got it out of my system.

Our kids are all gone. Grown-ups. Out of the house. Empty nest. Must seem like good timing. Of course, we could grow old and cranky together.

Things change.

Maybe they were always the same. She was more committed than me. Floyd's daughter. Came with him to visit me in prison. My prison Quaker angel. We wrote letters. Stayed true. Together we believed in an idea, but I turned out to be just a man.

Believe me. I've thought about all the reasons. Women have to give up too much, lose their careers to raise kids, follow us around. Maybe we seemed exotic at the time, but after too many years, imperfections and old habits chafe. Better to leave than to become bitter. Besides, were you a jerk?

Yeah.

Yeah. And then there's that thing we couldn't figure out.

Race?

Yeah.

We thought it didn't matter.

But look out here. I gestured to our protest. *Matters.*

Didn't seem to matter to us. What were we blind to?

Color blind. Supposed to be a good thing but the kids have to deal with it.

Thing is, we did what we did because of love.

Are you going to tell that to the kids?

Yeah, have to tell my kids.

No, I mean these kids out here. I pointed at a contingent of marching Asian American students, fists plunging the frosty San Francisco air.

What do you think?

No. They think you acted entirely on principle. We have to set an example.

It might be wiser to tell them.

It's the wrong story, and they won't believe you anyway.

It will never be the wrong story. Couldn't have happened without love.

DANA: Six Persimmons

DANA

That was the year the persimmon tree exploded with fruit. One day when I got home from classes she was on a ladder with shears snipping persimmons and handing them to my mom below, who was filling buckets and shopping bags. Pooch Maxie was in sit-position next to the tree like he was going to get a treat. She was trying to reach higher into the tree, but Mom said, *That's enough. Leave them for the birds. Anyway, there's more that need to get ripe.*

We hauled the heavy buckets and bags into the kitchen, and she picked through them. *Do you mind if I take a few?*

That one's not ripe, Mom said.

That's fine, she answered. *I need them in different stages, different coloring. Not perfect. This one.* She picked up a bruised fruit pecked by the birds.

Shapes? I asked, and handed her a really squat one.

Okay.

This one is huge.

Okay.

We cradled the fruit loot in our arms, and Maxie and I followed her downstairs to the bedroom next to the rumpus room, plopped them on the bed. She looked over the persimmons and chose six, placing them on the desk, arranging them carefully in a row, then exchanging one position for another, replacing one or another, setting them forward or back, scrutinizing each for blemishes, turning them in the light.

She was born in Manzanar, ended up no-no at Tule. That's what I heard on the drive over to Santa Rita. It was the night before Thanksgiving, and the roads were socked with traffic. The trip should have taken a half hour, but that day it took two hours. I asked, *Why do we have to do this today? Can't it wait?* My folks are nisei, so of course they ignore stupid complaining. Finally, we saw her. Guards brought her out of her jail cell. She looked like any other sansei, older than my sister, but not by much. It was a meet-and-greet thing where we said we'd be her host family. Took another two hours to drive home, but my mom, right away, got her room ready downstairs.

She didn't want to talk, really. At the time, I was at Cal, majoring in math. I could have dormed in Berkeley, but living at home was cheap and came with home cooking, mostly Dad's, who liked to cook, and free laundry. My sister left when she was sixteen and never looked back, but I was used to it.

People like her were always in our house. My folks turned the place into Asian American Movement Central. I couldn't come home without finding some long-haired movement type trying to get my dad to elaborate on prison reform or another following my mom out of the kitchen with a bowl of sembei or furikake mix, pouring tea and sodas to feed some committee. Student organizers, Marxist theorists, Asian Black Panthers, radical pastors, prison activists, political poets—you name it, they made their way up the twisting road to 7028 Colton, like it was a hillside hideout for revolution. A few years back, it was strategizing for a Third World college, then the occupation of Haviland Hall to forestall the fall of the School of Criminology, and now it was her Fair Trial Committee. The committee organized to hire attorneys, reduce her bail, then pay it. Twenty-five thousand. Out on bail, she lived at our house.

My folks met at Cal in the fifties, postwar. Dad came out of Manzanar, Mom out of Rohwer, nisei who intuitively got politics from living in concentration camps. Didn't have to explain it to each other, but that's what bound them together to the end. Turned out they were both activist social researchers on the more radical end of the nisei spectrum. I figure Mom was smarter than Dad, actually came from privilege, was completely bilingual, had an upper-class education in Cleveland Heights, but then her family got caught in the internment. Dad's side were strawberry farmers in the Sacramento Valley, but he claimed to have been a spoiled son with two sisters, privileged in that sense. His memory of grammar school was two rooms, and after that high school, one year of junior college in Sacramento. He said school was easy, but then came Manzanar.

ONE PERSIMMON

Traditional Japanese watercolor is impressionistic, quick deft brushstrokes, graceful and precise, negative space implicit. Delicate petal and stem, tossing koi, prancing horse, a winter landscape—all envisioned in black sumi.

In this scene, it's a hospital barrack lined with cots, a rudimentary setup run by nisei doctors and nurses who desperately try to stretch meager resources. On night duty, a young orderly moves around the cots, all the patients asleep in one position or another, huddled under scratchy green blankets. The orderly wears an army peacoat. Despite the stove at one end of the barrack, it's freezing in the room.

Black to gray tones embellish a soft light, illuminating the face of one patient, a young man of twenty-one, his breathing erratic. The orderly props the man up, securing a tin cup of water. The patient is feverish, grabs the orderly's arm. They stare at each other, knowing they are the same age, that one life could be exchanged for the other, but the patient is Jim Kanegawa, caught, five days ago, in the camp riot, in the confusion of tear gas and machine-gun fire, shot in the back. He whispers to his young caretaker, *I don't want to die.* All through the night, the orderly, bereft of skills, left only with orders to remain on watch to record, if necessary, the time of death, hears Jim repeating his prayer mantra, *I don't want to die. I don't want to die.*

Turn the page of the sketchbook: a month later, in the same hospital, a baby girl is born.

CRIM 100

My lecture today will be on bias in the justice system. We assume the law is blind, but people are not. Officers of the law, district attorneys, judges, juries, prison personnel, parole officers, social workers, all who participate in the administration of justice are subject to the social and cultural bias of their personal vision of justice. The system is far from perfect.

My guest here with us today is a victim of racial and class bias. Her story parallels the history of race prejudice in California and U.S. immigration laws, the incarceration of Japanese Americans during World War II, and the current movement for black and ethnic studies at this university.

Recent events on our campus, the employment of police against students and the subsequent violence is an example of the bias to which I am referring, but in fact police violence is condoned on a daily basis in poor and minority communities. Please refer to the statistical evidence in my article in your reader.

I will conclude this lecture with suggestions for steps toward community policing to effect change.

TWO PERSIMMONS

This scene is in charcoal. A ferry crosses from Hiroshima to the island of Etajima in the Seto Inland Sea. The ferry passes the port of Kure, an old naval base and, during the war, Japan's largest ammunition arsenal. Scars of heavy bombing are still evident. Fishing and freight boats crisscross the sea with the ferry, passing the great remains of tremendous warships, partially sunken, now rusting in the strait, small tugs lugging away salvage. Looking back toward Hiroshima, over the rolling spume in the ferry's wake, one sees the afterimage of the blasted remains of the iconic dome, the leveling of an entire city, and now, a scant year later, teeming with people struggling to survive.

On deck, a toddler girl of two years sits on a bundle of belongings, one hand grabbing the nearby skirt of her mother. Her father grips the railing, his thoughts distant but perhaps perceptible. He's been to Hiroshima, searched for his ancestral home, where he was sent as a boy to be educated. Nothing left. Those who survive say, *You speak English, luckier than us; you can get a job with the Americans.* They don't say, *Please go; leave us,* but it's obvious they don't want to share their meager and precious means. He's left them a box of cigarettes, which can be exchanged on the black market, but he clutches the stash of American cash he's hidden, sewn into his chest pocket.

He looks at his wife and tiny daughter. They've followed him to this mistake, and at all costs he must make it right. The Occupation has set up headquarters in the old imperial naval academy on Etajima. It's not just that he can speak English. He was once, by birthright, an American citizen—he and his wife and his little daughter. He breathes in the sea-salty spring air.

Ten years from this moment, he will receive a letter from an American attorney in San Francisco, Mr. Wayne Collins, settling their case, repudiating their renunciation.

In the next scene, the toddler girl of now twelve. She sits in a second-grade classroom in Fresno, California, towering over the other children and wondering why.

DANA

She was a chain-smoker. I used to go downstairs and smoke with her. Maybe she'd be sketching something, planning out a lithograph. She'd smoke and work, and I'd hang out, to avoid reading or some paper I should have been writing. Maybe I missed my sister.

I don't know what I assumed, but I guess I was surprised to find out she had a life before she came to live with us, that she knew plenty of folks—rich, by our standards, and white—all around the Bay Area. Instead of us, she could've probably lived with any one of them. She could've gone back into hiding and disappeared forever, but I figure that gets old.

Who she didn't know was us, Japanese Americans, what we were now calling Asian Americans. She could name music venues, coffee shops, and bars in S.F., but none of the restaurants and local hangouts in J-Town.

She didn't grow up in our community, even though she could speak fluent Japanese. That was reserved for her parents. They were far away back in Fresno and had no idea what she was up to. It must have been a big surprise to see her on the front page of the *San Francisco Chronicle* with the heiress of that newspaper.

As far as I could tell, all her friends were white hippies. Everyone who read the papers assumed those friends were terrorists. The truth of those stories only she knew. I never asked, and anyway they weren't the secrets we shared in the rumpus room. Well, wasn't that the point of living with us? To change the story. To claim her as one of us. There were legitimate reasons she got involved in radical politics, like the injustice of concentration camps she'd personally experienced. And any one of us sansei could have been, like her, picked up because of friendships and close encounters with the revolution. But would we get a fair shake? The community had risen to save her. Eventually I realized that getting saved was one thing; being the one saved was another.

About the time, at the age of twelve, she moved from Japan to Fresno, I was born in Boyle Heights. In L.A., Dad was a parole officer for drug offenders, a lot of them Hollywood types, jazz musicians, some of them pretty famous. That was when he started his research, realized he was working for injustice just as often as justice.

THREE PERSIMMONS

This scene is in pen-and-ink. A frosty fall morning around six a.m. Along Sproul Plaza, the leaves on the London planes have fallen, exposing craggy trunks. The stillness of the cold air portends none of the tumult that will follow in the next weeks and months. A contingent of Asian American students congregates at Sather Gate, its ornate copper blue-green arch framing the top of the scene. To one side, the great oak. Several students staple gun posters to sticks, prop signage against its trunk. THIRD WORLD LIBERATION FRONT. TWLF. ASIAN AMERICANS FOR SOLIDARITY. ON STRIKE! The sign of the fist thrusts upward. SHUT IT DOWN! YELLOW POWER! STOP THE GENOCIDE. ETHNIC STUDIES NOW! The students are various versions of Asian, clad in heavy green army surplus, well padded at the shoulders, said to help sustain police clubbing. Some sport hachimaki tied around foreheads, though helmets would probably be more appropriate. They pen an emergency phone number onto their wrists, press beef jerky, corn nuts, and dimes deep into pockets. Ready for a confrontation.

One by one, they start the routine, snaking a figure eight in and around Sather's three entries, pumping fists and posters into the air. Someone's got the bullhorn, pumps up the crowd with chanting. At this hour, scant few are there to observe their protest. It will be a few hours before the crowds trickle in. The Asians get the morning shift because, frankly, they might be more organized, don't mind getting up early for classes.

In the distance, they can see a nisei lady with a big thermos and a bag with a box of doughnuts hurrying up the plaza. They say, *Mrs. T, what are you doing here? It's dangerous!* She looks around the empty campus and laughs, passes out cups, pours hot coffee. They choose sugar or jelly. She insists they all get napkins. She'll be there every morning until they send in the riot squad with clubs and tear gas.

DANA

One day she came back to the house with a new haircut. When we first met her at the Santa Rita jail, she had it permed and wavy with a part to the side. She let the perm go, got it straight with bangs like me. I guess we could have been sisters.

Maybe I wanted to know what it was like to live undercover, on the run, on the road. Up until then I'd mostly been around California. Farthest I'd been was Canada, on a family trip to visit my dad's friend Gordon. The world—politics and protest—just seemed to arrive in our house. I paid attention to and ignored arrivals depending on whether they were of interest to me. Eventually I followed some collective types out the door, went to work at a factory because I was supposed to unionize it. It was a hippie candle operation, sculpting amorphous candles in sand. The employees came to work in their pajamas. No one there needed to be unionized.

It was good to have her there for a while to complain to, to compare notes. Still, I never got her inside story, and maybe that was the point. There was no inside story. She had just been at the wrong place at the wrong time. She could have been me, working in a hippie candle factory that could have been a cover for a white bomb brigade. Anyway, that was what her attorneys would argue.

Dad got a feeling for research in the legal system, wanted more of it, and went after his Ph.D. at Stanford, then got recruited to teach in Criminology at Berkeley. He got tenure there and became associate dean of the school. He put together a radical posse of attorneys and legal philosophers to create the theoretical side of criminology. One side of the field was about forensics and practice and the other side was about the system. It might not make sense, but the system side called itself radical criminology, and their purpose was, well, to abolish themselves. He and his cohort started the *Journal of Social Justice*. It was about this time also that Orientals became Asians, and my dad and mom got anointed godparents of Asian American students at Berkeley protesting for the establishment of a Third World college.

CRIM 100

My lecture today will trace the historical origins of our American prison system. I begin my talk with the Walnut Street Jail built in 1790 in Philadelphia, considered to be the first penitentiary with its use of individual cells. Tall narrow room, grated window near the ceiling, single mattress, water tap, and privy pipe. This system replaced jails designed to house large groups, which became overcrowded, unsanitary, and disposed to inmate violence. Walnut Street was considered improved and enlightened, and from that example evolved the Eastern State Penitentiary, also built in Philadelphia in 1829—a castle fortress constructed around an array of seven corridors with five hundred cells and, at its center, a central surveillance point.

The central surveillance point or panopticon was an idea developed by Jeremy Bentham, eighteenth-century philosopher, founder of utilitarianism. The architect of Eastern State was John Haviland, who adopted Bentham's idea. (Incidentally, Haviland Hall is not named for that architect, but I find the name an interesting coincidence.)

Now, pay particular attention to the word "penitentiary," attributed to the Quaker belief in penitence and self-examination as a route to personal salvation. If we are to reform and dismantle the American prison system, it is, I believe, important to recognize its Christian assumptions and influences. The practice of solitary confinement, originally meant to be a kind of forced monastic seclusion to induce reflection, has become an inhuman, unusually cruel method of isolation and punishment, said to be reserved for incorrigibles and death-row inmates.

Please refer to articles in your reader on the psychological effects of solitary confinement and exclusion.

FOUR PERSIMMONS

This scene is in pastels. A hundred and fifty students march into Haviland Hall, chain-lock the doors behind them. They open the third-floor windows and unfurl a banner over the balcony: SAVE THE SCHOOL OF CRIMINOLOGY!

It's a takeover. An outside contingent sets up on the ground for the duration, walkie-talkies back and forth. The inside crowd sits tight for one week. They fashion a pulley and haul up provisions in baskets from the balcony. The outside contingent rallies, marching around with bullhorns. Speeches from the balcony. Cheers and chanting responses from below. *Save Crim! Radical Criminology against Inequality, Injustice, Exploitation, Patriarchy, and White Supremacy! Prisoner Support! Down with the Military Industrial Prison Complex!*

One day, a troop of police in full riot gear scuddle in heavy boots to Haviland, cut the heavy chains on the doors, pound their way up to the third floor. By now the hundred and fifty has whittled down to a dozen; those with state funding and scholarships have sloughed off. Police handcuff and arrest the remaining Haviland dozen.

A month later in June 1974, the Chancellor, with the blessing of UC Regents, initiates the closing of the school.

DANA

She moved out of our house after a few months. I guess I should have predicted it. I was used to the rules, being a good sansei kid and all that. My folks were activists, but they were still nisei. And after all, she was a grown-up who'd been on the run, had boyfriends and intimate relationships, navigated the streets. She'd crossed the country, did a stint in Cuba. The hardcore sorts who came into our living room were mostly playing hardcore. She was the real deal, but nothing about her life made her mean. Somehow, she moved about easy, kind of goofy and just vulnerable enough. I could see how trust and curiosity might get her into trouble. She wasn't breaking rules to provoke my mom. She was just living her life. Anyway, my mom lost control, but to be fair, she thought she was responsible for the public face of the Fair Trial Committee. I didn't want her to leave. I called my sister in New York. *Mom's pissed.* My sister answered, *So?*

She found an apartment in north Oakland, Rockridge, and we reconvened the Fair Trial Committee work there. I scooted between her apartment and Glide Memorial on Ellis.

I joined the subcommittee for the jury pool, working on surveys to determine anti-Asian bias. We were there to screen the jury selection, then try to determine their moves. I remember there was a fat bald guy who we thought could be a swing vote, and we tried to figure out how to swing him. In those days, we assumed that discrimination was a conscious thing, that prejudice just had to be revealed, and you'd make a conscious decision to change the course of history. Boy, were we dumb in those days. The judge was Martin Pulich, a tough-on-crime Republican; his subconscious bias was hidden under a paper-thin veneer.

When it was all over and we'd lost, I was there in her Rockridge apartment. The attorneys were there, too, that night. I brushed away tears, apologizing that I didn't work hard enough on those jury surveys, that we could've done this or that, that I'd failed her.

She chuckled. *Oh,* she said, *don't beat yourself up. You did the best you could.*

I couldn't believe it. She was going to prison. *Don't worry,* she smiled. *We'll see each other again.*

FIVE PERSIMMONS

This scene is inside a color television. ABC Channel 7 Eyewitness News. Friday, May 17, 1974. The television set could be in any American living or hotel room in metropolitan L.A. It's the evening news report: *They say police fired more ammunition than they'd ever fired before in a single assault. Just who are the five persons killed? That still is not known. We still have nothing official at this hour to say with certainty that the five persons who died in the shootout were actually members of the Symbionese Liberation Army. Coroner Dr. Thomas Noguchi is even now trying to identify the bodies, some of which were burned beyond recognition.*

Earlier that day, continuously, for two hours, television cameras focus on a yellow one-story stucco house in South L.A. just east of the Harbor Freeway, on Compton Avenue and Fifty-fourth Street. Those who tune in to ABC sit riveted to the tube—sound of popping gunfire, dramatic reporting by film crew and police, women and children fleeing the house and houses nearby, and finally, orange flames roiling from windows, black smoke spurting skyward. It is said to be *the most dramatic gun battle in Los Angeles history,* and Angelinos across the city watch it all in real time, live.

DANA

People want to know what happened. They think it's over so it's okay to talk, but it's really not. There is always a chance that some DNA test could put someone in prison, even years after it happened. You'd think people would forget and forgive. Let people who made mistakes when they were young get on with their lives, live into old age peacefully. But revenge is built into the justice system and never lets go. Dad thought it was bias and eugenics, but it's more than that. He started something, even if he didn't realize it. Now they call it abolition. Abolish the prison system. Until that happens, some secrets have to die with you.

I drove out to Corona, down south toward the Inland Empire, prison for women. On the way, I stopped in Fresno, picked up a package of art supplies from her mom. I brought her that and cigarettes, then sat around and smoked like old times, kept her company for an afternoon. She was there for about a year. After her parole, I visited her at the Juice Bar Collective on Vine. She blended me a nutritional drink, called it Sunset, orange and carrot juice. I told her that my mom died of a heart attack. I thought she should know.

She said, *Everyone loved your mom like the activist mom they wanted to have.*

I chucked. *Yeah.*

Well, you got your doctorate before she died. I bet she was happy about that.

That was true.

How's your dad?

He'll survive.

We walked over to her studio. I hung around looking at her watercolors of fruit. I figured she brought fresh fruit home from the bar and painted them. Until you see her work, you don't know that watercoloring can be like photography. That's her genius. As I left, she handed me a watercolor of six persimmons. They call it still life, but I swear those persimmons are not still. Life is not still.

CRIM 100

My lecture today will trace eugenics as an accepted scientific study of racial difference, positing IQ tests and cultural and social measurements of achievement as valid comparative evidence of racial superiority. Eugenics as a methodology of distinguishing racial groups has been largely discredited. This is due to its ignominious connection to the Holocaust; however, the residue of its thinking still persists.

For example, the findings of standardized tests have been used to compare student achievement, and in the case of Japanese students in America and Canada, tests have demonstrated their superiority over white students in the areas of math and science, while lagging behind in language literacy. The scholastic achievement of Japanese American students, despite lower economic status and settlement in poor and ghettoized neighborhoods, has been attributed to cohesive familial structure, community organization, and ascribed cultural values.

Today, I want to dispute what I believe are assumptions that have not been statistically researched nor confirmed by critically honest methods of investigation. A kind of cultural essentialism continues to pervade our thinking about racial difference, makes erroneous comparisons that divide us, place us in unnecessary and destructive competition.

Please refer to the reader, to chapters from Ruth Benedict's *Chrysanthemum and the Sword* and David Starr Jordan's *Human Harvest.*

SIX PERSIMMONS

These scenes are expressed in vibrant watercolor. Watercolors of natural life have a long history, including Carl Linnaeus in the eighteenth century, who created a system for classification and botanical illustration.

In one scene, there are six varieties of persimmon or kaki, astringent and nonastringent, represented in varying sizes—large orbs, squat tomatoes, oval or pear-like, and the many colorations of fall—deep orange, yellow, purple to brown.

In the second scene, the persimmons are all of a kind, hachiya perhaps, in different stages of ripening. Bite into an unripened hachiya: The mouth and tongue recoil, pucker: dry and bitter. Bite into the fully ripened fruit: soft, pulpy, honey-sweet. This is the variety that hangs strung by stems, under winter eaves, dry ripened in snowy climes.

In the third scene, the kaki are all fuyu, squatly orange, some supple with crunch, the scent of cinnamon and cloves, others mushy with syrup and the sweet alcoholic stink of rot.

The persimmon tree renders its fruit in autumn, at year's end, when its deciduous leaves turn orange, flutter away, leaving branches naked but for that glorious harvest of golden globes turning in October light.

AIKO: Final Report

[T]he "Japanese American Evacuation and Resettlement Study" was set up under the directorship of Dorothy Swaine Thomas, then a University of California Professor of Rural Sociology and a skilled demographer. Her staff included a broad spectrum of social scientists, but curiously did not include either professional historians or archivists.

—Roger Daniels, *Concentration Camps USA*, 1972

Tuesday, August 11, 1981
National Archives & Records Administration
Washington, D.C.

Peter jogs out of the Library of Congress. It's his birthday. He turns forty today. Ninety degrees in August in D.C., humidity at 65 percent. He makes a runner's decision, around the Capitol, down the grassy mall, past the Smithsonians. At the LOC, flipping through the card catalog, a few books had turned up, but none on the legal cases. Nothing on Korematsu. Nothing on Hirabayashi or Yasui. Wide-open territory; could be his next book. Heading toward the National Archives, driblets of salty sweat pasting shirt to back and armpits, he turns past the giant front portico, pillars supporting grandeur, where the tourists line up to view the Declaration of Independence. At the back entrance, level with Pennsylvania Avenue, he saunters through the brass doors flanked by sword-bearing Roman reliefs. No backpack to check, into cold air-conditioning. Talk to Marian. She'll help. She's the one who pointed him to *History of Supreme Court Cases*. Korematsu was a footnote, and footnotes are like small diamonds scattered at the bottom of pages. Marian likes him, though maybe she likes everyone, treats every visitor with the same smile, the same archival hospitality, not just him, but he's personable, never rude, cracks jokes, has a slightly needy demeanor. Besides, she wants to help, be useful, and what's not to like? Innocent flirting over arcane knowledge. Throw some sparkles into the dusty archive. Marian the librarian.

Marian walks him into the stacks. Trust her; she's been here since the thirties. *Let's see: WRA solicitor files.*

What's WRA?

War Relocation Authority. They administered the internment of the Japanese during the war. Oh, it's all checked out. She points to a huddle of carts all surrounding one table in the center of the hall. Hey, that must be everything. No one should be able to hoard everything. This is a public entity, criminy crickets. But, he can't show irritation. Dear Marian smiles. He's got to wait his turn.

He's got a lanky stride in his blue Adidas. Can't hurt to take a look, hover, just to let the person know he's in line, waiting. As if it's a crowded restaurant and he's got a reservation too. And check out if it's really the stuff he needs to see. Behind the carts, hidden between stacks of documents, a tiny woman is bent over a yellow pad, scribbled end to end, thick with pages and pages of notes. And let's be more specific; the tiny woman is Asian, a wavy swirl of coiffed gray and glasses, oversized frames hiding her features. Later he'll find out she's nisei. She never looks up, so immersed is she in work. He sneakers around, checking the labels on the folders and boxes. Oh, she's reading from the record: *Hirabayashi v. United States, Opinion of the U.S. Supreme Court.* He peers through the lower end of his glasses, reads it over her shoulder. Her fingers tap nervously, then follow the sentences, reading the paragraph slowly once and then again.

> The indictment is in two counts. The second charges that appellant, being a person of Japanese ancestry, had on a specified date, contrary to a restriction promulgated by the military commander of the Western Defenses Command, Fourth Army, failed to remain in his place of residence in the designated military area between the hours of 8:00 o'clock p.m. and 6:00 a.m. The first count charges that appellant, on May 11 and 12, 1942, had, contrary to a Civilian Exclusion Order issued by the military commander, failed to report to the Civil Control Station within the designated area, it appearing that appellant's required presence there was a preliminary step to the exclusion from that area of persons of Japanese ancestry.*

He's too close, close enough to hear her soft groan. Plus, he's still a little sweaty from his run; it must give him away.

She turns to confront him. *Are you looking for something?* Her voice is low; its growl pushes into the floor.

Well, yes, I, well, aren't these the WRA—he smiles to himself, quick learner—*files for the wartime internment of Japanese?*

Yes.

He clears his throat to create an air of propriety. *Well, I'm interested in the legal cases that contested internment.*

Are you a lawyer?

Yes.

Oh good. She knows white men and their proprieties; they can be useful. *Read this. What does it mean?*

He continues to read:

> The conviction under the second count is without constitutional infirmity. Hence we have no occasion to review the conviction on the first

* 320 U.S. 81 (1943).

count since, as already stated, the sentence in the two counts are to run concurrently and conviction on the second is sufficient to sustain the sentence. For this reason also it is unnecessary to consider the Government's argument that compliance with the order to report at the Civilian Control Station did not necessarily entail confinement to a relocation center.*

She's patient and attentive when he speaks. *Well,* he says, *the court separated Hirabayashi's conviction into two counts: one, his failure to report to be evacuated, and two, his failure to obey curfew. They ruled on number two, that he disobeyed curfew, and they argue that, in time of war, curfew is justified, so he's guilty. They skirted the issue of evacuation.* He paused. *They do this all the time. Decide on a case so narrowly, so specifically, that it sounds reasonable. Did Hirabayashi disobey a law? Yes. Then he's guilty. The end.*

Oh, you're very good at this. Why didn't they just say what you said? She quickly scribbles his explanation onto her yellow pad, and says appreciatively, *You could be a teacher.*

I am.

She finally turns in her chair to look at him squarely. *Are you saying that if they'd ruled on the first count forcing Hirabayashi's exclusion, Gordon might have, well, all of us, could have been freed?*

Yes.

She points at the carts loaded with file boxes. *There's a mountain of evidence that shows we were loyal citizens imprisoned in concentration camps because of racial prejudice. What you're saying is that they avoided the big question in order to condemn us anyway?*

Oh, she gets it. It's a rhetorical question, but he answers, *Yes.*

She peers at him over her glasses. *They lied to us.*

I think so.

We need to prove that they lied. You're a lawyer. Do lawyers lie?

They shouldn't.

Seems to me that lawyers change the way they say things so that it doesn't sound like a lie. It's very confusing, but I suspect only a lawyer like you can find the lie. I mean, she pauses to stare down a man on the next table who coughs to show his irritation. She lowers her voice. *I know there's a lie in there, but can you expose it?*

---

* 320 U.S. 81 (1943).

He leans in conspiratorially. *Maybe.* He looks over at the man at the other table; that guy doesn't realize this little Asian lady is a force with a mission.

She points to the chair beside her. *Sit down. I need your help. We have to find every document in this mess that proves them wrong. I don't understand the legalese. It's confounding.* She pushes a file toward him. *Here, find what's important. What's hidden. I don't want to miss anything significant.* She passes a clean yellow legal pad in his direction and commands, *Copy down everything, and don't forget to note the document number, what file, what box, what record group.*

She's got a pile of pink papers cut into three-by-five cards. He's dumbfounded and in awe. She's cataloging everything, and she has a system. Better to be obedient, sit down, take a file, read. If he wants to see these files, better do as she says.

Periodically she looks over, observes his work, maybe his handwriting skills, and nods approvingly. After several hours, she taps him on the shoulder. *Time for lunch,* she announces.

Why not? he thinks, and sneakers behind her to the lockers.

She says, *Usually, my husband meets me, but today he made me a tuna fish sandwich. We can share. Not much, but you must be hungry.*

They sit outside on the lawn. She rips open a bag of chips, pours tea from a thermos. He offers her a cigarette. They blow cool smoke into shaded humidity. After a moment, she smiles and asks, *Now, what was your name?* She giggles, low and taunting.

I'm Peter. He juts his hand forward.

I'm Aiko, she says, still giggling, then laughs out loud. It's infectious.

They laugh hilariously for a long while.

I'm so sorry, Aiko sputters into sincerity. *I didn't think you'd stay. But, you're doing an awfully good job. Now I can't let you go. I really need your help.* She snatches under the clear rims of her glasses at laughing tears, then speaks seriously. *I can explain. I'm the archivist for the CWRIC, it's the official commission on the incarceration of Japanese during the war. A public hearing is going on right now in San Francisco. After that, it's Seattle, Alaska, Chicago. We're on a deadline, gathering the material for the written report.*

So you're a historian?

No. I'm a retired mom. She feigns an annoyed look. *Do you know Michi Weglyn? She wrote the book* Years of Infamy.

He feels sheepish.

Well, you need to read it. Michi was a costume designer for Perry Como. She's my inspiration. But what about you?

I came down from Boston to research a book on the FBI, but it's five thousand rolls of microfilm in random chaos, so I've abandoned that. Now I'm thinking I'd like to study the Korematsu case. Also Hirabayashi and Yasui.

She nods approval. *Those guys contested internment. Cases went to the Supreme Court.*

Yes. I'm curious about the decisions.

Why? I mean, she pauses, *what's your beef?*

He studies her poker face and decides. *I burned my draft card to oppose the Vietnam War and went to jail. I went to jail because it's the law, but I thought, what's the law? So now I study it.*

Oh. She smiles.

Anyway, you know these archives. To be frank, you've got all of them.

Yes, I have official commission status, priority access. Actually, I probably shouldn't be sharing this material—Aiko crunches a chip, licks the salt from then rolls a pointed finger in the air like a magic wand. *But*—she points the same finger at him—*you know the law.*

If I help you, then?

Yes, okay, she says sweetly. *It's a deal.*

A deal.

Half a tuna fish sandwich is not much of a deal. She pouts. *I can make it up to you. Jack will be here at six. Dinner?*

Tuesday evening, February 17, 1942
1669 31st Street NW, Washington D.C.
(home of Francis & Katherine Garrison Chapin Biddle)

Dramatis Personae:

Francis Beverley Biddle, Attorney General of the United States, age 56

Katherine Garrison Chapin Biddle, poet, librettist/playwright, wife of Francis Biddle, age 52

Edward J. Ennis, director, Alien Enemy Control Unit, Justice Department, age 35

James H. Rowe, assistant to Attorney General, age 33

John J. McCloy, Assistant Secretary of War, age 47

Allen W. Gullion, Provost Marshal General of the Army, age 62

Karl R. Bendetsen, Major, liaison, and later Colonel, assistant chief of staff to General John L. DeWitt, General of the Western Defense Command and Fourth Army, age 35

Peter H. Irons, civil rights attorney, political scientist, and legal scholar

Aiko Herzig-Yoshinaga, political activist, lead researcher for the Commission on Wartime Relocation and Internment of Japanese American Civilians

Scene:

Georgetown, nineteenth-century pre–Civil War fifteen-room home of Francis and Katherine Biddle

PETER: What are we doing here?

AIKO: We're future ghosts.

PETER: Is there such a thing?

AIKO: Why not? We have a right to be here. I have a right to be here. These men determined my young future and destroyed it. Right here, in this dining room. Cut glass, fine china, silverware, over Irish lace.

PETER: Are you sure it was dinner? Did they make their decision before or after?

AIKO: Had to be after. How could Ennis and Rowe eat after?

PETER: An after-dinner decision over drinks.

AIKO: Don't forget, technically, the decision had already been made.

PETER: Only Ennis and Rowe didn't know. Look, there's Attorney General

Francis Biddle, confident, with his comb-over, hairy brows, and thin moustache, sitting at the head of the table. He's proposing a toast.

AIKO: At the other end, Mrs. Katherine Garrison Chapin Biddle, tonight her hair slightly graying. They're both in their fifties, two sons, one dead at age seven. Son Edmund in college. She's worried he'll register and she'll lose him too. Sad eyes.

PETER: Katherine wrote the libretto for the opera *And They Lynched Him on a Tree,* music by the African American composer William Grant Still.

AIKO: To support an anti-lynching bill.

PETER: I read there were two choruses, one white and the other black.

AIKO: Segregated?

PETER: The bill failed in Congress. Point is, this table is set with liberal politics, old Philadelphia abolitionism in the middle of conspiratorial D.C.

AIKO: There's something thin, brittle about that couple. But, *Mr.* Biddle is not *Mrs.* Biddle. Now, *she* might have had the backbone.

PETER: Notice how they're lined up on either side of the table. On one side, the military brass: provost general Allen Gullion, old hard-liner in full uniform flanked by younger yes-men, Assistant Secretary of War John McCloy and Gullion's deputy, a major also in uniform, Karl Bendetsen.

AIKO: Bendetsen works for DeWitt, too, ping-pongs back and forth between the two old generals.

PETER: On the other side, the opposing team, Biddle's suited young cadre of New Deal lawyers: Edward Ennis and James Rowe.

AIKO: War to the right. Justice to the left. Truth is, they're all FDR New Deal.

PETER: Versions of the New Deal. But here, the Biddles are presiding. What will they eat?

AIKO: There's a black cook in the kitchen. I read the menu: filet mignon. Sautéed medium rare with shredded heart of artichoke in Madeira. The sides are broccoli polonaise and wild rice au gratin.

PETER: In wartime?

AIKO: The servant is pouring Paul Garrett sparkling burgundy.

PETER: You notice who's relaxed and who isn't.

AIKO: War has at least two glasses. Justice just sips. They finish with Lady Baltimore cake. Who's Lady Baltimore? Cake looks yummy.

PETER: Angel food cake, nut and raisin filling, Swiss meringue frosting. What were you eating in camp at the time?

AIKO: Don't go there.

PETER: Oh listen, Bendetsen is lying about his ancestry to Mrs. Biddle. She got him to admit he's not a Harvard but a Stanford man.

KATHERINE BIDDLE: Major, might you be related to Bendetson Netzorg, the illustrious pianist?

PETER: That Bendetson is definitely Jewish. She's fishing.

KARL BENDETSEN: I don't believe so, ma'am. We're Danish, from Maine.

AIKO: Bendetsen was born Jewish in Aberdeen, Washington. One lie leads to another.

PETER: And another. He's a young, handsome climber for sure. Looking like a movie star, perfect hair combed back and parted just right of middle.

AIKO: Arrogant bastard, calculating subservience, flying back and forth between the generals, Gullion in D.C. and DeWitt in the Presidio, a lousy liaison manipulating racist egos.

PETER: Listen. Gullion is quoting from Shakespeare like an aging theatrical actor. Iago's lines from *Othello.*

ALLEN GULLION: *The Moor is of a free and open nature / That thinks men honest that but seem to be so, / And will as tenderly be led by th' nose / As asses are—*

AIKO: Mrs. Biddle is impressed. She'll better him.

KATHERINE BIDDLE: *I have't. It is engendered! Hell and night / Must bring this monstrous birth to the world's light.*

PETER: Applause around the table.

AIKO: The New Deal Justice lawyers, Ennis and Rowe, glance sideways at each other. Poke at their wild rice like they're looking for nuts. Personally they hate the racist old general.

PETER: Gullion could be making fun of his lackey Bendetsen, clueless to Shakespeare. But if Bendetsen is Iago, who is Othello?

AIKO: DeWitt? Now there's a clueless man.

PETER: Susceptive to rumors for sure. The old codger DeWitt's just like us, ghosting this table. Gullion's dear old friend, for whom he speaks and makes the fool.

AIKO: Record shows, originally, DeWitt was against mass evacuation. Then for it, then against it, finally all over it, signed the order on the dotted lines. Shrewd Bendetsen pushed all his shiny buttons. Wishy-washy.

PETER: Can you reach into McCloy's mind? There he sits at the end of the table, attentive to Mrs. Biddle, self-satisfied, swishing down the last of his burgundy. Assisting war. In the end, the shrewdest mind in the room.

JOHN MCCLOY: [interior thoughts] That old fool DeWitt, put out to pasture on the West Coast. If the West Coast were really ever under attack, we're lost. Man hasn't got a thought of his own, rising through the ranks by taking on the opinion of the last man who convinces him.

AIKO: Trusty Bendetsen made sure he, Bendetsen, was always *that* last man. A secondary character, low on the military totem pole, Bendetsen's the architect of the evacuation. His fingerprints are on every document DeWitt ever signed. If only I could strangle him now.

PETER: They're moving from the dining table to the relaxed comfort of the living room.

AIKO: Mrs. Biddle retires, leaves the men to their dirty work. Now Biddle is pouring scotch. The war department guys all tap cold golden glasses. Biddle's a brandy man.

PETER: A black servant brings hot black coffee on a silver platter for the Justice men.

AIKO: Unlike booze, coffee must be getting scarce. Drink it while they can.

PETER: Watch McCloy get his briefcase. Pulls out his ever-present yellow legal pad. Can't think without it. Even with a fait accompli he's going to take notes.

AIKO: Get ready for the fireworks.

JAMES ROWE: I was in San Francisco in early January and spoke with General DeWitt. He said that an evacuation was damned nonsense. All he wanted was the establishment of restricted areas A and B.

BENDETSEN: Around the same time, I had meetings with the state attorney general, Earl Warren, and Congressman Leland Ford and others, and they are extremely concerned about sabotage. I believe General DeWitt is now of the opinion that an evacuation of the Japanese population is the only answer to protect restricted areas.

EDWARD ENNIS: Mass evacuation is still damned nonsense. If this is the case, what about the entire East Coast and all the Germans and Italians residing there?

BENDETSEN: We've been concerned, for example, with Los Angeles, where you have so many industrial installations over the face of the city that, if you attempt to establish a protective island around each of those installations, you would find first that those circles would soon overlap, and also, of course all the supply lines and power lines. The map of the restricted area is certainly much greater than previously anticipated. And as you may know, the California plan was to remove all Japanese from coastal areas to the interior and put them in agricultural labor camps.

JAMES ROWE: Those California politicians are just nuts. Caving in to them is out of the question.

MCCLOY: It's true the Army cannot take a position even in conversations with political figures out there that it favors a wholesale withdrawal of Japanese citizens and aliens from the coast.

ENNIS: Citizens?

MCCLOY: There are a number of complications, which we have not yet seen the end of.

ENNIS: That's stating it mildly.

MCCLOY: We've reached the point where we felt perhaps the best solution is to limit withdrawal from certain prohibited areas. In the first place, there are so many legal problems involved in discrimination, that is to say discerning the difference between the native-born Japanese and the aliens.

ROWE: Native-born Japanese are aliens.

MCCLOY: I mean American-born Japanese citizens and aliens. Where was I?

BENDETSEN: Second place?

MCCLOY: In the second place, so many people would be involved in a mass withdrawal, and the social and economic consequences would be so great that we would like to go a little more slowly on it.

BENDETSEN: General DeWitt has made it clear that, although we haven't gone through the details of it—

AIKO: He means *he* hasn't gone through the details.

BENDETSEN: It would be no job as far as an evacuation were concerned to move one hundred thousand people. We could do it in job lots. Four to five thousand a day.

MCCLOY: We've been a little afraid that if it gets about out there that the Army is taking the position of mass withdrawal, it may stimulate panic.

BIDDLE: The question of whether Japanese should be evacuated, citizens or not, necessarily involves a judgment based on military considerations. This, of course, is the responsibility of the Army. I have no doubt that the Army can legally, at any time, evacuate all persons in a specified territory if such action is deemed essential from a military point of view for the defense and protection of the area. No legal problems arise when Japanese enemy aliens are evacuated; but American citizens of Japanese origin could not, in my opinion, be singled out of an area and be evacuated with the other Japanese.

GULLION: Listen, Biddle, do you mean to tell me that if the Army, the men on the ground, determine it is a military necessity to move citizens, Jap citizens, that you won't help out?

BIDDLE: That is correct.

ROWE: You and the War Department are on your own.

ENNIS: Look here. The Justice Department, the War Department, all of us who work for this government, this nation, have an obligation to the Constitution. What you are suggesting goes against the laws of this country. Wartime or not. We've made an oath. If not, what are we fighting this goddamn war for?

ROWE: The Justice Department cannot go on record to isolate one group of people, one race of people for mass evacuation. Isn't that what Hitler is doing to the Jews? In America we have habeas corpus.

GULLION: Young man, we are at war. To hell with habeas corpus.

MCCLOY: You are putting a Wall Street lawyer in a helluva box, but if it is a question of the safety of the country and the Constitution, why the Constitution is just a scrap of paper to me.

BENDETSEN: As Mr. Biddle has previously suggested, we might accomplish the removal of citizens by evacuating all persons in the area and then permitting back those whom the military authorities believe are not objectionable from a military point of view.

ENNIS: Why are we even speaking of removal of citizens when this is clearly unnecessary? There have been no instances of sabotage. The FBI, J. Edgar Hoover himself, has said so. He's stated that over two thousand arrests on the Custodial Detention ABC list have been made since December 7. The entire first-generation Japanese leadership has already been detained. This constitutes the major danger of any fifth column activity.

MCCLOY: Now, we cannot take lightly any possibility of fifth column activity.

BENDETSEN: General DeWitt has been carefully tracking evidence of Jap submarines and ship-to-coast radio activity.

ROWE: But there's no evidence whatsoever of any reason for disturbing citizens. The Navy conducted an investigation. By an officer named Ringle, the one who broke into the Japanese consulate. He and Mr. Munson both agreed there's no necessity for removing the Japanese. No evidence.

GULLION: No evidence? Your department is trying to cover yourselves and lull the populace into a false sense of security. If our production for war is seriously delayed by the sabotage of the West Coast states, we stand very possibly to lose the war. I have not personally inspected the situation in those states, but from reliable reports from military and other sources, the danger of Japanese-inspired sabotage is great. That danger cannot be minimized. No halfway measures based on considerations of economic disturbance, humanitarianism, or fear of retaliation will suffice. Such measures will be too little or too late.

ROWE: Officer Kenneth Ringle, I believe, is a reliable source, considering his expertise in the Japanese culture and language. He is one of our few experts in the field.

GULLION: Young man, I saw service during the Moro Rebellion in the Philippines. I am familiar with the Oriental mind. More significantly, I fought with Pershing in the Kentucky Second Infantry over the Mexican border, and I personally met the Japanese spies we sent in to poison Pancho Villa. I know the tenacious inscrutability of the Japanese and their willingness to work for any side.

AIKO: Oh, that's bizarre.

PETER: Rowe's about to jump out of his chair, but McCloy changes the subject.

MCCLOY: I assume you've read Lippmann's column.

PETER: Oh, look, he's pulling *The Washington Post* right out of his briefcase.

AIKO: Walter Lippmann cozied up to DeWitt and Attorney General Earl Warren, then wrote that piece of yellow journalism.

MCCLOY: [quoting Walter Lippmann] *[T]he Pacific Coast is in imminent danger of a combined attack from within and without. It is a fact that the Japanese navy has been reconnoitering the Pacific Coast more or less continually . . . There is the assumption [in Washington] that a citizen may not be interfered with unless he has committed an overt act . . . The Pacific Coast is officially a combat zone. Some part of it may at any moment be a battlefield . . . And nobody ought to be on a battlefield who has no good reason for being there. There is plenty of room elsewhere for him to exercise his rights.*

BIDDLE: That's the absolute nonsense of an armchair general.

PETER: Good dig at Gullion.

ENNIS: There is no evidence of planned sabotage.

BIDDLE: I have designated as a prohibited area every area recommended to me by your department. We've got no dispute here between the War, Navy, and Justice.

ROWE: The evacuation of ninety-three thousand Japanese in California is unnecessary. It will disrupt agriculture production, require thousands of troops, tie up transportation, and raise very difficult questions of resettlement. And under the Constitution, sixty thousand of these Japanese are American citizens.

BIDDLE: It is extremely dangerous of journalists, acting as armchair strategists and junior G-men, to suggest that an attack on the West Coast and planned sabotage is imminent when the military authorities and the FBI have indicated that this is not the fact. It seems close to shouting FIRE! in the theater; and if race riots occur, these writers will bear a heavy responsibility. Either Lippmann has information that the War Department and the FBI apparently do not have or he is acting with dangerous irresponsibility.

GULLION: Biddle, we've been in consultation with General DeWitt and upon our recommendation he is preparing for the record his recommendations and his reasons for his recommendations, based on his assessment going up and down the coast.

BENDETSEN: Yes sir, I believe that General DeWitt is preparing a document that can support and confirm Lippmann's statements.

AIKO: Oh there it is. He's preparing DeWitt's *Final Report*, the report that will justify FDR's executive order and our incarceration as a military necessity.

GULLION: Gentlemen, I believe we can all agree that only presidential action from the commander in chief can intercede to enable us to take necessary and vigorous action. We need not mention the evacuation of citizens or make any racial distinctions. We only need a general proclamation, establishing military oversight of restricted zones. We may call them proscribed military zones from which anyone can be excluded.

MCCLOY: The President has given us carte blanche to do what we want. Well, he has said, *Be as reasonable as you can.*

ENNIS: What does that mean?

PETER: Here it comes. Gullion is reaching into his pocket. He's got a sheet of paper folded up.

GULLION: Now, as Mr. Biddle will explain, we spoke with the President this morning, and we, Bendetsen and I, have been working all afternoon to draft this executive order. Of course, we ask you Justice men, who have the full authority and expertise, to finalize the legal language appropriate to our situation.

ROWE: [astounded laughter]

AIKO: Look at Ennis. His face is beet red. Enraged. He's staring aghast at Biddle. It hits him. Betrayed. Rowe looks like he's about to gag.

PETER: Filet mignon and Lady Baltimore vying for escape.

AIKO: Gullion unfolds his draft.
GULLION: [reads]

> Now, therefore, by virtue of the authority vested in me as President of the United States, and Commander in Chief of the Army and Navy, I hereby authorize and direct the Secretary of War, and the Military Commanders whom he may from time to time designate, whenever he or any designated Commander deems such action necessary or desirable, to prescribe military areas in such places and of such extent as he or the appropriate Military Commander may determine, from which any or all persons may be excluded, and with respect to which, the right of any person to enter, remain in, or leave shall be subject to whatever restrictions the Secretary of War or the appropriate Military Commander may impose in his discretion. The Secretary of War is hereby authorized to provide for residents of any such area who are excluded therefrom, such transportation, food, shelter, and other accommodations as may be necessary, in the judgment of the Secretary of War or the said Military Commander, and until other arrangements are made, to accomplish the purpose of this order.*

* Executive Order 9066, February 19, 1942.

Tuesday, September 29, 1981
Department of Commerce
Washington, D.C.

By now, going back and forth, Boston to D.C., he's been staying at Aiko and her husband Jack's place in Maryland. As their research gets focused, he realizes that the WRA files are just one part of what's required. He's got to get files out of the Justice and War Departments and the Supreme Court. Assisting Aiko, he's found little sheets of paper, not even cards, with case numbers and names, scattered within the documents. Follow the trail. He's put in a FOIA request but has little expectation. Between teaching classes at Amherst, he gets the call, and books the train to D.C.

Freedom of Information, indeed. Three boxes of Justice Department wartime docs sit on a desk in the FOIA Commerce office. They'd been in storage in Maryland and misfiled there with Commerce, specifically, the knowledgeable old archivist says, with the Custodian of Enemy Property. Enemy property? There's irony. He stares at dusty boxes bound by twine and digs his nails into the hairy strings, manages to pull them apart, pries open the cardboard flaps, and coughs in the spray of fine dust. Files in manila folders are thrown in like they were pulled randomly from cabinets and stacks on desks. He imagines the end of war, offices closed; on to the next situation, next administration, next political drama, the next war. Sweep out the old and make way for the new. This stuff couldn't be trashed, so it was stored. Condemned to history.

But, it wasn't history yet. People had to live and experience it first. Isn't history always after the fact? What's the point of history that drives accountability after everyone is abused, killed, and dead? Okay, they say that history repeats itself, so, in other words, don't repeat history, but history is always repeated again and again and again. And then there's the law. Turns out the law is fickle, and there's a history of that too. Even if we don't survive the consequences of history, what's left of it becomes a record, stored on hundreds of metal shelves in acid-free boxes, forming an endless labyrinth. Of course, it's just saved stuff.

He opens Box 37 tagged *Korematsu v. United States*. When musty dust settles, he reads the memo sitting on the very top: *Enemy Alien Control Unit Assistant Director John L. Burling to Solicitor General Charles Fahy, April 13, 1944*:

> We are now therefore in possession of substantially incontrovertible evidence that the most important statements of fact advanced by

> General DeWitt to justify the evacuation and detention were incorrect, and furthermore that General DeWitt had cause to know, and in all probability did know, that they were incorrect at the time he embodied them in his final report to General Marshall.*

Holy shit. It's the smoking gun! His heart beats faster, but he needs to look placid, like it's just paper, more of the same archaic bureaucratic pulp that boring legal historians like himself find fascinating.

Just so happens the FOIA deputy chief is out that day, so he says to the old archivist, *This is lot of material. Do you mind if I take it away, take my time with it?*

It's not my area, but I suppose you can tag what you want, and we'll copy and send that to you. Probably have to go through it first to make sure it can leave the archives. These are ancient, but they're still official records.

I see. He could just steal the top pages, but beneath it could be a minefield. He spends the rest of day clipping pieces of paper to particular documents, but there's no way he can read three boxes in the hours that are left, and even if he tags the pages, when they figure out what it is, he probably won't see this stuff ever again. He looks at his watch. *Do you mind if I make a call?*

Help yourself. Phone's over there.

Aiko's at the commission offices today. *CWRIC*, she answers.

Aiko, I'm here at Commerce. The Coolidge Building. You know those Justice Department files? The ones I requested FOIA? Just opened them. I believe you'll find them pertinent to our research. He turns away and whispers, *Aiko, we've got to secure this stuff. Trust me. This is it. They won't let me take it out, but if I leave it here, we might never see it again.*

Aiko replies, *Stay where you are. I'll be there.* And hangs up. Twenty minutes later, she walks into the office waving a piece of paper at the old archivist at the desk. *I understand these boxes contain documents required by the Commission on Wartime Relocations and Internment of Civilians.* It's a mouthful, but she says it to stun the man. *May I have a look?*

They pry open all the boxes and pull out and set aside whatever looks significant and as much as they can carry away. She points at their selected pile of a several hundred pages and announces to the archivist, *We'll be needing to copy these.* And miraculously, Peter follows Aiko out the door, hugging the smoking gun.

* Peter Irons, *Justice at War* (University of California Press, 1983), p. 285; Burling to Fahy, April 13, 1944, Box 37, Folder 3, Fahy Papers, Franklin Delano Roosevelt Library, Hyde Park, New York.

Monday, October 16, 1944
Supreme Court Conference Room
Washington, D.C.

Dramatis Personae:

Chief Justice Harlan Fiske Stone, 71
Justice Owen Josephus Roberts, writing dissenting opinion, 68
Justice Hugo Lafayette Black, writing concurring opinion, 57
Justice Stanley Forman Reed, 59
Justice Felix Frankfurter, writing concurring opinion, 61
Justice William Orville Douglas, 45
Justice Francis "Frank" W. Murphy, writing dissenting opinion, 53
Justice Robert Houghwout Jackson, writing dissenting opinion, 51
Justice Wiley Blount Rutledge, 49

Scene:

Supreme Court Conference Room. Justices, dressed suited but informally—jackets cast aside, ties loosened, pipes and cigarettes smoldering—are seated in nine leather armchairs around a large conference table over a Persian carpet. A fireplace warms the room at one end, and chandeliers above and a large window light the dark wood-paneled room inset with shelves lined with leather-bound legal texts.

AIKO: Where are we now?

PETER: Supreme Court conference room. Deep innards of the court. Nine old white guys come here to deliberate justice. They are convening on Korematsu.

AIKO: To decide my fate.

PETER: Whether Executive Order 9066 was constitutional.

AIKO: Where are the clerks, their minions?

PETER: Only these nine are allowed inside this sacred room, but there's a hierarchy. Last guy appointed has to go to the door to ask for water and clerical assistance.

AIKO: Who's that?

PETER: Wiley Rutledge, confirmed last year, February 8. He's been on the court less than two years. He's their water boy.

AIKO: The chief is at the head of the table?

PETER: Harlan Stone. Elevated to Chief in 1941, but he's been here already eighteen years, since 1925. Originally a Columbia man, Attorney

General under Coolidge. Today he's seventy-one. He'll die in a few years. Just months after the atom bomb.

AIKO: If Rutledge is the last, what's the order?

PETER: Top dog: Stone. Then Roberts, Black, Reed, Frankfurter, Douglas, Murphy, Jackson, Rutledge. They'll go around the table in that order.

HARLAN STONE: Are we confined to the exclusion order or was it so tied in with relocation orders that it must be considered? The court cannot say as a matter of fact that one who goes to an assembly center will go into a relocation center, since we cannot say such an order would ever be made. We must read the order as if it said he should go to an assembly center and stay there subject to further orders. We should treat this merely as an exclusion order.

AIKO: Oh, he's doing that thing again. Confining the argument.

PETER: Narrow the decision to whether Korematsu disobeyed exclusion orders. If they rule on that, then the case is settled.

AIKO: Always evading the question.

PETER: Here's Roberts next. Big man sitting catty-corner to Stone. He's the swing vote, the only justice not appointed by FDR. Considered a former conservative, turned coat. Now he'll show his swing. He went along with the Hirabayashi verdict, agreed to narrow the decision to a curfew violation, but not this time. He's going to dissent.

OWEN ROBERTS: This is not a case of keeping people off the streets at night . . . nor a case of temporary exclusion of a citizen from an area for his own safety or that of the community, nor a case of offering him an opportunity to go temporarily out of an area where his presence might cause danger to himself or his fellows. On the contrary, it is the case of convicting a citizen as a punishment for not submitting to imprisonment in a concentration camp, based on his ancestry, and solely because of his ancestry, without evidence or inquiry concerning his loyalty and good disposition toward the United States.*

PETER: They go down the hierarchy. Stone is counting votes. He wants consensus on his side, and he gets the next three to concur: Black, Reed, Frankfurter. Hugo Black is that fit old gent who plays tennis. Stanley Reed's the balding man with spectacles, longtime New Deal monetary policy man. Felix Frankfurter, short guy also in spectacles, is the only immigrant, Jew born in Vienna, Harvard professor. He was Reed's mentor at Harvard; they usually vote together.

* 323 U.S. 214 (1944).

AIKO: So far, it's four to one. Who's next?

PETER: The guy with the nose, William Douglas. Born in Minnesota, raised in Washington, he's unhappy in the court. He'd rather be president. Tried to be VP, but Truman shoved him off the ticket. When FDR dies, Truman will get the job.

AIKO: What kind of president would he have been?

PETER: A wild card. They call him Wild Bill. Also, they say, a womanizer. Married four times to successively younger women.

AIKO: Very presidential. But what's his call?

PETER: At first, dissent.

WILLIAM DOUGLAS: DeWitt's evacuation program had every earmark of good faith as a measure designed to prevent espionage and sabotage. The assembly centers were conceived as the device for compelling evacuation and making it more orderly and efficient. Public Law 503 does not mention any authority to detain, but the power to detain stems from the power to exclude. If DeWitt had the power to order Korematsu's exclusion from San Leandro, the right to do it by force if necessary must be implied. And any forcible measures must necessarily entail some degree of detention or restraint whatever method of removal is employed.*

AIKO: How is this a dissent?

PETER: Remember, they are trying to disassociate the exclusion order from detention. If it's the same thing, they have to decide whether it was unconstitutional to detain Korematsu. But Douglas moves over to Stone's concurring side in exchange for the following language:

DOUGLAS: Some of the members of the Court are of the view that evacuation and detention in an Assembly Center were inseparable. But whichever view is taken, it results in holding that the order under which petitioner was convicted was valid.†

AIKO: It doesn't make sense.

PETER: Think of it this way. They decide what side to take, then work backward. In the process, they do some horse-trading.

AIKO: With my rights?

PETER: There's a war going on, and FDR is up for a fourth term. Except for Roberts, these men are all FDR appointees. They hold off their decision until after the November elections. Then Frankfurter and Biddle time

* Irons, *Justice at War*, p. 333.

† 323 U.S. 214 (1944).

the announcement of the Endo decision for December 18, the day after the War Department rescinds exclusion from the West Coast.

AIKO: Very convenient. Mitsuye Endo along with several hundred other California State nisei employees were fired after the outbreak of war, but only she has to spend all those years in camp just to be a JACL test case.

PETER: Endo is deemed a loyal citizen, and they agree you can't detain a loyal citizen.

AIKO: So they finally officially release us from incarceration end of 1944.

PETER: The Court is unanimous for Endo, but they blow up over Korematsu.

AIKO: Who's left?

PETER: Murphy, Jackson, and Rutledge.

AIKO: Murphy must be that thin man with the bushy eyebrows and big forehead.

PETER: Born and educated in Michigan, judge and mayor of Detroit. Governor of the Philippines, then governor of Michigan. FDR appoints him Attorney General, then to the Court.

FRANK MURPHY: That this forced exclusion was the result in good measure of this erroneous assumption of racial guilt rather than bona fide military necessity is evidenced by the Commanding General's Final Report on the evacuation from the Pacific Coast area.*

AIKO: Now I remember. Murphy's dissent is mostly over the footnotes in DeWitt's *Final Report.*

PETER: I bet you read every footnote.

AIKO: I did.

MURPHY: I dissent, therefore, from this legalization of racism. Racial discrimination in any form and in any degree has no justifiable part whatever in our democratic way of life. It is unattractive in any setting but it is utterly revolting among a free people who have embraced the principles set for in the Constitution of the United States. All residents of this nation are kin in some way by blood or culture to a foreign land. Yet they are primarily and necessarily a part of the new and distinct civilization of the United States. They must accordingly be treated at all times as the heirs of the American experiment and as entitled to all the rights and freedoms guaranteed by the Constitution.†

PETER: Robert Jackson writes the third dissenting opinion.

* 323 U.S. 214 (1944).
† 323 U.S. 214 (1944).

AIKO: Why didn't they write one dissenting opinion together?

PETER: Subtle differences in legal language. Jackson agrees with Roberts that exclusion is unconstitutional but differs over judicial review.

AIKO: Meaning?

PETER: Meaning Jackson believes that the courts can rule over the military. Justice trumps War.

AIKO: And Roberts sides with military necessity.

PETER: But Jackson still says military judgment is not the judgment of the court. He's not an expert.

AIKO: Too subtle for me.

PETER: Robert Jackson does write the phrase that will be most quoted in the future.

ROBERT JACKSON: Much is said of the danger to liberty from the Army program for deporting and detaining these citizens of Japanese extraction. But a judicial construction of the due process clause that will sustain this order is a far more subtle blow to liberty than the promulgation of the order itself. A military order, however unconstitutional, is not apt to last longer than the military emergency. But once a judicial opinion rationalizes such an order to show that it conforms to the Constitution, or rather rationalizes the Constitution to show that the Constitution sanctions such an order, the Court for all time has validated the principle of racial discrimination in criminal procedure and of transplanting American citizens. The principle then lies about like a loaded weapon ready for the hand of any authority that can bring forward a plausible claim of an urgent need. Every repetition imbeds that principle more deeply in our law and thinking and expands it to new purposes.*

AIKO: *The principle then lies about like a loaded weapon . . .*

PETER: Gun metaphors. His final sentences show more clearly his position. He, like everyone else, had to toe the line with FDR, even though he read the *Final Report*'s military necessity as nonsense.

JACKSON: My duties as a justice as I see them do not require me to make a military judgment as to whether General DeWitt's evacuation and detention program was a reasonable military necessity. I do not suggest that the courts should have attempted to interfere with the Army in carrying out its task. But I do not think they may be asked to execute

* 323 U.S. 214 (1944).

a military expedient that has no place in law under the Constitution. I would reverse the judgment and discharge the prisoner.*

PETER: Two years from now Robert Jackson will take a leave from the Court to serve as chief prosecutor for the Nuremburg trials. Korematsu is a prelude.

AIKO: Roberts, Murphy, Jackson. Three dissents. They disagree on legal points, but they clearly understand that Korematsu has been convicted because of racism and military lies.

PETER: Chief Stone is on shaky grounds. If Douglas defects, Rutledge might go that way too. Black could also defect. He could lose. He gives the guys a pep talk.

STONE: If you can do curfew for Hirabayashi, you can do exclusion for Korematsu.†

AIKO: Five to four. Four to five. Now what?

PETER: Stone makes Hugo Black write the concurring opinion for Korematsu, and makes Rutledge write for Endo. Keeps them busy with the problem.

AIKO: Hugo Black, the tennis player?

PETER: Senator from Alabama. After his court confirmation, it's leaked that he'd been a Klan member. He rejects the Klan to became strong on civil rights. They say, as a young man, he wore a white gown to scare the blacks; as an old man, he wore black to scare the whites.

HUGO BLACK: Our task would be simple, our duty clear, were this a case involving the imprisonment of a loyal citizen in a concentration camp because of racial prejudice. Regardless of the true nature of the assembly and relocation centers—and we deem it unjustifiable to call them concentration camps with all the ugly connotations that term implies—we are dealing specifically with nothing but an exclusion order. To cast this case into outlines of racial prejudice, without reference to the real military dangers which were presented, merely confuses the issue.‡

PETER: Black has to negotiate all the concurring opinions into one compromising concurrence. He has to use Stone's premise on separating exclusion from detention, and get Frankfurter, Douglas, and Rutledge

* 323 U.S. 214 (1944).
† Irons, *Justice at War*, p. 322.
‡ 323 U.S. 214 (1944).

in on the deal. Their messy concessions are all over Black's opinion. In the end, Frankfurter writes his own opinion.

FELIX FRANKFURTER: I join in the opinion of the Court, but should like to add a few words of my own. The provisions of the Constitution which confer on the Congress and President powers to enable this country to wage war are as much part of the Constitution as provisions looking to a nation at peace . . . And being an exercise of the war power explicitly granted by the Constitution for safeguarding the national life by prosecuting war effectively, I find nothing in the Constitution which denies to Congress the power to enforce such a valid military order by making its violation an offense triable in the civil courts . . . To find that the Constitution does not forbid the military measures now complained of does not carry with it approval of that which Congress and the Executive did. That is their business, not ours.*

PETER: He's an ardent FDR man, protecting the power of the exec. It's his manipulation among the justices, the Court, Biddle in Justice and McCloy in War, that moves the opinion.

AIKO: What about separation of powers?

PETER: This is our lesson, isn't it? The political moment dictates the tilt of justice. Black's final words:

BLACK: Korematsu was not excluded from the Military Area because of hostility to him or his race. He was excluded because we are at war with the Japanese Empire, because the properly constituted military authorities feared an invasion of our West Coast and felt constrained to take proper security measures, because they decided that military urgency of the situation demanded that all citizens of Japanese ancestry be segregated from the West Coast temporarily, and finally because Congress, reposing its confidence in this time of war on our military leaders—as inevitably it must—determined that they should have the power to do this. There was evidence of disloyalty on the part of some, the military authorities considered that the need for action was great, and time was short. We cannot—by availing ourselves of the calm perspective of hindsight—now say that at that time these actions were unjustified.†

AIKO: I cannot accept this.

---

* 323 U.S. 214 (1944).

† 323 U.S. 214 (1944).

November, around Thanksgiving, 1982
Herzig-Yoshinaga home in Maryland

He's flown in from San Diego. Jack asks, *How's the teaching?* He pulls out a glass, fills it with ice and scotch, hands it over.

Good. Good. I like my new job. I'm a natural.

They toast.

Priscilla?

Officially now my ex. She hated the move to San Diego, but she's writing now. And working for El Salvador solidarity. She's an amazing writer, beautiful poet. Peter jiggles the ice in his scotch. *I get it. Time to get on with what she wants of her life. She's always been there for me, when I burned my draft card, those years in prison. We'll always be best friends. I'm just glad I got to spend some time with a smart woman.*

Jack nods. *I know what you mean.*

Peter looks around the small living room. Every time he shows up, there're more boxes of documents. The room he stays in is filled to the ceiling. The bed just fits. Good thing it's not California. Earthquake country. An LP plays in the background. Jazz piano. *Who's that?*

You don't know? Aiko comes in from the kitchen and pretends to be shocked. *That's Billy Taylor. I used to work for him in Harlem.* She puts down a bowl of sembei, those little rice crackers bandaged in nori. *Don't snack too much,* she advises. *I made Chinameshi.*

He looks curious.

Don't get too excited. It's just fried rice. How close are you to filing those coram nobis cases?

Jack asks, *Explain again coram nobis?*

It's a writ to correct an error of judgment by presenting new evidence.

Our smoking gun, asserts Aiko. *That memo you found that shows the DOJ covered up DeWitt's lies.*

So we can reopen Korematsu and the other cases, Hirabayashi and Yasui, and get them vacated. We're close. In San Francisco, January. But keep it quiet. Don't want the JACL or any others to upstage this thing. Yasui can't keep quiet.

Jack says, *He's a lawyer. Likes to talk.*

Caught us off guard.

Turf wars. Jack shakes his head and smiles. *You are aware, we work for all sides.*

Peter nods and continues, *I've got to say, you are a very organized people. Passed it on to the next generation: Dale, Lori, Don, all of them, working their butts off but like a well-oiled machine. They've got charts, schedules, keep everyone on their toes. Serious business. Opened offices in Seattle for Hirabayashi, Portland for Yasui, and San Francisco for Korematsu. When I introduced them to Fred, he was puzzled. Who are these kids?*

Aiko takes a sip of Jack's scotch, and her voice trails back into the kitchen. *Asian American Law Caucus kids, that's who. Smart sanseis.*

But then, in between, it's Nerf balls and Pac-Man. Jack, you ever play Pac-Man? He sips the scotch and holds it up. *Takes the edge off. Promotes camaraderie, I'd say. Could have used it at SNCC.*

You were in Snick? Jack pronounces the acronym.

Yep. Voter registration. Mississippi Summer of '64. Left before Stokely, though.

What're you talking about? Aiko returns and growls. There it is, her Lauren Bacall smoker's voice. *That yellow arcade ball that eats?* She passes her hand in front of his face in chomping motions.

That's it. All the rage. I'm pretty good at it myself.

Jack says, *Arcade games, they say, train the mind.*

Yeah, Aiko interjects, *to shoot.*

Jack smiles. *Japanese invented the game. Part of peacetime remodeling. Subliminal consumerism.*

Peter laughs and grabs a handful of sembei. *Anything new to report?*

I found this document. Aiko walks over to the dining table piled with her research. *Now where was that? Here it is. Signed by,* she reads, *Warrant Officer Theodore J. E. Smith. Says: I certify that this date I witnessed the destruction by burning of the galley proofs, galley pages, drafts and memorandums of the original report of the Japanese Evacuation. This is proof that there was a previous version.*

He reads and repeats, . . . *burning of the original report of the Japanese Evacuation. DeWitt's Final Report?*

There were ten originals, told to burn them, but—Aiko shakes her finger. *They could only account for nine destroyed. I just know that out there, somewhere, there's a survivor. If I can find it—*

We can bag Korematsu.

Jack observes, *They destroyed the originals with the lies.*

They were all filled with lies, Aiko quips, then wiggles the paper at him. *Can you use this?*

New evidence. Build that paper trail. He gestures at the stacked boxes along every wall.

Aiko sighs, *Foolish bureaucrat. Theodore J. E. Smith, burning paper, making paper.*

Crumbs in a forest.

Jack jokes, pointing at him, *And Pac-Man follows, eating it all up.*

Several days later, November, 1982
National Archives & Records Administration
Washington, D.C.

Peter and Jack follow Aiko back to the National Archives and hang around waiting for her appointment. Plan is to go on to lunch after.

The archivist is out helping another researcher. Aiko's eyes scan the desks, always the hawk searching down her prey. Hmmm. She fingers a book, *Final Report: Japanese Evacuation from the West Coast.* Looks like another copy of the *Final Report.* There, DeWitt's signature. And the date: *April 1943.* Wait. She recognizes the name penciled in the inside cover, Robert Myers. The editor. Turning pages. Handwritten notations in the margins: *Delete. Scratch. Change. Move.* All fifty-five changes noted in this only surviving copy. It's the tenth copy that the bureaucrat warrant office Theodore J. E. Smith couldn't find to burn and destroy, probably lost at the Whitcomb in DeWitt's very offices at Western Defense. Makes sense. Keep an old version to edit the new. Aiko has found the original *Final Report* with the original lies. She is breathless. A moment only a dedicated archivist can appreciate. Hallelujah! Hours of tedious meticulous notations, week after week, document by document, deciphering the maze to find the story.

Peter and Jack gather around Aiko, flip to the accusing page.

> To complicate the situation, it was impossible to establish the identity of the loyal and the disloyal with any degree of safety. It was not that there was insufficient time in which to make such a determination; it was simply a matter of facing the realities that a positive determination could not be made, that an exact separation of the "sheep from the goats" was unfeasible.*

Aiko pulls out the revision:

> To complicate the situation, no ready means existed for determining the loyal and the disloyal with any degree of safety. It was necessary to face the realities—a positive determination could not have been made.†

The sheep from the goats. Bingo.

---

* John L. DeWitt, *Final Report,* April 1943.

† DeWitt, *Final Report,* June 5, 1943.

MICHAEL: Racial Formation

By any criterion of good citizenship that we choose, the Japanese Americans are better than any other group in our society, including native-born whites. They have established this remarkable record, moreover, by their own almost totally unaided effort. Every attempt to hamper their progress resulted only in enhancing their determination to succeed. Even in a country whose patron saint is the Horatio Alger hero, there is no parallel to this success story.

—William Petersen, "Success Story, Japanese-American Style," *The New York Times Magazine*, January 9, 1966

La raza cosmica. Some say it was born in Mexico, but truth be told, it was born in Hawaii.

The professor shifted uneasily in his chair, red pen wavering over the sentence on the page. He flopped the stack of papers on his lap to the floor and stood up to mute the television. It was something about Eminem outselling Snoop Dog. He didn't know either of them. Not his kind of music. His son would know, then laugh when he assumed they were both black. He bent over and drew back the pile of student responses. *Just get through this before dinner,* he thought.

If we think about the model minority on a global scale, they are the Japanese and Germans, WWII enemies who came around to become America's closest allies.

Good grief, the professor muttered to himself. Maybe it was time for that scotch. He got up and walked to the kitchen, opened the freezer, pulling out the ice tray, twisted the plastic, plopped ice cubes into an empty glass. Poured a golden shot.

Anyway, these student responses were his fault. He asked the question, suggested prompts, keywords, wrote them on the board. Write what comes to mind. What to you is race? How do you live with race? It was a starter query they could look back on at the end of the course, see how far they'd come, what they learned. Right here, in his lap, were the general comments that ought to help him launch the course. Collect ten observations and build ten lectures. Some were repeating themes; he tossed those into one pile.

Aren't we all one race, the human race?

I don't really see race. I don't see color. I try to treat everyone individualistically.

His son sauntered in. *Papers?*

Yeah.

Why you assign them if you don't want to read them?

I didn't say that.

Well, you got the scotch out early. His son loitered around the room. *I was thinking.*

Oh?

I have to write this paper on race.

Is that so?

Race is your thing, right? He held out the textbook.

The professor glanced at his published book, the one that got him tenure.

I'm serious. I'm even reading it. It's pretty good shit.

Thanks.

I need to impress this teacher, see. No one's gonna know I'm your son. I can write the paper myself. I just need a little encouragement.

I encourage you to write the paper.

But what's my hook?

Show me your first paragraph, your thesis. Then we'll talk.

On Racial Formation: The Racial Project in *Blu's Hanging*

> Guided by the theory of racial formation, race in this paper is understood as a category interrelated with categories of ethnicity, class, nation, and gender. Even if we can "see" race, it is not biological. It is a social formation. The theory asserts that race and racial categories are constructed via processes that are social, economic, political, historical, and, I will argue here, also literary. In the words of the theorists, racial formation is "the sociohistorical process by which racial identities are created, lived out, transformed, and destroyed." Because race is a formation, it can become and change. Racial formations have consequences that are positive and negative; that is, a racial formation can be a template for oppression or a template for resistance. Thus, studying racial formation is necessary to understand and oppose racism.

Blu's Hanging?

I saw the book on your desk. It looked interesting. It's an English class. I got to read something.

An English class on race?

Ethnic literature.

It's not the same thing.

Yeah, but. Are you going to help me or not?

Keep writing. What's the book about?

You don't know?
Of course I know. The professor resumed his perusal of student responses.

I'm a biology major, and I really wonder if we should be talking about race at all. I mean we're about to crack the human genome, the blueprint for human life. In the end, all we really amount to is a DNA string.

Times are different. We live in a multicultural society and are given the possibility of learning about and living with other cultures. It's a great experiment, and we should embrace it.

I'm here with an open mind, but frankly, in my opinion, ethnic studies balkanizes people.

Race is embedded in everything. People can't walk out of their houses without confronting it every day. Walk into any place and open your mouth. What do you get? "Your English is so good."

> This paper examines the novel *Blu's Hanging* as a racial project that demonstrates the complexities of racial formation on micro and macro levels.
>
> *Blu's Hanging* is the coming-of-age story told by Ivah, the teenage daughter in an impoverished Japanese American family living on the island of Molokai. Suffering the traumatic death of her mother, Ivah becomes a maternal surrogate, bound to raise her brother Presley and sister Maisie and to keep house for and feed her grief-stricken father Bertrand. Presley is nicknamed Blu, after the film *Blue Hawaii*, starring Elvis Presley. Blu, who eats obsessively and dreams of food, is overweight, and Maisie, since the loss of her mother, is mute. The secret stigma that isolates the family is that the parents, Bertrand and deceased Eleanor, were once confined in Molokai's leper colony, likely the common though unspoken humiliation of the surrounding community. Struggling with the confinement of family trauma and ghettoized misery, Ivah must find her way.

Dad?
He opened his eyes.

You asleep?

No.

I'm thinking about Japanese Americans in Hawaii. Arguing that this community on the island of Molokai is a racial formation. You know you only have one paragraph on Japanese on page thirty? He pointed to the paragraph.

Book's not about one group.

What's JERS?

What it says. Japanese Evacuation Resettlement Study. Sociological study of the Japanese in the camps.

Were the camps racial formations?

Expressions of.

Hmm. His son wandered back to his room.

> Ivah's narrative is infused with pidgin dialogue in contrast to the arrogance and imposition of proper American English of outsiders and, in particular, teachers. The inflection, play, and humor of pidgin throughout the book is revelatory and provocative. Most resonant is the representation of education in Hawaii as a struggle to perform proper English. While pidgin is the common vernacular uniting a community characterized as working-class poor, ethnic differences are recognized as divisive and hierarchical—haole and Portuguese being toward the top, then Japanese, Filipino, and native Hawaiian. I will elaborate later on this matter as it relates to the racial project that concerns this paper.

The professor adjusted his slumped position and read on, tossing responses to the floor. His thematic piles became a messy jumble on the carpet around his feet.

> Supposedly university culture is built on diversity, but I see everyone gravitating into their separate clusters. And each cluster can be pretty specific. For example, all Asians aren't alike. You got your Taiwanese, your mainland Chinese, your Hong Kong, your ABC, and that's just the Chinese. What about the Khmer, Laotian, and Vietnamese? And some of them are Chinese too. Then I know Chinese Mexicans and Cubans. They all got their groups, their food, their in-jokes. And that's just your Chinese.

Is Asian a race? I'm confused.

> In Hawaii, the phrase "hang loose" is accompanied by the shaka hand sign, meaning "all right," or "right on." Thus, the metaphor of *hanging* for Blu is popular, but also literal and multiple. As a joke, Blu accidently *hangs* himself on a tree, but is saved by the cracking branch. Although made comical, the symbolism of lynching likely underlies this act. Blu *hangs* on to his dead mother's ghost and memory, his family members, the animals that come to populate the house. Dead cats are ominously *hung* on the clothesline. He plays *hang* man with his sister Maisie. Blu, though alone and ostracized, pretends to be immune to his status and manages to *hang* out with every sort of misfit in their ragtag community. Blu's desire for food and sexual pleasure, his intimate care for his mute sister Maisie, his goofy creative schemes, performative talent, and his resistant and resilient character represent a different version of a blue Hawaii, blue in the sense of jazz and the recurring song his father Bertrand can never finish singing, "Moon River." *Hanging* loose, Blu's blues is replete with foolish antics, melodrama, and nostalgia. While Ivah narrates the story, and the plot is whether or not she will stay or leave, Blu *hangs* at the center of the novel.

I'm 100% Filipino.

I just read Joel's response. He's sitting next to me. I'm Filipino, too, but what's he saying? 100% of what? Do the math. Google says we've got 7,641 islands, and we were colonized by Muslims, Spanish, American, and Japanese. Not only are we the rainbow coalition, the great convergence. We work everywhere in the world, colonizing global worker bees.

The professor's son returned to the living room. He stood in his socks beyond the scatter of papers and stared at the muted television. *Are you watching that show?*

What show?

Survivor.

No. It's muted. Just background in case something interesting comes up.

They're really in survivor mode, you know. On an island with nothing but their wits and their physical agility, or something like that. I bet it's all staged. Where's Borneo?

Over there. China Sea, I think.

Borneo people are Asian?

Pacific Islanders.

So, they're filming live these white Americans trying to survive in the tropics. Why don't they send our people? We know how to survive.

We do? By the way, that book you're reading. Remember we were in Hawaii a few summers ago?

Yeah, that was awesome.

Well, while you were trying to surf, there was a conference going on, and people were fighting over that book.

Really?

Look it up. That's my contribution to your paper. Don't thank me, but you should cite my book. And use the second edition. You don't have to put my name on it, just Howie's.

Thanks, Dad.

> Originally, the choice of this novel for examination assumed a redefinition of a racial formation. However, it was surprising to learn about the controversy surrounding its publication in 1997. In the following year, at the annual conference of the Association for Asian American Studies (AAAS) hosted by the University of Hawaii at Manoa, the novel was awarded the association prize for fiction; however, under protest, the membership voted to rescind the award. AAAS, founded in 1979, over twenty years ago, is the academic association that supports professional research and teaching of Asian American studies, an interdisciplinary field created out of the movement for Third World liberation in the 1960s. The record shows that the association has granted book awards since 1987.
>
> In 1994, the author received the fiction award for a previous book, *Saturday Night at the Pahala Theater.* Apparently, there were questions about the racial stereotyping of Filipino characters in that book; however, when the author was again awarded this distinction for *Blu's Hanging,* these complaints became pronounced. The concerns addressed the character of the Filipino

uncle Paulo who sexually abuses his nieces and finally the boy Blu. There are other negative representations of racialized characters—Mrs. Ikeda or Icky, the abusive dog breeder; old Mr. Iwasaki who exposes himself to passersby; Miss Tammy Owens, the imperious white racist school teacher—but Paulo is the most perverted. Analyzing the text, it is difficult to understand why Paulo abuses Blu, and the rape, consequential in the story in an extreme way, seems gratuitous. At the same time, the exploration of sexuality, its flagrant in-your-face images and expressions are part of the book's narrative appeal. It's the insider world of young people on the underbelly of a vacation paradise.

The professor stood and stretched, stepped over the papers, headed for a brief bathroom break. Then back in the living room, he continued his students' racial surveys.

People talk about diversity being a good thing. I mean, I think it's a good thing, but frankly it's a lot of work. You get a diverse group of people together, and they can't agree on anything. It takes a lot of energy, and in the end, people want to stay in a safe situation and just get along. Why is anyone surprised when violence happens?

I've been concerned about settler colonialism. I'm a mixed Japanese and black from Hawaii. When I'm in Hawaii people think I'm native because I look the part, but then they tell me I'm really from settler colonial stock. I'm thinking when did my people ever colonize Hawaii, though technically we settled from elsewhere. I think I can't go back to where I came from because where would that be?

The phone rang. He let the answering machine run, then heard his sister. *Pick up, will you? We need to talk.*

He grabbed the phone. *Can you cover for me next week? I've got a deadline. Just go over and see Mom, bring her the paper, maybe some makizushi.*

Okay.

All she talks about is camp. Can you believe it? They wouldn't talk about it when it mattered, and now that's all she talks about. For godsake, we got reparations already.

Are you complaining?

No. Dementia is tiring.
When you get dementia, just remember I was the best brother ever.
Oh shut up. The phone went dead.

The AAAS conference was held in the Ilikai Hotel on Waikiki Beach. Those familiar with professional conferences understand how keynotes, panels, roundtables, and caucuses are organized within hotels and convention centers—air-conditioned rooms provided with mikes, podiums, slide projections, coffee, tea, and water. In Hawaii, one imagines that conference members also don muumuus and pineapple shirts and join excursions to Pearl Harbor and Diamond Head, surfing and hula classes, with the usual bar down-time mai-tais, leis and luaus. Bunches of professionals momentarily let loose in a tropical paradise. The AAAS conference was probably no different, except that Hawaii is also the home of Asian Pacific Americans, and in a sense, conferees might have felt they had come home. Ironically, however, they had granted a local novelist a coveted award, which they also came to take away.

For me feminist and gender matters are of greater concern. Misogyny, masculinity, homophobia. These issues press against my life more than race.

What I don't like is being yellow in the middle, like I'm the baloney between the white sourdough and brown rye.

I have a question about what theory to embrace. It seems like there should be a theory that explains my socio-historical situation as a racialized person. But then I think well, what do I choose? Marxism? Feminism? Socialism? Then if I really get into it, will I get free?

Research reveals that months before the actual conference, a storm was brewing mainland-side, headed for the islands, organized by the Filipino American Caucus and the Anti-Racist Coalition. The fiction selection committee refused to change their decision. The association president and the board of directors, given full warning, were forced to consult an attorney. By the time of the conference in Honolulu, the script was

> pre-written: at the final association meeting, the board announced the book awards and handed the fiction award to three Filipino American students sent by the author to receive it. Protestors armed with black bands, stood, held hands, and turned away from the stage, while the author's students tearfully received the award and spoke on her behalf. Then, the board, en masse, submitted their resignations and left the stage. A single Filipino American board member was left to conduct the discussion on the resolution to revoke the 1997 AAAS Fiction Award. In a vote of 91 to 55, the award was rescinded.

I know this might sound strange, but these days I'm thinking about humans as living animals, and I'm thinking of identifying as a mammal.

It used to be Irish and Italians and Jews were (excuse my English) micks and wops and kikes, but now they're white. Now, they are at risk of becoming white supremacists.

In my opinion class trumps race. If all the working-class folks would just get together and start a revolution, that would include everyone that matters.

> On a micro level, we can analyze the novel, its individual characters and story and meaning. We can also research the Japanese American author, her personal background and writing, and her Filipino American students. Although the novel is considered fiction, how much of it is tied to life experience? No doubt attention to its story is also attention to its authenticity of voice. We can also discuss the arguments for and against the resolution to revoke the award, committee determinations, the attorney's recommendations to the board, pronouncements and letters speaking for first amendment and authorial rights, academic and intellectual writing on literary and narrative point of view and narrative responsibility, arguments over art versus politics. Finally, we can discuss the personal trauma of racial stereotyping, historic divides prompted by wartime memories of invading Japanese soldiers and the colonial state, family histories and embedded postwar prejudices.

> This was a personal matter to each individual involved, a war that hadn't ended.

As a mixed-race person, this question of race is personal. I get it all the time. "Where are you from?" "I'm so jealous. Mixed race people are so exotic." Then I get this: "You have it easy when it comes to race because your body reflects the many. You can be outside of prejudice."

What I don't understand is how if I am pro-Palestine, I'm anti-Semitic.

I just read about Tiger Woods who won the US Open. Not that I follow golfing, but my dad does. Woods says he's ¼ Thai, ¼ Chinese, ¼ Caucasian, 1/8 African American, and 1/8 Native American. He's Cablinasian.

> On the macro level, the novel itself invites the larger questions of racial hierarchy, exposed even in a marginalized and impoverished community—the underlying polemic of ethnic hierarchy of Japanese and Chinese over Filipinos in jobs and politics. Within a larger historical context, the story reflects the history of Hawaiian sovereignty stripped open to the American colonial project. The novel's story is about the residue of migrant labor, disposed from sugarcane and pineapple plantations, and the marginalization of Molokai as leper colony. To wit, post-plantation life.

> Similarly, the AAAS had to reckon with its own plantation hierarchy, the marginalization of Filipino American scholars within who used the dissolution of the award as an argument to expose the internal racism of the group. The celebratory solidarity of the pan-Asian Pacific project of Asian American studies imploded right there in paradisic Hawaii. The AAAS tasked with addressing racial formations at the macro levels of colonialism, imperialism, and state violence, struggled at the micro level with self-identifications of race in art attributed to itself.

I've been a member of the Asian American Student Union since freshman year. I get the history of struggle even though I wasn't there, but

> I get tired of those members who, I figure, to stay politically relevant, try to be the most radical participants.

The sweet buttery smell of popcorn wafted from the kitchen. The professor could hear the corn popping in the microwave. *Hey, Dad, time for a snack.*

They stood there for a moment watching the bag inflate. His son asked, *So, why sociology?*

What?

Why'd you become a sociologist?

You know Dana's dad? He was my professor. I majored in sociology, went over to Criminology to take his courses, and when I graduated, I told him I was applying for law school. He said, "Plenty of Asian American lawyers out there. You should become a sociologist."

After this paper, honestly, I'm thinking about law.

They both laughed.

So, what did you think of the book?

Good book. Fun read. Kinda like hip-hop. I think it's a precursor, you know. It's the rhythm in the pidgin, in your face.

Didn't think of it that way.

Yeah, when we were there, hell, Hawaii was paradise, but this book shows the other side, what I'm calling the underbelly. You'd never know there were ghettos in Hawaii.

You all right with the rape thing?

No, not at all, but when you compare, it's tame.

Compared to what?

You know Fresh Kid Ice? Not that I follow his stuff. He's Chinese Trinidadian, from the Floridian ghetto.

Yeah?

So, he has these songs, about hos and his Chinese dick. You wouldn't approve. It's not for you.

I guess not.

> In conclusion, there is no conclusion. The theory of racial formation enables us to dissect the problem but not to resolve it. However, in the process, we can recognize unequal racial hierarchies and intra-ethnic racism, and that is perhaps the most positive ongoing outcome of this particular struggle. What is

> interesting is that a work of fiction and a boy hanging blue were the inadvertent catalysts. Some things are fiction, and some things are not.

Does anyone know the story of Vincent Chin? He was mistaken for a Japanese and bludgeoned to death by two white men who accused him of making Japanese cars and causing them to lose their jobs.

For me race is like this. It's literally a race. So, you get in a race and you win it. And they say, hey, you had an advantage; it's those tennis shoes. I bet you can't win if you race without them. So, you race barefoot, and you win the race. So, they say, no way, you got to lose a toe. So, you lose a toe, and you still win. So, they say, no, got to lose another toe. And it goes on like that until you have to run without feet.

Personally, I think my race is the best race.

Rapping race
Yo, professor
Let's talk race
Let's talk race

BRUCE: The Jetty

This is the story of two people haunted by memories not their own.

In the case of the man, he remembered his brother's memory. His brother, a boy of three, wanders after a dog in the desert. Maybe the dog is following a man who feeds it. Maybe there are three of them walking each alone in the desert. They follow a path leaving footprints, broken cracks in the earth, a dry meringue clay. His steps go *crunch crunch*. The air is cold. He follows the dog along a barbed wire fence. In the distance, a man in a tower. It will be years until the boy understands that the man in the tower is a soldier with a rifle and that the fence is barbed wire. A shout comes from the tower. The dog runs into the path of the walking man. Maybe the dog chases a lizard under the fence. Maybe the boy chases the dog. A small dog can scoot under barbed wire. The man's attention follows the dog. *Hey, come back here.* Maybe the soldier's aim follows the dog like a deer or coyote; he's a good shot. Wherever the aim, the shot follows the man, charges into his back through thick clothing, shattering bone and skin. The boy sees the man kneel, his arms flung upward in surrender and supplication, sees the man fall, blood pooling into meringue soil. The dog circles back. The man's mouth is an O. The boy runs away. He is lost to his parents for hours before they find him, but they will never know what he has seen.

In the case of the woman, she remembered her sister's memory. Her sister, also three, is holding a wooden skewer of dango in her small hand. She's walking with her parents away from the carnival. She wraps her teeth around the top dango, sticky with teriyaki sauce, stuffs it into her little mouth. Her mother reprimands her to wait to eat when they get home. She runs ahead to get there sooner, mochi clinging to the roof of her mouth and teeth, black sauce running down her chin. She knows the way, little feet kicking up sand and dust. Years later she will understand that home is makeshift and temporary, a tarpaper barrack with wooden steps. Shouts growl and men scatter. She sees the familiar face of her uncle, sprawled backward on those steps against the door, blood spilling from his nose and mouth, his throat slashed, head twisted, eyes aghast. Her fingers grip the skewer raised like a weapon. The texture of mochi, taste of sweet shoyu, from that moment, is anathema to her senses, but she will not remember why.

Both events occur at twilight, moon rising as sun sets. The soldier climbs down from his tower. The killers flee with their knives. Two men stare into the eyes of terrified children, their faces a last fading vision. The children—a little boy and a little girl—impressed with a first memory, lose speech. Even when they do not know that speech incriminates, they lose speech, go silent for many years. Each soul stands at a crossroad of three paths; only one leads to freedom, the unknown, the provocative.

In the aftermath, years after, the man and the woman are born. They are born outside and distant from the bleak circumstances of their older siblings, and for a short moment they experience sunlight and seaside. But a cold war follows, and they follow their siblings into an underground cadre of the people. The memory of sea and sand glistens in their eyes, ties them nostalgically. They fall in love. Now, they sleep together in the underground, each haunted separately by a repeating nightmare they cannot decipher. They come to know that the nightmares are the reason they are underground. When it is time to sleep, they hold hands and whisper. *You are trembling. Wake. It's your nightmare again. Tell me. What do you see?* They learn to see in the dark.

Learning to see in the dark, they make films.

The woman is obsessed with making films to remember the way it used to be aboveground in the light. She makes films to recall and unravel the moment mistakes were made, to spy on the past to see when and how the evil began. She makes films to return, to understand and discover how to start over again, how to make something new, how to climb out from under, if it's possible to turn a thing inside out.

The man is obsessed with films he remembers seeing, films that had nothing to do with his own life, filled with people he didn't live with or know, filled with romantic stories of other lives that probably never happened. These remembered films fill his memory, substituting the past with an imagined past. He recreates these old films, collecting pieces, picking through his fractured memories of them, zooming in, interrogating the fuzzy details, collaging pieces and merging stories, repurposing them to reveal feelings he used to have when they lived aboveground.

When the woman makes films of her memories, the man takes her films, cuts, collages, and rearranges them. He turns some of her images into stills, then reframes them. Her films, once linear, stutter, fragments of her memory turned into his new film.

When the man makes his films, the woman cuts out segments to use in her films, adds a voiceover to connect his segments into her narrative. She uses his newsreel flashes, his cartoons, his iconic Hollywood moments, his images of natural life—water, waves, fish, birds, sky, and snowy peaks—to make poetic sense.

Because they see memory differently, sometimes they argue. They yell and cry, but they always get back in bed and have sex. But, one day, although it is never day and only time, the woman makes a film to retell the man's nightmare, a memory of his brother's memory of a man and a dog walking in the desert. The man becomes upset because the woman has used his memory in her film. She says it was not his memory anyway, and besides, was he saving it for something? *One of your art films that nobody understands?* The man decides to make a film of the woman's nightmare about a girl with a dango skewer slitting a man's throat. His film is stop-action and horrifying, and the woman screams. After this, they don't speak to each other or have sex for a long time.

Eventually, however, the filmmakers reconcile. They are given the task of creating a film that is a video game that will time-travel so that it may be possible to find the moment that caused the evil that forced them into the underground. The woman believes that this might be possible. The man has no such illusions, but he believes that, maybe, this is a way they can escape.

They make a prototype confined to a concentration camp. The goal is to get out. The player must answer a series of questions on a questionnaire. The critical questions are questions 27 and 28. There are eight possible answers: yes-yes, yes-no, no-yes, no-no, blank-yes, yes-blank, blank-no, no-blank, and blank-blank. *But* or *if* answers are useless. In fact, any answer other than yes-yes is problematic. Answering yes-yes makes the game shorter, but you don't necessarily get out or win. Staying alive long enough to leave is not easy. You can be killed several ways: suicide, disease, old age, inadequate hospital care, work accident, stabbing, gunshot. It's possible to leave as a soldier, but then you can assume, for purposes of the game, you die anyway. Depending on your answers, you are assigned a number and a barrack. You do have some agency; for example, at the outset of the game, there's a pull-down list of age, gender, and generation: issei, nisei, kibei, sansei. There's also a list of jobs: nurse, cook, fireman, block manager, teacher, police, co-op worker, journalist, artist, social worker, preacher, etc. You can choose your avatar. Now you need to familiarize yourself with a map of the camp—the mess hall, latrines, and boiler rooms, hospital and administrative offices, schools and churches, baseball fields and gardens, stockade and jail. And don't forget the perimeters of the camp, the lookout towers, the borderlands beyond. Now, depending on your generational choice and answers to 27 and 28, the game may situate you as loyal or nominally loyal or disloyal, and you must navigate a complicated journey through the camp. The journey will bring you into contact with the JACL, with pro-Japanese nationalists, gamblers, social researchers, draft resisters, draft officers, FBI, military, camp officials, the Spanish consul, and ACLU lawyers. Remember, it doesn't matter what you think or believe; only your answers to 27 and 28 matter.

So, this is the filmmakers' videogame prototype. However, games have rules. Time travel also has its rules. The filmmakers discuss these rules and think there must be a way to break the rules. They strategize that, before anyone is allowed to leave the concentration camp, the man shot in the desert and the man stabbed on the wooden steps have to be saved. Maybe this is the key to the game. The men must live to leave so that the little boy and the little girl can also leave.

The filmmakers decide to test their theory. They assume their avatars, as little boy and little girl. They enter the game.

YUKI: Rashomon

You saw nothing in Hiroshima. Nothing.

—Marguerite Duras, *Hiroshima Mon Amour,* 1959

The important thing is not to blink.

—Susan Sontag, *On Photography,* 1977

I studied the little girl and at last rediscovered my mother.

—Roland Barthes, *Camera Lucida,* 1980

The task of a philosophy of photography is to reflect upon this possibility of freedom . . . in a world dominated by apparatuses . . .

—Vilém Flusser, *Towards a Philosophy of Photography,* 1984

Narratives can make us understand. Photographs do something else: they haunt us.

—Susan Sontag, *Regarding the Pain of Others,* 2003

THE CHILD

In the photo, I am two. I am enemy and prisoner. In the future, I have no memory of the moment because memory does not begin until later. I say, *Yes, that must be me.**

And this photograph here?

In the photo, I am nine. I am survivor and orphan. I remember my baby brother dies. I run from yellow smoke, clothing evaporating, skin burning. I say, *Yes, that is my naked body.*†

And this photograph here?

In the photo, I am twelve. I am refugee and exile. I remember my mother. I stare at the machine, pointing like a gun. I could be brave. *Maybe,* I say, *that is me.*‡

And this photograph here?

In the photo, I am fifteen. I am alive. I remember my mother and I bathe together. I say, *Yes, that is my floating body.*§

The inspector nods gravely. *We have tests to know the truth. We can look into the iris of your eye and match the iris in the photo. Then we can be sure.*

You mean, you don't believe me, that that is me.

This photograph has historic significance. The child in the photograph can't be just any child.

I could be any child.

But not necessarily the child in this photograph.

I am no longer the child in that photograph.

This is true.

The child blinks. The camera blinks.

THE PROFESSOR

I have computed the Iris Codes and calculated the Hamming distance in each of the eyes, comparing the photographic images in the child eyes and the adult eyes. The algorithms show a match such that the mathematical odds against such an event are six million to one in the right eye, and 10-to-the-15th power to one for the left eye.

---

* Yukiko Okinaga Hayakawa Llewellyn, April 7, 1942, Santa Fe La Grande Station, Los Angeles; Clem Albers and Russell Lee, photographers.

† Phan Thi Kim Phuc, June 8, 1972, Trang Bang, Vietnam; Nick Ut, photographer.

‡ Sharbat Gula, 1984, Nasir Bagh refugee camp, Pakistan; Steve McCurry, photographer.

§ Tomoko Uemura, 1971, Minamata, Japan; W. Eugene Smith, photographer.

Iris Code:

3F3EDCE173FFFF8F00405C7FBF93416080FF7E7AE1F93E32A141409090508020
20A0E0E0203000004 0E0E0C0202000000000181A01000000030F0F0F0C080001
030F0E0A0000010F0F0800000B07010C0E1E1000303D7F6E44021A2B17F7FA79
298004062028FFDFDD4DB76200043DFFC302005DFEBFF8E0495FFFFE0000C17D
BCF0FDFFFF9F8040407E3F9F81C1C0FCFE7E78793331014040C0D090002020E0
E0E0E020000000E06060202000000000000180000000010F0F0F0C080001030F
0E0C0000000F0E0C08000303030D0F1E021010383D3E4606020F3FFFFFF9E121
00000434FEDFDFDD612000001DFFEB8202547FFEFCE0E97FFF3E028081433F3E
FF1FA71EED7DFFFFFFBFDFFEFFFB7FDE969CFFD34EFEF8C2D1F1F0E0800000C0
C000E0E0E0C0C0E0A0E0E0C0206000202000181E1F0F0F0F0B0F0F0C0D0F0F0F
0B0F0D0D0F0F0E0F0E090F0F0A0B0F0B1F1F0F3F373F7F7DBBFFC7B8C7F7F86D
325E787861E1B4DE6860202CFCF27CFFD2FCFCDC7CFEE27F967DFF3EFD7EFFB5
1DE3FBFFFFFF7FBFFFBD5FE7FF7FDEFDFF7FFC7E70F1D1B070E0A080C0C0C060
E0E0E0E0C0E0E0C060602020002000000018080E0F0F0D0F0F0F0D0F0F0E0F0F
0E0F0F0F0E0D0E0F0B0F0F0F0B0D0F0F050F1F3F3C0F3D79FFF2E7F7FFFD665E
7A79F961BCFCFD79C4FCFCF44CACF23EBCB85CFCFEF666797F7EFFFEFF39BFBF*

Iris recognition is regarded as the most accurate and reliable biometric identification system available.

It is confirmed. The child in the photograph is the woman in the photograph.

But there is a disconcerting complication. Hovering above the iris, a reflection on the lens. What the eye sees enters the mind to disappear into memory. What the eye saw is captured residue and accusation. I have seen what the child's eye saw.

THE CAMERA

Graflex 4x5 Speed Graphic

Speed Graphic features include Graflex focal plane shutter, interchangeable lenses, flash synchronization, eye-level view finders, accessory coupled range finders, ground glass focusing and long bellows draw. The new Miniature Speed Graphic has in addition: built-in focal plane shutte flash synchronization, dual

* https://web.archive.org/web/20120113013321/, http://www.cl.cam.ac.uk/~jgd1000/afghanscreendump.txt, https://web.archive.org/web/20120113013327/, http://www.cl.cam.ac.uk/~jgd1000/irisrecog.pdf.

> focusing knobs, accessory internally coupled range finders and extreme compactness.
>
> All-versatile Speed Graphic cameras are priced from $111.00; with coupled range finder, from $138.00.

I have a rhythm. Press here to open my cover. Focus me by twisting my knob to slide my accordion backward or forward. Use a separate meter to determine available light. Confer with the table inscribed on my plate. Check my tension, release or wind. Set my aperture. Crank my shutter speed. Click my tension. Release my shutter to change the settings. Depending, insert a bulb into my flash attachment. Frame the shot in my viewfinder. Compose. Insert into my back my preloaded film cartridge with twelve septums of 4" by 5" sheet film. Pull my slide out. Trip my shutter. Reset my mirror. Discard and change my flashbulb. Flip my film holder. Cock my shutter. Ready to shoot once again. Move with my rhythm: tension, wind, focus, trip, mirror down, shuffle film, slide out, fire. This time: discard flashbulb, insert flashbulb, then again: tension, wind, focus, trip, mirror down, shuffle film, slide out, fire.

THE PHOTOGRAPHER

I was born in Michigan, grew up in Berkeley. I was a teenager when I got hired as a journeyman photographer for the *San Francisco Bulletin*. Later I joined the staff of the *San Francisco Chronicle*. My biggest assignments included photographing the construction of the Golden Gate and Bay Bridges. I used a Graflex 4" x 5" Speed Graphic press camera equipped with rapid film changer magazine, range finder, and viewfinder, a camera commonly used by press photographers.

In 1942, from March to early May, I got a short-term contract with the War Relocation Authority's Information Division, to cover California and Arizona. A third of the photos I took were of Manzanar, where I worked for just a couple of days in April 1942. In those days, the camp was still under construction. Military police units still lived in army tents while the first inmates were arriving. I also shot photographs at Poston and Tule Lake. I covered the expulsion and assembly process, capturing Japanese Americans as they boarded buses and trains and disembarked at the various detention centers. In addition to photographing the mountains of baggage and long lines found at every camp, I turned my camera on the stark conditions of the barracks and aspects of their traditional culture.

I guess my experience as a press photographer influenced my ability to document the incarceration with a professional eye. My training taught me to work quickly. I wanted to capture the contradicting realities of the government, public perceptions, and of the Japanese people themselves. I didn't hesitate to reveal the primitive conditions in which the evacuees were placed, their grim and frightened expressions. My best camera work relied on serendipitous contrast and sardonic details. I wanted to capture the emotional and physical discomforts, gallows humor, and full range of facial reactions—frowns, grimaces, even a beguiling smile.*

THE CAMERA

Contax Model 1

This camera will record the ethereal pattern of a dragon fly's wing in a 7" close-up . . . will snap vivid pictures indoors in ordinary artificial light . . . will take informal, express portraits. Contax offers new, fascinating possibilities—in full color as well as black and white. Unposed action photos or still pictures now possible under adverse light conditions. Pocket size camera. Ten speeds up to 1/1000 second, 36 pictures, 1" x 1 1/2", permitting remarkable enlargements. Loads as easily as any roll-film camera. Ever-lasting metal shutter. Built-in long-base range-finder focuses automatically. Choice of 15 interchangeable Zeiss lenses.

Camera with Carl Zeiss Tessar F/3.5, 50 mm . . . $174.00 (black) $218 (chrome)
Camera with Carl Zeiss Tessar F/2.8, 50 mm . . . $184.50 (black) $228.50 (chrome)

His hands caress me. Sometimes he wipes me with a soft cloth, peeling away each piece of me, polishing, and tenderly remounting my body, turning my ligaments, pushing my buttons. I am never far from his touch. I hang from his neck by a leather strap. His heart beats, his lungs breathe, his stomach growls, inches away. In an instant, I can feel his panic or excitement,

* https://encyclopedia.densho.org/Clem_Albers/.

grabbing and pressing my body to his face, his one eye fluttering, peering through me. His fingers are delicate and exacting, move with precision, adjust and tune until my focus is sharp. Sharper yet. He holds his breath. Steady. Wait. Wait for the light. Frame and capture. There. And then again. There. The moment rising, fading. Moving. And again and again in anxious waves.

THE PHOTOGRAPHER

Every phase of the photographic process fascinates me. I am an engineer-chemist who loves the technical aspects of my work. I mix my own chemicals and push the film from a normal rating of ASA 32 all the way up to ASA 100. I've discovered the possibilities of open flash and have begun to experiment with flash synchronizers.

I see the world through my viewfinder. I find expression in the quick-caught images. They call me a taxonomist with a camera. I want the understated, yet to reveal every element. While other photographers favor natural light and rarely go inside buildings, I use direct flash to record my subjects inside their environments. At times I go for a stark, glaring light with my flash. This can lead to harsh shadows but also yield details. I want the details. I'm probably the most prolific of the FSA photographers, producing in series while others are constantly seeking one great image.

In the field, traveling alone, I keep my technique simple. My 35 mm Contax camera is small and quiet and allows me to get up close and personal. I like to pick up a conversation, inquire about daily routines, establish a rapport.

Now, with the war, Farm Security getting transformed into the Office of War Information, things have changed. It's one thing to document rural poverty, but this West Coast military removal of Japanese is different. I talked to Dorothea about it. The gov controls our work. Likely no one will ever see what we've seen. Thankfully my wife, Jean, has joined me. With Jean, I can get into their homes, follow them selling their belongings and moving inland to the camps. We've seen these people herded with tags on them, their little houses and businesses with FOR SALE signs. The inland camps are decent enough, but desolate. Since April of 1942, I've shot nearly six hundred images of Japanese Americans in California, Oregon, and Idaho.*

---

* https://encyclopedia.densho.org/Russell_Lee/.

THE BOY

I followed him to the backside of camp, next to the cemetery, over there behind Block 24. It was a cold spring morning, but he had me carry the tripod and his bag of film all the way from Block 30, so I'd worked up a bit of sweat.

He waved to the soldier in the guard tower, who waved back. He nudged me to wave too. I waved. He pointed to his camera, to the snowy mountains, and shouted, *Beautiful day! Light's perfect.* I handed him the tripod, and he set it in the sandy soil and tumbleweed near the fence.

Hey, he yelled up at the soldier. *Do you mind?* He set his boot on the bottom wire of the fence and with his strong fingers pulled up on the next wire, motioning me to go through.

The soldier looked on, bored.

To get a sense of perspective, he yelled. *Got to get beyond the wire.*

Yeah, fine, the soldier replied.

I ducked and scrambled to the other side. I thought I was a sure shot from up there where the soldier had his sights. He could pick me off easy. Anyway, there was nowhere to go, and nowhere out there was a long way away.

We walked away from the tower, me outside the fence, he inside. I watched a lizard skid out under the sage, and I kicked up some dirt after.

He kept setting the tripod down and looking into his camera, focusing back at the tower and the mountains, then telling me to keep walking until he could get a good sight. We were maybe about fifty feet from the tower when he said, *Okay, stop here.*

I pressed my hand against the fencepost to take a rest.

He looked from around the camera and said, *No, press your hand into the wire.*

I tugged at the wire, back and forth, and chuckled.

He said, *You ever wonder why they used barbed wire?*

Of course I'd thought about it. Who didn't? I looked through the fence back into camp, at my home in those barracks. Some obachan came out with laundry, struggling with her basket. She hitched it to her hip, walked away crookedly, dust swirling around her feet. I watched her figure get tiny.

Don't move, he said.

THE SON

The war was ending. We were the people left behind. It was then that my dad set up his own shop, got his old equipment out of storage, used a real camera, bought film and chemicals and had them delivered, hired me as an assistant. The excuse was that we had to have photos of special events like weddings and funerals, like family photos before guys left in uniform for the front maybe to die, like yearbooks for high school graduations. Wasn't that what a local photographer would do for his community? He could walk around in the open with his cameras, set up his tripod, point at whatever he saw, even snap the shutter himself. We were no longer a threat. This was not a secret. No one cared anymore.

THE SHADOW

Morning arrives from the southeast, washes at an angle down the long fence, surprises the snow-covered sierras, their contrasting and haunting glare outlined against azure sky. I fall starkly in intervals attached to fence posts and tower, but otherwise the view opens into endless and glorious natural landscape. I do not become jagged lines imprinted on desert sand and sage; rather, those barbed wires cut across the air, framing the height of the boy, a scar against his face, his sky and horizon split. The sun caresses the back of the photographer, and I fall into tumbleweed, a corrupted but organic version of the man, forecasting another moment of my documented appearance, blasted into concrete at precisely 8:15 on an August morning.

THE FILM

You saw nothing in Manzanar.

I saw everything.

You saw nothing.

I saw the hospital. It exists. How could I not have seen it?

You didn't see the hospital.

I saw the museum.

What museum?

I saw people walking around, lost in thought, among the photographs, the reconstructions, the explanations. I was hot in the sun. One hundred and ten degrees in the sun. I know it. How could you not know it?

*You saw nothing in Manzanar. Nothing.**

* *Hiroshima Mon Amour.*

THE JOURNALIST

He agreed to the interview. I had prepared my questions.

When you smuggled in the camera lens and the film plate, what were your original motivations?

What photos did you take with your handmade camera? For example, during the camp riots, where were you? Did you document the violence?

Will you ever show in exhibition the photographs you took with your handmade camera?

What do you think of the work of white photographers, those outsiders who took officially sanctioned photos? As an insider, how do you compare your work to theirs?

How would you characterize your photography? Would you say it was a form of resistance?

What do you think about the depiction of you by the actor in the movie version of the incarceration?

Today, looking back in time, what would you say is the message of your camp photography?

THE LUNCH BOX

Steel, wood, aluminum (H 14, W 14, D 19 cm).

They call me the lunch box. I am a wooden box, handsomely handcrafted from scraps of wood—ash, mountain mahogany, and locust. My cover flips up, held open with metal levers. My Wollensack Rapax lens and shutter are welded to the male end of a 2" drainpipe. This pipe screws into a female pipe-end attached to my wooden frame. A piece of ground glass clips to my back side. Under a black cloth, look through the glass to see the image upside-down. Turn the pipe over its threads to focus my lens. Close my shutter and set the F-stop on the nose of my lens. Unclip my ground glass and replace with my 2-shot film holder for 3.25" x 4.25" sheet film. Pull out the dark slide from my holder to expose the film. Release my shutter.

THE PHOTOGRAPHER

I had a responsibility to record. But that was not the entire reason. I knew I could not be separated from my camera. That would have been a kind of death. To be without the tools to make my art. Like a painter without a brush, a writer without a pen, a musician without an instrument. When life and all reason are the floor that drops from beneath you, you grab what matters. I grabbed the shutter lens and the film holder, hid them among the stuff we could carry. I would find a way.

I had friends: a wood craftsman and an auto mechanic; they constructed the lunch box. It turned into a small masterpiece using all our precise skills. Imprisoned, what else was there to do? We turned our hands to tasks to keep our minds busy, our hearts still.

Then it turned out the camp supplier for hardware was an old client and friend. He'd arrive and say, *My coat is hanging in the hallway*, or, *My truck's over there; the blue one, plate 8J 90 66*. I'd get a nisei officer to pick his pockets: lenses, meters, odd attachments, or to pick up the stuff in his truck: film developer, chemicals, paper.

In those first six months, I woke up early or wandered around when folks were eating in the mess halls, avoided the patrols. I took scenic photos, to be safe, but eventually everyone knew about the camera, wanted family photos, especially photos of their sons before they left for military service.

Finally, I got the director to sign me on as camp photographer. Maybe he appreciated my tutelage under Edward Weston, my friendship with Ansel Adams. It still didn't matter. I still had to follow the rule: I could set up the shot, but I couldn't trip the shutter. They hired a white kid from L.A. to do this. Every night the kid removed the camera lens and took it home. One day, I had two hundred people lined up for a shoot, and the kid removed the lens before I'd removed the film. Exposed everything. I was hopping mad. The kid quit. Then they hired these white ladies, wives of camp employees, to sit in my studio and just watch. I made sure they had nothing else to do, so eventually they got bored and quit. The director gave up, said he had trouble seeing anything to his left, which I took to mean he'd turn a blind eye.

Finally, I got the freedom to do my work. I sent for my equipment stored in Los Angeles. I started a studio within the co-op and went to work. We only had so much film and supplies, so I limited sessions to two customers per block, and two shots per person. We charged $10 for a dozen mounted 8" x 10" wedding photos, $9 for a dozen family and $8 for a dozen funeral shots. I got a wage of $19 a month. My assistants got about $12 a month.

Folks just wanted to take pictures of their kids growing up, keep a record and the memory. In camp, they lost that opportunity. They saw time pass like it didn't matter. It should have been easier. What I did was mostly formal portraits, but I did the best I could.

When I left camp in 1945, I'd taken 1,500 photos of the way we lived and died, on the inside, for folks on the inside. I took the photos people wanted to see of themselves. All our work, our celebrations, weddings and funerals, church and school, holidays and sports events, dances and shows, the special and the routine. We weren't criminals, and my camera wasn't a spy.

EYE CAMERA

In the past, present, and future, I am an irresponsible machine, a magical pandora's black box. My focusing lens captures light, whether a flash of image against chemical emulsion or digital capture. My magic is technical, transforming my user into magician, player, artist, or mere functionary. Through me, a moment of the real may be transformed, orchestrated, framed, selected from time, no longer real. I am truth teller and spy, memory and spectacle maker, framer of facts and lies. The image I release can be exhibited, interpreted, exploited, augmented, reproduced, consumed, worshiped. Take care, for you may, through me, capture an image, after which your life will never be the same. But as I've said, I am irresponsible.

THE PHOTOGRAPHER

Like a lot of sansei, I learned about camp by chance. Came home from school one day and asked the folks about it, and they said, *Yeah, that happened.* They'd been silent about it for years, and they weren't going to break that silence.

I yelled, *Whadya mean that happened!* I was outraged, and it took me a long time to understand they were steaming in their silence.

My uncle offered, *See this photo? That's me. I was just a kid in the day.*

Maybe that's why I became a photographer, because this photo was proof that you could be silent for years, but the story would be told. I kept that photo, always staring into it, searching for more.

I told my uncle, *Let's go back to that place and take another photo of you today.* That's how it started.

One day I got hold of an archive of photos, and I went looking for the people. At the time no one bothered to get their names or even permission to snap those shots. The captions said: *With the owner scheduled to be evacuated, a store front is boarded on Post Street.* Or: *Just about to step into the bus for the assembly center.* Or: *Child on the way to Manzanar.* Sanitized entry data like people just moving on, living their lives in benevolent imprisonment. Who were they? What did they remember? Where were they now? I had to find out. One by one.

The little girl sitting on a bundle with her apple in one hand, her purse in the other, waiting alone for a train. The boy at the barbed wire, watch tower and snowy mountains behind. Where were their parents? What was beyond the frame? Were there multiple shots? What happened after? Who did they become? Were they still alive? I went searching.

THE SHOEBOX

1. Spray or paint the inside of a shoebox with black matte paint.
2. On one end of the box, cut out a small 1/2" opening.
3. Cut out a square from an aluminum can and sand it down. Punch and pull a needle through the aluminum to make a pinhole.
4. Tape the aluminum piece over the 1/2" opening. Use more tape to make a shutter cover over the pinhole.
5. In a dark room, tape photo paper to the inside of the box opposite the pinhole. Close the box with tape. Make sure no light can enter the box.
6. To take the photo, position the shoebox. Remove the tape covering the pinhole for 20 seconds to several minutes, depending on the light.
7. Open the shoebox in a dark room to remove the photo paper for developing.

THE PHOTOGRAPHER

My dad showed me how to take pictures with a shoebox, with a pinhole and film on the inside. We prepped a bunch of these boxes, so I could get one photo per box. Then we went on a road trip to visit the internment camp where Grandpa and Grandma were sent during the war.

We located this concrete slab where, according to the map, the hospital used to be. Dad said that was where he was born. I set one of my shoeboxes down on the concrete at the far end of the slab, pulled open my tape shutter, counted to twenty, then closed the shutter.

When we got home, we developed the pictures. Mostly I got these pictures that look empty. Okay, not really empty, but looking into the deep desert, greasewood growing over rubble like it's been bombed out.

But in this one picture, you can see a fuzzy figure of my dad in his aloha shirt and shorts, a Dodger cap shading his head. Corroded bars and dried weeds shoot out of the cracked surface. Rusted nails and wires are tossed around his tennis shoes. Maybe it doesn't look like my dad exactly. His Ray-Bans reflect the sun back like spotlights. Maybe he's squinting, but I know better.

THE SMART PHONE

> iPhone 12 Pro Max: 6.7" all-screen OLED display; 5G cellular; A14 Bionic chip; Pro camera system—ultra wide, wide, telephoto; LiDAR scanner for night mode portraits and next-level AR; compatible with MagSafe accessories
>
> Telephoto: 65 MM; new 5x optical zoom range
> Wide: faster *f*/1.6; 1.7 µm pixel sensor; 87% more light; sensor-shift OIS
> Ultra wide: 13 mm; night mode
>
> 5G goes Pro. A14 Bionic rockets past every other smartphone chip. The Pro camera system takes low-light photography to the next level—with an even bigger jump on iPhone 12 Pro Max. And Ceramic Shield delivers four times better drop performance.
> From $41.62/mo. for 24 mo. Or $999 before trade-in*

I am precision-machined from stainless steel with a tough ceramic film on my face. My big sensor dramatically increases detail captured and improves low-light performance by 87 percent. My custom-designed LiDAR scanner provides advanced mapping technology, revealing a new world of possibilities for augmented reality. I am a high-quality video machine. I can make movies. I can capture, play back, and edit 10-bit HDR footage with Dolby vision.

I'm a flat surface pulled from your purse or pocket, capturing the intruding moment digitally, exactly mapped and dated, saved and multiplied endlessly, social significance shared in repeating banality. Feel free to play with me. No worries, no mistakes. See the little trashcan icon? Just delete. Have a favorite? Heart that. Selfie that. Meme that. Face filter that. Send.

---

*https://www.apple.com/iphone-12-pro/?afid=p238%7Cs1S1i1fjK-dc_mtid_20925d2q39172_pcrid_499637092459_pgrid_114217449311_&cid=wwa-us-kwgo-iphone--slid---Brand-iPhone12ProMax-Avail-.

Friend. Thumbs up. Thumbs down. Emoji that. On May 3, 2022, for example, share your photo memory.

THE PHOTOGRAPHER

My dad is out there in the heat. He's got a pinhole attachment on his Nikon, and he's trying to take photos of a slab of concrete foundation. He's yelling at me to come out of the car, or he'll turn it off, shut down the air, and take away the keys. Give me a break. It's 110 degrees. No shade. No breeze. No WiFi. No way. Okay, he said Grandpa was born here. That's like eighty years ago or something. When Dad was a kid, he took this fuzzy black-and-white photo of Gramps, right here in this place. He wants to recreate the same photo with me in the picture. I look at the old photo of Gramps left on the dash and take a picture of it. Then I take some pics from the car. Even through the glass, I know my photos are way sharper than his. I check out my images. There's five of him setting up his tripod. Another five just standing there looking nowhere. I point my phone to his nowhere. Could be a coyote. My eyes see a little kid out there, but my screen zooms in on dust. I delete them. I take a selfie with him out there. When he comes to the window, I take a video of him with a coyote face and show it to him. He's all animated and looks crazy yelling through the window. I message it to Mom, who sends me an lol. Then I lock the doors and go back to Minecraft.

THE PHOTOGRAPH

One day in the future, you become.

But in the future, no one will remember this future. They will only remember the past, recorded forever in one spot, globally positioned and timed precisely by a cruel accident of history and the happenstance of photographic capture, the technology of time travel, imprisoned in the virtual eternity of a museum, saved in its infinite brain—attic, cloud—buried alive. But beautiful. Because innocent children are beautiful, and everything held dear, the tenuousness and fragility of their expectations, seeing beyond and into, hope before closing eyes nightly and finally.

You were so little then. A toddler. Here you are alone. You look abandoned, but of course your vigilant mother is never far away. She told you not to move. She's watching the men surrounding you taking your photo like paparazzi. They shoot with flash and discard the bulbs everywhere. She steps aside, hides to avoid their surveillance. Good thing she got you that new red corduroy outfit with red boots and little matching purse. Here, the viewer cannot see the composition of red: outfit, boots, purse, and apple, the lively shock of color in the gloom of cold morning. You exist as an idea in reportage black and white. Your mother also cut and combed your hair, shiny with a halo in the flash of light. What was she thinking? You and she are well-dressed prisoners, soon to be separated from ordinary people.

Who do these photographers think they are? They shoot from about six feet away, so you don't notice at first, not until the flash blinds you, and you search with worry for your mother. By then, the photographers have moved on to other scenes. They forget you until they see you in the developed photos. It will be years before anyone, including you, sees your image here. Sees the beauty in your pathos. The war will be over, and this censored photo will be hidden in an acid-free box. The heart-tug of your sad sweet image won't have changed anything. But, you were real. You were really here. You saw nothing. You saw everything. Years later, your own child will look upon you as this child, astonished.

One day, they'll recreate you from this photo to show the future what this moment of injustice was like. From your image, they can make a virtual prison that others can wander into and experience what you experienced and therefore feel empathy for your historic situation. You will return from death. Reality will be enhanced by a technologically induced lucid schizophrenia. What happened will be remembered, and people will learn the lessons of the past. It will be like time travel to change the future.

EPILOGUE

DANA: Telephone Call

Professor Takagi?

Yes?

Professor, we understand you are in possession of the WRA computer database for the World War Two internment of Japanese Americans. Can you tell us the codified meaning of the last five digits?

The last five digits?

Yes, the last five.

You mean you don't know?

No, we thought you might have deciphered their meaning.

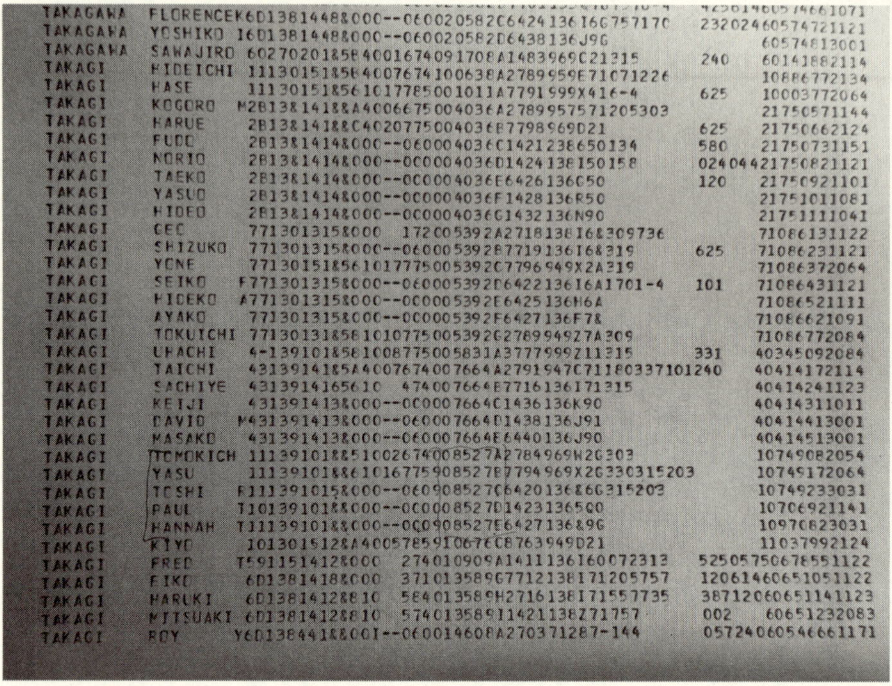

```
TAKAGAWA  FLORENCEK6D1381448&000--06002058206424136I6G757170   2320246057472112l
TAKAGAWA  YOSHIKO I6D1381448&000--0600205820643813 6J9G                 60574813001
TAKAGAWA  SAWAJIRO 60270201&5B4001674091708A1483969C21315       240    60141882114
TAKAGI    HIDEICHI 11130151&5B4007674100638A2789959E71071226            10886772134
TAKAGI    HASE     11130151&56101778500101 1A7791999X416-4      625    10003772064
TAKAGI    KOGORO  M2B13&1418&A40066750040 36A2789957571205303           21750571144
TAKAGI    HARUE    2B13&1418&C4020775004036B7798969D21           625    21750662124
TAKAGI    FUDO     2B13&1414&000--060004036C1421238650134        580    21750731151
TAKAGI    NORIO    2B13&1414&000--000004036D1424138I50158        0240442175082112l
TAKAGI    TAEKO    2B13&1414&000--000004036E6426136G50           120    21750921101
TAKAGI    YASUO    2B13&1414&000--000004036F1428136R50                  21751011081
TAKAGI    HIDEO    2B13&1414&000--000004036G1432136N90                  21751111041
TAKAGI    GEC      77130131 5&000  172005392A2718138I6&309736           71086131122
TAKAGI    SHIZUKO  771301315&000--060005392B7719136I6&319        625    71086231121
TAKAGI    YONE     77130151&561017775005392C7796949X2A319               71086372064
TAKAGI    SEIKO   F771301315&000--060005392D6422136I6A1701-4     101    71086431121
TAKAGI    HIDEKO  A771301315&000--000005392E6425136H6A                  71086521111
TAKAGI    AYAKO    771301315&000--000005392F6427136F7&                  71086621091
TAKAGI    TOKUICHI 7713013 1&58101077500539 2G2789949Z7A309             71086772084
TAKAGI    UHACHI   4-139101&58100877500583 1A3777999Z11315       331    40345092084
TAKAGI    TAICHI   4313914 1&5A400767400766 4A2791947C711803371012 40   40414172114
TAKAGI    SACHIYE  43139141 65610  4740076 64B7716136I71315             40414241123
TAKAGI    KEIJI    431391413&000--000007664C1436136K90                  40414311011
TAKAGI    DAVID   M431391413&000--060007664D1438136J91                  40414413001
TAKAGI    MASAKO   431391413&000--060007664E6440136J90                  40414513001
TAKAGI    TOMOKICH 111391018&51002674008527A2784969W2G303               10749082054
TAKAGI    YASU     111391018&61016775908527B7794969X2G330315203         10749172064
TAKAGI    TOSHI   F111391015&000--060908527C6420136&6G315203            10749233031
TAKAGI    PAUL    T10139101&&000--000008527D1423136 5Q0                 10706921141
TAKAGI    HANNAH  T11139101&&000--0Q0908527E6427136&9G                  10970823031
TAKAGI    KIYO     101301512&A4005785910676C8763949D21                  11037992124
TAKAGI    FRED    T591151412&000  274010909A1411136I60072313   52505750678551122
TAKAGI    EIKO     6D1381418&000  371013589G7712138I71205757   12061460651051122
TAKAGI    HARUKI   6D1381412&810  584013589H2716138I71557735   38712060651141123
TAKAGI    MITSUAKI 6D1381412&810  574013589I1421138Z71757      002    60651232083
TAKAGI    ROY     Y6D138441&&00I--060014608A270371287-144      05724060546661171
```

ACKNOWLEDGMENTS

Many years ago, Lane Hirabayashi sent me his just-published book, the edited work of Richard S. Nishimoto, *Inside an American Concentration Camp*. He noted that this material emerged from the JERS (Japanese Evacuation Resettlement Study) archived in the Bancroft Library at UC Berkeley, and that of some 355 boxes (250.5 linear archival feet), he opened maybe two boxes, the tip of an iceberg so to speak, about what we didn't know about the incarceration of Japanese Americans. Did anyone want to open the rest of this archive? I thought then—it was 1995—that about "the camps," we'd been there, done that, but as those who continue to research and write about these events know very well, it's never done. I mourn the passing of Lane, and perhaps this is my small promise to his continuing investigation, to learn and impart another way of seeing what happened to our parents and their families. Unlike Lane, I was never trained in anthropology, but I've attempted in my writing to see time, people, and culture through its lens. I wondered what JERS, an on-site sociological/anthropological investigation of Japanese American wartime internment, would expose. I began with the loyalty questionnaire, which I surmised was a kind of sociological statistical methodology for evaluating a group, but the questionnaire became for me labyrinthian, questions within questions. Perhaps I did not open 355 boxes; yet still I encountered the complex and unforeseen of Pandora. I devised a formal structure to try to contain time, investigative participants, hearsay and evidence, to build for myself a way to see and understand, yet I realize that I who've written all this into a book cannot fully see, cannot truly understand. Others with better intellectual skills and keener scholarship may unearth with time the particulars, reveal clearer epiphanies, come closer to knowing. In any case, my work is fiction.

In the research and writing of this book, I've imposed upon many folks to read, critique, share knowledge, inspire stories: Jasmine Alinder, Anjali Arondekar, Jane Beckwith, Howard Pat Boltz, Jane Tomi Boltz, Timothy

Anglin Burgard, Lucy Mae San Pablo Burns, Julie Cho, Alan Christy, Binh Danh, Gina Dent, Tommy Dyo, Masaki Fujihata, Kasey Furutani, Kimi Hill, Ruth Hsu, Peter Irons, Earl Jackson, Betty Kano, Mika Kasuga, Ikue Kina, Kerrily and Kimberly Kitano, Lynn and Christine Kitano, Norma Klahn, Andrew Leong, R. Zamora Linmark, Valeria Luiselli, Douglas Lummis, Boreth Ly, Nidhi Mahajan, Philip Tajitsu Nash, Steven Okazaki, Michael Omi, Roshni Rustomji-Kerns, Russell Wei Shen Soh, Stephen Hong Sohn, Amy Sueyoshi, Dana Takagi, Don Tamaki, Tosh Tanaka, Tina Takemoto, Adam Thorman, Tim Yamamura, Sharon Yamato, Lois-Ann Yamanaka, Kenneth Yamashita, Alice Yang, Bruce Yonemoto, Wendy Yoshimura. And thank you to the support of extended families: Beckwiths, Dyos, Furutanis, Kitanos, and Takagis. If I've forgotten anyone, please add your name and know my gratitude. It's been a long process.

Thanks to dedicated archivists: Monica deAtley, Tracy Fisher, and Maria Ordaz at the Center for Social Justice & Civil Liberties at Riverside Community College, for access to the archive of Miné Okubo; and Jamie Henricks at the Hirasaki National Resource Center at JANM (Japanese American National Museum), for access to the archive of Michi Nishiura Weglyn.

A big thank-you to Lawrence-Minh Davis, editor of *The Asian American Literary Review*, for the early publication of "Isamu," to *n+1* for early publication of "Tsutomu," and to Michael Emmerich of the Yanai Initiative at the University of California, Los Angeles, for the original publication of "Yuki's Rashomon," in the catalog featuring the JANM art installation of Masaki Fujihata: *BeHere/1942: A New Lens on the Japanese American Incarceration.*

Over a period of five years, I received support from the University of California, Santa Cruz, through generous awards from the Committee on Research and the Edward A. Dickson Emeritus Professorship. During this time, Yuki Obayashi collaborated in researching the life and writing of Etsu Sugimoto and translated, among several other Japanese texts, the nineteenth-century Japanese travel pamphlet *Come, Japanese!* Jonathan van Harmelen, while researching numerous resources, including the Library of Congress and UC Berkeley Bancroft Library's JERS, shared his meticulous archival skills and historical scholarship. Throughout the writing of this book, Jonathan's expansive knowledge of Japanese American history and his critical historian's eye opened paths of inquiry and kept me honest. Yuki and Jonathan, thank you so much. Your expertise and dedication made this book possible.

Thank you, Yuka Igarashi, editor extraordinaire, for your adept provocations and keen story sensibility and to the stellar staff at Graywolf Press. Thank you, Anya Backlund at Blue Flower Arts and Chris Fischbach, literary agent and dear friend. Thank you to my friends and colleagues at the University of California, Santa Cruz, most especially Micah Perks and Ronaldo V. Wilson. Finally, thank you to my family—Ronaldo, Jane Tomi, Pat, Jane Tei, Jon, Mary Jane, Lucy, Milton, Andrew, Andrea, Javon, Mizumi—for your patience and for always being there, making this world our home.

BIBLIOGRAPHY

BOX 1: Salvage

Yone:

Noguchi, Yone. *The American Diary of a Japanese Girl: An Annotated Edition.* Edited by Edward Marx and Laura E. Franey. Temple University Press, 2007.

Noguchi, Yone. *The Story of Yone Noguchi: Told by Himself.* Chatto & Windus, 1914.

Stoddard, Charles Warren. *For the Pleasure of His Company: An Affair of the Misty City.* San Francisco, 1903.

Sueyoshi, Amy. *Queer Confessions: Race, Nation, and Sexuality in the Affairs of Yone Noguchi.* University of Hawaii Press, 2012.

Kyutaro:

Azuma, Eiichiro. *Between Two Empires: Race, History, and Transnationalism in Japanese America.* Oxford University Press, 2005.

Azuma, Eiichiro. *In Search of Our Frontier: Japanese American and Settler Colonialism in the Construction of Japan's Borderless Empire.* University of California Press, 2019.

Ichioka, Yuji. *The Issei: The World of the First Generation Japanese Immigrants, 1885–1924.* Free Press, 1988.

Ishida, Kumajiro. *Kitare nihonjin* 来たれ日本人 [*Come, Japanese!*]. Kaishindo, 1886.

Scheiner, Irwin. *Christian Converts and Social Protest in Meiji Japan.* University of California Press, 1970.

Tsutomu:

García, Jerry. *Looking Like the Enemy: Japanese Mexicans, the Mexican State, and US Hegemony, 1897–1945.* University of Arizona Press, 2014.

Harris, Charles H., III, and Louis R. Sadler. *The Border and the Revolution:*

Clandestine Activities of the Mexican Revolution; 1910–1920. High-Lonesome Books, 1988.

Katz, Friedrich. *The Life and Times of Pancho Villa.* Stanford University Press, 1998.

Reed, John. *Insurgent Mexico.* Appleton, 1914.

Etsu:

Hirakawa, Setsuko. "Etsu I. Sugimoto's 'A Daughter of the Samurai' in America." *Comparative Literature Studies* 30:4 (1993).

Kuo, Karen, "'Japanese Women Are Like Volcanoes': Trans-Pacific Feminist Musings in Etsu I. Sugimoto's *A Daughter of a Samurai.*" *Frontiers: A Journal of Women Studies* 36:1 (2015).

Sugimoto, Etsu Inagaki, *A Daughter of the Samurai.* Doubleday, Page, 1925.

Sugimoto, Etsu Inagaki. *Memorial: Florence Mills Wilson* (1933), Cincinnati History Library and Archives.

Uchida, Yoshio. *Bushi no musume: Nichibei no kakehashitonatta etsuko to furorensu* [*A Daughter of the Samurai: Etsuko and Florence, a Japan–U.S. Bridge*]. Kodansha, 2015.

Yamato:

Bywater, Hector C. *Sea-Power in the Pacific: A Study of the American-Japanese Naval Problem.* Houghton Mifflin, 1921.

Bywater, Hector C. *The Great Pacific War: A Historic Prophecy Now Being Fulfilled.* Houghton Mifflin, 1942.

Chang, Gordon, ed. *Morning Glory, Evening Shadow: Yamato Ichihashi and His Internment Writings, 1942–1945.* Stanford University Press, 1997.

Honan, William H. [William Holmes]. *Visions of Infamy: The Untold Story of How Journalist Hector C. Bywater Devised the Plans That Led to Pearl Harbor.* St. Martin's Press, 1992.

Ichihashi, Yamato. *Japanese in the United States: A Critical Study of the Problems of the Japanese Immigrants and their Children.* Stanford University Press, 1932.

Ichihashi, Yamato. *The Washington Conference and After: A History Survey.* Stanford University Press, 1928.

Ichioka, Yuji. *A Buried Past: An Annotated Bibliography of the Japanese American Research Project Collection.* University of California Press, 1974.

Ichioka, Yuji. "'Attorney for the Defense': Yamato Ichihashi and Japanese Immigration." *Pacific Historical Review* 55:2 (May 1986).

Jordan, David Starr. *The Human Harvest: A Study of the Decay of Races Through the Survival of the Unfit.* Heintzemann, 1907. Reprint, Garland, 1972.

Miller, Lulu. *Why Fish Don't Exist: A Story of Loss, Love, and the Hidden Order of Life.* Simon & Schuster, 2020.

Waltonsmith, Ann, and Connie Young Yu. *Images of America: Hakone Estate & Gardens*. Arcadia, 2021.

Haruko:

Brown, Greg C. *Fair Market Appraisal of Original Japanese American Monochrome Sumi-e Illustrative Painting on Paper by Professor Chiura Obata*. Washington, 2017.

Burgard, Timothy Anglin, [exhibition] *Great Nature: The Transcendent Landscapes of Chiura Obata*. Fine Arts Museums of San Francisco. M. H. de Young Memorial Museum, Sept. 23–Dec. 31, 2000. Distributed by M. H. de Young. Exhibition catalog.

Hill, Kimi Kodani, ed. *Chiura Obata's Topaz Moon: Art of the Internment*. Heyday Books, 2000.

Obata, Chiura. *Sumi-e*. Berkeley, 1967.

Obata, Haruko. *An Illustrated Handbook of Japanese Flower Arrangement*. Obata Studio, 1940.

Ross, Michael Elsohn. *Nature Art with Chiura Obata*. Carolrhoda Books, 2000.

Wang, ShiPu. *Chiura Obata: An American Modern*. Art, Design & Architecture Museum, UC Santa Barbara. Oakland, California, 2018.

BOX 2: Spoilage

Isamu:

Duus, Masayo. *The Life of Isamu Noguchi: Journey Without Borders*. Translated by Peter Duus. Princeton University Press, 2004.

Noguchi, Isamu. *I Become a Nisei*. Isamu Noguchi Foundation and Garden Museum, 2020.

Noguchi, Isamu. *Isamu Noguchi: A Sculptor's World*. Harper & Row, 1968.

Violet:

Cristoforo, Violet Kazue de, ed. *May Sky: There Is Always Tomorrow; Anthology of Japanese American Concentration Camp Kaiko Haiku*. Sun & Moon Press, 1997.

Cristoforo, Violet Kazue de. "A Victim of the Japanese Evacuation and Resettlement Study (JERS)." June 30, 1987.

Grodzins, Morton. *Americans Betrayed: Politics and the Japanese Evacuation*. University of Chicago Press, 1949.

Hansen, Art. *Japanese American WWII Evacuation Oral History Project*. California State University, Fullerton, 1994.

Hirabayashi, Lane Ryo. *The Politics of Fieldwork: Research in an American Concentration Camp*. University of Arizona Press, 1999.

Howard, John. *Concentration Camps on the Home Front: Japanese Americans in the House of Jim Crow.* University of Chicago Press, 2008.

Ichioka, Yuji, ed. *Views from Within: The Japanese American Evacuation Resettlement Study.* UCLA Asian American Studies, 1989.

Murray, Alice Yang. *Historical Memories of the Japanese American Internment and the Struggle for Redress.* Stanford University Press, 2008.

Shallit, Barney. *Song of Anger: Tales of Tule Lake.* Center for Oral and Public History, California State University, Fullerton. 2001.

Tateishi, John. *And Justice for All: An Oral History of the Japanese Detention Camp.* University of Washington Press, 1984.

Takita-Ishii, Sachiko, ed. and trans. "Tokio Yamane: A Renunciant's Story." In *A Question of Loyalty: Internment at Tule Lake.* Shaw Historical Library, 2005.

Thomas, Dorothy Swaine. *The Spoilage.* With Richard Shigeaki Nishimoto. University of California Press, 1946.

Suzuki, Peter T. "The University of California Japanese Evacuation and Resettlement Study: A Prolegomenon." *Dialectical Anthropology* 10:1, 2 (1985).

Wax, Rosalie Hankey. *Doing Fieldwork: Warnings and Advice.* University of Chicago Press, 1971.

Weglyn, Michi. *Years of Infamy: The Untold Story of America's Concentrations Camps.* William Morrow, 1976.

Joe:

Aderer, Conrad, dir. *Resistance at Tule Lake.* Documentary film. 2017.

Benedict, Ruth. *The Chrysanthemum and the Sword: Patterns of Japanese Culture.* Houghton Mifflin, 1946.

Chin, Frank. *Born in the USA: A Story of Japanese America, 1889–1947.* Rowman & Littlefield, 2002.

Harrington, Joseph D. *Yankee Samurai: The Secret Role of Nisei in America's Pacific Victory.* Pettigrew Enterprises, 1979.

Hosokawa, Bill. *Nisei: The Quiet Americans.* William Morrow, 1969.

Inouye, Daniel K. *Journey to Washington.* With Lawrence Elliott. Prentice-Hall, 1967.

JERS *Japanese Evacuation and Resettlement Study Records,* BANC MSS 67/14c, UC Berkeley Bancroft Library Online Archive of California (OAC) Field-notes: Diary of S Yoshiyama; Joe Kurihara essays and correspondence; Moe Yonemura correspondence.

Masaoka, Mike. *They Call Me Moses Masaoka: An American Saga.* With Bill Hosokawa. William Morrow, 1987.

Mizuguchi, Kenji, dir. *The Forty-Seven Ronin (Genroku Chushingura).* Film. 1941.

Okada, John. *No-No Boy.* Tuttle, 1957.

Omura, James Matsumoto. *Nisei Naysayer: The Memoir of Militant Japanese American Journalist Jimmie Omura*. Edited by Arthur A. Hansen. Stanford University Press, 2018.

Tamura, Eileen H. *In Defense of Justice: Joseph Kurihara and the Japanese American Struggle for Equality*. University of Illinois Press, 2013.

Ueno, Harry Yoshio. *Manzanar Martyr: An Interview with Harry Y. Ueno*. Interview by Sue Kunitomi Embrey, Arthur A Hansen, and Betty Kulberg Mitson. Fullerton, Calif., 1986.

Wax, Rosalie Hankey. "The Development of Authoritarianism: A Comparison of the Japanese-American Relocation Centers and Germany." PhD diss. University of Chicago, 1951.

Yamane, Tokio. Interview by Sachiko Takita-Isii, Yoko Murakawa, and Noriko Kawakami. Densho Digital Archive, Visual History Collection Japan, May 23, 2004; https://ddr.densho.org/media/ddr-densho-1000/ddr-densho-1000-432-transcript-3f9b7a89d0.htm.

Yoneda, Karl G. *Ganbatte: Sixty-Year Struggle of a Kibei Worker*. Asian American Studies Center, UCLA, 1983.

Miné:

Beckwith, Frank A. *Indian Joe: In Person and In Background; Historical Perspective into Piute Life*. DuWil, 1975.

Hathaway, Heather. *That Damned Fence: The Literature of the Japanese American Prison Camps*. Oxford University Press, 2022.

Hong, Christine. "A Blueprint for Occupied Japan: Miné Okubo and the American Concentration Camp." In *A Violent Peace: Race: U.S. Militarism, and Cultures of Democratization in Cold War Asia and the Pacific*. Stanford University Press, 2020.

LaDuke, Betty. "Miné Okubo: An American Experience." In *The Forbidden Stitch: An Asian American Women's Anthology*, edited by Shirley Geok-lin Lim, Mayumi Tsutakawa, and Margarita Donnelly. Calyx Books, 1989.

Modell, John, ed. *The Kikuchi Diary: Chronicle from an American Concentration Camp; The Tanforan Journals of Charles Kikuchi*. University of Illinois Press, 1973.

Okubo, Miné. *Citizen 13660*. University of Washington Press, 1983.

Robinson, Greg, and Elena Tajima Creef, eds. *Miné Okubo: Following Her Own Road*. University of Washington Press, 2008.

Charlie:

Adamic, Louis. *From Many Lands*. Harper & Brothers, 1940.

Briones, Matthew M. *Jim and Jap Crow: A Cultural History of 1940s Interracial America*. Princeton University Press, 2012.

Ichioka, Yuji, ed. *Views from Within: The Japanese American Evacuation and Resettlement Study.* UCLA Asian American Studies Center, 1989.

Modell, John, ed. *The Kikuchi Diary: Chronicle from an American Concentration Camp; The Tanforan Journals of Charles Kikuchi.* University of Illinois Press, 1973.

Thomas, Dorothy Swaine. *The Salvage.* With Charles Kikuchi and James Minoru Sakoda. University of California Press, 1952.

Richard:

Bird, Kai. *The Chairman: John J. McCloy, the Making of the American Establishment.* Simon & Schuster, 1992.

Grodzins, Morton. *Americans Betrayed: Politics and the Japanese Evacuation.* University of Chicago Press, 1949.

Hirabayashi, Lane Ryo. *The Politics of Fieldwork: Research in an American Concentration Camp.* University of Arizona Press, 1999.

Nishimoto, Richard S. *Inside an American Concentration Camp: Japanese American Resistance at Poston, Arizona.* Edited by Lane Ryo Hirabayashi. University of Arizona Press, 1995.

tenBroek, Jacobus, Edward N. Barnhart, and Floyd W. Matson. *Prejudice, War, and the Constitution.* University of California Press, 1954.

Thomas, Dorothy Swaine, and Richard Shigeaki Nishimoto. *The Spoilage.* University of California Press, 1946.

Thomas, Dorothy Swaine. *The Salvage.* With Charles Kikuchi and James Minoru Sakoda. University of California Press, 1952.

Jimmy:

Hansen, Arthur A., ed. *Japanese American World War II Evacuation Oral History Project.* Part III, *Analysts.* K. G. Saur, 1994.

Hegselmann, Rainer. "Thomas C. Schelling & James M. Sakoda: The Intellectual, Technical, and Social History of a Model." *Journal of Artificial Societies and Social Stimulation* 20:3 (2017).

Ichioka, Yuji, ed. *Views from Within: The Japanese American Evacuation and Resettlement Study.* UCLA Asian American Studies Center, 1989.

Shibutani, Tamotsu. *Improvised News: A Sociological Study of Rumor.* Bobbs-Merrill, 1966.

BOX 3: Residue

Harry:

Broom, Leonard, and John I. Kitsuse. *The Managed Casualty: The Japanese-American Family in World War II.* University of California Press, 1973.

Crouch, Stanley. *Kansas City Lightning: The Rise & Times of Charlie Parker.* Harper, 2013.

Crouch, Stanley. *Victory Is Assured: Uncollected Writings of Stanley Crouch.* Liveright, 2022.

Ellison, Ralph. *Invisible Man.* Random House, 1952.

Kitano, Harry H. L. *Japanese Americans: The Evolution of a Subculture.* Prentice-Hall, 1969.

Kitano, Harry H. L., and Roger Daniels. *Asian Americans: Emerging Minorities.* Prentice-Hall, 1988.

Owsley, Dennis C. *Saint Louis Jazz: A History.* Arcadia, 2019.

Yoshida, George. *Reminiscing in Swingtime: Japanese Americans in American Popular Music, 1925–1960.* National Japanese American Historical Society, 1997.

Robert:

Anderson, Mark. *From Boas to Black Power.* Stanford University Press, 2019.

Benedict, Ruth. *The Chrysanthemum and the Sword: Patterns of Japanese Culture.* Houghton Mifflin, 1946.

Dazai, Osamu. *The Setting Sun* (1947). Translated by Donald Keene. New Directions, 1956.

Dower, John W. *Embracing Defeat: Japan in the Wake of World War II.* W. W. Norton, 1999.

Embree, John F. *Suye Mura: A Japanese Village.* University of Chicago Press, 1939.

Fleming, Ian. *You Only Live Twice.* Jonathan Cape, 1964.

Hearn, Lafcadio. *Kokoro: Hints and Echoes of Japanese Inner Life.* Tuttle, 1895.

Honda, Ishiro. *Gojira.* Toho, 1954.

Lummis, C. Douglas. *Boundaries in the Land, Boundaries in the Mind.* Hokkuseido Press, 1982.

Lummis, C. Douglas. *A New Look at the Chrysanthemum and the Sword.* Shohakusha, 1982.

Lummis, C. Douglas. "Ruth Benedict's Obituary for Japanese Culture." *Asia-Pacific Journal, Japan Focus* 5:7 (July 12, 2007).

McGowan, Dorrell, and Stuart E. Dorrell, directors. *Tokyo File 212.* Breakston-McGowan Productions and Tonichi Enterprises, 1951.

Nitobe, Inazo. *Bushido: The Soul of Japan; An Exposition of Japanese Thought.* London, 1899.

Ohnuki-Tierney, Emiko. *Kamikaze, Cherry Blossoms, and Nationalism: The Militarization of Aesthetics in Japanese History.* University of Chicago Press, 2002.

Price, David H. *Anthropological Intelligence: The Deployment and Neglect of American Anthropology in the Second World War.* Duke University Press, 2008.

Soseki, Natsume. *Botchan* (1906). Translated by Yasotaro Morri. Ogawa Seibundo, 1918.

Swift, Jonathan. *Gulliver's Travels.* Benjamin Motte, 1726.

Nobuya:

Kochiyama, Yuri. *Passing It On: A Memoir.* UCLA Asian American Studies Center, 2004.

Fujino, Diane C. *Heartbeat of Struggle: The Revolutionary Life of Yuri Kochiyama.* University of Minnesota Press, 2005.

Michi:

Christgau, John. "Collins Versus the World: The Fight to Restore Citizenship to Japanese Renunciants of World War II." *Pacific Historical Review* 54:1 (February 1985).

Christgau, John. *Enemies: World War II Alien Internment.* Bison Books, 2009.

Collins, Wayne M. Papers, 1918–1974. Bancroft Library, University of California, Berkeley.

Weglyn, Michi. Papers. Hirasaki National Resource Center, Japanese American National Museum, Los Angeles.

Weglyn, Michi. *Years of Infamy: The Untold Story of America's Concentrations Camps.* William Morrow, 1976.

Wollenberg, Charles. *Rebel Lawyer: Wayne Collins and the Defense of Japanese American Rights.* Heyday, 2018.

Yamato, Sharon. *One Fighting Irishman: Wayne M. Collins and the Tule Lake Segregation Center.* Short film, 2023.

Yamato, Sharon, and Nancy Kapitanoff. *Out of Infamy: Michi Nishiura Weglyn.* Short film, 2010.

James:

DeGraaf, John, dir. *A Personal Matter: Gordon Hirabayashi versus the United States.* National Asian American Telecommunications Association, 1992.

Hirabayashi, Gordon K. *A Principled Stand: The Story of Hirabayashi v. United States.* University of Washington Press, 2012.

Dana:

Choy, Curtis, dir. *Wendy . . . Uh . . . What's Her Name?* Film. 2006.

Platt, Tony, and Paul Takagi, eds. *Punishment and Penal Discipline: Essays on the Prison and the Prisoners' Movement.* Crime and Social Justice Associates, 1979.

Takagi, Paul T., and Gregory Shank. *Paul T. Takagi: Recollections and Writings.* Crime and Social Justice Associates/Global Options, 2012.

Aiko:

Bird, Kai. *The Chairman: John J. McCloy, the Making of the American Establishment.* Simon & Schuster, 1992.

Daniels, Roger. *Concentration Camps USA: Japanese Americans and World War II.* Holt, Rinehart & Winston, 1971.

Daniels, Roger. *The Decision to Relocate the Japanese Americans.* J. B. Lippincott, 1975.

De Nevers, Klancy Clark. *The Colonel and the Pacifist: Karl Bendetsen, Perry Saito, and the Incarceration of Japanese Americans During World War II.* University of Utah Press, 2004.

DeWitt, John L. *Final Report: Japanese Evacuation from the West Coast, 1942.* United States Government Printing Office, 1943.

Irons, Peter. *The Center Seat: Life and Death in the Supreme Court.* Novel. Self-published, 2016.

Irons, Peter H. *Justice at War: The Story of the Japanese American Internment Cases.* Oxford University Press, 1983.

Irons, Peter H., ed. *Justice Delayed: The Record of the Japanese American Internment Cases.* Wesleyan University Press, 1989.

Minami, Dale, and Peter Irons. *Petition for Writ of Error Corum Nobis: Fred Toyasaburo Korematsu v. United States, Crim. No. 27535-W.* Filed January 19, 1983.

Roosevelt, Kermit. *Allegiance.* Regan Arts, 2020.

Tanaka, Janice D. *Rebel with a Cause: The Life of Aiko Herzig Yoshinaga.* Biopicture. 2016.

Tateishi, John. *Redress: The Inside Story of the Successful Campaign for Japanese American Reparations.* Heyday, 2020.

United States Commission on Wartime Relocation and Internment of Civilians. *Personal Justice Denied.* University of Washington Press, 1997.

Weglyn, Michi. *Years of Infamy: The Untold Story of America's Concentrations Camps.* William Morrow, 1976.

Yang Murray, Alice. *Historical Memories of the Japanese American Internment and the Struggle for Redress.* Stanford University Press, 2008.

Michael:

Omi, Michael, and Howard Winant. *Racial Formation in the United States,* Routledge, 2015.

Yamanaka, Lois-Ann. *Blu's Hanging.* Farrar, Straus & Giroux, 1997.

Bruce:

Marker, Chris, dir. *La Jetée.* Film. 1962.

Marker, Chris, dir. *Sans Soleil.* Film. 1983.

Marker, Chris, dir. *Level 5*. Film. 1997.

Omori, Emiko, dir. *Rabbit in the Moon*. Film. 1999.

Omori, Emiko, dir. *To Chris Marker: An Unsent Letter*. Film. 2008.

Yonemoto, Bruce, and Norman Yonemoto. *Framed*. Video installation. Long Beach Museum of Art, 1989.

Yuki:

Alinder, Jasmine. *Moving Images: Photography and the Japanese American Incarceration*. University of Illinois Press, 2009.

Barthes, Roland. *Camera Lucida: Reflections on Photography*. Translated by Richard Howard. Hill and Wang, 1981.

Benjamin, Walter. "A Short History of Photography." Translated by Phil Patton. *ArtForum* 15:6 (1979).

Berger, John. *Understanding a Photograph*. Aperture, 1967.

Creef, Elena Tajima. *Imaging Japanese America: The Visual Construction of Citizenship, Nation, and the Body*. New York University Press, 2004.

Flusser, Vilém. *Towards a Philosophy of Photography*. Translated by Anthony Mathews. Reaktion Books, 2000.

Gordon, Linda, and Gary Okihiro. *Impounded: Dorothea Lange and the Censored Images of Japanese American Internment*. W. W. Norton, 2006.

Hirabayashi, Lane Ryo. *Japanese American Resettlement Through the Lens*. University Press of Colorado, 2009.

Kitagaki, Paul Jr. *Behind Barbed Wire: Searching for Japanese Americans Incarcerated During World War II*. Cityfiles Press, 2019.

Muller, Eric L., ed. *Colors of Confinement: Rare Kodachrome Photographs of Japanese American Incarceration in World War II*. University of North Carolina Press, 2021.

Resnais, Alain, dir. *Hiroshima Mon Amour*. Screenplay by Marguerite Duras. 1959.

Robinson, Gerald H. *Elusive Truth: Four Photographers at Manzanar*. Carl Mautz, 2007.

Sontag, Susan. *On Photography*. Picador, 1977.

Sontag, Susan. *Regarding the Pain of Others*. Picador, 2003.

KAREN TEI YAMASHITA is the author of nine books, including *I Hotel*, finalist for the National Book Award. Recipient of the National Book Foundation's 2021 Medal for Distinguished Contribution to American Letters, she is Professor Emerita of literature and creative writing at the University of California, Santa Cruz. In 2024 Yamashita was inducted as a Literature Fellow in the American Academy of Arts and Sciences.

Graywolf Press publishes risk-taking, visionary writers who transform culture through literature. As a nonprofit organization, Graywolf relies on the generous support of its donors to bring books like this one into the world.

This publication is made possible, in part, by the voters of Minnesota through a Minnesota State Arts Board Operating Support grant, thanks to a legislative appropriation from the arts and cultural heritage fund. Significant support has also been provided by other generous contributions from foundations, corporations, and individuals. To these supporters we offer our heartfelt thanks.

The text and display elements of *Questions 27 & 28* are set in
Aptos Narrow, Arno Pro, Freight Text Pro, Learning Curve, Source Serif Pro,
Times New Roman, and Trade Gothic Next LT Pro.
The cherry blossom image is designed by Freepik.
The origami boat image is designed by brgfx / Freepik.
Book design by Rachel Holscher.
Composition by Bookmobile Design & Digital
Publisher Services, Minneapolis,
Minnesota. Manufactured by Friesens on acid-free,
100 percent postconsumer wastepaper.